PRAISE FOR

THE GOOD DAUGHTER

"Alexandra Burt expertly weaves a rich tapestry of a story that is surprising at every turn and impossible to put down. I was incredibly impressed with her ability to take seemingly unrelated threads and connect each one to the core of the story. Excellent read!"

—Rena Olsen, author of *The Girl Before*

"Stunning. Every landscape, from rural Texas to the dark past of the characters, is intricately and beautifully crafted, pulling you in from the very first page to the very last. Rarely do we get to enjoy psychological suspense with such extraordinary descriptive narration. It's a wonderful read!"

—Wendy Walker, bestselling author of *All Is Not Forgotten*

"An eerily beautiful novel. . . . Alexandra Burt fills the Texas woods with her haunting prose and multiple layers of faithfulness, blood ties, and betrayals. The suspense draws you in those woods and keeps you there until the final page."

—Kathy Hepinstall, author *Blue Asylum*

PRAISE FOR

REMEMBER MIA

"As riveting as *Gone Girl*, but with an even sharper emotional edge, this story . . . will pull you in from the very first page. The fast-paced plot, psychological intrigue, and engrossing twists will have you flipping pages faster and faster as Estelle's memories are gradually uncovered and piece by jagged piece the puzzle comes together."

—Kelly Jones, author of *Lost and Found in Prague*

"*Remember Mia* is a twisty, gripping read—beautifully written and impossible to put down."

—Meg Gardiner, Edgar® Award–winning author of *Phantom Instinct*

"If you enjoy books that pull you in from the beginning and keep you so fully engrossed that you think about them even when you are doing other things, [this] is a book that you should not miss."

—Fresh Fiction

Berkley titles by Alexandra Burt

REMEMBER MIA

THE GOOD DAUGHTER

SHADOW GARDEN

Alexandra Burt

BERKLEY

New York

BERKLEY
An imprint of Penguin Random House LLC
penguinrandomhouse.com

Copyright © 2020 by Alexandra Burt
"Readers guide" copyright © 2020 by Alexandra Burt
Penguin Random House supports copyright. Copyright fuels
creativity, encourages diverse voices, promotes free speech, and
creates a vibrant culture. Thank you for buying an authorized edition
of this book and for complying with copyright laws by not
reproducing, scanning, or distributing any part of it in any form
without permission. You are supporting writers and allowing Penguin
Random House to continue to publish books for every reader.

BERKLEY and the BERKLEY & B colophon are registered trademarks
of Penguin Random House LLC.

Library of Congress Cataloging-in-Publication Data

Names: Burt, Alexandra, author.
Title: Shadow garden / Alexandra Burt.
Description: First edition. | New York: Berkley, 2020.
Identifiers: LCCN 2020002034 (print) | LCCN 2020002035 (ebook) |
ISBN 9780440000327 (trade paperback) | ISBN 9780440000334 (ebook)
Subjects: LCSH: Domestic fiction. | GSAFD: Suspense fiction. |
Mystery fiction.
Classification: LCC PS3602.U7694 S53 2020 (print) |
LCC PS3602.U7694 (ebook) | DDC 813/.6—dc23
LC record available at https://lccn.loc.gov/2020002034
LC ebook record available at https://lccn.loc.gov/2020002035

First Edition: July 2020

Printed in the United States of America
1 3 5 7 9 10 8 6 4 2

Cover art: *Figure in landscape* by Arcangel/Katya Evdokimova;
Face by Shutterstock/Nina Skarga
Cover design by Emily Osborne
Book design by Tiffany Estreicher

To Long Goodbyes

Why, what could she have done, being what she is?

—WILLIAM BUTLER YEATS

PART I

HELL

There is no greater sorrow than to recall
happiness in times of misery.

—DANTE ALIGHIERI

1

DONNA

Through the thicket of trees, the faint amber lights of a building appear. The sign catches me by surprise as if it isn't meant to be seen by just anyone. Like a hurried deer crossing the road it materializes, and below it, bushy sky-blue hydrangeas the size of human heads thrive.

Golden letters come into focus. *Shadow Garden.*

How strange. All these years I've lived here but I never knew this place existed.

"You think I'll get better soon?"

I turn and look at Edward, my husband. I shouldn't notice the heavy metal-alloy femoral head in my left hip but it weighs me down in more ways than one. Since the accident things have been difficult between us.

Edward stares straight ahead. His face hadn't been touched by a razor in months, not until this morning, when he decided to stop hiding behind a full beard. I study the profile of the face that has emerged, exposed and on the verge of being unfamiliar. A spot by his upper lip, a small blood-speckled wound from the razor blade. His fitted suit is no longer snug and I resist telling him to have the garment altered. I have become good at swallowing my words by visualizing pulling an imaginary zipper across my mouth.

A gate shuts behind us. I search for words to accurately explain myself but I'm distracted by shiny kaleidoscopic grackles of purple, green, and blue iridescence foraging with long dark bills. They peck at shamrock-green grass blades, have taken over the walkways and the shrubberies, they dot the lawn, sit perched on rims of copper fountains, bobbing their heads. As we pass them, the flock scatters off into nearby trees. In the fading light, their yellow eyes stand out in the otherwise emerald landscape. They settle nearby, invisible to the eye, but their calls are unnerving, like the sound of buzzing power lines.

I look out the car window so Edward doesn't see me tearing up. He hates tears. They unravel him, do him in. He's been composed so far, at least on the outside, but that's nothing to brag about; he's a surgeon, it comes to him naturally.

That name. Shadow Garden. How overly dramatic, as if ripped from a Victorian horror novel. It isn't until I'm shown the grounds that it grows on me. It has the feel of an Ivy League university surrounded by a vastness of jade, mint, olive, and sage—any hue of green the eye can imagine.

Shadow Garden is nothing to shake a stick at. It sits on a majestic estate of almost forty acres of hiking trails tucked away in the countryside at the end of a rural road. To call the estate a garden, even in a remote sense, is an understatement: The grounds are a burst of potted plants, bushes, shrubberies, and trees shading the paved walkways. Crape myrtles rise between the buildings, slender, with sinewy, fluted stems and mottled branches and bark that sheds like snakeskin.

"I guess I've turned into an old shrew, griping all day long," I joke but to no avail. Earlier, when I struggled down the stairs and limped over to the car, his eyes were fixated on me, watching my every step. He hasn't looked at me since. I wonder what he thinks of me shuffling around without any strength and confidence, and maybe he's run out of compassion. Just look at him staring straight ahead as if I'm not even here. "Did you hear me?"

"Bones heal, dear. That's what bones do. They fuse," Edward says as the corners of his lips form the imitation of a smile.

"You're the doctor, you ought to know," I say with a slight hint of sarcasm, but truth be told, it isn't my bones I'm worried about. I wish I could talk to Edward like I used to. I want to tell him how terrified I am. "I worry about Penelope," I add, barely a whisper.

His head swivels toward me when I mention our daughter.

"Marleen will be with you. No need to worry."

Marleen. My housekeeper. My steadfast soldier. Years ago, Edward and I traveled to Egypt. We toured a temple and the guide told us about a human entombed with nobility to serve them in the afterlife—a retainer sacrifice. Metaphorically speaking I'm a cast-off given a servant.

Later, Edward stands awkwardly blocking the front door. "I have to leave now," he says, and I blink the tears away.

"I don't understand why all this is happening," I can't help myself and before I know it, the words have escaped my mouth. They rest between us with all those other weighted things we have accumulated in the past.

Edward remains silent. I reach for his hand, which hangs lifeless and cold by his side. He seems jittery but maybe I'm reading too much into it.

"You'll be back to your old self in no time," Edward finally says without making eye contact.

Thirty years of marriage and I can read him like a book. Even he doesn't believe the back-to-your-old-self thing. The fabric between him and the truth is nothing but a smokescreen. As thin as paper. An illusion. The truth is our marriage is over and Shadow Garden is my consolation prize. That's the gist of it.

As I see Edward off, the lampposts flicker, and for a moment the night is so dark, it seems capable of devouring me. Like being swallowed whole.

2

DONNA

I tug at the crisp white sheet clinging to the corner of my vanity mirror. Yanking at it, I center the fabric. The sheet disturbs dust, which threatens to settle on every surface of my bedroom.

"I don't understand what this is all about," Marleen reprimands me as if I'm an unruly child. Her eyes pan back and forth between me and the mirror.

"This isn't nearly as dramatic as it looks," I say and reassure her I'm in great spirits. Just in case she thinks otherwise.

I've explained the entire mourning affair to Marleen but it must have gone over her head. My friend and neighbor, Vera Olmsted, told me about holding shiva for seven days, during which one shrouds all mirrors, but I'm Methodist and there's no need to follow the rules exactly. Loss comes in many forms and my state of mourning has to do with my marriage. For the longest time I counted on a reconciliation but months have passed and not a single phone call from Edward. Not one visit. And my daughter, Penelope, I haven't spoken to her either.

Voices drift toward me through the open window—a child, giggling, high-pitched, pit-a-patting, racing down the walkway with a joy that only children possess. A mother's voice responds gently, *wait, slow down, hold my hand*. I crane my neck to get a good look at them—the girl is about five or so—and seeing her is comforting at first but then reality sinks in.

When Penelope was five, we lived in Florida at the end of a cul-de-sac. I search my mind for fond memories of the bungalow but all I know is I wouldn't set foot in it today. A crooked fire hydrant in the front yard and a small square patch of grass. Every time the air conditioner kicked in, the lights flickered on trembling currents due to faulty wiring. We were able to afford the house because the interior was dated and overhead power lines cut through the backyard, mere feet away from the porch. Metal towers loomed above us and I often wondered if it was safe to live there.

For hours on end, Penelope played with her dollhouses, scooting across the cheap carpet until her knees turned pinkish red from the friction. She'd sit with what I interpreted as sharp concentration but as time passed I saw it for what it was: an obsession, a way of soothing herself. She rearranged plastic dolls and dainty accessories and when I interrupted her, she'd snap her head back and flip her ponytail by weaving her fingers through her hair, whipping it around.

Penelope—we called her Pea as a baby and toddler, Penny as a child, Penelope starting as a teenager—never made friends easily. She didn't care for other children. It sounds callous, but it wasn't so much her not liking others as her enjoying her own company. I found what I thought was the solution to her isolation and bought her an outdoor playhouse, hoping it would attract children from the neighborhood. I had an image of Pea and her friends having tea parties and tucking their doll babies in strollers, playing dress-up and wearing princess dresses.

I didn't read the description and the playhouse arrived in hundreds of pieces of wooden shapes with numbered and lettered plastic stickers and a bag of screws, nails, and hex keys. That Edward was going to put the playhouse together was wishful thinking on my part; he has not so much as hammered a nail in the wall.

I found a handyman in the Yellow Pages who put it together the very next day. After he left, Penelope stared at the house for a long time, then circled it as if she was pondering its intended use. "Go on," I said and watched her step inside as I stood on the back porch and beheld the structure: the scalloped cedar shingles, the cast-iron bell, the stained-glass window in the door which allowed plenty of sunlight to sneak inside, where a delicate heart-and-swag stencil pattern adorned the walls.

Penelope disappeared within the structure and a sudden gust of wind slammed the playhouse door shut and the stained-glass pane shattered though it took me some time to connect cause and effect. Penelope screamed and I ran to find her with a gaping cut from the tip of her index finger down the palm of her hand to her wrist. The cut bled so profusely, I was unable to staunch the bleeding. I rushed her to the ER and Edward did the sutures himself and eventually all that was left of that day was a faint white line in my daughter's palm. It seemed to float, to sit above her skin. Penelope didn't so much as shed a tear. She knew no pain. I say that without judgment, that was just the body she lived in.

There was something about Penelope, something that made me—

Outside my window heavy footsteps sound. More laughter. *I got you. Stop being silly.* The voices grow weak, then fade, swallowed by the lush landscaping until there's nothing but silence spilling into my room. There one moment, gone the next.

In the blink of an eye. That's my go-to comment when I encounter families in the park outside my window. "Children grow up so quickly," I say and smile though I shudder when small sticky hands reach for me. I bury my hands in my pockets and add, "Before you know it, they are grown. In the blink of an eye. Gone."

Like my daughter, Penelope. My husband, my entire life. Gone.

My mind bends in on itself, pondering my role in it all. There's a lesson in here somewhere, but what the lesson is I don't know.

3

PENELOPE

That playhouse. Penelope knew what her mother was trying to do: like the man in the book, the Pied Piper, she wanted children to march into the backyard and up the wooden steps into the miniature house with shelves and benches and tables. Those kids might appear but not a single one of them would stick around.

It wasn't her earlobes, which were flatter than any lobe she had ever seen—not even her parents had them and how she got them, she couldn't be sure. She didn't comprehend biology or genetics or inheritance quite yet but was told she had her mother's fine hair and her father's nose, so everything about her came from them but her lobes were a puzzle to everyone.

But that wasn't what made her different.

There was the accident in the cul-de-sac. A girl fell off her bike, having just learned to ride, still clumsy and off balance, teetering left and right. Penelope watched her glide across the concrete and come to rest against the curb. She imagined the girl's skin scraping against the asphalt and there was a lot of blood though Penelope's father later explained to her that head wounds always tended to bleed profusely. It wasn't the fact that Penelope had remained calm when the blood collected in the sidewalk dip—the very hollow in which a puddle formed and she jumped after a rain shower—it was the fact that all the kids who saw the blood gasped and turned pale. Even the boys backed up and one began to cry.

But not Penelope. She stood and stared at the blood pooling in the indent in the asphalt and the girl's mother came running and pushed Penelope to the side, pressing a handkerchief against her daughter's head.

The children were led away from the scene and huddled by a nearby tree. During the frenzy of cries and cars coming to a screeching halt offering help, Penelope wandered back and decided to observe the scene up close.

She stared at the pool of blood. It wasn't as scandalous to her as it was to the onlookers—she thought of the moment later, how it was twisted into something it was not—and she was merely attempting to see something up close she was fascinated by, not any different than looking at cells under a microscope, something doctors do, like her father.

Penelope kneeled down but couldn't get a good look at the blood and so she lowered her bottom, her legs turned out and away from her body, her thighs spread apart, her eyes hovering inches above the ground. Ever since then, the children thought her to be odd and all the playhouses in the world weren't going to change that.

The day the playhouse was put together and the window shattered—Penelope didn't have power over the wind, didn't slam the door shut, didn't make the window break, and therefore the entire affair was not completely her doing—Penelope took a shard and sliced her hand open. The cutting part scared her at first but once the skin opened up, she was mesmerized and felt no pain. Who is to say why she did what she did? To distract her mother? To spare herself the humiliation of playing alone? The anticipation of having her father spend an entire hour getting the sutures just right?

Penelope sat in a squeaky chair for the better part of an hour waiting in the ER. "Any doctor can suture that cut," the nurse said, but Penelope's mother wasn't having any of it. Only Dr. Pryor's expertise would do. Her mother trusted no one else to close the wound just right, and she didn't want *even a hint of a scar*, Penelope overheard her say to the nurse.

"My husband is an excellent plastic surgeon. I will not have my daughter's hand look like an experiment."

Her father came to stitch up the wound. In Penelope's mind, he had special vision: he saw how things ought to be righted that had gone wrong. How else was she to understand that he cut healthy people with a scalpel and then just stitched them up without having cured anything at all?

Penelope had expected the trip to the hospital—the first of her life, not counting her birth—to be a bigger ordeal. It was anti-climactic for the most part; there were no machines taking pictures of her bones, no cups she had to pee in, and no needles prodding her, they didn't even tell her to take off her clothes so they could put a gown on her. The highlight of the day was her mother inspecting the sutures and whispering over them as if she could will the skin to close and heal without a mark.

Later, at home, her mother sat down next to Penelope.

"What happened?" she asked and watched for words or gestures meant to expose Penelope somehow. Her mother was smart that way, capable of seeing signs that gave her away: the rapid blinking of the lids she had no control over, the trailing of her eyes to the left and downward, a sure sign of a lie to come.

"You didn't do this deliberately, did you?" her mother asked. There was a long pause as Penelope watched her mother brace herself for the answer.

Penny replied with a wobble of the head, which could have been a yes or a no.

"Did you?"

"I don't know what that word means," Penelope said instead.

"Were you trying to hurt yourself?" Donna rephrased but Penelope knew the meaning of *deliberate*.

"Hurt myself?" Penny said as if that was a question incomprehensible to her, like a concept that only adults understood and that didn't make sense to her at all.

Penelope felt desperation run through her mother, could tell by her breathing and the red rash on her neck. Penelope liked this spark she felt inside of her; it made her feel powerful. She closed her eyes, kept her breathing steady, afraid her mother might demand an explanation.

"Okay." Donna smoothed the pink duvet along the edges of the four-poster bed. "Okay. You go to sleep."

Penelope traced the cut with the tip of her thumb for years to come. There was an occasional tingling of severed nerves and the red welt faded into a barely visible white scar passing as a second life line, as if Penelope could pick one fate over the other.

4

DONNA

S oon it will be winter. Everything will cease to grow and thrive
and bloom. I'd like to have a word with the arborist. What he's
done to the crape myrtles is a sin and I want to tell him how to
properly prune them. Cutting them off at a certain height is the
lazy way out; no, each plant is different and requires individual
treatment. All one has to do is remove any dead flowers and seed-
pods and if you keep fertilizing, they will keep vigorously produc-
ing blooms until the first frost. I seem to recall purple blossoms a
while back but I didn't pay much attention; I wasn't in the right
state of mind then.

Though I've come a long way since Edward left me, I'm still in a
peculiar place. I told the therapist—also located in-house for our
convenience—I will always be Mrs. Edward Pryor and I insist on
keeping the Pryor name after the divorce, minus the house and the
husband. Though I told him, as a side remark, that keeping it was

something I feel compelled to do, the truth is I imagine with horror Edward demanding I take back my maiden name.

Belcher. Donna Belcher. It conjures up the picture of a matronly woman in sensible shoes and stiff Aqua Net hair waiting for her monthly check to arrive so she can go grocery shopping. I have zero proclivities to be that kind of a woman, ever.

Outside my window two women with visors walk past, their footsteps echoing sharply. They are dressed casually: jeans, fitted jackets, and neck scarves. Their arms and legs move in unison and I feel a pang of loneliness. Friendships are hard to come by, and I've been moody and ought to make more of an effort to meet people.

All day I've worn my hair in a bun, the bobby pins nipping and prodding my scalp. Without a mirror I struggle and they get tangled in my hair. I open a drawer and arrange the pins neatly on top of a sleek folder with a glossy cover and embossed letters in gold foil.

I had pulled it from the recycling bin within a stack of discarded newspapers. The folder was given to Marleen when I moved to Shadow Garden a year ago. She has removed most of the pages— the one with important phone numbers is tacked to the bulletin board in the kitchen, so is the waste schedule. *Garbage is to be placed on the walkways on Monday and Thursday between eight and ten, securely tied up in bags and left beside the columns by the front doors to be picked up by a maintenance crew member.* Marleen takes care of that and has the schedule committed to memory, I'm sure.

The back page of the folder is a map of the monarch butterfly migration, starting in Mexico beginning in March and subsequently journeying north to Canada. It's a nice touch, though I lack understanding of the connection to luxury apartments, but I appreciate the juxtaposition with my own life of, say, reinvention and determination of one's own journey. The calligraphy is exquisite and reminds me of invitations I used to send out. The rest of the pages I barely skimmed over but I recall sketches of floor plans with square footages, suggested furniture placement—management is a stickler for keeping the windows unobstructed by heavy pieces, for safety reasons I assume—reminders about the wildlife, and bait stations tucked underneath bushes and in the corners of breezeways. Apparently stray cats are frowned upon and rats are considered a nuisance, and just like in real life, friend or foe seem arbitrary but I keep my mouth shut.

I slide the folder back into the drawer of my vanity. So little privacy left with Marleen around every day but this drawer remains my very own space.

How long have I been sitting here, tinkering with my hair? The two women from earlier have passed by my window twice, maybe even three times. To lose track of time can be a blessing with the thoughts of—

The house phone rings twice. Always twice. Then it stops. How odd. I wonder what that's all about. From the kitchen the cabinet doors bang, the dishes clink like cymbals.

"Marleen," I call out. My voice sounds sharp. I'm not always kind to her and I promised myself I'll do better. "Marleen?" Softer this time.

She appears as if she moves about by hovering above the ground. "Yes, Mrs. Pryor?"

This is what it comes down to every day. "Any phone calls today?"

"No, Mrs. Pryor, no calls."

"I heard the phone ring."

"Oh, that," she says and cocks her head to the side. "Just someone at the gate punching the wrong numbers, I guess. It stopped ringing."

Marleen Clifford is a swift and practical woman. She's either a young-looking fifty or a hard-life thirty, it's difficult to tell. I don't ask her age, that would be rude. She appears in the mornings and without fanfare prepares my breakfast. She does my laundry, manages my appointments, reminds me of my schedule, and does everyday chores like vacuuming and dusting. She cooks and cleans, though the meals are not elaborate and the house seems to maintain itself.

I have no complaints but for this one peculiar habit of hers: she seems to think she's in charge of certain aspects of my life. She moves things around the house—vases, figurines, and glass bowls—puts them away altogether—mind you, I have observed this myself—and I'm convinced she was a clumsy child and had her fair share of scolding. Her disposition is one of anticipating the worst. I discovered my Meissen figurines in a box in the storage room. Marleen never told me she found them though I had specifically asked for them to be displayed. I have yet to mention that to her.

It took weeks to get settled and now there's that storage room left to tackle. Boxes pile up to the ceiling, leaving barely room to move. The peculiar thing is that the number of boxes never seem to lessen regardless how much linen we stack in closets or how many books we put on shelves. They multiply and when I comment on it, Marleen seems uneasy. I don't mention it anymore.

I've come a long way with my injury considering I was in excruciating pain when I began walking again. But I pushed through. Though my hip gives me problems on certain days, I have taken up running again. I've been hiding my recovery from everyone—Marleen, the doctors, even my friend Vera.

I check my running shoes for the proper tie and I head past a cluster of cast-iron chairs and a table tucked away underneath the silver maples where leaves have left unsightly stains on the ground. The courtyard has changed into its fall clothes and is no longer in bloom with colors of ferns, pears, and lime peels, has months to go before nature will emerge triumphantly.

I head down a walkway, past a fountain covered in algae, its copper spigot a pale green, and take the steps up to the walking trails where cast-iron poles indicate color-coded routes.

A trail of blood leads from the path onto the lawn. A grackle struggles within the green lush blades, one wing spread, the other tucked underneath its body. It wobbles and tips to the side, the long keel-shaped tail unable to keep it upright.

Around me, numerous grackles croak as if in protest, followed by a high-pitched whistle like a rusty gate swinging open. The calls of the birds are interrupted by a sound of scraping metal, which sends dozens of them bursting from surrounding trees.

A man in Dickies shovels what looks like a heap of black iridescent feathers into a metal bucket, repeatedly grating the shovel against the stones. There are countless dead birds scattered all around him but the man—I recognize him as one of the handymen but I don't know his name—moves his large frame as if to conceal their scrawny legs sticking up into the air.

From the corner of my eye I see a shadow. I brace for impact and instinctively raise my arms. An owl—face round like a disc, head pulled back, and talons spread wide open—pounces on the struggling bird and then thrusts upward, spreading its wings, carrying the fidgeting grackle with it. The man and I stare at each other, then we gaze up at the sky. The owl has disappeared.

"Well, I'll be damned," he says and the shovel lands with a clunk on the walkway.

Tipped-over rat bait stations and green chunks lie scattered about. Didn't they mention something about the sanctity of wildlife in that brochure?

Neither one of us mentions the dead birds.

Marleen told me there was a mix-up. That's not what she said, her words were quite harsh and there were lots of tears, more a stern lecture to not mess with the bills, those were her words. *Mess with.*

A month ago I came upon a contractor's estimate for the kitchen renovation at Hawthorne Court. Some oversight while packing, the paperwork must have ended up with my bank statements. I would have discarded the papers altogether if it hadn't been for the rather silly logo that jogged my memory: two gnomes with red pointy hats, *Kitchen Magic, Inc.* The cheapest estimate by far, yet it took two months for the kitchen renovation and delayed our move to Hawthorne Court by weeks. I feel anger when I'm reminded of Edward's constant miser mode. Before I knew it, I tore at the papers, shredding them, wanting to gnarl at them like a wild animal.

I must have ripped up other paperwork in the process and thrown out bills that subsequently didn't get paid and then the phone rang, one call after the other, and Marleen was upset, so much more so than anyone should be over paperwork, and I remember thinking *why doesn't she just put someone in charge of the bills?* But she *is* the one in charge.

Marleen made me promise not to go through the drawers again but the incident also opened a floodgate of emotions: finances, bank statements, insurance policies, legal contracts, everything pertaining to my financial situation is unknown to me. Edward takes care of all the financial affairs though I'm not aware of any settlement or if he has filed for divorce. No one's served me with papers, I've never signed any kind of documents relating to anything financial, nor have I been contacted by a lawyer. There's no prenuptial agreement—neither one of us brought anything into the marriage but our good intentions—and I have signed neither a lease nor anything related to utilities. I'm not aware of a health or life insurance policy, of investments, annuities. Was there a settlement? Is there alimony? Or is Edward paying for Shadow Garden as long as he sees fit? Until . . . until? No contract I can hold Edward to, no agreement of support. What would I do, where would I go?

I'm hardly prepared to support myself and what happens if Edward decides to abandon me completely? And mostly, why would he not? I'm not worth anything to him, the smidgeon of loyalty he has left for me will eventually fade.

I get angry, mostly at myself. For not knowing. The scenarios I imagine create a panic I can hardly contain, not a hypothetical panic, not some made-up situation, no, I've seen some Donna Pryors around here. I've seen them on the trails, well off, just look at their clothes and shoes, and those handbags they carry, their nails immaculate, not a wrinkle in their clothes, not a scuff mark on their shoes. I've also seen husbands trade in wives for younger women, I've seen how easily alliances shift and money gets tight, I've seen men live it up with the new woman and call destitution in front of a judge. I've known court cases to drag on for years.

I open the drawer where Marleen keeps all the files, but they are gone. She must have moved them because all they contain is a bare minimum of flatware and kitchen utensils where the files used to be. In the drawer below that, underneath a tray of sterling tea strainers, bouillon scoops, cheese picks, cake servers, and caviar forks, I find a folder but all it contains are medical bills. There's not a scrap of paper relating to a divorce or a settlement.

Now that my head is clearer, I should get legal advice. I flinch when I imagine a version of myself scraping by in an apartment with cheap carpet, laminated countertops, and a small storage room on the balcony. It's not an image I plan to entertain. I didn't go to medical school but I had just as much to do with Edward's success and anyone who wants to say otherwise, I challenge. We did good things and good things came to us.

If Shadow Garden is my consolation prize, what's Edward's? I've fretted endlessly about it, have weighed the options, teetered from guilt to *he would never* to *how much do we really know another person?* Is keeping Penelope from me his final revenge? I'm not insinuating Edward is capable of hurting Penelope—that's not at all what I'm saying—but maybe Edward wants Penelope all to himself? Some sort of psychological manipulation when parents separate, which happens every day in so many families. The fact that both have cut off contact with me makes me suspicious of Edward.

He was the kind of man who went to work every morning, face cleanly shaven, shirt starched, tie knotted, forever cheerful and personable with his employees and patients, just to come home and take critical glances at renovations and new furniture. Money was one thing—there was lots of it—but Penelope was another, an only child getting caught in the crosshairs of our squabbles. He complained how I monopolized her and he blamed his trouble connecting with her on my taking up so much of her time. We clashed about everything pertaining to Penelope's future. It all came to a head when I had my mind set on having her attend the International Debutante Ball.

"What's wrong with a grand ballroom where young women from all over the country are introduced to society?"

"This is clearly out of our league," he replied.

Attending etiquette classes and preparing for the ball would take years and Edward visibly cringed at the thought of it all. I had envisioned the gown—Spanish guipure lace and three-dimensional flowers—but participants had to excel in something. Hadn't one of the girls been an award-winning math scholar a couple of years back?

"What a parade of clowns," Edward said and put his foot down. "For one, it's an archaic notion," he said, but I understood his issues to run much deeper; it was just another activity that he'd feel left out of. Like the playhouse, which had drawn harsh words from him, especially because it wasn't something we could afford then. "I know I spend a lot of time at work but I'd like to . . ." He couldn't find the right words. "You two have this connection," he said, "and I feel I'm on the outside looking in."

But Edward was all talk and no action. He hadn't had the patience to practice division and subtraction with Penelope nor had he witnessed how difficult she could be. I had never explained to him how unsettled I was by some of her behavior, never mentioned when Penelope regressed to wetting the bed at eight.

I don't know what it all means. Was I given a task to complete as a parent and I failed? Was I tested? Is that what this was all about? I am always searching for answers in the dark, always wandering aimlessly to understand.

Outside my window I see a couple, a man and a woman. The man does the gentlemanly thing and lets her rest her arm in the crook of his. I find it romantic, so much more so than holding hands. I'm oddly moved by them. My mind retreats into memories of my marriage. There's the happy part, and then there's reality. Stark and relentless: I have no clue what will become of me if Edward decides to cut me off financially.

The gibberish rush in my mind cumulates into one single thought: no sense in kidding myself, I'm at the mercy of Edward Pryor.

5

EDWARD

The cast-iron gate closed behind Edward. With one final shudder, the wheels rolled across the tracks, the chain quieted. Shadow Garden sat like a barbican, all that was missing was a drawbridge and a moat. As he drove off, the road dipped down and the building disappeared in his rearview mirror.

He was in a state. As if the gate's final tremor had kindled his brain's neurons, a dozen things were knocking on his door waiting to be acknowledged. Edward took stock: this was it. Donna was gone. Not *gone gone*, but gone from his life.

He had never taken the time to reflect. It wasn't for a lack of want or need but for a lack of time. His parents, though they had the financial means to put him through college, had insisted on him working and grinding away and had turned him into a workhorse. He didn't harbor any resentment regarding the money part, but they had all but expected him to practice family medicine, not that his parents knew what was best for him or what his dreams were, they wanted a son who was a local doctor in the town they'd lived all their lives.

What do parents really know about their children anyway, right?

Penelope was his only child so there were no feelings or money or time to be divvied up, it was all her all the time, yet he knew nothing about her. He was now convinced all he had ever seen of his daughter were versions of her, adaptations. Renderings, at best.

He'd always wanted a family. The thought of children had manifested long before the marriage part. The woman who would be the mother of his children remained elusive. There were girlfriends, of course, quite a few, but it wasn't until he was halfway through medical school that he began to think about the kind of wife he wanted, though he had always been clear about the qualities he wanted to instill in his children. Five kids sounded about right to him. One would become a physician like him, one would turn into something lofty like a writer or painter—which was bound to happen with a gaggle of children—two of his daughters would marry well, among them there might be one or even both tying the knot due to an unplanned pregnancy, nothing to be embarrassed about. He imagined a dark horse somewhere in there, one child that would emerge within the competition that was inevitably going to ensue among so many siblings, one who seemed unlikely to succeed yet would prove everyone wrong, would live out his or her dreams, whatever living out one's dream meant.

His father had had a vision for his family. Edward's brother, George, ran a gas station and a car wash, his sister Victoria was a teacher, and Denise, the youngest of the siblings, had four foster children. As soon as one aged out of the system, she took in another. He used to be closest to George though they hadn't spoken in years. Four siblings, one to heal, one to educate, and one to care for others, an entire family seeing to the success and health of humanity, and George, well, George was George and he liked to spend his money on trips to Atlantic City, had a couple of failed marriages and children from them, though that part wasn't talked about. He was that one loose brick, yet the family foundation didn't crumble. *You are your choices,* Edward's father used to quote some philosopher, then add some gems of his own making—*a path of your own design,* and *every choice you make makes you in turn*—and Edward had by all accounts done the right things and had imagined his life to take shape accordingly, the way puzzle pieces automatically click into place.

He often pondered an existence in which he'd never met Donna, never married her. It had been a slippery slope lately, one he tried to avoid, but it was a thought he had been entertaining. Say, if he had married another woman. Become a father to another woman's children. He didn't want to think of Penelope as not having come into existence, yet here he was, wondering what his life might have been like without her or her mother.

Edward accelerated. Suddenly he couldn't get away from Shadow Garden fast enough. He had no clue if he was doing the right thing—he had just dropped off his wife like a pesky relative who had overstayed her welcome—and just like that, guilt saw an opening and swooped in, and a fair share of guilt at that. He couldn't help but think he should have known, seen the signs.

There are none so blind as those who will not see.

It all started out with so much hope. He had met Donna in the ER at Houston Methodist, where he worked as an intern. When he rubbed the stethoscope on his thigh to warm it up, her childlike voice spoke of flu symptoms: cough, aches, nausea, fatigue, and a fever. He observed her being short of breath and she complained of short and stabby chest pain. An X-ray showed atypical pneumonia and he treated her with antibiotics. Donna caught his eye not because she was beautiful but because, though she was flushed and coughing and unable to keep food down, she was looking to him to make her well. He had made people well before, as much as an intern can whose every diagnosis and test is signed off by a resident, yet he caught himself checking in on her more often than he had to.

It wasn't a grandiose and sweeping love affair, Edward wasn't looking for that, figured what came on quickly and powerfully waned just as fast, while slow and steady would win the race. The relationship began with a natural ease, revolved from acquaintances to friends, from friends to lovers, though it took them a year to become a couple. They married informally at a justice of the peace. No family attended.

He had wondered about that often, why they didn't have a big wedding with family and cousins and people flying in from all over the country. To his recollection, Donna said she needed time to plan the wedding but then came the residency, and Penelope's birth, the move to Florida, the modest house they bought, and then she seemed to have lost interest. How could she have been such a frugal and pragmatic person then, compared to the woman who ended up throwing parties with tents and caterers and valet parking? Once he generated a fortune, she was all about showing it off, had the mentality of someone winning the lottery just to end up destitute within two years' time. It was a gradual change, he liked to think, and therefore it was hard to pinpoint the moment she changed, and he often saw himself as a lobster in cold water and Donna turned on the burner and he happily drifted off into a stupor.

Edward had learned a lot about himself when he became a father. The way the world tilted the moment he held Penelope, the vulnerability six pounds of flesh created inside of him, a helpless bundle wrapped in a generic hospital blanket, a milky white synthetic material with thin stripes in blue and pink. Her mere existence opened him up to so much more than anything he had experienced thus far. But his love for his daughter was complicated by the detachment he had cultivated and refined over the years. It was not something that had come easy to him, it was a rather unnatural skill, he was not *not* compassionate, but he had to learn to suppress this innate sympathy. It had taken him years to get to that point but he eventually came to see death as the result of a disease and not of the care he gave.

Edward balanced on that fence for a while—the detachment on one side, this crushing love for his daughter on the other. It was impossible to teeter back and forth between those extremes. The physician in him was trained to disconnect and though it was useful and necessary, he might have taken it too far. He ended up with a limited capacity for caring altogether and a sense of distance snuck between him and the rest of the world and ultimately Penelope got caught up in that. One day he awoke and no longer embodied his role as a father.

Though he blamed Donna for monopolizing Penelope, it wasn't up to her to foster their father-daughter relationship, but he knew it was the sting of *I'm-not-a-perfect-father* that made him fault her. He knew that about himself but he didn't want to admit it to Donna, didn't want to complain, saw it as some kind of ungratefulness—because look at what they had achieved, look at this life, this house, the cabin by the lake, the cars, the money, their standing in the community.

He'd achieved his status by choosing detachment from those around him, coupled with an innate need for proficiency, and add to that his curiosity, his way of wanting to get things done faster and more efficiently. That was what had led to his patents and one day he realized he had made a name not only in the community but worldwide, was asked to speak at international medical conferences, and was given awards. He was a success, he had arrived.

He was man enough to admit the sacrifices he'd made to himself but Donna was a different story altogether. The past couple of years or so distrust had crept in and burrowed itself a den. Donna told little lies Edward ignored for the most part, and when he did ask her about inconsistencies—money she'd spent or another renovation she didn't tell him about, issues concerning Penelope—she blamed it on absentmindedness and maybe she was a bit of an airhead after all, something his mother had alluded to. But when did all this mistrust start? This deeply entrenched wariness he felt toward Donna, it couldn't have been that far back—or could it? This needle was hard to thread.

Here he was again, obsessing about Donna when he should have . . . Then the thought comes, a good-for-the-goose-good-for-the-gander moment; maybe he too had been taught to look the other way, like his parents did when it came to George, his brother, who gambled and had more money problems than anyone cared to admit. One of his sisters, Debbie, had problems too, but no one ever acknowledged that either. She was an alcoholic, had been sober for decades now, but back then they all looked the other way. Had he and Donna brought their own little carry-on baggage to this marriage, were they both to blame? All along he thought this life had come with some sort of a guarantee, and it wasn't until he left Shadow Garden and Donna behind that he understood his limitations.

Edward took a deep breath and straightened his tie by slowly running his hand from knot to tip. How eager he had been all these years to stay trim and fit and how loose the fitted shirt was now. Nothing was right, not his clothes, not his life. Not this car, the house. It had all become ill fitting. *Disengage,* he told himself. It's done. *Disengage* and *separate.*

Except, he couldn't free himself of Donna. She tore at him. The way she had clowned around even on the ride to Shadow Garden, how she cracked jokes about everything. Old shrew this and weeping hag that. It was all a joke to her. One big goddamn joke.

He floored the gas pedal, turned onto the highway, and true to its German origins, the car remained stable even as he accelerated way beyond the speed limit. The signs flew by, cars honked at him or hastily switched lanes to allow him to pass. When he reached the underground toll lane, the concrete barriers propelling him forward like chutes, he felt a sense of calmness. Just a twitch of his arm and the car would turn and collide with the concrete wall and that would be the end of it. Nothing lives that hits concrete at this high a speed. He wasn't planning on doing just that, but it felt good to know the tunnel wasn't going anywhere.

As he turned onto his street, a neighbor passed him. Edward panicked, didn't know if he should smile or wave or not do anything at all. It might come up later, how he acted in the aftermath of it all. Edward slowed and lifted his fingers in a greeting while his hand remained on the steering wheel, that's what he'd normally do. He'd have to get used to that—being normal.

When he reached his driveway, he sat in the car and his body wouldn't move. He stared at the inlayed brick, the house number, the name, *Hawthorne Court*, the cursive letters—what was it with people and naming houses, he'd never understand. Something struck him: it was the first time he'd come home and Donna wasn't waiting for him—burden or gift, he wasn't sure.

He cut the engine and got out, unlocked the front door, but his hand hovered over the doorknob. He had no way of knowing if he'd done the right thing but it was the only thing to do, or so he told himself, and therefore he should be absolved from guilt.

6

DONNA

Marleen extends a round porcelain bowl with pills. I scoop them up, put them in my mouth, and take a sip of water from a glass on the nightstand. She leaves the room and I lean back and listen to the sounds of the house. Marleen karate-chops the throw pillows on the couch (I don't care for that look but I won't correct her) and wipes the kitchen counters (there is the tearing of a disinfectant wipe from the container, followed by the sound of the garbage can lid clinking shut shortly thereafter). Her heels clack, make their way down the hallway and into the powder room, followed by a silence during which she undoubtedly straightens towels on the shelf.

The house phone rings. Marleen's explanation about someone punching in the wrong numbers at the gate sounds contrived. I want to get up, hurry from my bedroom down the hallway and into the kitchen, want to get to the bottom of this—want to grab the receiver and demand to know who is on the other end of the line— but the phone stops ringing. I don't want to be in this state of mistrust but—

That book on the nightstand. I hadn't noticed it before. Its pages are tightly bound, I can barely see the beginning of the lines. As the spine cracks open, the glue dissolves and pages are loosening before my eyes. A piece of paper falls out. One of those lists I make to remind me of all the things I have to do? I unfold it. It's a drawing. A child's drawing. Penelope's drawing. Large heads on small bodies, fingers like tentacles pointing upward, then turning into scribbles all over the page as if she were trying to erase it all. Dozens of colored markers, yet she drew exclusively in black and red. Never a rainbow, never a field of flowers. When I carefully probed about the intended meaning, she just shrugged. Or said it's what's in her head. Or something like that. So many years have passed, I can't read into it now.

Ch'trik. The front door locks.

There's a pull behind my eyes. My limbs are heavy, something lures me to sleep.

It seems as if—no, I'm pretty sure of it—there's a sleeping pill among the statins and the anti-inflammatories. A sleeping pill so potent that I don't recall ever having woken up in the middle of the night since I've moved here.

My last thought is of Penelope. And like so often, the last image is of her face, evanescent, as if behind a bridal veil—always a bridal veil—and it's hard to interpret. I want to think it's a clue that she's happy somewhere. But I also see a slick wet pool of red. As if on cue, my heartbeat slows to a peaceful rhythm, and like counting backward before surgery, the curtains come down all at once. First the world as I know it is there, then it isn't.

It's not until morning, until I get out of bed and step on the book, that I remember the drawing. For a few minutes it all feels like a dream. I protest but Marleen gathers everything and stuffs it all into a garbage bag and the garbage bag into a bin.

Between keeping the house neat and tossing the drawing, I wonder if Marleen was out of line on that one. I'll mention it to Vera later, she is good at putting things into perspective. I do confide in her a lot, maybe more than I should. Edward wouldn't approve if he knew how much I tell her about my former life. He'd turned into a strangely private person and I can admit that now, he went from clearheaded to paranoid. Edward being paranoid—that goes against all reason, or does it?

Occasionally Vera reads from one of her novels in the space off the lobby with fireplaces and immaculately polished hardwood floors. It's a special occasion and that afternoon, I get my nails done in a salon in the main building. I take my time picking out a color, nothing fancy, a nude shade will do, yet I'm forever undecided—Flesh, Ballerina, Anonymous, Jade Rose, Incognito—and later, we take our seats in rows of chairs.

It has taken me quite some time to warm up to Vera. For the longest I couldn't remember her name, Valerie or Vivian or Viola, but once we got talking, we felt comfortable around each other. Vera and I, we both had a moment in the limelight. Vera was catapulted into fame almost overnight with a book, and I, I was Miss Texas 1985. My winning gown and sash are now memorialized in a shadow box. I just had the gown dry-cleaned and reframed and Penelope has yet to see it in my bedroom above the fireplace.

I'm always looking forward to Vera's readings, her novels have garnered critical acclaim in Europe, there's a lot of loathing and suffering and I feel an instant kinship with her characters as they seem to be in a constant state of existential threat.

A podium has been set up, staff in black pants and white shirts pass trays around. The hors d'oeuvres leave a lot to be desired, avocado and crab toast and some shrimp on a stick. I must mention this to Vera, she relies on me to tell her such things, her head is always in the clouds and I'm her voice of reason in these matters as she is mine when it comes to my emotions.

Vera takes the podium. She commands it, her oval tortoiseshell glasses high on the bridge of her nose, pausing intermittently for maximum impact, the breaks arranged so perfectly that her words connect instantly with the audience.

Vera reads an excerpt of one of her novels. Ludvig, a boy from a remote farm in Sweden, is expected to slaughter a pig but he dreads the blood, the taking of a life. To teach him a lesson, his family abandons him in a vast and surreal landscape. He sets out on a path, past rolling hills, a setting as dramatic as his feelings about nature, and ends up in the mountains, where he encounters a sounder of starving boars and witnesses a wolf devour them. He could intervene but he doesn't and so the boars meet their fate.

I watch the people seated in front of me, the way their heads snap sideways, making eye contact during the gory parts. Throats are clearing, there's twitching and sneezing, not everyone enjoys this violent and dark tale. In front of me a couple exchanges glances during the grisly tearing apart of the boars, behind me I hear nervous tappings of feet, and a couple of people get up and leave the room. Two women talk too loudly—their voices travel in the large space—and are asked to leave. There's a loud huff from a woman behind me. "Why is she doing this?" she asks, and the person next to her whispers in her ear. I throw a dismissive look at them, then focus my attention on Vera.

I'm captivated by the story, and the abandonment of a child, though clearly fictional, stirs up something inside of me. I imagine Penelope being lost in the dark of night, endlessly wandering in unfamiliar surroundings. But I see myself in Ludvig's resolve and like a needle scratching off a record, my instincts are roused: the drawing in that book, who put it there, what was it meant to convey? I'm unwavering and being unwavering is one of my strong suits. Edward will tell you that. Something is afoot. A blind woman could see that.

The alarm clock LED display is the only light in the room. Marleen's nightly preparation of the house plays out: doors close, cabinets bang, the venetian blinds go *krrr-krrr-krrr-krrr*. Footsteps approach.

 8:45.

Marleen presents the small porcelain dish with my medication. I scoop up the four pills but instead of dropping them into my mouth, I tuck them underneath my thumb, pressing them into the soft part of my palm. I tilt my head back and take a sip of water. As Marleen pulls the duvet taut at the end of the bed, I stow the pills underneath my pillow.

 8:46

Marleen's heels click on the hardwood floors. In the parlor, she closes the drapes and slides the metal hook of the tassels back on the tieback. Her heels make their way through the apartment with long strides and intermittent pauses. The hinges of the linen closet shriek.

 8:58.

The toilet in the powder room flushes and the lid clanks shut. From the kitchen familiar sounds of putting away dishes fill the house. Marleen's shadow passes by my bedroom twice—she has turned off the lights in the hallway by then—her keys clink, a sign she's about to leave.

I do something I've never done before. I stand by the bedroom door and watch her.

Marleen places something on the fireplace mantel, slides it toward the back, where her hands pause, fiddle around as if she's making sure it sits in a very specific spot. Keys jingle again and weather stripping sweeps across the marble floor. The front door lock snaps in place. A gate slams in the distance and for a long time there are no sounds.

9:08.

Sliding my fingers underneath the pillow, I dig until I hold the four pills in my hand. There's a tiny orange pill, a statin. The white oval is an anti-inflammatory for my hip. The round pale yellow one is an allergy pill I was prescribed after I complained about itchy eyes. The pastel green round pill, I have no idea what it is.

9:09.

I wait.

9:14.

My bare feet don't cause so much as a creak on the hardwood floors. The bedroom door swings open without a sound. In the parlor, I push up the dimmer and the light fixture spreads a soft shimmer across the room. The drapes are closed.

On top of the fireplace sits an array of items that don't quite go together. A vase, candlesticks, a statue—I've developed a fondness for the depiction of the woman cradling a child in her arms—and as I run my finger down it, I am surprised it is cold to the touch. It's not resin after all, is it? Off the cuff, I push it aside a few inches. It's heavy but it budges though it bumps the bottom of the vase which I barely keep from tumbling to the ground. A key is tucked behind it, a gold key with long teeth and I am not sure if this is the item Marleen was placing so perfectly. Is it one of the spare keys she leaves in the house in case she misplaces hers? I have told her a copy in a kitchen drawer would suffice.

Marleen misplaced her set of keys before and once locked herself out of the house. There were meltdowns during which she was almost in tears, once pounding on the front door. Another time she rapped on the window. I didn't question her theatrical behavior nor did I try to understand it though I thought it to be overly dramatic.

She does get worked up about things a lot, I wish she didn't but that's part of her constitution.

I attempt to insert the key into the front door but it doesn't fit. The only other door with a lock is the one leading out of the storage room.

There, boxes are stacked on top of one another. Though the room is a mess, it seems methodical somehow as if the boxes are supposed to create a path. The light entering from the hallway is enough for me to look around, and though I've been in here many times—usually poring over a box Marleen has picked out—this time the shadows are different, the chaos seems to be held at bay by the limited light. There's the door behind a tower of boxes, but it is not an interior door, it looks sturdy, and once I make my way down what feels like an aisle in a grocery store, I put my hand on it. It's made of metal, like an exterior door. I slide the key into the key-hole without resistance. It grips and unlocks.

The opening leads outside, into the breezeway where the dead birds were. As I peer around the doorframe, moths as large as hum-ming birds whir around electric lanterns emitting a faint glow. Os-cillating carbon filament bulbs swing rapidly from side to side, mimicking a flame. Lampposts cast shadows, elongated, dark, and menacing. There's a flashlight in the kitchen drawer but using it would only draw attention to myself.

I step into the night and look up into the starry sky.

Edward and I own a cabin in Angel Fire, New Mexico. We spent a week there now and then, whenever he could make the time. I called it *a dip into the mountains* and at night it was so dark we once observed the zodiacal light. One must understand how uncommon such an occasion is during which millions of light particles com-bine to create a cone so long it touches the horizon like a worldly connection to the stars above.

Just look, Edward said, one arm wrapped tightly around me as he pointed at the band of light in the night sky. *Do you know how rare this is?* he added.

Almost as if we're chosen, isn't it? I asked and meant it.

The sky is for everyone, Donna, he said.

We are chosen, I insisted and Edward didn't object.

My thoughts are caught up in the memories of the cabin when on the other side of the courtyard, beyond the lawn, I hear a clacking sound. I step behind a large myrtle. A woman is coming down the walkway across the lawn, dragging a bag behind her. A clacking of bottles on the lawn, all the louder for the absence of daylight and people. I recognize her. I don't want to embarrass her and remain in the shadows.

Vera has mentioned her peculiar fascination with people's garbage—*but don't go around gossiping about it, I don't need people talking*; she uses it for inspiration for her writing, her exact words were, *I can tell a lot from people's garbage*—but I imagined her retrieving papers or discarded mail. I never so much as thought that she'd go through garbage like a raccoon in the middle of the night. Vera tows the bag to her front door, then slogs it over the threshold, a key scrapes in the lock, and her front porch goes dark.

That's what you get for snooping, I think. *You see things you can't unsee.*

A light comes on in what seems like my foyer. I rush across the lawn. My blinds are shut only halfway. Are people talking inside? I step closer but there's a concrete stoop below the window and I misjudge its height. My right foot, muddy and wet and smeared with filth, taps against it. I stumble, hit the ground, and break the fall with my left knee. I manage to get up. With my heart pounding, I shoot around the corner but before I can slip back into the breezeway and the storage room, I hear footsteps. They sound out of nowhere, there isn't a buildup in volume or a quickening of pace, they are just suddenly *there*.

I step behind a tree but the thin trunk leaves me exposed. I crawl into the mulch behind the shrubs but this isn't a sufficient place to hide either. I listen into the dark night but hear nothing, not a footstep, not the opening or the closing of a door. Nothing but a hum in the air, an anticipation of something I can't put my finger on. The hum intensifies. A whisk and a tick. With a *sssssssh-chk-chk-chk sssssssh-chk-chk-chk*, sprinkler heads emerge from the ground. In an instant my clothes cleave to my body like a second layer of skin.

Voices. They linger, nameless at first, then my mind shifts into reality. I recognize the silhouette. I *think* I recognize the silhouette. The way he walks, moves. It's Edward. As peculiar as this is, on the borders of my consciousness, there's another voice. Marleen's. Then they're gone.

I root the lawn, scan the courtyard, then the breezeway. I part the bushes and shrubs. I turn around quickly as if I'm attempting to catch someone standing behind me. There's no one, not in the breezeway where the man swept up the dead birds, not down the path. I turn again, just to make sure, but the walkways remain deserted and not a soul is about this time of night. Farther down, the silvery sidewalk fades between the buildings, disappearing into complete and utter darkness. I make a run for the breezeway and go back inside. I lock the door behind me.

I should have followed the voice. Should have confronted Edward right then and there. *Should have. Could have. Would have.* Was it Edward after all? I'm reminded of the night I woke and thought I was still living with Edward at Hawthorne Court. It was a bewildering feeling, like memories competing for priority. Getting out of bed there was a straight shot, but here the bathroom door is off to the side and so I stood with my hands pressed against the wall and felt my way around. A moment of confusion, like feeling disorientated by accidentally getting out of a hotel elevator on the wrong floor.

I must admit at times I jostle with recollections of Hawthorne Court and Shadow Garden. They overlap. My brain plays with both before settling on the correct one. Losing my former life is a difficult thing to come to terms with and sometimes I struggle to find the right memory but in the end my brain resolves the conflict.

Marleen's voice? While I've been busy organizing and moving in, getting my life down to a schedule that resembles some sort of existence, the voices I heard have confirmed what I've been thinking for a while: I no longer trust her.

When I allow myself to state it so matter-of-factly, it sounds menacing. I wonder what's easier: to be confronted with the facts or to forever imagine the worst.

The next morning, to occupy my mind, I look around the living room as if I'm seeing it for the first time. My apartment at Shadow Garden is a beautiful place, I have to admit as much; the fireplace to my right, carved marble with soft beige undertones and veins swirling together, is slightly too small for the room but that's not what bothers me: the mantel appears disjointed, off balance. A vase. The one I nearly dropped last night. It's a tacky thing I don't recall purchasing or having received as a gift. It sits on the left side, shoved to the back, throwing off the symmetry of the pillar candles on the right. It's ugly and maybe I ought to get rid of it altogether.

A leather-bound book on the coffee table strikes me as foreign, an intruder in my familiar surroundings like a visitor's forgotten umbrella leaning in a corner, but then I recognize it, the cover embossed with a golden globe. I open it and a sudden rush of excitement surges through me as the veillike glassine sheet crumbles, then comes to rest.

The pictures are decades old: in one my hair is long and parted in the middle, before Penelope was born, on our honeymoon; the cabin in New Mexico; sitting on a rock at the edge of a lake, snow-capped mountains in the back, Colorado maybe? Some photographs have a bluish tint to them, taken before there was digital photography, when pictures came out the way they came out and you got what you got and you didn't complain. We had a camera with so many functions it boggled my mind and I eventually bought a point-and-shoot camera.

A series of images on a beach. I can almost smell the salty air, feel the wind in my hair, my skin dry, my lips cracked. Penelope, about four, building a sand castle with her legs folded up under her. Edward is scooping sand in a bucket. They both look into the camera, happy, carefree. I don't recall the moment but I probably said *smile*, or maybe I just caught them in a moment of happiness. Penelope's mouth is open as if she is saying something to me.

Most of the photographs are overexposed, the sun like a floodlight streaming in from the back, beaming rays not meant to be a special effect but a failure on my part. But still, the images are beautiful, anything but perfect, but beautiful. Look at those boats bobbing on the waves! The colors are striking, the pale sand and the waves whitecapped in the breeze, like brushstrokes placed by a painter. I'm not ready to abandon this scene to memory just yet, but a vibrant color catches my attention: the trip to a strawberry farm. Penelope clutches a basket full of berries, puny little things, barely a third the size of the ones in supermarkets. Red smudges around her mouth, smeared across her cheek with the back of her hand. Penelope's outfit was ruined that day, but the fun we had.

Like a gift from an unknown benefactor these photographs are conduits to the past, stuck to cardboard pages with glue, separated by flimsy paper to keep them from becoming worn and damaged.

I'm not naïve. Photographs are a world of make-believe. You have to look beyond the colors and the setting, the smiles, to recognize what they're really about. I turn the page and there it is. A portrait of Penelope. I stare at her face caught in a moment of perfection. Focusing on her eyes, I'm taken aback by how they glisten with the twinkle of laughter. The happiest memories hurt the most, cut the deepest. I clutch the album tight against my body.

The photographs remind me of what I've lost and that's all it takes for me to burst into tears. This is all that remains of those days, of our happiness. Marleen pries the album from my hands. Her eyes are wide and glaring, her eyebrows raised.

If I didn't know any better I'd say she's mad at me.

Later that afternoon, at my physical therapy appointment, I follow the instructions given to me. I stretch and extend, adduct, abduct. I complain about a lack of range of motion in my hip.

"You've been making super progress compared to where you started," the physical therapist, a stout blond man with a red beard, says and furrows his brows. His name is Jed and he wears L.L.Bean jackets. I feel compelled to roll my eyes every time he uses the word *super*.

"I'm still not where I want to be," I say as I turn on my side, knees bent to provide support. I straighten my top leg and slowly raise it. I hold for five, lower it, relax, and repeat. He doesn't know how well I am. Keeping my recovery a secret, I wonder what the point of it is.

My *super* recovery. The only thing I can imagine is I don't want Edward to find out yet. Maintaining this secret gives me some sort of power I can't quite put my finger on. My ace in a hole or up a sleeve, I forget how the saying goes.

I think of the wristwatch I bought Edward for our anniversary a couple of years ago, the way the jeweler had explained the apparatus, how springs were regulated by more springs, unwinding into a controlled and periodic release of time. Gears oscillating back and forth, and with each swing of the balance wheel the hands move forward at a constant rate. He'd wanted the watch for a while, was giddy with anticipation, and that's how it feels, my hidden recovery. Groundwork, I don't know for what, but I hear a constant *tick tick tick* in the background.

7

EDWARD

Edward Pryor, the scientist, believed in principles and reliable data which then led him to inevitable conclusions—that's how problems were solved. But even the most perfectly laid-out plans derailed at times and here he was, stuck in traffic. The last operation of the day would have to be bumped off the schedule. The proverbial monkey wrench in his game plan.

As he sat tapping his fingers on the steering wheel, an explosion sounded in the distance. The boom was followed by a ball of flame and a fist of gray smoke. Maybe he should offer his help, though the OR schedule would really be shot for the rest of the day, but it was the right thing to do. Just as he was about to reach for the door, an ambulance passed by him. Sirens and blinking lights, police cars and ambulances, they came and went and finally the traffic inched forward. He passed a car with a smashed hood, another fifty yards and a dented fender was left discarded by the side of the road. In a field a car sat reduced to a muddle of parts and broken glass, nothing but a skeletal burnt frame, the earth scorched around it.

His phone rang but he swiped the call away. Donna. Last night they'd settled it: no more back and forth half-hearted ultimatums and lax demands. They had finally agreed that Penelope had one more month to get it together. It was time to move out.

"I'm not holding my breath on this one," Edward told Donna, who was preoccupied with three packages of English muffins. He watched her ponder each bag—white, whole grain, and low fat—the way her eyes squinted at the labels. Penelope had specific preferences and most of the time Donna aimed to please her but usually Penelope took one bite and the rest ended up in the bin. Edward wanted Donna to stop indulging her every whim but who says that to a mother?

Donna swept up the muffins and stuffed them in the fridge.

"We should have done this a long time ago, maybe that's what she needs. An ultimatum, a clear line in the sand. We are doing her a disservice by coddling her," Donna said and checked her wristwatch. "She'll be twenty-nine. At twenty-nine . . ." Donna's voice trailed off but Edward knew what she was going to say. How they had to make do when they were young, make adjustments, and how this generation was pampered, carrying their anxieties with them like a designer purse, *look what I got,* expecting everyone to acknowledge and pander to their emotions.

"I paid her credit card yesterday. You should see those charges," Edward said.

"What kind of charges?"

Edward glanced toward the stairs but it was before seven, Penelope was upstairs asleep.

"All retail. And restaurants. And cash withdrawals. Who gets cash advances on a credit card?"

"Well, it is what it is."

But was it really? Edward wasn't sure.

His phone rang again and he let it go to voice mail again. Donna was going to give up eventually. He'd be prepping for surgery in fifteen minutes, he'd be in scrubs by now if it wasn't for this accident, and any minute she would give up pestering him.

Donna's steadfast resolve to support Penelope had waned and he couldn't blame her for it. Edward had been fed up for a while himself and finally they were on the same page. He had spent a fortune renting apartments and houses—had never seen the deposits back on any of those—had offered to pay for college, proposed to invest in a business (once she'd come up with a viable business plan) but Penelope had decided on a real estate license. She had, to both their surprise, taken all mandatory classes and certifications. Maybe this was the progress they'd been waiting for and the looming move might do the trick. And according to the credit card charges she had also rented an office at a real estate firm.

"It's not an office. More a cubicle in a strip mall," Donna said. "It needs fresh paint and new carpet."

Edward imagined Donna dropping by the office in sunglasses high on the bridge of her nose, her coat collar popped up, asking to use the bathroom, snooping out the place. Office or cubicle, he was torn about the real estate thing. Penelope wasn't a people person and it wasn't what he wanted for her but it was an honest profession. He could live with that, had learned to be comfortable with being uncomfortable when it came to his daughter.

He saw Penelope at dinner every night. On the surface she seemed poised but there was something about her he couldn't put his finger on. Like she was constantly on edge. He could tell by the way she turned into a know-it-all, had an answer to everything, and quarreled with Donna about unlocked doors and dirty laundry left in heaps for days on end. Penelope acted agreeable enough, promised to do better yet never followed through and argued afterward about what she had meant. It made him bristle, her flighty behavior, avoiding eye contact.

"I said I'd do it. But don't tell me when and how."

This teenage rebellion behavior she should have outgrown by now, Edward recognized it for what it was: neglect of *anything not Penelope*. That's what he called it. If it didn't directly benefit her, it was a low priority.

It had been six months and Penelope living with them had begun to take a toll on Donna. She wasn't herself—he could tell by the way she forgot things, mixed up dates, an overall state of decline—as if Penelope's moods were rubbing off on her. A month prior, Donna had let the housekeeper go. She alluded to wanting to hire someone else but Edward knew without a doubt that she didn't want any witnesses to the volatile mother-daughter relationship. She feared gossip and Donna did her best to keep up with maintaining order in the house but the pristine condition he was used to was long in the past.

Edward had finally given Penelope an ultimatum. "One more month," he had told her. Penelope hadn't responded but got up and stormed out of the room, leaving Donna and Edward staring at each other.

With all this on his mind, the traffic cleared and moved, first at a snail's pace, but then the speed picked up. The scent of gasoline hung in the air and Edward fumbled with the recirculate function on the dash. The phone rang again. He almost answered it, his hand reached but then he decided otherwise. He refused to argue with Donna again. She went from *let her stay* to *make her move* to *tell her to leave today* and this morning there had been another quarrel right after, in which Donna once again doubted she was doing the right thing, never sticking to her guns when it came to Penelope.

"We said we'd see it through, Donna. The ultimatum was she has one more month to move out. It's only a few more days. Allow her that time, wait it out, and then we'll get on with our lives."

"I can't do it another day, Edward."

He wasn't going to budge. He wasn't going to answer his phone and argue about it, and a few more days weren't going to kill anyone.

As he got out of the car in the parking lot of his practice, there was yet another call. He ignored it. By now Donna was worked up about him not answering his phone, about not being able to get off her chest whatever had prompted her and Penelope to quarrel. He used to intervene but over the past few months their behavior had become increasingly difficult for him to navigate, and he was tired of walking around on eggshells in his own home and had a hard time shaking it all off and didn't they know the pressure he was under? They'd understand if any of them had any responsibility, held the lives of others in their hands like he did.

Once in the office, he checked labs and X-rays and prepared for the first operation of the day. A straightforward lipo followed by a mastopexy.

Every surgeon he knew performed rituals, every single one, and he was no different. He had always found the following to be true above all else: there was tremendous solace in rituals, in symbolic behaviors. The entire preparatory activity calmed his mind in ways nothing else could. It created control and reduced uncertainty.

Time to scrub in. A glance at the clock above the sink and he began timing. *Tick tick tick. Leave nothing to chance.*

He focused on the antimicrobial cleanser turning from yellow into white suds as he scoured his left hand with a brush. Scrubbing each finger and in between, the back and front of the hand for exactly three minutes, he moved on to the forearm, consistently keeping the hand higher than the arm at all times. Time check. He repeated the process on the other hand and arm, envisioned cuts and proportions, sutures and muscle fiber, existing scar tissue, and then he imagined the perfect end result.

Tick tick tick.

The operating suite phone rang. He looked up in surprise. It was unusual for a call to be put through once they had all gathered and were prepping for a procedure. Some last-minute funky lab result? Once a patient's husband had a heart attack in the lobby, such things happen.

A nurse answered on the third ring. "Dr. Pryor, it's your wife. It's urgent."

The nurse was unrecognizable behind her mask and splash guard—Connie maybe, or Debra, he couldn't tell—all he saw were raised eyebrows. The nurse glanced back and forth between him and his hands as she held out the phone.

"Put it close to my ear," Edward said and proceeded to scrub the left arm to three inches above the elbow for exactly one minute. An *emergency*. He couldn't deviate from the inescapable ritual, he had to adhere to his self-imposed constraints.

Tick tick tick.

"Donna. What's going on?" he asked, keeping his ear a safe distance from the phone to avoid contamination. She was breathless. He only comprehended every third word. *Here. Penelope. Come home. Need.* How glad he was he hadn't told the nurse to put the phone on speaker. "Focus," he said. "I don't understand what you're saying."

Hands in the air he stood, the nurse moving the phone in closer as she shifted from one leg to the other. He jerked backward. If the phone touched his mask, he would have to change his gown, would have to repeat the entire procedure. He rinsed his hands and arms with one single movement from fingertips to elbow by passing them through the water.

He had lost his momentum. He was supposed to be draped in a yellow paper gown in the operating suite, yet there he stood, hands above elbows, not understanding Donna's words. He glanced through the door into the operating suite where a nurse stood with a sterile towel in her outstretched hands, waiting to dry him off. A third nurse stood holding his gown and sterile gloves.

"Start from the beginning. I don't understand what's going on." He listened intently, even closed his eyes attempting to better con-

centrate on Donna's breathy words. "What happened? Repeat that?"
The nurse holding the phone looked past him as if to give him
a semblance of privacy, while the others were clustered in a far
corner.

Much was made later of this phone call. Each nurse had a different recollection of his reaction. One said he seemed impatient, another said he was business as usual. One said he balled his hands
into a fist. In reality he said—and these were his words verbatim—
"I'm scrubbed in. I'll call you back," and all the while he attempted
to maintain a sense of order. There were no balled fists, and it
wasn't business as usual either, but there were no harsh words, no
gasping, no argument. Nothing of that sort.

What he did do was tell the nurse to hang up the phone. Standing off to the side, waiting for the anesthesiologist to give him the
nod to begin the procedure, he attempted to focus on the patient in
front of him, her areas of perceived plumpness; the body lined and
dotted by permanent marker in front of him like a rudimentary
map. The man in him saw the body on the table as perfect, the plastic surgeon recognized areas for improvement.

He couldn't get Donna's voice out of his head, winded words escaping her mouth, *come home, come home, come home,* the slurring of
her words as if she couldn't be bothered to enunciate each syllable.
He felt his breathing become rapid and shallow and a primal urge
to flee the OR came over him and there was a momentary silence
in the room but for the beeping of the machines behind the patient
when he thought he might lose control. He would remember this
day with absolute clarity later: this epiphany, this moment of knowing something horrible was going to happen.

How many times had he returned home from work and watched
Donna set the table, impeccably dressed and poised and put together? They would have dinner and not until they went to bed
would she tell him of something Penelope had done and he wanted
to scream *how did you just get through this dinner without telling me?*

How did you just sit there and eat and make small talk when your daughter has become unhinged again? How did she get through all this unscathed, at least seemingly so? And now this, a breathless stuttering phone call, her incoherent carrying on.

Behind the blue drapes the anesthesiologist leaned to the left and glanced at him. The nurses became aware of his hesitation though he didn't know what they were thinking of this entire affair. He cleared his mind, willed himself to concentrate on the task at hand. After all, attention to detail was second nature to him, just like compartmentalizing had become a strength of his, cultivated by all these years as a surgeon.

"Let's do this," he said and nodded at everyone in the room.

He worked quickly and with focus. He injected diluted local anesthesia to reduce bleeding and swelling. Once the tissue was swollen and firm and the epinephrine took care of possible bleeding, he made a series of tiny incisions around the navel and one on each side of the patient's flanks. He inserted a thin hollow tube through the cuts and loosened the excess fat with a controlled back-and-forth stabbing motion. He reached farther and farther to the outskirts of the markings on the body in front of him while holding the tip of the tube down with his flattened hand so as not to puncture the skin. In a radiating pattern he pushed the cannula into layers of fat, creating tunnels, sucking liquid until the tube refused to give up any more blubbery secretion. The contents of the plastic containers, which were marked with lines and numbers, settled as the fat floated to the surface.

By the time he completed the left side of the abdomen, tension began to grow in the back of his neck like a tumor spreading at warp speed. It wasn't until the nurse was about to fit the compression garment, as he inspected the exposed chest of the patient, in that moment of mental easing that his mind produced images of his daughter: Penelope breastfeeding. Her first steps, first day in school. By then Penelope was elusive to him, no longer the small child holding on to his hand. He had maintained an image of her as being perpetually four years old with wispy hair blowing in the wind, cheeks flushed and hands sticky after a day at the beach, never as a grown woman. Did he want her to remain forever dependent on him or was it a wish on his part to return to happier times?

Etched into his brain stem was Penelope's perfect face with long lashes around green eyes the color of seaweed. So poised and graceful even at that age. *She knows things about this world other children don't,* he thought. How composed she was. Donna had called her Pea back then, and told him proudly how unruffled she was, how Pea couldn't be thrown off by anything. *She's so brave,* Donna said. *She never so much as grimaced when she got her shots.*

Donna's pride was one thing, but Edward was taken aback by Pea; was it normal for a child her age to ask to use the restroom when children her age still had accidents or wore training pants at the very least? Pea sought out adults rather than children, who didn't seem to be worth the bother. She was intellectually ahead, breezed through elementary school, picked up on reading and writing as if it was the most natural thing but Edward had always thought Penelope's maturity uncanny for a child, saw how she observed other children as if taking clues from them, watched and studied their mannerisms and sometimes she did something completely out of character because she'd seen another child do it. And with every incident he became more alarmed, and it dawned on him that he wasn't witnessing just his daughter's copying others but also feeling bewildered about how to be in this world.

Sooner than most children knew how to use their clumsy little hands, Penny insisted on using a fork, wouldn't eat unless they handed it to her. Maybe they shouldn't have allowed her such a thing—was that why she stabbed a child at a birthday party? Out of the blue, Donna told him, Penelope had raised a plastic fork and slammed the tines into a child's forearm.

How absurd it all sounded, melodramatic and removed from reality, and Edward caught himself ranting on in his mind like Donna had done earlier. Donna had just exclaimed to him the other day that she was no longer able to drive because of all the stress with Penelope and he didn't know what that was all about and suggested she get her eyes checked, to which she responded, *bless your heart, but it has nothing to do with my eyes.*

His stomach locked up tight.

"Dr. Pryor."

The voice of the OR nurse pierced through his thoughts, as if she had been attempting to gain his attention for a while. "The patient is ready for the next procedure. Everything okay?"

He wasn't okay. He was worried and the truth was, he had been for a while. Donna was acting peculiar and she couldn't be trusted. And Penelope. Her state of mind. He hadn't had a conversation that made sense with her in a week or two. Good at picking up on changes in her mood and variations in her verbal patterns, he had years of experience spotting something off.

"Scalpel," he said and reached for the shiny metal object but stopped just short of allowing it to make contact with his hand. There was a slight tremor in his left pinky finger. He wasn't concerned—his father and grandfather both had the same tremor, it was a non-specific tremble, nothing to worry about—but he had observed it lately while tying sutures, had cut himself shaving even. All this stress with Penelope and Donna didn't help.

Suddenly the marked body in front of him seemed like an abomination. This was a forty-year-old woman who looked like she was supposed to look; slight drooping of her breasts, a minimal amount of excess skin around the navel from three pregnancies, nothing he considered imperfect. But he would cut open her skin and stanch the bleeding, he'd tug and slice her breasts, had already ruthlessly stabbed her hips with a tube sucking out fat. It was a disgrace really, to spend his talent and his time with these surgeries when he could do so much good in the world. He would talk to the office manager as soon as he finished for today, would tell her to keep a week or so free so he could do some work abroad, like reconstructive surgeries, cleft palates, facial abnormalities, benign tumors disfiguring otherwise healthy bodies. Plastic surgeons had their root in postwar reconstructions of faces blown apart by grenades, skin grafts of mutilated bodies, the surgeon a tool of more than healing physical wounds, but restoring patients to their former selves. Not middle-aged men and women wanting to compete with a younger generation. He couldn't help but draw parallels to his very own life.

There he was again, ranting. *Focus,* he told himself. The woman's upper chest was sufficiently full, no implants needed. Raise the nipple, reduce the size of the areola, and remove excess skin. He knew every move, every single cut he had to make, could do so blindly guided by muscle memory alone, had done thousands of these lifts. Yet the tremor wouldn't stop.

"Dr. Pryor." The voice of the OR nurse ripped him from his hypervigilant state. "The patient is ready. Are you okay?"

"Scalpel," he said, and this time he grabbed the shiny metal object the nurse extended to him.

In the background were the soothing rhythmic sounds of the heart monitor and the gentle lifting of the oxygen sleeve. He poked the breast with the tip of his finger. The tissue was spongy, bounced back. He touched the body with the tip of the scalpel, increased the pressure, and watched the blood appear. The nurse wiped the scarlet line with gauze.

That tremor, he felt it more than he saw it, and hoped the nurse wouldn't pick up on it. He shifted in place, willed his mind to engage. A perfect circle around the areola. The second cut: vertically down to the breast crease. He knew every slice and tuck in his sleep, could reshape the tissue to improve contour and firmness in the dark, remove excess skin to compensate for a loss of elasticity with one eye closed. The third cut: horizontally down to the breast crease. He repositioned the nipple and areola to a natural and youthful height.

He stepped around the table and began work on the right breast. When the incisions were concealed and the sutures layered deep within the tissue and in the natural breast contours, he stepped back and motioned the nurses to prop up the bed, allow gravity to take over. The symmetry was perfect, the patient was going to be very happy.

He reached behind his back and pulled the strings, loosening the coat. He tucked the gloves within the fabric and tossed the bundle into the bin.

What the next step with Penelope was he wasn't sure. He'd been kidding himself. Penelope would never make it on her own. But what did his involvement look like? He couldn't lock her up, put her away in a box underneath the ground to keep her safe. Donna had used those words and he was taken aback by them then. He imagined a box in the ground, just how had her mind gone that far? Donna had her faults but she was a good mother, and for her to use those words frightened him.

He had one wish: to be able to alter Penelope's brain like he altered breast tissue and nasal tips and eyelids, to cut away the things that were not meant to be there. So easy to fix a body, make it look young and firm and perfect. He was capable of rewinding time but how could he fix a brain, one in which something malign did push-ups every day?

This he knew for sure: Penelope wasn't a model or a scientific equation. She was a human being and he'd failed her. That was certain, and for that he didn't need to run labs, check blood, or observe a cutting site. Failure. In all his years as a plastic surgeon he had never known what failure was.

The tremor was gone and his confidence returned. He could fix anything. He had successfully operated on a nose and septum once that was nothing but a gnarly pulp. Sometimes he had to perform controlled fractures, had to make it worse to make it better, and that's what he'd do, with mallet and chisel, he'd do what he had to do to make it all better.

8

PENELOPE

Penelope's mother spent hours looking at old photographs. She made Penelope sit next to her and pointed. *Here is your first time at the beach. Look, your first birthday. Remember the day you learned to ride your bike?*

Penelope stared at pictures of a girl in front of dollhouses, at beaches, and in the family cabin. Her mother remembered years and places—1993, Florida, Disney World; 1995, a cruise to Mexico—and recited the details like an itinerary. She never got confused, never mixed up the details, never said *wait a minute, what year was this?* There were photographs of a girl hanging upside down on monkey bars, a girl at birthday parties blowing out candles, a girl in a room filled with the quintessential childhood of American Girl dolls and Boxcar Children books.

Penelope believed her mother was telling the truth, didn't assume those stories to be lies. She recognized the girl in the pictures, yes, it was her, she was sure, but most of the details her mother relayed seemed made up. *You loved the beach*—Penelope broke out in hives within minutes of being exposed to the sun, tiny bumps merged into raised patches on her chest and arms—and how did her mother come up with having a fondness for animals? That was some far-fetched tale. There were photographs of Penelope kneeling next to a dog but they'd never owned a pet. Her body language clearly showed she was reluctant around the animal, she could tell by her forced smile and how she leaned away from it and her mother would never allow hair on furniture or the destruction of her immaculate lawn. There was a faint memory of a wooden swing, the creaking frame, swinging back and forth, feet lifted upward—a recollection of being suspended—but there was no picture of a swing anywhere. Her entire life felt that way, her mother relaying some picture-perfect past for which Penelope dug in every corner of her mind, yet she came up empty as there was never any proof for what she clearly remembered.

Penelope was about ten when those stories began to lead up to another activity: Her parents handed her paper and markers. Penelope looked forward to this and their undivided attention, and they didn't stare at her directly but clandestinely, via peripheral vision or random glances, they watched her. Later they'd gather the drawings to give them to someone to look at. Penelope knew that because a doctor asked her once about oversized hands she had drawn on herself and she told him those were leaves and not hands. Though there were red veins but he never asked about those. What she drew seemed to be very important to everyone.

Draw a picture of your parents.
Draw a picture of your house.
Draw a picture of your friends.
How childish to make her color as if she were a toddler, but she

liked how pushing down on the tip extracted the ink and dried out the once-vibrant marker until the paper dissolved and soiled the table underneath.

She couldn't explain the drawings, it wasn't anything recognizable or real. Once she drew a picture with waves coming out of her head. That was the closest thing to getting people to understand how she felt.

And so she drew happy pictures of happy houses with crooked roofs and crooked flowers bigger than the house itself and her happy family holding happy hands behind a crooked fence, the crooked slats taller than the happy house but spaced so you could still see the happy people in the yard. But that was not what was going on in her head. The inside of her was much darker. She imagined the doctor's thoughts, how they contemplated a possible switch between good and evil within her though they didn't call it good and evil but *right* and *wrong*.

Her mother was very specific about what was right and what was wrong. Right made her mother smile, like displaying concern and positive interactions (her mother's words) with other children. Her mother called it "lovable qualities" which in turn made up for her infractions, as if good deeds canceled out the wrong, as if pretending to be good made the wrong inside of her bearable.

And how exhausting it was to hide the wrong parts of her, with her mother always being around, watching. Penelope didn't pretend around her father as much, for one she hardly saw him but on the weekends, but she could somehow be herself around him, he never saw anything *nefarious* (her mother's word) in her every action. He asked her about the fork incident. That's what everyone called it as if she hadn't just planted fork tines in the forearm of a girl who chewed with her mouth open. The girl also moved her arm when she lowered the fork, which made it all worse.

Dad asked her why she did it.

The question rattled around in her head, and she kept her hands steady. *It builds up, and then I have to do it, I can't keep it away.* Penelope didn't say that. Even she knew that would be cause for concern.

"You didn't do it deliberately, did you?" he asked but Penelope remained quiet. "You weren't trying to hurt her?"

Penelope sat, listened, and concentrated.

"Was it an accident?"

Penelope moved her head in what could pass for a nod.

"I'm sorry," she said.

"It's okay," her father responded after a long while.

They played board games, but mostly he read to her and afterward she thought of alternative endings, born of her own imagination, and sometimes she got carried away, adding dark twists and turns. She was glad they never asked her to write but to draw instead.

Later, Penelope overheard a conversation between her parents. She stood in the dark behind her parents' bedroom door, which wouldn't shut because her mother had the door and the frame around it replaced for the third time.

"She was in a mood, all those kids and the noise," her mother said on the other side of the wall. "Should we take her back to the therapist, you think?"

"She's just a child, and we have to help her learn to function in the world, it's not rocket science," her father said.

Her mother's voice then. Solemn. Calm. "I don't want to see the other shoe drop."

Her father mumbled something Penelope couldn't make out.

"Don't be dramatic," she heard her mother's voice, followed by a door slamming and water running.

I am a shoe waiting to drop. It sounded sad but powerful at the same time.

Back in her room, Penelope colored over the lines of the paper and onto the table. Her mother would be mad.

The next day, after school, she could tell that someone had scrubbed the table clean. She asked her mother if she had touched anything in her room but she said no. Penelope observed marker stains on her mother's fingers, the kind that would take forever to disappear.

9

DONNA

I step outside and something stirs to my left. It's Vera, slouching her way to the common area with a book in one hand, wrapped in a wool shawl she is clutching with both hands. I watch her as she lowers her body into a metal chair in slow motion.

Every Wednesday, a man in a black suit leads Vera along the walkways as she hooks her hand around his upper arm. There is a certain familiarity between them. For a long time I believed he was her son who lived in the city somewhere but found out later it was her driver taking her on errands.

As I watch Vera, her face tilted back, toward the sun, her eyes closed, I'm reminded of the cabin in Angel Fire. I wonder if Edward has sold the cabin, maybe he'd be willing to put it in my name? I always enjoyed the leisurely weekends there and I suddenly long to be at the lake. In the mornings, the water condensed into mist as it rose from the lake, and the waves lapped the shore, where here, at

Shadow Garden, man-made fountains with electric motors pump water out of algae-covered copper spigots.

Vera sits, her mouth drooping, her neck now tilting sideways. What if she was dead, I think, how long until someone realizes? I slam the patio door shut. Vera jerks awake, puzzled. She lifts her hand and waves at me by merely wiggling her fingers about. I wave back. I motion to her with my hand and point at the chair next to her. Vera nods. When I drop into the chair, I look left and right to make sure there isn't anyone within earshot.

"Vera," I say and grab her book from her lap. I'm not interested in the book itself but I don't want her to get distracted, and she will, she always does. "I've made a decision."

"What's that, dear?"

"I'm going to see Edward. I have to talk to him." My breathing is heavy.

I wait for her response but there's none. Her face is turned toward the sun, her eyes are closed. After a long while, she speaks. "Edward?" she finally says. "You haven't spoken to him in months. Are you sure that's a good idea?"

"I don't care." I feel myself getting worked up, tears about to stream down my face. I've kept the desperation at bay but it's about to pour out of me. Vera has never seen me cry, though apart from exchanging pleasantries and gossip, she knows the gist of my story. I've spent hours relaying my life to her.

I take in a deep breath. "This is about money. I need to talk to him. I can't find any paperwork regarding a divorce or a settlement, anything about alimony."

"Why are you crying?" Vera asks, my tears throwing her off.

I go on and on, explaining how I should have insisted on legal papers, how hush-hush the time was just before Edward discarded me, how nebulous the weeks before, how I couldn't get out of bed, the melancholy—I want to avoid the D word at all costs—how my overall state of mind was neither here nor there, and how the edges of that time are no longer clear. And Penelope, I worry about Penelope. Always I worry. Always.

"Penelope hasn't called in months. I've no idea where she is or if she's okay. It's driving me nuts. And Edward, Edward doesn't know the half of it, he's not prepared to deal and so much has been happening, I . . ."

Vera doesn't display any negative notion though I can tell by her pursed lips that she has some sort of feeling about my disoriented stream of words.

"She's grown, but who doesn't call their mother?" I add.

"I don't call my mother."

"Your mother is dead, Vera."

She cranes her neck to look past me. A family with two small children approaches. One of them, a boy the age of five, maybe six, runs after a ball. It bounces and then rolls over the grass, toward us. He picks it up but then stares at us as if he wants to talk.

"Hi," he says and holds the ball in front of him like it's a big belly. "What are you doing?" He sounds squeaky and high-pitched, still so many years before he will lose his childlike voice.

Vera opens her mouth but before she can say anything, a woman appears and grabs the boy by the hand, pulling him away. He tugs on her arm but can't get loose. Her hands close around his twiggy upper arm, and she all but drags him a few feet.

"Parents are so rough these days," Vera says, loud enough for everyone to hear.

The mother—I'm willing to make that allowance and call her that since I spot a slight resemblance around the eyes and the nose—bends down and whispers in the boy's ear. I can see how tight her grip is around his arm, how she's attempting to keep him in check. And we don't know anything, maybe the mother is trying to protect the child, she doesn't know the first thing about us, apparently the boy is too trusting. I want to say all this to Vera but she doesn't have children, she wouldn't understand. The boy reminds me of

Penelope, she too was a headstrong child. *Don't judge her,* I want to say. *Maybe the child's a handful, a terror. You can't tell by looking at them.* It's always so convenient to say if a child goes wrong, look at the family. That was the very reason I never employed a nanny. How do you have strangers in your home, how do you act, how do you maintain privacy?

The family disappears around the corner and I turn back to Vera.

"Can you help me? Can you drive me to see Edward?" I ask.

"I don't have a car. You know that. We talked about that, Donna, dear, do you ever listen when I talk? The point of my being here is not to go anywhere. I have so much work to do and so little time. I'm not getting any younger." She hesitates as if she's searching for something to say but is immediately distracted by a door opening in one of the buildings farther down the path. A woman and a man with a Chihuahua emerge and the man drops the dog in the grass where he immediately squats. The woman scoops him up and off they go.

"Vera . . ." I say, not knowing how to go on.

"I'm sorry. I'm digressing, what's this all about?" Vera asks. "What's that got to do with Edward?"

"What will become of me?" I ask.

"Think of your daughter. She—"

"She won't speak to me," I interrupt. "But I won't allow him to keep Penelope from me."

"Keeping her from you?"

Vera is a writer. She picks words apart. *Keeping her*—the expression bothers her, I can tell. *Keeping her* implies he's physically restraining her somehow. It seems like an odd realization, the possibility of such a thing.

"You believe Edward is keeping Penelope from you?"

"When I say he's keeping her from me, I don't mean physically, I mean maybe he didn't tell her where I am. Or he told her lies about me. Or maybe . . . maybe she isn't well."

"What makes you say that?"

"Marleen . . ." I pause. How do I tell her about the voices I heard? The pills Marleen gives me. The key she hides. Do I say *a series of strange and unsettling incidents has occurred over the past few days*? No, that sounds melodramatic.

"Vera, I need you to do something for me."

"Okay?"

"Your driver." I pause briefly. I must think this through, slow down. "I want your driver to take me to see Edward. I want him to take me to Edward."

"Do you even know where he lives? I thought you haven't been speaking to him? He might be remarried. Have you ever thought about that?"

"I don't care, I need to talk to him."

"Maybe Marleen—"

"No, I don't trust her," I cut Vera off. "I don't trust her anymore."

Vera takes in a deep breath and blows it out. She isn't fond of Marleen.

"That one," Vera says and her lips turn downward, "I've never been sure what to make of her. I have an eye for such things, you know."

My phone beeps. It says, *your appointment with Dr. Jacobson is in 10 minutes*. I have all but forgotten about it. I need to talk to some-body about what's been happening to me and what's been making me so anxious. *Restless*, Marleen called my mood and made an ap-pointment.

Vera stares at my phone and chuckles. "Jacobson, huh? Quacks they are, all of them."

"Please call your driver, Vera."

"Of course, dear. Don't you worry."

. . .

Dr. Jacobson's office is in the west wing of the main building. There's also a dentist and a chiropractor. Right next door is a movie theater made to look like one of those old-timey cinemas with Art Deco features back when movies were a big deal. It has velvety red curtains and a carpeted floor and I have to say they keep it immaculate. No lopsided seats or abandoned popcorn boxes—I used to take Penelope to many movies when she was young—but I'm not fond of the movie nights Vera tries to talk me into. Too much whispering and overly air-conditioned, people stepping on your feet when they pass. I have seen a couple of movies with Vera but I always show up late to avoid the previews.

I pass the marquee of the theater and enter Dr. Jacobson's office. Her waiting room smells of some artificial fresh linen scent, nothing one would encounter in real life. I might tell her a bamboo plant would go a long way in freshening up the air but seconds after I push the button to indicate my presence, the door opens. I hardly have enough time to look around.

Dr. Jacobson is younger than I expected. Black, shiny hair, not a single line of gray disturbs the perfection. Her front teeth overlap, which gives her a touch of approachability. She's petite, her skin flawless. We shake hands and hers is cool to the touch as the alcohol of the hand sanitizer wafts off her skin.

"We haven't met yet, have we, Mrs. Pryor?" she asks.

"You must know everything about everyone living here? Oh, the gossip you could share," I reply. Vera would never forgive me if I didn't ask.

"I can't tell you any gossip, you know that," she says and winks at me with her left eye. "Let's get acquainted, shall we?"

Dr. Jacobson's office is a beautiful space. I assess the candleholders and the paintings, the rug, the desk. Everything is styled to perfection, the color scheme is taupe, white, and sapphire blue. The chair is a deep azure velvet, her couch the finest Italian leather. I sit and my hands stroke the cushions. Its soft surface is, like her, exquisite. The windows are set high so there's really no view to speak of. I wonder if she wants her patients not to get distracted. I assume her to be in her late forties, maybe early fifties, her face too slim and structured for jowls to give her age away, one of those women who has never gained or lost a single pound, which is really the only way to keep a face in shape. She wears lots of eye makeup, which distracts from her slightly drooping lids. I decide on forty-five, which seems like a safe bet.

"Tell me why you wanted to see me."

"There's been some anxiety lately," I start off and cross my legs. Ten years ago we might have been friends, yet here we are, doctor and patient.

"I haven't heard from my daughter in over a year. I'm not sure what is going on and my husband . . ." I pause then correct myself. "My estranged husband won't return my calls."

A pause. "Are you divorced or estranged?"

"I wouldn't know. Estranged for sure, the rest is just a formality, right?"

She writes down every word. Entire sentences—I can tell by the way the pen stroke reaches from the very left of the page all the way to the right—not just bullet points. I can't imagine that I'm telling her anything that needs writing down.

"Tell me about Penelope?"

I don't remember having mentioned her name. I give her the story in a nutshell: my marriage, Penelope being a difficult child, a trying teenager, the ensuing tension. My accident. The shattered hip. The subsequent depression. My recovery.

"What role did Edward play in all of this?"

I don't recall having told her his name either but maybe I have. I must have, how else would she know? Assigning guilt is difficult. It challenges the limits of my memory—which is not the same thing as lying at all—but I don't know what to make of his role.

"We did not *not* split on good terms." I remain vague and un-cross my legs. "But I think he was trying to get rid of me. That's why I have a suspicion that he's keeping my daughter from me. Or maybe he told her lies about me. And there is a possibility that everyone is in on it but me."

She remains quiet and takes notes.

"Everyone," I repeat and watch her closely.

"Your daughter is how old?" she asks, ignoring my comment altogether.

"Twenty-nine."

"What makes you think she's unable to make contact?"

"She should call," I burst out. I hate myself for it. "Every single day I ask Marleen, every single day, *has Penelope called?* Every day those words come out of my mouth and every single day she tells me, *not today, maybe tomorrow.*" I scoot forward. "I don't know what to do. I need to see Edward. I need to sort this out."

"I understand. What do you think needs sorting out?"

I stare at her. Talking about money is tacky.

"Edward pays for everything. All this," I say and swipe my hands at my surroundings. "Medical care, rent, my housekeeper, my bills. But for how long? I can't help wonder what will happen if he has a change of heart?" I sigh. Heart is not something Edward has, after all. He got rid of me in my darkest hour. I can almost see him roll his eyes about my choice of words.

"Your worries are financial, regarding your future," she jumps in.

"I have no proof of divorce, there's no paperwork, no settlement, no alimony. I need answers."

"And then there's your daughter."

"I wonder about her, too. Yes. I need to know she's okay."

"Would you describe for me what you remember about the last time you saw her?"

"We were in her room, I sat on her bed. I held her hand." That's not true at all. I made this up just now. I don't know where the image came from but it becomes an instant memory. I claim it, file it away. I operate in good faith here, we all know how faulty memory can be. That's what our last encounter shall be, one of devotion. My daughter is grown, why I would sit at her bedside and hold her hand is beyond me but so be it. I can't bear digging into hiding places so I keep eye contact and say with a firm voice, "I'll sort it out."

"It seems like you need answers to all those questions."

I fold my hands in my lap. This gesture always works, pious motions move the heart, I have always believed that. You pull a child into an embrace, you close your eyes, hold them tight. People assume devotion.

"I think I just got carried away. Coming here"—I want to say *was a mistake,* but instead I lower my voice—"wasn't necessary. I'm fine. I just had a moment."

My thoughts are like a runaway train: Edward has Marleen under his spell. Money does that; it buys you things that are not natural. When confronted with the immensity of it all, I realize I have to be a fortress, keep myself from harm. I'm a distrustful person, I know that about myself, but instead of worrying about what others can do to me, I'll strengthen my resolve. It's really the only way.

Vera told me not to trust Marleen and now Jacobson . . . I can't trust anyone. Especially Edward. He's got them all fooled, even Dr. Jacobson. Explain to me how she knew their names?

Back at the apartment, a sandwich in cellophane sits on the counter and beside it a small teapot. I unwrap it and behold it. Turkey. Swiss cheese. Romaine. The lettuce leaf is in between the cheese and the turkey and I want to take it apart and reassemble it but I'm not supposed to be picky about food, a promise I made to myself.

I listlessly and without joy eat my lunch. I feel like I'm forced to, Marleen will give me a lecture if she finds food in the garbage. *No need to make a fuss about it.* Those are the exact words I used to say to Penelope. I have to practice what I preach. That's what they told me, the therapists, *children don't listen to you but they watch you all the time.*

Food had always been a disaster with Penelope. I'd prepare things that I thought children liked—pancakes in the shape of dinosaurs and cheese turned into building blocks, eggs into canoes, I painstakingly picked letters from alphabet soup to write simple words—but they ended up mushed up or splattered across the floor.

Penelope was Penelope, it's as simple and as difficult as that. How endlessly I pondered her motivations—energetic or hyperactive, impulsive or living in the moment—which one was it? The spin was endless, but there came a point I had to acknowledge that—

But am I in the dark about something else? Is there something I refuse to realize? So many thoughts in random order. I'm not crazy, you know, I've seen her drawings when she was a child, those horrid unsettling drawings—

That's why I worry. That's why Edward can't be left alone to deal with her. He doesn't understand the complexity of it all.

Memories of Penelope appear like shadows, suddenly, without warning. Tucked away for decades but then suddenly they long to be recognized. How could I have paid attention to all the details but missed the big picture?

10

PENELOPE

"They locked me in a cupboard," Penelope said. "There was nothing I could have done."

The doctor stared at her but eventually broke eye contact. Penelope was aware of how unbelievable, unlikely, even preposterous that sounded.

"I swear they did. Why would I make this up?" she added.

"Your mother tells me—"

"That's your first mistake. Talking to my mother."

"Your mother tells me," he goes on, "the police got involved. It was a break-in. They interviewed people in the neighborhood."

"They locked me in a cupboard," Penelope repeated, staccato this time, robotic.

"They? It was more than one?"

"I was in the cupboard, I don't know."

There was no cupboard and no *them*. It was a party Penelope had organized. The house under construction was at the end of a cul-de-sac, with no one around for a mile or so. The party had gotten out of hand but once the cupboard lie was told, it was hard to take it back. Everything after turned into a lie and taking back hundreds of them was, well, difficult.

Her mother made Penelope see this doctor because she was mad at her and for no other reason than forgetting to feed the stray cats while her parents were gone for the weekend. It wasn't that Penelope didn't want to feed them, but before she knew it the weekend was over and her mother only knew because she counted the cans she had bought and left on the kitchen counter.

While her parents were away, Penelope had gone out back but the cats were shy and feral and didn't really want any affection. One of them, a tabby with large eyes, tiptoed sideways at the drop of a leaf blowing by. Penelope grabbed her and held her tight as she wiggled. One of her friends wanted a kitten and there were so many of them and Penelope took it inside the house and made calls about the party.

There was this new subdivision with Mediterranean-style houses and it was the weekend after Thanksgiving and no one was working and Penelope told her friends to cut the lights and park in the area by the side of the house, which was invisible from the street. Three cars with five people each, altogether there were twenty. A few came on foot. There was alcohol. They did tequila shots straight from the bottle. No one brought lime or salt or anything, and the liquor burned going down, making their lungs feel on fire.

Someone played "I Got 5 on It" and they swayed and rolled their hips in a two-step motion, snapping their fingers.

From the corner of her eyes Penelope observed a group by what looked like the initial stages of a fireplace. A short thin girl lit a blunt. Her chest expanded as she inhaled and faint trails of smoke escaped from her nostrils. The kitten Penelope had handed her poked its head out of the pocket of the girl's jacket. Penelope wished her mother could see how she spooned against her, safe and warm.

A guy, Eric, came on foot. He brought the coke. He poured the powder on the countertop and cut it with a credit card in short stabbing motions, and dragged the plastic over the counter to form lines.

As Penelope bent over, her hair grazed the lines. Eric gathered it in the nape of her neck, his hand hot against her skin. It felt sensual and Penelope used the middle part of an ink pen and snorted the dust, sucking it in so deep she had to take a breath to keep from fainting.

A guy came up to her and asked, "You're the girl from that private school, right?"

Penelope didn't answer. She felt her mood drop but honed in on the sense of surety that began to form as the coke kicked in. Soon the most thrilling phase of them all would begin—feeling physically overly competent without the awareness to restrain herself. That was Penelope's sweet spot. Remaining there had proven difficult. Another line, another rush.

"What about the blood?" the therapist asked and took notes as if he wanted to avoid eye contact.

"What blood?"

Penelope remembered screaming *let the games begin*. She hurled a brick. There was a crash of glass in the front part of the house. A volley of stones followed, smashing glass, sharp fragments bouncing off the walls. That was the last thing she remembered clearly.

11

EDWARD

Edward often thought the objective of being a father was to keep Penelope from harm, like a little bird fitting into the palm of his hand. He had made it his duty to keep an eye on her, like a fragile creature sitting on a padded cushion, but he hadn't thought any further than that. He hadn't been prepared for any setbacks, had not expected bad things to happen to them. That's what he thought of his family, a good family. *Proper*—a word Donna used.

There were random memories that stuck out, though he couldn't remember her first day of school to save his life, but for some reason he remembered Penelope learning to tie her shoes. How persistent she was, folding laces into bunny ears, crossing and looping through and over, pulling a loop to each side. She did it with such determination and wouldn't quit for anything.

So much about her childhood remained elusive to Edward. He had to admit he had watched from the sidelines. Every morning, he woke at the crack of dawn and glanced into Penny's room to make sure nothing had caused the fledgling creature distress overnight. Burrowed within duvets and blankets she was invisible but he observed the shelves crammed with dolls touching at the shoulders, propping one another up. After a day working in the OR and catching up on charting, he returned to a home where Donna chattered on and on about parties, vacation homes, schedules for trips, and functions she had committed him to.

If Donna strived for perfection and social obligations, Penelope was determined to endlessly create her own world with the wooden people in her ghastly dollhouses. When they lived in Florida, Donna once had spent money they didn't have on a wooden playhouse she had built in the backyard. When he saw the monstrosity, he wanted to tell Donna off but the same day Penelope cut her hand on a shard and he was called in to do the sutures. Donna had insisted on it, the nurses had thrown him sideway glances at her sheer panic and her insistence that Edward treat their daughter's palm. He was taken aback by Penelope's bravery. There wasn't a tear when he numbed her hand and closed up the wound.

The question of a sibling had come up when Penelope was about three and just about every year thereafter.

"I'm not sure," Donna said, "Penelope's a handful. I'm so busy with everything, I don't know if we should or not."

Edward didn't know what being *busy* meant. He only knew what he had experienced himself: a childhood home full of siblings and chaos, modest but happy Christmas mornings, and yearly trips to state parks.

Over the years, Donna's running of the household had turned into a well-oiled machine: twice a week help came to pick up the house, and once every quarter the windows were cleaned and women in white uniforms dusted the chandeliers one crystal at a time. Paint was touched up once a year though he'd never seen a smudge on a wall, the exterior stonework got the pressure washer treatment and the chimney sweep was also a yearly thing. Caterers prepared even the simplest meals and his parents had more than once commented— never in front of Donna, though—how formal his life was.

Donna kept her distance from his parents. They never vacationed with them, never spent Christmas together, the most Donna made an allowance for was Easter brunch and an egg hunt for Penelope and her cousins. No one spent the night at Hawthorne Court; Donna always made reservations at hotels.

"They'll be so much more comfortable in a hotel," she said. "And Penelope tires easily. Let's just all put our best foot forward and not step on each other's toes."

Once he insisted on a vacation with his parents and his siblings and their children but the planning got out of control and no one could manage to come up with a date that fit in everyone's schedule and after dozens of emails and phone calls and being unsure about a place that could accommodate such a large group, he gave up. It saddened him, he wanted Penelope to know his family. Time had slipped away from them and they never got around to having another child and the thought of Penelope being all alone one day pained him. Before he knew it, Penelope was a senior in high school and he felt disarmed by the fact that he had missed it all. The challenge was over and there was no more input on his part.

He had never told anyone but he imagined opening his hand and flattening the palm and allowing the fledgling to scuttle off. Penelope had come to embody the image of a bird striking a window and slithering toward the ground. But those were thoughts that over time he learned to repress and from there on out he kept his fingers crossed.

There was no warning, no transition, no proclivity to violence. Then the vandalism at the construction site occurred. After Edward smoothed the waters with the builder and wrote a check, he demanded to know Penny's reasoning but she just raised her shoulders as if his guess was as good as hers.

The next day, an envelope addressed to him arrived in the mail. It said *Care of Edward Pryor* in a cursive handwriting, jagged letters without any discernible style. He remembered thinking that it was an odd way to address a letter.

Mr. Pryor. We don't know each other . . .

His fingers felt thick and clumsy as he pulled the pages closer.

. . . but I think you ought to know what happened that night.

His first thought was how much was this going to cost him?

You don't know the half of it.

Edward dropped into the chair behind his desk.

I have enclosed pictures my son took that night.

He stuck his hand inside the envelope and pulled them out one by one.

I thought you ought to know. If this were my daughter . . .

He sat with a churning stomach, clutching the pictures. He must have been pale as the wall behind him. *Snowbound by Sherwin Williams.* What an odd detail to remember. He couldn't show Donna the pictures, it would break her heart. This is how it began, this mishmash in his mind, the moment he pondered if *some thing* lived beneath Penny's skin.

About the cat, he read and willed himself not to flinch.

He jerked when he heard Donna's voice behind him.

"What's this?" Donna asked.

"Just catching up on charting," Edward said and tucked the photos underneath a pile of paperwork.

Donna stood with her teeth tucked over her bottom lip. How long had she been standing there, looking over his shoulder?

Donna took his hand and pulled it toward her chest, where he felt her heart beating.

"You work too much. Let's go away," she said with a faraway look in her eyes. "Just for a little while."

Edward glanced at the files in front of him, the calendar and his OR schedule, the paperwork under which he had tucked the photographs. It struck him how they could both look at the same thing yet draw different conclusions.

They looked out the Tudor window, across the dew-wet lawn, the panes of glass in a crisscross pattern, distorting the view. Everything—the trees, the driveway, the fence, the road—all seemed warped.

Except the expanse of the lawn. That remained in focus. And vast. So vast.

12

DONNA

I turn it over in my head: how to confront Edward. What to say to Penelope, once I see her. A malaise overcomes me like a wave. It sloshes over me like a leg cramp gone too far, unable to stretch the muscle to alleviate the pain. I have to stay busy, do something, until then, and maybe somewhere in my house is a sign of her, a phone number, anything. Somewhere in this place there must be a sign of Penelope other than the framed picture in the parlor.

"Marleen," I call out. "I'm going to be in the storage room for a while. Sooner or later we'll have to get this mess cleared out," I say in a dismissing tone, resisting the urge to raise my voice. I twist the doorknob to the storage room. It turns but the door doesn't budge.

"Let me unlock it for you."

I spin around, surprised by her closeness. Marleen reaches into the pocket of her apron and unlocks the door. I want to scold her for scaring me but I don't. And her appearance, that meek black skirt and blouse and that apron—have I not told her repeatedly not to wear anything so dated? I grab her by the arm and walk her toward the kitchen.

"Don't mind me, just carry on with what you were doing. I'll be just fine. Time to go through those boxes anyway. And if you have a moment to spare, if you can give the silverware a good cleaning, that would be great. I'm thinking about having a dinner party. Invite some people. You know, have some fun. It's been rather dreary here."

That's a lie, I don't know anyone who I'd want to have a dinner party for. Marleen stalls, or maybe I just imagine it, but I continue to nudge her into the kitchen.

I open the first box. My Meissen figurines. Unrolling the packing paper, I catch the tumbling shepherd in my hands. Followed by the winged cupid figurine, a group of hunting dogs, and a girl in a blue dress walking a goose on a leash. One by one, I cradle them in my hands. They used to sit on the mantel at Hawthorne Court, but here at Shadow Garden, Marleen is dead set on keeping them packed away for fear they might break. After I fold the tissue paper around each one, I attempt to close the box lid—I watched Marleen once, the way she tucks the corners under without ever using a piece of tape—but I can't manage to do it and I give up.

The second box contains painting supplies. I had taken a private art class once from an artist who painted beautiful landscapes, but I'd never gotten around to actually attempting a project, and so the canvases and paints have been sitting untouched, the oil and tempera, and the water colors, the paint dried in the tubes after all those years, the brushes brittle. I should make an attempt now since I have not much else to do. Come to think of it, I could paint Penelope the way I remember her that one summer at the cabin when her hair turned golden from swimming and lounging in the sun. How beautiful she was and how I'd suggested she should go even blonder, how it suited her, especially when unruly freckles appeared on the bridge of her nose. Penelope always dyed her hair two shades too dark, which made her look pale and aged her, but that too was a battle I shouldn't have fought.

The next box clinks with flatware, the holiday sets, and I won't trouble myself with pulling a single piece out of the velvet-lined containers. Stuffed below are greeting cards, too many to count, with Penelope's childlike scribble, oblong hearts and flowers with round petals, clumsy crayon strokes within the lines, others just a chaos of scrawls and colors.

A book catches my eye, on top of three stacked crates. I stroke the worn and cracked sleeve, its pages swollen with water damage. I don't see how I'd keep a book so old and torn and damaged, unfit for a shelf, the jacket so faded I can hardly make out any words—must be one of those book club selections that seem cheesy but turn out to be an entertaining read over a summer vacation—and I almost toss it aside but then my eyes scan the faded title.

My heart stumbles—it's a book about a girl and a dollhouse. The dolls move, talk, play instruments, lead a secret life of their own which the humans know nothing about. I scramble to recall the story, remember a girl searching for her missing sister who has vanished and the doll family go about their clandestine mission to find her, at night, when the house goes dark.

The cover, though the story is uplifting, is rather dark; a girl kneels in front of the dollhouse with her back to the onlooker, hand suspended in midair, taken by the fact that the dollhouse is deserted. It's just a book, yet it's not that simple; it disappeared years ago in some drawer, stashed away on a shelf or cubby at Hawthorne Court, leaving Penelope upset when she couldn't find it. For months there were endless questions and a stubborn insistence we turn the house upside down to look in every nook and cranny, but we never located it. How did this book end up here, on top those crates full of linen and silverware and odds and ends, here at Shadow Garden? And why is my heart beating so fast as I'm holding it in my hand?

I don't want to be disturbed, want to be left alone with this memory, but Marleen's voice trails in from the kitchen, the words being swallowed somewhere along the hallway. Parts drift in through the open door, urgent words and a tone that defies her usual quiet and eager to please demeanor.

The book cracks open at will and unfolds on a page, a piece of folded paper stuck in between like a bookmark. I attempt to lift it off the page—is it a note or part of a note? Words, one line after another, like a tally or maybe a list of some sort. The dots above the I's appear a letter or so later than they ought to. I recognize Penelope's handwriting, hasty and messy, the words have gaps between them, not like after a period, but random spaces that make no sense at all. Penmanship has always been a pet peeve of mine, cursive especially, and I had scolded Penny often but looking back at it now it wasn't worth the fight, didn't warrant any harsh words.

I snap the book shut. I unfold the paper and smooth it with my palm. My mind goes to work, I scrutinize every letter, over and over. I can't make out the words. I try and try but the letters are more an attempt at practice than formed words or sentences. My cheeks turn hot and I feel the blood rushing in my ears.

I have a thought. It's random, I realize that, yet it is powerful. *Penelope made sure this book made it here so I'd know she needs me.* She is trying to tell me *something*, not with the words themselves but with the fact that her lost book ended up with a box that ended up here at Shadow Garden. On top of a box with bedsheets, a box to be unpacked first. Everybody puts sheets on first after a move but there are so many boxes, other boxes with other sheets, and maybe if I hadn't dillydallied I would have seen this months ago.

"Mrs. Pryor." Marleen's voice behind me makes me jerk. "I have some news."

I clutch the book to my chest and turn around. My mind unfolds: This is a sign. This is not a breadcrumb indicating where Penelope is but an omen foretelling what is about to happen, signifying the advent of *something*. A divine message: Penelope called. I know it. She called and she's all right and I've imagined it all and she's on her way or she'll be here tomorrow or whenever but she is all right.

"She called," I say matter-of-factly. I can't contain the joy. "Penelope called?"

I'm still guarded, *cautiously optimistic*, I have hope, yet I don't dare hang my happiness on it, like a nail unable to support a heavy frame. Marleen isn't surprised by my question at all. Quite the contrary. She wears an expression void of emotion and her demeanor is at a level of confidence that suggests she knows what to say next.

"Did Penelope call?" I repeat and sound harsh, though I immediately regret it.

"There was an accident," Marleen says. "Please don't be alarmed. Nothing life-threatening or even remotely worrisome."

"Penny?" I ask, breathless. *Accident. Don't be alarmed*. It rings true in an odd and sinister way. A memory unfolds, pristine and clear like a winter wonderland no human has set foot in. There *was* an accident. "What's happened to Penny? Is she all right?" *Accident*. My daughter is . . . had an *accident*? The horror of that thought, it tears at me. It's something that can't be reasoned with.

"No, not Penny. It's Vera. Your neighbor Vera Olmsted. She took a fall. They found her and she said to let you know."

Marleen's chatter is now nothing but white noise in my mind. "Penny." I say it again. Penny had an accident. I know this to be true. I can't explain it any other way.

"Mrs. Pryor, please. Listen to me. It's not Penny, this is not about your daughter. I don't know anything about Penny. It's about Vera. Vera Olmsted, your friend."

Not Penny. But Vera, poor Vera.

"Is Vera all right?"

"Nothing to worry about. A fall. But you know, at her age, it's difficult."

"I should go see her."

"She'll be up and about in no time."

Is Marleen a doctor? How does she know that? How dare she give such opinions? Always placating, always soothing and pacifying me like a child.

"How do you know?"

"Aubrey called."

"Aubrey?"

"Her niece."

Aubrey's not Vera's niece. She looks at her like a niece. Just goes to show how little Marleen knows about any of this.

"She's not her niece."

"I thought she—"

"So Penny didn't call?" I interrupt her. "Maybe tomorrow. Maybe tomorrow she'll call," I add, aware how this is just a farce at this point. Penny hasn't called and she won't call but something inside of me compels me to repeat this every day. Not until I say it do I realize how little sense it makes.

I tuck the book in the box with the linens. Panic narrows my focus. I have to walk this off, have to purge my thoughts. From the kitchen into the parlor and down the hallway. Walking helps my thoughts propel forward; there's a door that needs opening—not a literal door, no, but access to a memory that is difficult to get to. My steps are measured and with each one the word *accident* echoes in my mind. It sounds like something I recognize, not Vera's, not my own, but Penny's. It rings true, there's no other way for me to explain it.

Marleen passes by me for the third time. She seems to be keeping an eye on me. In the bedroom, I can't decide what to wear. I lean toward pants, a blouse, and a light jacket. No one cares, no one will give me a second look, but I've been this way since I can remember.

Here I am in my underwear, staring at a garment that is laid out on the bed. This dress. Long sleeves, V-neck, a self-tie sash, lynx print. A cocktail party dress, not something I've worn in a long time. Who put it here?

"Marleen," I shout, a couple of notches too loud. I feel horrid about it all, all of it: Penny, Vera, Edward, the way I talk to Marleen. I know that about myself, this inability to do what's right.

Marleen's face pokes into the bedroom.

"Do you need help picking out an outfit?" she asks as if it is the most ordinary thing. When does she ever pick out my outfits? I want to make a snarky remark—something along the lines of *what would you know about outfit choices?*—but didn't I just scold myself for being tactless, and look at me, here I go again.

"Who put this dress on my bed?"

She hesitates.

"Where did this dress come from? I don't understand."

"I'm sorry." Marleen slides between me and the bed and scoops up the garment. "Let's just put it in the closet."

Marleen rushes to the closet, returning the dress to its proper place. I want to ask *why are you doing this?* I want to repeat it over and over. It's like a game she's playing—they are playing. Like the doll people in Penelope's book, they go about it in the dark of night. But why? Why are they doing this?

I crane my neck as I approach Vera's door. Two women in scrubs stand there and chat. They are part of the cleaning crew. Every morning, they spill from a van with tinted windows reminiscent of an airport shuttle bus. I've watched them through my bay window before as they walk to their respective buildings. By now they have begun to look familiar: one wears a turtleneck, and according to Vera, she's covering up a tattoo. Some of the women are young, others in their fifties. They carry large purses and lunch boxes.

I'm distracted by a woman pacing up and down the walkway.

Her cell phone is pressed to her ear and she seems worked up about something. She is wearing regular clothes, not scrubs, so she could be Aubrey, Vera's assistant. I've heard Vera speak of her—*she is like a niece to me*—but I've never met her.

Aubrey is in her mid-thirties, her mouse-brown hair is up in a sloppy bun and she wears ghastly cat-eye glasses. That's all you see when you look at her, a face dominated by thick frames flaring out at the temples. I wonder if she knows those are ill fitting. Black slacks stretched tightly across her stomach and a white blouse would make her look put together if it wasn't for her sloppy cheap flats with scuff marks on the back.

"You must be Mrs. Pryor. I'm Aubrey."

"How's Vera?" I ask.

"She's been asking for you," Aubrey says.

"I didn't bring anything," I say.

"Don't worry about that. She'll be glad to have company. She's worked up about something. She mentioned your name but I couldn't make sense of it."

Vera does her fair share of complaining about Aubrey, though she's quite fond of her. She can be overbearing, just like Marleen. Her responsibility, as far as I know, is the preservation of Vera's estate, specifically organizing and transcribing notes Vera writes on canary legal pads, which she leaves on her kitchen counter by the dozens.

When I met Vera, I did my fair share of snooping. I ran across articles and photos of her; wrap dresses and tailored skirts with knee-high boots. She was casual yet effortlessly chic in her ribbed Henley shirts with her long hair parted in the middle and prominent eyebrows. In one picture she leans against one of those Mercedes roadsters, in another she sits in an overgrown yard with a typewriter on a weathered table. There are pictures with headscarves and large round sunglasses. She is still slim bordering on emaciated, her clavicles poking from beneath her translucent freckly skin. I saw a photograph of her once with Lagerfeld in a black suit and a ponytail, dark shades, huddled together as if they were the best of friends. She has replaced her cashmere sweaters and scarves for kaftans and loungewear these days but she's still beautiful.

How odd I've never been to Vera's apartment. "I have stuff all over the place, research and such, it's really not in the condition for visitors," she told me once and I accepted it. "I try forever to keep up with the clutter but it always gets away. You know how things get away sometimes, don't you?"

I wouldn't know but I nodded. Poor Vera suffers from some sort of brittle bone disease. She must be careful not to fall or even bump into things. Born with a broken collarbone, she was predisposed even before birth, which I assume lent itself to spending lots of time indoors as a child. There's also some issue with her connective tissue, a rare disease which can be controlled but not cured, though it is manageable as an adult, but I don't know the specifics. You wouldn't know any of this by looking at her. She is one of those women who spent her life indulging in artistic endeavors, traveling and never wasting a thought on having a family. Vera's wealthy. She doesn't talk about money, that's how I know, people who are don't ever do.

Standing in Vera's foyer, I'm taken aback. I all but expected her house to be messy but not unbearably so. I imagined it to be minimally furnished, an artful bohemian aesthetic mixed with vibrant and rich colors, textures and patterns, handmade and vintage pieces. A hand-carved bench from Sweden, a velvet couch in a jewel tone with embroidered kilim pillows and plush rugs. Somehow I thought her home to be her greatest work of art but this place looks like all work but no art.

Crowded seems too trivial a word for what this is: tables with randomly stacked books, some of the backs show but most are upside down, titles illegible. Papers, so many papers. Reams of them stacked on tables, not even real tables but plastic folding things, and cardboard boxes with indecipherable black felt-tip marker scribblings in the corner. What good can come from being this disorganized? The walls are bare and devoid of any framed art. Black bags are lined up on the kitchen floor, the veined marble underneath stained with dirt and smudges. One bag is leaking some sort of fluid. My mind makes the connection and horror overcomes me as I realize what they are: garbage bags.

I enter Vera's bedroom. She's propped up by multiple pillows and her legs rest elevated on a wedge-like Styrofoam shape. Her mouth is open and she seems to be resting. Dots travel along her upper arm as if fingertips have dug into her, one bruise reaches all the way to her elbow. Purple, as if she had fallen on something oblong, but there are lots of bruises in yellow and green which must have been hidden by her kaftan sleeves.

The front door slams and Aubrey mumbles something under her breath. I can see the parlor and the kitchen from the bedroom door and I watch Aubrey stuff leaking bags into a larger one.

"Aubrey," I call out into the hallway. "What happened to Vera?"

Aubrey pokes her head into Vera's bedroom.

"Just a slip."

"What happened?" I repeat, this time with a sharper tone.

"She fell but she's fine. The doctor said not to worry but she needs some rest." She pauses for a second. "She was upset with me earlier, I needed to step outside for a moment."

"Why was she upset?"

"She was upset when she told me about you two having plans so I called Marleen to let you know," Aubrey says and tucks a messy strand of hair behind her ears.

"How did she fall?" I ask and hold my breath.

"It was really just a slip in the kitchen. I don't know if she told you about her"—there's a pause, during which she lets out a deep breath—"her habit of going through peoples' bags. She leaves them in the kitchen and she won't allow me to tidy up."

Vera is stirring, then fiddles with the blanket.

"Your friend Donna is here, Vera," Aubrey says and then lowers her voice. "I know this place looks alarming but I'm organizing her notes. She's working on so many projects. There'll be a collection of essays and a short story collection, maybe even two. And she is working on a novel. At this point there's so much material I don't even know where to begin. We're imaging some of her hand-written notes so editors can get a better look at them. You know, the anniversary of her book is coming up. Thirty years. There'll be a special edition and we want to include some new content. It's a lot of work, as you can see." She nods toward the hallway and the stacks of papers.

"Donna." Vera struggles to make her voice boom.

"She's been very difficult all afternoon."

"I'll keep her company. Don't concern yourself with that."

I turn as if to dismiss her but I see Aubrey flinch. I sound harsh again. I don't mean to.

I step toward Vera and lower myself carefully onto the bed so as not to bounce the mattress. "Vera, what happened?"

Her eyes are open now. Her helpless posture makes her look even more fragile than usual.

"I slipped in the kitchen and everyone is making a big deal about it. My ankle hurts but no sprain or break." She lets out a deep breath. "Yet here I am. In bed."

I stroke her hand and swipe her hair from her forehead. I'll make sure someone touches up her roots and keeps up her nails. I vow to have her hair done in that strawberry blond that she loves so much, if it ever comes to that. I tell her none of that—that would be macabre.

"I'm so sorry about—"

"Don't worry about anything," I say and turn to see if Aubrey has left the room. I hear the pipes humming and water running in the kitchen. A mop lands on the tiles with a clatter. A door slams.

Vera looks at me for a long time. "What's the matter? You look worried. I'll be back on my feet in no time. Promise me you'll drop by every day."

"Of course."

"So what's the sour face all about?"

"I was just thinking."

"About the driver, about going to see Edward?"

"Yes." I hesitate. It made much more sense in my mind but saying it out loud seems foolish. *I think Edward had something to do with your fall.* "I don't want to burden you with this." My voice sounds breathless, almost as if I'm winded, having ran or exerted myself. "But I have to tell you something." I lower my voice even further. "I swear, I'm not making this up but I heard them two nights ago."

"Heard them?"

"I heard Edward talk to Marleen."

I'm hearing voices, is the gist of it. I ponder the comment *I heard Edward's voice.* It does sound daft, I agree. I have no explanation for it but I know what I heard.

"What were they talking about?" Vera asks, not doubtful at all.

"I couldn't make out the words. But I've been thinking. Marleen, she gives me pills and they make me loopy but I stopped taking them. I'll get to the bottom of it. But I need you to know, I need someone to know. They are in on it."

Vera blinks twice in rapid succession. "In on it? On what?"

"I'm not crazy, you know."

"Oh, Donna. Of course you're not crazy. Who said you were?"

"Not in those words but I swear, Marleen babies me like I don't have any sense whatsoever. My wardrobe, she now selects my wardrobe." I stand up and twirl. "Do I look like I need someone picking out my wardrobe?"

"You look lovely, my dear. You always do."

"See. See." I poke my finger at her.

Vera yawns. Her head rolls from one side to the other.

"Donna." So soft, like a feather floating. Vera is restless, as if there's something on her mind.

"What, Vera?"

"I wish things were different."

"Different how?"

"Donna, I'm so sorry. I wish I could do something."

Vera reaches for my hands, clutches them against her chest. It strikes me as dramatic, not something she's ever done before.

"Do something about what?" I ask.

"About what happened to Penelope."

"What do you mean? What happened to her?" My heart races. "What do you mean?" I repeat.

"Two nights ago, I heard a sound, somewhere in the house, but, you know, these walls, I don't know, there're lots of noises at night. The building settling, maybe. I don't know. I'm not sure what I heard. I couldn't tell where it was coming from, so I went outside. I saw someone, a man. He spoke to me. He asked me questions."

"Questions about what?"

"About . . ." Her voice gets weaker and weaker, the word is barely a whisper.

"Was it Edward?" As I close my hand tighter around hers, I position my ear close to her mouth so as to not miss a single word. "What kind of questions did he ask you?" She doesn't answer. "Vera?" Her breathing becomes deeper, her head slouches. "Vera, tell me. Vera . . ." Her hand loses its strength. She's asleep.

I'm eager to wake her, make her tell me about this encounter. Impatience can't get the better of me, I won't allow it, and I pull my hand away from Vera before I wiggle this fragile woman's bony shoulder to get her to talk to me. I feel myself shake with anger. Anger toward Edward but mainly anger at myself, how I had turned into a woman with a subservient streak the days before he dumped me here at this place. Even the employees here come and go as they please, yet here I am, trapped. How clear it all is now. They don't want me to leave Shadow Garden. Edward is behind this.

On my way out, as I pass the accent table in the foyer, I see a pair of scrubs draped over a table, atop a stack of papers. What I do next I can't explain. I grab the scrubs and I don't even bother hiding them, I walk past Aubrey who is elbow deep in a garbage bag, the sleeves of her white shirt cuffed.

Outside, an army of men in khaki pants with orange vests and baseball hats has descended upon the grounds. There are hedge trimmers and riding mowers for the large expanses of lawn, and pushing mowers for the smaller areas. I rush toward my door and I fumble with the lock. My shoulders brush against ivy that has made its way up the storm drain, a couple of leaves touch my mailbox already, so resilient and gritty, snaking its way up and over.

In the bedroom I turn on the radio to drown out the droning mowers. It makes things worse. I feel like crawling into a corner and pressing my palms against my ears to escape the hurricane-force noise. I understand more than people give me credit for. Penelope was my garden. I didn't tend to her as I should have. Maybe I'm getting what I deserve.

Marleen leaves early—*I'm very tired, all that walking exhausts me and I'm worried about Vera, I think I'll just turn in early*—and then I'm alone. The sky is dragon-fruit pink and soon it'll be dark. I don't know what it is about this time of day, as if there's a magnetic pull, but panic rears its head as if I've forgotten how to maneuver in the dark. A house ablaze with chandeliers and sconces is where I should be, that's how I see myself, and those memories have me on edge and all I want are for the sharp corners to dull, for the shadows to become less menacing.

Penelope used to hide in closets. There's an urgent need to trace my way back like a ball of yarn. And a plan forms in my mind.

13

PENELOPE

Penelope watched the guests and their children arrive at the party. Her mother had told her she was allowed to invite a friend from school. Shannon had been her friend for the better part of a year but for no reason they stopped talking and Penelope was perfectly fine with it.

"It's just a casual open house and it would be rude to exclude children. But please keep an eye on them," her mother told her but Penelope was taken aback that her mother would trust her with such a responsibility.

Women's heels clicked across the marble floors, the men wore casual dress shirts with gold watches on their wrists. She noticed even grown-ups formed cliques. Penelope understood the concept but not the reasoning behind it. The women admired the floors, the walls, the ceilings, they ran their fingers over counters and the men stood on the back patio, looking left and right and toward the neighboring house in the distance where the lawn blurred into the woods. *None of this is real,* Penelope kept thinking. How her mother chatted on and on about where the chandelier was from or what country in Europe the counters were imported from. It felt like some tedious social experiment.

As she observed the caterers busying about, she was determined to follow her mother's instructions: smile, stay with the children, don't bother the adults, and most of all, don't get into any trouble.

Through the patio doors, those large panes reaching from floor to ceiling, a family arrived with a boy with pale skin and black hair. Her mother greeted them, air kisses and all, and pointed at Penelope across the room as if to say *that's my daughter, you'll be safe with her.*

The day after the party, her mother asked Penelope about her "take" on that day as if there was a range of interpretations that lend themselves to an analysis. As if Penelope, at thirteen, could interpret what had happened.

She remembered hiding in a closet until her mother found her. She also recalled the smell of ammonia, and something else—a whole complex array of odors—and her skin itching. Through the slats of the closet door, out of the corner of her eye, she saw flashes of lights in all colors, red, blue, and amber, as if from a rotating beacon.

"Tell me what you remember of that night, Penny. You were there." Donna was harsh in her delivery, keeping eye contact, not allowing her daughter to falter.

Penelope thought of it as a clever game of realities. She was short in turn, said, "I only know what you told me."

14

DONNA

Penelope didn't make it through two months before I was summoned to the Academy. As I parked the car, I recalled my high school and the breezeways thick with the smell of chicken broth, a maze of empty hallways, and a single counselor who was a hideous man in a wrinkled shirt.

The administration wing of the Academy resembled more an office suite filled with conference rooms, upscale furniture, and executive office equipment. A secretary led me into a room and though I wasn't sure what to expect, I knew it wasn't going to be good news. The counselor had an untrustworthy feel about him with his small light-brown eyes, bulbous nose, and softly shaped jaw. He wore a flannel shirt and I remember thinking how odd that was for this time of year.

I dropped into a chair and crossed my legs, inspecting the room. I jerked as he closed a drawer. Without much fanfare he told me

Penelope led a group of girls attempting to enter the school building at night. They didn't succeed. "If they had, it would be breaking and entering, assuming they didn't destroy anything, which would be vandalism on top of that. They were lucky they got caught before it got out of control." He emphasized she wouldn't be suspended but we needed to address her behavior. He softened somewhat when I asked why there were no other parents waiting to be seen, why Penelope was being singled out as the culprit and accused him of making her out to be a leader of a rabid gang of girls when it was merely a teenage indiscretion.

He made multiple attempts to gain insight into her motivations. His questions felt intrusive and misplaced for the price we paid at such an institution. I answered sparsely, bewildered by his audacity in thinking a school counselor was remotely equipped to get to the root of who Penelope was.

I'd heard professional opinions over the years, first I consulted a pediatrician who specialized in childhood disorders, and then there was a psychiatrist who recommended weekly appointments during which I sat in the waiting room staring at a red light above a door.

One day I drove her back to school after an appointment and she was in a mood. I pulled into the overflow parking lot of the Academy and told her to walk the rest of the way.

"Drop me off at the front door," she said and didn't as much as reach for her seat belt.

"Penny, it's literally right there, don't make me drive through this maze of cones and speed bumps every ten feet. Go to the office and give them the note so they don't count you as absent."

"I'm not walking, drive me to the front."

I asked her five times and five times she refused. I had been steadfast in my resolve, but just like water filling small cracks in a rock, as the water freezes and expands, the cracks widen and split apart the rock. I lost my patience.

"Get out of this car and walk into the building and if you don't, I will pull you out and throw you on the lawn," I yelled.

Penelope stared at me, still not moving.

I reached for the door handle. Penelope releasing the buckle, opening the door, and storming out was all one action. Putting the car in drive, I looked over my left shoulder for oncoming traffic and simultaneously stepped on the gas. Something told me to look straight ahead and I saw her just in time, standing in front of the bumper. I hit the brakes and the car stopped but her body rocked gently backwards as the car bumped into her. Rule number one had always been, *you walk behind the car, never up front.* She told Edward I hit her with the car in a fit of anger, which was not even close to the truth. I wondered how far she'd go to prove a point.

After I left the Academy, thoughts tumbled through my mind in restless succession, fears that had been growing steadily. What had begun with a plastic fork at a birthday party embedded in the arm of another child, a shard of glass in a backyard in Florida, had turned into destructive behavior. Another notch in her belt. I felt guilty for thinking this way but one thing I knew for sure: once there was an official stamp on her forehead she wouldn't be able to erase it.

I tend to be overly dramatic and blow things out of proportion, I know that about myself, but I had to shut this down. I had to shut down the pediatricians and psychiatrists and psychologists, the therapists and counselors. I shut it down for her. For Pea, for Penny, for Penelope. For all of them. I shut it all down before it got away from me.

She's just difficult and most important of all, she'll grow out of it. That story became fixed, frozen, unchanging. I could live with that.

15

DONNA

Reconciling what happened the day of the housewarming party, that's where my mind is stuck. I realize truth and memory aren't the same thing but if they were, could both be faulty? My mind is finicky that way.

Here is a fact: by recalling an incident, you corrupt it. If you want it to maintain its pristine and virgin state, just let it sit, don't disturb it. I've been playing that game for a while and it's time to blow away the cobwebs and look at the truth, even if it isn't pretty.

The move to Hawthorne Court had been a long time coming. We bought the Tudor in spring and renovated all through summer and finally, a week before school was to start, we moved in. The renovations had taken much longer than we anticipated—I had the kitchen countertops replaced because the color wasn't quite the shade I had picked out, which in turn delayed the backsplash installation, which in turn delayed the cabinets and to Edward's dismay it was a costly affair for which I was solely to blame—and though we hadn't unpacked all the boxes yet, the main part of the house, the first floor, was perfect. Edward had just opened his practice and I looked at the housewarming party as the debutante ball of our family and so we invited the who's who of the medical community.

The invitations were a piece of art. *We are home!* it said in an elegant cursive font. I had pondered over the invitation for days—*6 pm to 9 pm* or *Six to Nine o'clock*—and the quote took me a long time to select. *Bread, that this house may never know hunger. Salt, that this life may always have flavor. And wine, that joy and prosperity may reign forever,* from *It's a Wonderful Life*. I had an oversized invitation framed and displayed on a floor easel, had staged a table with a loaf of bread, a bowl of salt, and a bottle of merlot at the entrance. There was champagne, valet parking, bartenders, and servers, we had spent a fortune on the catering though I no longer recall the menu.

We were off to a rocky start. The gardener, a haggard and sunburned man who often smelled of alcohol, was still attempting to create lined lawn patterns with the mower. I had made a sketch for him but the stripes were crooked and I told him to just store the equipment away in the pool house, where lawn furniture was stacked in corners and pool chemicals and paint cans sat forgotten. The pool had been cleaned and filled with water but we hadn't bothered beyond that. I scratched the outdoor bar at the very last minute.

Inside, everything seemed to go well. The servers were swift, the party planner made sure glasses were full and appetizers circled around. Children ran around in the backyard, an unfenced lawn bordering the neighbors' property, a farmhouse that could only be seen from the road. It was a beauty with regionally quarried stone, white fiber cement clapboard siding, and horse stables. Between the gardener running late and hunting for the box which contained the punch bowl, I was distracted.

I can't help but wonder, if I hadn't insisted on so many intricate details, I could have paid more attention to what was really happening.

Guests came and left and if anyone had asked me later about faces and names, I would've drawn a blank, that's how much coming and going there was. I frequently checked up on the children running around in the back. The fence around the pool was sturdy and the gate was locked—I shimmied it twice—and I didn't give it a second thought after that. None of the parents voiced any concerns, and at some point children tossed toys over the fence into the pool. Penelope was there in the midst of the laughter and screaming and I made a mental note to have a talk with her about that.

Later, as I stood in the kitchen and beheld the empty trays and bowls and the kitchen staff buzzed around me, I thought how odd, *it's so quiet out there.* All the children must have left and Penelope was nowhere to be seen and as quickly as I thought there was something amiss, I just as quickly was distracted by the caterer coming up to me with a question or Edward wanting me to see someone off. I didn't have time to hover over Penny, had given her clear instructions, and we were at home, literally the invitation stated *We are Home!* and I did see a glimpse of her long hair at some point, by the back door or in the butler's pantry, just a hint of her like you see someone in passing and you think *I'll talk to her later,* but instead I chatted with Edward's colleagues and their wives and tried to remember everybody's name.

It wasn't until later, after it was dark and the dirty dishes were packed away and the trays sat stacked in the catering van, when I handed the caterer the check in the driveway, that I saw the shattered window on the east side of the pool house. I still didn't think much of it, I assumed the children had played around with a bat or a ball and broken the window and I wasn't going to dwell on it and call up the parents to get to the bottom of it the next morning. I'd just get it taken care of and never mention it again.

I was still staring at the shards when a couple approached me. He was a plastic surgeon and his wife a philanthropist for children's causes—muscular dystrophy, I believe—and they looked around with worry.

"Have you seen our son?" the wife asked, and I tried to remember her name but my mind was blank.

"What's his name again? I haven't seen any of the children, I thought everyone had left," I said, and I attempted to lead them toward the French doors into the house.

"Gabriel," the mom said, as she scanned the yard. Then she eyed the pool.

We stepped up to the fence, my heart beating a thousand miles a second, as I remembered headlines of children drowning. How often had I heard about drowning accidents with adults literally feet away? Nothing but toys floated on the water's surface.

We searched for Gabriel, we called out his name into the dark toward the black stretch of grass leading to the neighboring estate. I thought about mentioning the stock pond past the trees but then I didn't. I had only been there once since we bought the property, and it was nothing more than a watering hole used for livestock long before Hawthorne Court was built, and I couldn't imagine anyone walking all the way across the lawn and past the trees and through such a heavily wooded area.

I made idle conversation to keep it light, didn't want the parents to worry, but more than once Doug, the father, all but pushed me out of the way as if I was a hindrance in the search for his son. I might have been too slow and when I remarked on the plans of renovating the pool house he looked at me with disdain, his eyes narrow, and he grabbed me by the shoulder and moved me aside to look into the broken window. It was too dark to see inside though there was accent lighting around the pool, and he didn't mention the shards in the grass.

I tried to picture the boy but I couldn't—was he old enough to stand in some dark corner kissing or making out with Penelope? That would be different than him being too young to be out here alone.

"Let's check in the house," I said and hooked my hand underneath the mother's arm, Beatrice I think; I heard him say her name though I didn't recall a formal introduction. She turned toward me and I saw the panic in her eyes and I wanted to reassure her, *this is a good home, we'll find him, please don't worry.* "Let's go upstairs and work our way down," I said and rushed ahead.

We passed by Edward, who was on the phone and his voice was loud and happy and I didn't dare say anything about the missing boy and the broken window and we slipped by him, up the stairs.

The door to the playroom was wide open, the lights were on. The room was empty. Penelope's bedroom was dark. The closet door was ajar and when I opened it, Penelope sat on the floor, leaning to the left, propped against the wall. She was asleep.

There was a rule, *no children in the house upstairs during a party,* there was a bar in the master bedroom, a small table with a mirrored top, a few decanters, and whiskey and sherry and bourbon, elderflower liqueur. There was also a balcony and though I had locked all the doors I didn't know if children would think so far as to search for keys or use tools or anything like that to pry open doors. Between the broken window and the balcony it would be a lie if I said I wasn't worried.

"Where is Gabriel?" the mother called out and Penelope roused.

"Where is your friend? Gabriel?" I asked and held Penelope's hand as if to keep a grip on her. I smelled a floral sticky scent on her breath.

"Gabriel?" Penelope furrowed her brow. "I don't know. Everyone left a while ago."

The parents stormed by me, downstairs, and past Edward, who was still on the phone in the foyer. He threw up his hand and waved and mouthed a thank-you to the couple, unaware what was going on.

"We can't find our son," the mother said out loud and I was glad the guests and caterers had left and I imagined this entire scene playing out in front of everybody, envisioned heads snapping around and people gasping.

"Have you seen a boy about Penny's age?" I asked Edward and he stared right through me. "There's a broken window in the pool house and Gabriel, their son, is missing." We exchanged glances. "Penny is upstairs," I added and he looked away and followed the parents outside.

I scanned the surface of the pool again and inspected the floating toys more closely. An inflatable beach ball bobbed on the surface and diving rings shimmered on the bottom rendering their shape distorted and warped. As I walked by the fence around the pool, I jingled the lock. The gate didn't budge.

My thoughts tumbled: Should I have locked the pool house? Is there even a key; the gardener had stored the tools and he had just finished putting down the mulch and trimmed the bushes and tamed the ground cover, and I don't want to make a fuss about this; there need not be a commotion. All this planning and here we were, a child gone missing.

The boy's mother was in tears and though I wanted to console her, I felt frozen in place. Instead, I thought of Penelope upstairs in her room. How odd to fall asleep in the closet, she hadn't done that in years. Edward held me around my shoulders to keep me from crying or from losing my balance, maybe both. I did what I do when I need to regain control of myself and I asked, "How do I look to a casual observer?" and that always allowed me to take a step back just long enough to reclaim my self-control.

We didn't get anywhere with the search. The police were summoned, though I don't remember who made the call. The many flashing lights were unnerving. As two officers combed through the house and the backyard, the energy changed. Police stopped dead in their tracks and huddled in a group. Between the crackling sounds of the shoulder microphones and the coded language, I couldn't make sense of their conversations. The parents were rushed to a police car and I watched them drive off, my heart hammering in my chest.

Later, we received a call. The owners of the farmhouse heard noises in the barn and found the horses in a state of pandemonium. They thought a bobcat had gotten into the structure—there had been numerous sightings in the area, though I often wondered if it wasn't just a stray cat, people loved the country setting but weren't accepting of wildlife—but they found the missing boy, Gabriel, in a horse stall. He was unconscious. Barely breathing.

Edward rang Gabriel's parents the next day. After he hung up the phone, I asked him how the boy was doing.

"Not good," he said and ran the palm of his hand over his face as if trying to banish the memory of it all. "He'll be in the hospital for quite a while."

I thought how cruel for someone so young having to spend a long time in bed. I asked Edward what to tell Penelope but he was short with me.

"Did she ask about him?" Edward wanted to know.

"No," I replied.

"Don't say anything to her. Not a word," he said with such an edge to his voice that it startled me.

Fall came and went. The Shumard oaks turned from dark green into a vibrant scarlet red color, yet the leaves remained, though dead and brown, but they hung on nonetheless. During the winter, whenever I was out back feeding the stray cats, I glanced toward the property. The farmhouse sat hidden behind the oaks, which were planted tight like slats of a fence. There wasn't so much as a clapboard visible, not even the tip of a roof emerged from the wooded property. I wondered how Gabriel had ended up in that barn, how he even knew it was there. I had a hunch but I pushed that hunch into the shadows, where it remained with all the other monsters one prefers not to look at.

PART II
PURGATORY

No one thinks of how much blood it costs.

—Dante Alighieri

16

DONNA

I open a window. Shadow Garden lies quietly. The mowers and trimmers have fallen silent. The scent of just-mowed lawn in the air. I strain to see the buildings beyond, in the east, and I have to crane my neck to get a good look at a garden gate stuck in between brick walls. The brickwork is more substantial and the windows are covered with iron grates. I have yet to venture that far back into the property.

A woman, elfin compared to the building, walks into view. She plants herself on the walkway as if waiting for someone. It's just a few minutes before five. More women spill from the doors. I can't help but remember how they arrive in the mornings; their steps swift and their scrubs pressed clean and fresh, but in the afternoons, having spent hours cleaning and dusting and vacuuming, there's a certain apathy about them as they walk toward the parking garage.

There's no warning, no transition, just knowing now is the time. I put on the dirty scrubs from Vera's apartment and gather my hair in a ponytail. I stuff money from the kitchen drawer into a purse: $184.

I step outside and join the women, carefully mimicking their steps. I keep my head down, my hands in the pockets of the scrubs from Vera's house. If they were washed and pressed, it would be a dead giveaway, but there are stains across the front and they are wrinkled and I blend in. I'm one of them.

We take a breezeway between buildings and end up by a brick wall near the parking garage. I stand off to the side. The women's hands are red from scrubbing and cleaning and polishing silver. I keep mine hidden in the pockets so my fresh Chanel Rose Caché nude manicure doesn't show. The women chat away and eye me suspiciously but no one asks questions.

A vehicle approaches. It's much larger than a van but not quite a bus, more reminiscent of an airport shuttle. I get in line and then step into the interior, the smell of pine needles and dankness overwhelming. A surge of panic—what if there aren't enough seats for all of us?—but some remain empty. I don't know if the driver takes count or if he relies on some sort of system but there doesn't seem to be a method to all this. The sliding doors close.

I attempt to focus on what's to come to get out of my own head but all I can do is sit tight and wait to see where the van is taking me. The driver turns on the radio. The noise level rises as if someone has given the women the go-ahead to come to life. They giggle and joke and there's this overall cheerfulness filling the van.

As I'm twisting my diamond ring—it's looser than it used to be and I fear it'll slip off and get lost—I realize I absentmindedly put on a wide gold cuff bracelet when I visited Vera earlier. On my middle finger is a ring Edward gave me for an anniversary, a garnet surrounded by twenty small stones resembling the seeds of the pomegranate, Penelope's birthstone. Don't garnets bring misfortune to those who act improperly while wearing them? What an odd thought to have, I think, and slide the jewelry off and tuck everything into an interior pocket of my purse.

I fashion my behavior after the only other woman who isn't talking—indifferent toward everyone, not making eye contact at all—and like her, I stare off into nothingness through the tinted windows. We sit and wait and then the van takes off down the long winding road leading away from Shadow Garden.

Leaving Shadow Garden behind, possibilities are opening up but I'm also reminded of my shortcomings. First, my vision is weak in dim light. How fast darkness has descended, how stubbornly my eyes fail to adapt, looking from the road up into a lit window my eyes don't respond and for a few seconds I see nothing but vague floating spheres. Those sudden shifts from dark to light to dark, are those lights approaching cars or are they moving away? Secondly, as we pass street signs, names sound familiar, but I don't recognize much else, not the roads, not the buildings, especially when we get into the city. I don't put too much stock into this, not yet, I have always been directionally challenged.

A realization grows astronomically with every passing second: all this newfound confidence isn't worth anything knowing I'm about to be confronted with my old life. All those months at Shadow Garden I have become invested in the past and maybe I've lost myself in memories that can't be true? They can't be true because—

A dip in the road sends me off my seat. The van's movements rock me side to side, the driver brakes and the front dives, he accelerates and the rear end squats. I take long deep breaths and plant my feet on the floor of the van, where they stick to soda spills and popcorn remnants, but still my heart is whopping in my chest.

I sit paralyzed, want time to stop to get my thoughts together but that's not going to happen. I can't imagine what's about to happen, there's no way of knowing—I keep repeating it to myself *I can do this I can do this I can do this*—but I have hardly any time to figure anything out because the van merges onto the highway. Two exits and we turn into a grocery store parking lot. The doors open and two women get off. As quickly as the doors have opened, they shut and we merge back onto the freeway.

If I had been dropped in the middle of a foreign city, I couldn't feel more disoriented. There's no stopping this ride, there's no getting out, and nothing I can do but hold on to my purse. Some street names seem familiar, but I can't be sure. Memory can be faulty; as a matter of fact, memory *is* faulty, I know that much.

17

DONNA

I'm going back to Hawthorne Court. I repeat it to myself to make it sound real, *I'm going back to Hawthorne Court*. But there's a feeling of paranoia accompanying me like some talisman I'm carrying in my pocket. I can't resolve the memories, like two columns never adding up; regardless how often I go over the numbers, they just won't reconcile. The gaps that need filling are like hollows, about what happened before I left the Tudor mansion. I didn't trust myself then and I don't quite trust myself now because there's this sharp and clear understanding of a lack of credibility on my part.

Blurred trails of light zip by, the springs of the seat whine with every dip in the road. The exits and street signs mean nothing to me until I spot a white building with a dainty lace appearance—but the closer we get, the less familiar it looks. We take an exit and the traffic slows, so many cars, at times I feel as if the van is slowly inching its way backward but that can't be. Lights move like tracers through my field of vision, one second I'm in a dark tunnel, the next in a brightly lit area. Nothing feels right. Before I know it, we have left upmarket stores and smooth black glass exteriors behind and we come to a halt at a gas station where two women exit and get into a car idling in the parking lot.

By now the women have begun to whisper, one of them turns around and looks at me, all the while they speak fast and furiously. One of them eyes my purse. Though there's an aisle separating us, there's no doubt she has recognized it for what it is. Though I have picked the most unassuming bag in my closet, an inconspicuous and ordinary black hobo bag, it's a Valentino Garavani for $2,500. I'm clutching the softest calfskin money can buy.

I stuff the purse between my body and the window and close my eyes. *Just for a minute,* I tell myself. Images are painted on my eyelids, images of Penelope's face, smeared with blood. Fear shoots through my body, my lungs panic for air. My arms flail and I'm reaching for something to hold on to. When I rip open my eyes I find my Garavani hobo bag in the aisle, its contents scattered across the grimy floor. My rings and the gold bracelet have come to rest on the dingy carpet for everyone to see.

"Hector," a woman calls out to the driver. She speaks rhythmically, melodic words strung together, one laced through the next, *robato* and *bolsa* and what are the odds that the only sentence in Spanish I recall is *cuántos libros hay en la bolsa*? I don't know the word *robato* but it's self-explanatory, and the women are shouting and carrying on, pointing at the jewelry, at my purse, at me.

The van comes to a halt and I steady my body by pressing the palm of my hands against the seat in front of me. My tongue sticks to the roof of my mouth. Hector unfastens his seat belt and walks toward me.

"Where did you get this?" he asks and points at the jewelry strewn across the filthy carpet.

What are they thinking, I stole it?

"What are you saying? Are you accusing me of stealing?"

"Did you?" His face is a blur, his body so mighty and hunched over me.

I lose my confidence and shake my head *no* and rise from my seat. *No no no no no no no no. It's mine, it's mine,* I repeat, over and over. I drop to the ground, on my knees in that small space that Hector leaves for me, and I scoot across the aisle of the van, over the filthy floor. I gather the jewelry pieces, hear myself say *mine mine mine,* and I hear the words coming out of my mouth, *this is mine, I don't want you to steal it.* That's not what I mean and maybe all they hear is steal and that's all it takes. I try to push my way past Hector, I want to sit down, fold in on myself, want to become invisible, but he looms over me and he stands uncompromising.

"No," he says in a menacing voice. "You get out of here."

"No, please, no. I don't know where I am. Please don't—"

"I'll call the police if you don't," Hector says and reaches into his chest pocket, and a cell phone appears in his hand. "Leave and don't come back."

"No, no, no, you don't understand," I say without a hint of authority in my voice. "Don't call the police," I add and reach for his phone. I want him to put it back in his pocket but he's not having any of this. Instead of backing up he takes a step toward me and I rise to my feet. "Okay, okay, I'll leave."

I pull the door handle and yank it toward the back but my hand slips off the smooth metal grip. A couple more pulls and the door opens. I step outside but my purse strap catches hold of an armrest. Hector slides it off and slams the door shut. The van speeds away.

Gasoline wafts at me. Run-down pawnshops, liquor stores, and dingy supermarkets. Behind me the gas station, on the left a taqueria, on the other side a warped parking lot with cracked asphalt bordering against a brick wall. I clasp my purse against my chest. I want to cry.

People pass by, some nod, some bump into me as if I'm in the way. My hands are shaking but I manage to get my phone from my purse. GPS. There's a map function on my phone and Marleen has explained it to me but I don't recall a single detail. It sounded logical and listening seemed unnecessary and I couldn't imagine a scenario in which I'd need to know my location. I give up and enter the gas station.

A woman sits on a stool behind a counter. She is young, almost childlike with her clean face, impeccable skin, and dark hair down to her shoulders. She apparently wants to look older with her airbrushed brows and her winged eyeliner. Her teeth are crooked and she smiles with her lips together, except when she forgets.

"Next," she says without looking at me.

"Hi." I try to sound cheerful.

"Yes?"

"Do you have maps?" I ask.

"Maps?" she asks and raises one of her perfect eyebrows. "Like paper maps?"

"Yes, a map, a regular map. You know, one you fold out, with streets and directions," I say, not wanting to sound sarcastic but I can tell I do.

"No one uses paper maps anymore, lady. Don't you have a phone?"

"I do," I say and offer it to her.

"You can use it like a map. See." She grabs it and her fingers swipe across the screen, two, three times. She hands it back to me. "Google Maps, here you go."

I stare at the screen. I see a map, partial at best. I still have no idea where I am. "How does it work?" I ask.

Customers behind me impatiently shift their weight from left to right, their irritation palatable, annoyed that I can't comprehend the smallest of things.

"You are here," the clerk says and points at an address. "Just type in where you want to go and it'll give you instructions. You paying for gas?" she adds and I realize she's talking to the person behind me. I step to the side.

I type in Preston Hallow Road and the map shifts, zooms out, changes angles. A blue rectangle with the words *Get Directions*. I click on it. Now there's a blue line and a red dot. It says thirty-eight minutes to get there. I click on the green GO button and the map shifts and zooms in once again. The gas station is the starting point, my destination is Preston Hallow Road. Arrival at 7:42 p.m. In 38 minutes: 14.8 miles.

"Turn up the volume," I hear the girl's voice call out to me. "If you turn up the volume, it'll tell you when to turn. If you're driving and can't look at the map."

"Thanks," I say. "But I'm going to need a taxi."

"Just call an Uber."

I look at her, puzzled. I have no idea what she's talking about. This is what it must feel like being released from prison and having ended up in some sort of futuristic science fiction world, almost as if a time machine has catapulted me here.

"A what?"

"It's like a taxi, but cheaper. There's an app. You download it and it tells you how long until the car gets here. But you're gonna need a credit card."

Marleen handles everything money related including my credit cards. I have less than two hundred dollars to my name. I open, then close my mouth.

"God, lady, where have you been?" she asks but not without empathy. "Let me call you a taxi. You have money, right?" the girl asks, one eyebrow raised as she eyes my stained clothes.

"I do."

"Okay. Wait outside. I'll call you a taxi. But download that Uber app or put a cab company in your contacts. Makes life easier."

"I will," I say though I have not understood a single word. "Thanks," I add and grab a bottle of Coke from the cooler. I feel compelled to buy something though I don't see how this is of any significance. I pay and step outside. I haven't had a Coke in I don't know how long.

A group of teenagers spill from a convenience store and bump into me without apologizing. Across the street is a park and I sit on a lopsided bench by the entrance. I smooth my hair back and realize the ponytail has come undone. Behind me in the park there is a screaming match going on, and the cars in the nearby parking lot rev their engines. I open the Coke bottle and it fizzes and spills all over my hands and thighs.

The taxi arrives. The driver has closely shaved dark brown hair, wide shoulders, and strong arms. He adjusts the mirror and makes eye contact as I tell him where to take me. Preston Hallow Road in Highland Park. I'm asking him to take me to a place where strangers on bikes cause people to call the police for fear of thieves and robbers staking out the neighborhood. He holds my gaze via the rearview mirror, and I can almost hear him think; I'm not a Highland Park resident, not with my stained scrubs and messy hair, but I pass for one of the invisible ones, the ones who tend to the rich, someone who has employee business there.

"Highland Park?" he asks and rolls down the window.

"That's what I said. Is there a problem?"

He raises his hands, palms up, as if to apologize that he overstepped his boundaries.

We take off and outside the exits fly by; Fourth Street, Mockingbird, Bender Lane. It isn't until we leave the city behind and he takes the Preston Hallow exit that a familiar feeling sets in and I remember every curve in the road, every sign, every tree, every open field, every fence, and every house.

Preston Hallow Road is the major artery leading to Preston Hallow, an enclave of the city but really a town in itself. How often, at parties, we talked about how Preston Hallow came to be: the first house a farmhouse with horse pastures and stables, then whatever farmland acreage was left was carved into rectangular parcels and then money moved in, a community of doctors, entrepreneurs, industrialists, and lawyers.

Preston Hallow is an accumulation of Colonial and Greek Revivals on plats large enough to keep styles from clashing, mansions set back at the end of winding driveways, most of them disappearing behind tree lines. Pure perfection with columns and gabled roofs, handwrought cast-iron gates, the landscaping rivaling country clubs; a perfect balance of lawn, pathways and plants, groundcover and trees. Most of all, beyond the stucco and the bricks and the oversized front doors, the families living within those walls, so onlookers imagine, are the luckiest and happiest of them all.

I used to believe that, too.

18

DONNA

"Pull over right here," I call out and point at a three-story building to the right. We are a quarter mile or so from Preston Hallow Road. "Can you let me out here?"

My voice sounds impatient, and he stops the car and I get out and hand him the money before he can answer. Twice I close the door too softly and it isn't until the third time that I manage to put enough strength into it and slam it shut.

The light is perfect, a soft dusk turning the sky into shades of pink and peach. The tall metal streetlamps cast an artificial glow onto the walkways below, illuminating fallen leaves. In front of me sits the Preston Hallow Academy, a private school we called simply the Academy. The building looks peculiar in the dark, lit by floodlights pointing at a large plaque. A sapphire blue coat of arms, a banner proclaiming *Truth, Beauty, and Goodness*. They must have added another building, it's been a decade since Penelope graduated, so it's not at all odd that it appears foreign to me.

I enrolled Penelope in Preston Hallow Academy when she was thirteen. It was her first private school, and when I told her before the semester started that uniforms were required, she thought it to be a joke—khaki skirts and navy-blue shirts seemed laughable—but I had stocked up on skirts and socks and shoes and polo shirts. Though Edward had complained that Preston Hallow Academy tuition was expensive, I had insisted.

Penelope's first day was in stark contrast to my first day of high school. The Academy had a three-story atrium made of glass and looked more like a college than a high school and according to the map we were given, there were three gyms, one weight room, a pool, and two libraries. As students and faculty moved from building to building between classes, they got to enjoy sculptures and pottery and perfectly pruned groundcover within its predetermined boundaries. My school was a square one-story building with chain-link fence and a small LED marquee with crumbling blacktops where we ran laps in a stuffy gym without air-conditioning.

Standing here, so many years later, I can almost hear the footsteps of the stream of students emerging from the front doors, echoing in the deserted square. An image of Penelope, lanky and tall, rushing up those steps in the morning, dark marks on her back from her still-wet hair, smelling of Dana Love's Baby Soft Cologne.

Every morning I gave Penelope an encouraging nod as she exited the car and every afternoon I sat in a line of SUVs with other mothers where, at pickup, school employees not only opened and closed car doors but called out a joyful *don't forget your seat belt* and *have a great day*. Among all those students, a man in blue overalls shuffled about with a toolbox, getting lost within the sea of school uniforms and groups of students moving about. Every day I sat in the parent car line and fought the memories of my childhood.

I'll spare you the details but I walked to school except when it rained, when I rode in the passenger seat of my father's Buick Century, with the transmission slipping every few minutes. My father, a janitor, was diagnosed with lung cancer a year into his retirement. Thirty years of unclogging toilets, tightening door handles, and replacing broken windows and one year was all he got. It tore at me on certain days, some more than others. Once, I cried, holding up the line and cars honking at me as Penelope snarled at me, *go, Mom, go, everyone is staring.*

The Academy. Passing below the banner promising *Truth, Beauty, and Goodness,* I wonder what else this night will have in store for me. I walk and walk what seems like a long way but then I see it in the distance. My house. There's no going back. Why stop now. I have come this far, have I not?

If a universal memory of Penelope is storming up school steps, Hawthorne Court's is that of a Tudor in silent repose with precision landscaping, perfect proportions of shrubs, and mulch surrounded by lush green grass. If it were daylight that's what would reveal itself, but everything appears dull and monochrome, only a sliver of a moon hangs in the sky but that's more than enough light for me to find my way around. I know every inch of this property, I know where the power lines are buried, where the underground cables snake below the lawn to light the corner posts in heritage-red brick.

Hawthorne Court is a gray blur but soon it'll come into focus.

Down the street, though *down the street* doesn't sound right, it's a quarter mile or more, there is Ward Quentin's house, partner at a midsize law firm, previously based in New York. Bachelor. Always brought different dates to parties. To the right of Hawthorne Court sits a Colonial: Jane and Erwin Goodward. Erwin owns car dealerships all over the state and it's impossible to count the cars on his lots, that's according to the TV commercials he runs excessively. *I got more cars to choose from than you can count.* He paid $4.19 million for the house. I have trouble remembering him, but I knew his wife, Jane, the book club hostess.

I wonder if they still meet, women sitting ramrod straight on couches with hard cushions, balancing teacups atop saucers, Villeroy & Boch, white with gold rim. I loved the sound, the chatter of it all. The conversations—every first Tuesday of the month, three to five o'clock—centered on our children once we got the book talk out of the way.

"How is Penelope doing? Is she still at the university?"

"Well you know, she's trying to find herself. She isn't sure what her passion is quite yet."

The facts were Penelope skipped classes and was expelled but I didn't say that. What was there to say? My daughter, though intelligent and bright, can't manage to make it from one semester to the next, can't keep an apartment, and can't keep her head straight for anything? In conversations with friends and neighbors, I might have mixed up the lies I told, about college and traveling and finding herself. They probably thought me to be scatterbrained or dishonest, or both.

When Penelope came home for the summer for what we thought would be two months before returning back to college for her sophomore year, she left a few days after her arrival at Hawthorne Court and we didn't hear from her. Days turned into weeks. I inquired at a precinct without mentioning my name and that's how it was explained to me: *She is free to come and go, she is an adult. Unless there's reason to believe a crime has been committed. Or if there is a history of mental problems.* I hung up the phone then. Penelope was twenty-two. A foggy time during which we should have come up with a more logical approach to her unpredictable behavior. She told us later she went hiking with friends but forgot to tell us where and with who. She returned like one of those stray cats with a dull coat and bald patches, in need of deworming. She slept for days and that was that. Is that something that needs discussing at book club meetings and cocktail parties?

The house to my left. The Atwals. The husband Indian, the wife Hawaiian, but I can't be sure. It's not polite to ask people about those kinds of things. I recall the family owning gas stations but it could have been something else. Hotels maybe. There was the wife and there were other women living in the house, his mother or sister, I believe. Their daughters were of breathtaking beauty, all three of them. Not one ugly duckling among them. I often wondered where this would lead, three girls each a year or so apart. They'd all reach their teenage years around the same time and I thought *better you than me*. The Atwals did come to the housewarming party and they loved the house, they were oohing and aahing plenty. They never attended any functions after that, though I invited them. I'd like to think their social life was just ascetic. Their lawn needs watering, those yellow patches are unsightly. Was there a reason they avoided us after that night? I don't—

Look at those silver maples! I planted them, what, five years ago? They have come along nicely. I would have preferred a creek or waterway nearby—one drought and they'll pay the price—but the roots have taken hold and deepened. They haven't been pruned in a while, the branches are too long and delicate, flimsy enough so a high wind or even a layer of ice can snap them off, and the rods I had put in to assure a straight growth pattern are tilted. Why would Edward allow such a thing, young trees are so susceptible to growing crooked if not corrected, one storm and in the morning you wake up and there it is—a leaning tree.

The house. There it is.

Ivy twirls undisciplined and shameless around the brick posts by the front door, sticky leaves have climbed upward, have attacked the house like an aggressive invader, and soon it'll attach itself to the oak, vines will climb up the tree trunk and envelop branches and twigs, blocking sunlight to the first then the second floor. I picture the brickwork overcome by rootlike structures. So much ivy. It's everywhere. A stem, thick as rope, sends runners over the stones. To my horror the mortar has cracked and blades of grass emerge in between them. The oak by the driveway, its leaves chatter above me, tell me I was supposed to care for the house, protect it. But I had not. I had not. Because Edward—

I wonder, do the neighbors still welcome Edward into their homes, invite him to parties? Will they welcome him with another woman? I bristle at the thought but I follow the easement line toward the house, cut across the lawn, and step onto the old stone path leading to the house.

I make my way to the front door. That door knocker. An ornate head of a woman with a bursting sun behind her like a halo I had come across at a salvage company on a trip to the Gulf Coast. The door's brushed bronze, exquisitely hand-forged hardware, the cut stone set back into a brick wall, make the entrance feel like stepping into a fortress. Having gained distance from my former life, I now understand what I tried to do here: it was my way of clearing the trees and preparing a plat, building dams and levees around it to keep predators at bay.

That day Edward dropped me off at Shadow Garden, I was beside myself and didn't think . . . What did I think, exactly? Having been cast off like a worn sock, I didn't have the strength to demand what . . . Should I have insisted on the key? This was my home and not being able to just enter through the front door makes me pity myself. Typical me, disappointment churning in my gut but I also haven't so much as wasted a thought on how I'd get *into* Hawthorne Court, having spent all that time wondering how I'd get here.

To my left the marble fountain prattles away. I dip my fingers in the water and quickly jerk my hand back. Algae sticks to my fingers and a scummy layer covers the entire basin, the water babbling and splashing but the gurgle is slow. Soon the pipes will be blocked.

I look up, second floor, second window, that's where Penelope's room is. I count the windows, locate my former bedroom. Is another woman sleeping in my bed?

Following the path, I end up at the metal gate leading to the service entrance. It was part of the original floor plan, from a time when employees entered the house and I had thought it quirky and charming and kept it, though we hardly used it.

Edward often forgot to lock the doors at night but the alarm system might be enabled and I don't dare cause a commotion of epic proportions; shrill alarms and blinking lights, and the security firm showing up. How would I explain myself, that's the conundrum, but I can't resist the urge to look through a window and if I'm careful enough, I won't trigger an alarm.

I part the potted gold dust aucuba by the service entrance which will allow me a view of the butler's pantry and the kitchen. The ground is nothing but knotted roots and I shuffle my feet to get closer to the window, but before I know it the vines have wrapped themselves around my ankle. Sharp English ivy leaves poke at me. I stumble as I break free, reach for the windowsill to steady myself but the house is so close—or am I closer to it than I thought?—and the palm of my hand hits the windowpane with a loud smack which echoes into the night like a slap on bare skin. I crouch and wait. I slip behind the flowerpot the size of a bathtub. Nothing stirs. No alarm. No footsteps, no lights. I wait a while longer to make sure. I sit in the dark, hidden by the six-foot-tall aucuba, the green, gold-spotted leaves wide and long enough for me to disappear behind. The irony of it all. As I cower in the corner, an ace tumbles out of my sleeve.

The first time Penelope hid from me, she was five years old. It was innocent enough. We had just moved to Florida, and the house was so small it took me less than thirty seconds to run from room to room. I checked the door but she was so little and could barely reach the lock. I opened cabinets and closets but there was no sign of her; I ripped shower curtains and checked the backyard for holes in the fence. I found her underneath the dinner table, calm and poised. Had she not just seen and heard me running through the house, screaming her name, banging doors and cabinets? Why was she so composed, as if it was a game we had played, when I was clearly out of my mind with worry?

She didn't stop there. She'd walk home from school and take a wrong turn or wander off in another direction and the entire neighborhood was looking for her while she sat on a bench pretending she didn't understand what all the hoopla was about.

"You can't just wander off. Don't do that again," I'd say to her.

"Don't do what again?"

"Wandering off. You scare us when you do that."

"But I'm just taking another route."

"It's embarrassing to alert the school and neighbors and the police and then we find you and sometimes I think you do this on purpose." I joked then, "Penelope, you are my only child, I don't have a spare. If I lose you, I have nothing."

I followed her once. Penelope was seventeen, and I happened to drive by her school and saw her get into a car. She had missed curfew again and we had taken the house keys because otherwise she'd come and go as she pleased and we needed her to know that we were keeping track of her. I trailed the car. The driver was too old to be a student, though I couldn't be sure. I eventually lost them in traffic but was worried when she didn't return home that day. I said to Edward, "Maybe we should lock her away in a box underground to keep her from harm," but it sounded macabre and I regretted it right away. That night I stayed up dreading the moment she'd stroll down the street like a wayward girl with the entire Preston Hallow neighborhood looking on.

She materialized out of thin air in the early morning hours. I watched her through the window as she approached the front door. She stood idly and then turned on her heels as if the front door was some sort of orientation point. It was an eerie sight to behold, my seventeen-year-old daughter taking strides through the yard at four o'clock in the morning like a mad soldier marching to the tune of a maniacal drum, stopping and changing directions at random. I wanted to go outside and assure her that everything was all right, but she stopped suddenly and proceeded east across the lawn, then back toward the house, then trudged with stiffness and determination until I realized she was counting her steps. She bent down and retrieved something from the lawn. She entered through the service entrance door. I stood in the sunroom that night, in the dark, pressed against the wall attempting to keep my breath steady.

The next day I searched the lawn and not until I came upon what I mistook for a crooked sprinkler head did I see it: a black film roll container buried in the soil. To the naked eye the round top looked like a sprinkler head, but inside she had hidden the key to the house.

It's been years but maybe it's still there?

Edward's neglect has contributed to my finding the key in the no-longer-plush grass. Underneath the oak the soil is prominent and the tree roots are visible, snaking about, stealing water from the grass, sparse patches are covered in stolon-like strands stretching from dirt patch to dirt patch, struggling to fill in the gaps. I take my steps deliberately, locate the spot, and the crooked canister materializes within the soil. It takes me only seconds and I tug at the container and it breaks free. The top comes off easily, the key is in pristine condition.

I walk to the front of the house and turn right, down the walkway back toward the service entrance. I gauge the distance to the army of maples on the edge of the property, just in case. It will take me about twenty seconds to get there and that's where I'll hide if the alarm goes off. All I have to do is be quick and it will seem like a fluke of the security system.

It dawns on me that I haven't felt my hip act up since I left Shadow Garden, I haven't so much as wasted a thought on it. All those walks, all those runs have paid off. It almost seems as if I've been preparing for this moment.

The key slips into the lock without hesitation. Feeling my heart all through my fingertips, pounding along metronome-like in a timely beat, I enter Hawthorne Court.

19

DONNA

I suck in the air and there's something unsettling about it. The scent is giving me images of a house locked up during a long absence, a buildup of time, yet it has a familiarity that is taking me back to a life that no longer exists. The kitchen under-cabinet lighting throwing shadows into the butler's pantry and Viking stove is familiar. As if queued, the specs run through my head: *induction, forty-eight inch, stainless steel, griddle, porcelain-coated cast-iron burner grates, royal-blue finish.*

With bold confidence, I enter the kitchen. I run my fingers across stainless-steel appliances and Italian marble counters and follow the house's natural flow, to the left, into the step-down living room with barrel ceilings and hardwood floors. On first instinct I want to rush to Penelope's room but I resist. I must start in the basement and work my way up strategically.

The basement construction had been a point of contention when we renovated the house.

"It'll cost more to excavate than our first home. Donna, you can't be serious," Edward said after I asked about an engineering survey. "This is more difficult than you realize," he added after I insisted on sitting down with the contractor to discuss it. "The ground swells up, then it shrinks. There are too many forces at play. You can build an entire guesthouse for the price of a basement."

I didn't budge. "Edward, you are not thinking clearly," I countered. "What about a shelter? There are tornadoes around here, where would we go?"

"It's cheaper to build up than down. You want another floor? Pick one or the other."

In the end we compromised; there was a small basement and the third floor was a split-level. To think how long and fervent that argument was, how trivial it seems now. I'll never think of the expense as a waste of money. In all those years I've never regretted going the extra mile when it came to Hawthorne Court. I still believe the basement came in handy, even if I don't live here anymore.

All Edward ever did was complain what things cost instead of soaking in the house and letting it make you happy and full, like a stray kitten after a saucer of thick cream. I feel anger rise but I need to keep my wits about myself and so I do what I have become accustomed to: I tell myself that the best part of memory is being able to forget and I push Edward momentarily out of my mind.

The door to the basement is ajar and that alone strikes me as odd; as a rule we left the door locked. I remember the first step down appearing suddenly, the stairs altogether steep, the drop-off abrupt and I had always been wary about a fall. I take short floating steps, but still they sound loud in the dark and quiet house. I tiptoe onto the first landing and pull the door shut behind me. My steps no longer travel, my breathing is now cushioned, and my breaths bounce off the walls instead of echoing through the house. The air is stagnant and there is a claustrophobic layer with space so limited, walls so close to my left and right. I descend on shallow treads, even the smallest wrong movement will send me tumbling down.

In the dark I reach for the string I remember dangling off the ceiling. It magically ends up in the palm of my hand. I loop it around my finger, pull on it, and the light comes on. Passing underneath the bare bulb forces me to hunch over as I count my steps. It strikes me as silly—it's not as if Edward has added any—but all the while it seems appropriate and when I land on the last one, I know why.

My foot slips as if on a patch of ice. I catch myself. How could I forget? I had made it a habit to hold on to the railing and caught myself every single time. Like now. *Muscle memory.* The concrete step had begun to crumble years ago, a big chunk had broken off. The slightest contact will deteriorate the jagged rectangle until there's nothing left but cement turning into dust. Eventually the sudden drop-off will feel like drifting off to sleep and catching yourself jerking awake, all the while you are tumbling into the dark.

The first door on my right swings open with ease. Mildew blasts at me. A few wooden boards are haphazardly cast onto the floor. I'm about to turn when I spot chairs in the back corner. One propped up upside down on the other, six altogether. They are covered in brown stains and I can't help but think of blood but then I catch myself. It terrifies me to know that's where my mind goes.

The room on the left is a wine cellar intended to shelve vintage wines but I lost interest—between the cost of vaults and temperature control units and logs one should keep—and Edward didn't want to spend more money and so I gave up on it altogether. Behind the next door is nothing but an old bike leaning against the wall, rolls of wrapping paper in a bucket, bent at the top as if they have been down here for decades. The last room contains nothing but cobwebs, spider nests, and rat droppings. Close to the ceiling are elongated windows, slit like cuts into the walls and even during sunny days they didn't provide enough natural light to see every nook and cranny. One window has been left ajar.

Back upstairs, in the kitchen, I listen to the house. The refrigerator hums, ice cubes drop into the tray. My movements are cautious, I pass from room to room, timidly, afraid I'll knock over a vase, bump into a chair, and send it screeching across the floor, or a rug will trip me up.

The dining room. I remember it as a long and narrow room with the original hardwood floors, the perfect size for a table that would seat a dozen people. In the best of days we'd had dinner parties and anniversary gatherings here, held charity functions, and even the mayor came for a brunch once. When Edward opened his practice, guests gathered in the foyer and upon my direction the staff pushed the doors open and the grand space revealed itself. I watched the faces, how their jaws dropped. Over the past year at Shadow Garden, I have imagined this room often: the mahogany table taking up most of the room, impeccably set with heavy silver cutlery; etched wineglasses luminous in the early evening light; candelabras on each end of the table; ornate place cards.

The starburst pendant hangs above. It's a work of art and a genius move to place it here, that one modern accent completing a room of antiques. Such a powerful statement, the perfect piece for the space. I wish I could see the room the way it used to look, the way the light danced off the walls and reflected in the windowpanes like a lustrous crown manifesting our place in the world, but I don't dare turn on the light.

I move on into the foyer and the double flight of stairs invitingly wind upward in front of me, but I hesitate, I'm fearful I'll give myself away if the stairs creak. I needn't worry, though; the construction is sturdy and up I go, ignoring the second floor with guest bedrooms and a library and make my way to the third floor. I want to *rush rush rush* but I stop myself from getting carried away. If I get careless, it'll only be a matter of time until I run into a chair, knock something over; eventually a mistake will be made.

At the top landing, the hallways to the left and right lie abandoned and I'm disoriented; furniture is missing, the hallways lack accent tables, the silk curtains are not there either and it strikes me—the entire house is furnished sparsely. I look left, then right, left again. The hallways are long square chutes, like shipping containers, leading into gradual darkness.

Above me, though shrouded in darkness, is a masterpiece. Just knowing it's there is consolation enough, even though I can't see it. The hours I spent on picking it out are incalculable, and the designer had advised against it but I told her if something works, you keep it around. From Versailles to Buckingham Palace, its appeal was time tested and if it was good enough for them, it was perfect for us: an early nineteenth-century French crystal chandelier draped with bead roping, heavy pear-shaped drops, an iron structure with fluted arms. I had purchased the chandelier behind Edward's back and had it electrified. I have no qualms with saying I would have spent double the money if I had to. How do you put a price on something so perfect? Every time I turned it on, it was like plugging in a Christmas tree.

Taking in a deep breath, I feel a tickle in my nose. Those dirty drapes and windows. Is it neglect or my presence sending a vortex of dust into the previously stagnant air? A house this size requires dusting twice a week or it turns into a dust trap, and judging by the state of it all, Edward hasn't hired a housekeeper. There's an expression physicians use: circling the drain. Talk for a patient whose death is unavoidable, a medical term for someone in rapid decline: this house is circling the drain. It's fixing to die. This isn't a house neglected, not a house in flux, in a state of unrest, but a house about to perish.

A ghost house is what this is. One moment there was a landing I used to navigate from but now there are so many rambling hallways, half stories, offset stairs, it's no longer simple and easy to get around, and everything is complicated and overthought. The transition between floors makes my head spin. I'm tangled within these walls. Maybe it's just the dark inducing some sort of bewilderment? That's what I tell myself: *the darkness is playing tricks on me.*

The hallway unfolds and there's panic. Has the house morphed into a labyrinth? There's this sinking feeling of despair, a lack of confidence in finding my way around, and is this warped house no longer willing to accommodate me? I might as well admit it to myself: I am lost. How does one get lost in one's own home?

Making my way back down the stairs, I end up in a passageway with a round table and a hideous horse statue. A glimmer of a memory in this otherwise unaccustomed space—Penelope in pajamas, a Christmas morning, her calling out to me, mere seconds and she was down the stairs tearing wrapping paper, Edward saying from above, "Would you look at that, Santa's been here!"—but then my heart sinks right through my body onto the floor. Is that where we used to put up the Christmas tree? I don't remember the area being so spacious. Why would I not remember the very house where I raised my daughter and where I lived for almost twenty years?

If I were in court, if someone made me rest one hand on a bible and raise the other, I'd say this isn't my house. But that is just silly. *Silly.*

20

DONNA

Down the hallway, a window looks out onto the neighboring property—the St. Clairs—the house is barely a faint light in the distance. What a pretentious name. The interior is decorated in white, *all white* mind you, even the bricks are painted white. Any designer or real estate professional will tell you that's a sin.

There were nights at Shadow Garden I dreamed in such vivid details about Hawthorne Court that when I woke I often forgot for a fraction of a second where I was. Though the muddle of the layout continues, to my surprise, I find the door to Penelope's room just fine. The more I hype myself, the heavier my heart gets.

Why haven't you called me or visited?

If you think I'm mad at you, I'm not.

I love you, that's what mothers do.

Your father told you lies about me, is that what this is?

I grasp the glass doorknob and I stand there, unable to move. The knob turns and the door swings open. I hover on the threshold. Paralysis isn't an exaggeration, for once I'm not being dramatic. I don't dare enter because the very end of the room disappears into blackness.

21

DONNA

A nostril flare confirms the carpet smells stale, unaired, yet there's something else, a tinge in the air, a trace of something I can't quite place. Though I'm unable to make out details in this faint light, I know Penelope's room by heart, every inch is etched into my brain. Though impossible to validate in the dark, the walls are painted in a soft daffodil yellow with gold flecks mixed into the paint.

Three framed prints on the opposite wall centered in a horizontal grouping tell a fictional story of an accumulation of bad choices. One: a girl leaning out of a window as she brushes her long hair. Rapunzel was the epitome of Penelope, mainly concerned with herself, up in a tower, but also, and I hate to admit it, due to the actions of her parents she ended up in the hands of a witch. In the second print, the girl sets off into the forest, carefree, her dress bil-

lowing, and her head high. A fearless heroine, Penny the adoles-
cent, curious and unafraid in everything she did. I have since
abandoned that belief and replaced it with a complete absence of
self-awareness, ignoring the dangers of the world rather than being
daring. Unprepared and ill equipped. In the third print the girl
comes upon wild animals in the woods, battling them, her dress
torn and her hair undone, unable to fight them off. I shiver.

The light and the darkness in the room create confusing and
obscure shapes and nothing about it says it has recently been occu-
pied. There are shadows on the floor, on the walls, on the shelves.
There's no nightstand, no vanity. No couch. No chair. No coffee
table. No white fluffy rug. The bookshelves are there but only a few
sad editions rest flat on the dusty surface. Nothing is as it used to
be, it's a dollhouse without furniture, empty and unassembled.

Drawing conclusions is difficult with just the faint moonlight
coming through the window and I won't know until I turn on the
light. I close the door gently so as not to make a sound. Pushing the
dimmer to the bottom, I switch on the light and move the knob up.
The light in the room is barely more than the flickering of a candle,
yet I see the floor clearly: dark squares and light rectangles in the
shape of tables and couches and chairs. No one had been here to
move furniture to allow the wood to evenly lighten. Ruined. It's all
ruined.

Penelope's not here and neither are her things. Do I check every
room of the house to find her? That seems impossible in the dark—
too many rooms, too much can go wrong. *Look for signs,* I tell myself. *Look for signs and clues about Penelope.*

I step toward the window and peer outside. The oak is too tall to
see Preston Hallow Road. Placing my hand on the windowsill and
leaning forward until my forehead touches the glass, I run my fingertips across the wooden frame. Splinters and slivers and bits of
wood dig themselves into my skin. The window casings are pep-

pered with holes, numerous wooden chips have gathered on the sill, I feel deep grooves beneath my fingers like someone took some sort of tool to the frame and hammered away.

The closet door is open and in the corner, like an array of sticks, sit floorboards with nails sticking out. In the far end of the room is the bed frame—just a mattress, no sheets or pillows—a skeletal piece with four posters. Draped over the footboard is a pillowcase, left behind in a hurry, as if its existence has escaped the person who removed everything else from the room. Even the fabric that was used to create the canopy is gone.

The shapes on the walls must be my imagination. Square, the size of an index card. Brushstrokes, they look like? Someone sampling shades and color choices before making a selection?

Pulling the pillowcase off the bed, I bunch it up and with my foot shove it into the gap underneath the door to keep the light from escaping into the hallway. I push the dimmer up another notch. The dark corners of the room illuminate and the angles and curves are now clear for me to inspect. Dings and dents everywhere. I recognize the indentations on the wall for what they are: square holes with jagged edges.

I inspect the bookshelves. The ledges are spare, only a few books remain flat on their backs, toppled over as the adjacent ones were removed. They are dusty, though the pages are immaculate as if they've never been cracked open. I stroke the spines as if the physical touch will make my mind recall them, yet none of them look familiar. I study the titles, make an attempt to recall the covers and stories, but I can't seem to make a connection. I can't quite get there. All those dollhouses Penelope had are so vivid in my mind—chairs, vanities, coat hangers, and fireplace stokers, no feature left neglected. How does one remember one detail but not another?

I switch off the light and push the pillowcase away from the crack underneath the door, turning to look at the room one more time.

There's a shiny object on the floor. I step toward it and get down on my knees. My hand passes through it and I realize it's just a sliver of moonlight coming through a crack in the window. My veins are prominent, my bones protrude. There's a shift, a slight flicker, real or imagined, who's to say. Old houses do that, make the world fluid, like a double exposed photograph. Am I caught in overlapping timelines? Or have I been in a coma and the world has gone on without me and I'm just now catching up to it?

One vivid memory pops into my head, from a time long ago. I take a deep breath, hold it. There's a question in my head, a loop without beginning or end, like a corkscrew, it spirals down, *down, down, down,* to the bottom of the steps. Out the door and to the place where I must go.

That's where I will find the truth about Penelope.

22

EDWARD

Edward awakes to a thud. A tree touching a window, a falling branch, he can't tell. He stares off into the darkness. There's the sound of breathing that isn't his own, a labored heaving like someone having exerted themselves. Probably his very own breath waking from a nightmare he no longer recalls. The duvet lies bunched up next to him and the night is cold. Maybe he neglected to shut a door or close a window? He's been forgetful lately.

He's aware of the shadows in the room, so familiar in the space he used to share with Donna. He could swear she's standing next to him, he smells the scent of her lotion hanging in the air. He's imaging this, must be, her perfume probably trapped in the bedding.

His forehead is hot as if he has a fever. He sits up in bed, sweating and chilled at the same time. There's a humming in his ears. He hasn't been himself lately, feels dizzy all the time. A constant spinning sensation, his body is no longer his own, hasn't been familiar to him in months. His bones must be leaking calcium, his wrists are weak and his muscles have lost their strength, how else is he to explain that he can't open as much as a jar without straining?

Even though he's grown accustomed to it, he loathes staring into the dark. The blackness around him multiplies his anxiety as if the night has studied him and seen to it he wakes. He evens his breathing, and then he hears the floorboards creak. No, it's more than that. It's not the house settling, this time it's different, he knows *something* is there. He wants to reach for the light switch but then he doesn't. All those hours he's been wandering around this house in the dark, he knows every inch of it. No need to turn on the light. But he'll take a flashlight. Just in case.

23

DONNA

As if teleported, like a figure in a dollhouse plucked from one part of the house and discarded in another, I find myself on the first floor.

I remember something else now—the months of my depression. How easy it has become to call it what it was: my depression. The misery of it all, like vapors it hung in the air. The staircase, the winding one, echoes with Edward's voice, *why why why did you do that?*

There was this long, drawn-out period of behavior that was odd, to say the least. It began with a rather short temper I suddenly felt prone to, its origin not something I could put my finger on. I was lashing out, in the beginning I had enough insight to be aware of it. I blamed Penelope for it, her living at home.

"The strangest things are happening to me," I'd told Edward and described one of the incidents to him. I called a cashier a name because she didn't bag my groceries fast enough, waiters also got the brunt of it, I'm embarrassed to say—I was so relentless in my pursuit to hurt people and dash out insults.

The next thought comes to me in a random fashion. *That's what this house does, it makes it all come back.*

Down the hallway, there's a window open inward, like a door. From there I see the pool and parts of the pool house. A cast-iron bench sits observing the night.

I pause in front of my former bedroom—*our* former bedroom. *It's time. It's time. It's time.*

It's all there, plain as day. All those years, an entire lifetime sloshes over me. I will my breathing to slow as if my beating heart is echoing off the walls. I turn the knob and I enter the room.

The cedar closet door on the far end is open. Even in the dark I can make out the room, the furnishings, even the corners in their entirety. It's odd and disjointed, none of the furniture I remember is here, how can that be? Those wingback chairs with the glass tables are an atrocity. I walk backward and bump into something. A wooden banker chair with wheels screeches across the floor. A negligent move on my part, reminding me to be more careful, be on my toes, have my ducks in a row. I bump into a wall—*why is there a wall?* This house, this room, it's like my body doesn't know where it begins and where it ends or maybe the house is encroaching on me? I know there's no such thing, it's not like the house is alive. Is it?

The bed is no longer on the east wall but in front of the windows facing the back of the house. A single body forms an outline underneath the duvet, chest uncovered, expanding then lowering. One must ask questions to keep sane and so I allow myself: What if the man in the bed isn't Edward at all? What if he sold the house and there's someone else sleeping in this bed? It's not a woman, not a child—a man for sure—but maybe even that's a lie my mind is telling me. The body stirs but there's not enough light in the room to see his face.

I step carefully toward the bed. I reach out and pull the duvet off the man's shoulders, away from his torso. He turns and rolls over, mumbles in his sleep. He reaches for the duvet, pulls it back over himself. The man stills and I dare not move. My brain is sending weird signals. All those things happen simultaneously and all I can think of is how I would have preferred to have some sort of a weapon in my hand, in case he charges at me.

What I do next, I can't explain. Not in the moment, not later on. My arm hovers in midair, my hand floats above him. Once that movement is made, everything after is hard to undo. I touch his cheek ever so lightly as if I want to wake him gently. The man sighs and that's when I know it's Edward. I can tell by the way he releases a breath, the minute pause he makes after he has completely deflated his lungs. I take a step back and that's when he opens his eyes.

I have retreated far enough into a dark corner, where I remain invisible. I reach back to steady myself but the wall behind is out of reach. I don't remember the room being this large.

Edward sits up and looks around, disoriented. He gazes in my direction, yet the shadows protect me from his view. He reaches for his glasses but they slip out of his hands. They land softly on the carpet. Quietly I take another step back. The wall is now cold against my back. One more step to the left and I'm in the bathroom. I slip into the space where the commode is. If he switches on the light, he will see me. I don't know what will happen after, I have no plan for what to do or what to say.

Edward is up and about. A drawer opens and closes, followed by a beam powering through the darkness. How silly of him to use a flashlight, why not switch on the overhead light?

He leaves the bedroom and I follow him, the beam of light alternating between illuminating the ground in front of him as if to make sure there are no surprise obstacles, then pointing straight ahead to find his way. I move about the edges of rooms, my body brushing against woodwork in hallways. I slide behind a column or remain on the other side of a doorway, in corners, that's where the shadows are best, where I feel secure, as if I've just been handed an invisibility cloak.

Following Edward feels peculiar. The flashlight dangles lifeless in his hand and underneath an accent table it reveals rolled-up rugs. Edward isn't looking for an intruder, he's predictable in his movements, no sudden turns, and most of all, he sees what I see, the chaos of this house, yet he's on autopilot, robotic in his steps, as if this is some sort of nocturnal pastime. His gait is that of a man overwhelmed, as if something has been claiming him bit by bit. I know him, know him too well, this is, *was*, my husband, how would I not?

The beam shoots upward as we reach the living room, spotlighting a cluster of photographs—strange apparitions as the light passes over them—there are so many gaps and the ones that remain are crooked. The mantel, so stark and empty. And above it all, the disarray, the missing furniture, the disorder, lingers the scent of old ashes, the raised hearth is sprinkled with debris.

We reach the entrance to the kitchen, a rectangular space, where it's not impossible for a light beam to catch me. There is nowhere to hide, crouching behind the island is all I can do, I have to *think think think*—I won't see him coming if I stoop behind it—and I panic.

The man, who had just barely shuffled through the dark, stops dead in his tracks. Like in a game of freeze I pause, mere inches from him. I'm his shadow, that's how close I am. Nothing but a swift swivel on his part and the light will expose me. To the right, past the butler's pantry, is the back door. I stare at it, prepared to make a run for it. I'm overheated and my heartbeat pounds in my ears but I don't waver, I have to trust myself.

How absurd to follow Edward, yet how essential it was just ten minutes ago. As if he heard something, he turns and moves past the opening into the kitchen and back to the living room. His pace even slower now, defeated. I stare at the back door, imagine the pebbled back porch underneath my feet. The path to the pool house.

It still bears the same memory—the hodgepodge of discarded outdoor furniture and lounge chair covers and umbrella stands—but there's something else. I can't come up with a clear understanding of why I do it, but I abandon Edward, leave him to his nocturnal stroll, and silently slip out the back door.

Like a ghost in the night I make my way to the pool house. The door is unlocked—still, we have never been able to locate the key and no one's ever bothered to replace the lock—and though it was an unfinished thought just seconds ago, I now feel compelled to search the entire place. I turn to look back at the house and there's Edward, standing on the lawn, his legs in a stance as if in anticipation of a gust of wind about to knock him over. He points the flashlight across the expansive lawn, as if he's expecting to see someone rush away from the house.

I slip into the pool house and pull the door shut behind me. I don't know how much time I have, I better be quick.

A kayak leaning in the corner. Followed by a reaction, like a glow stick breaking, and I know that this is where I will find the answers I need. How I ended up with that thought I don't know, it's like one of those hallways in the house, first I'm lost in the dark, then I've arrived in the light. I open the kayak compartment and within it is a plastic bag covered in dust, dead bugs, and round silky spider eggs. I grab the bag and unfold it, reach inside. It's full of pages ripped from one of those spiral notebooks. *Penelope's letters.* The ones the therapist told her to write.

A spear of light penetrates the window of the pool house. I must duck down, crouch between wall and kayak, or he'll see me. I don't know if my hip will cooperate, I dread the speed with which I have to move, but I must hide and do so quickly. I crouch down. A whimper escapes my mouth. The pain has another unpleasant side to it, there's nausea, too. Searing agony radiates from hip to knee, leaving me wanting to roll up in a ball, but I'm afraid I won't be able to get up. Light travels across the wall. Voices are calling out, *hello hello hello,* but maybe that's my imagination. There are footsteps now, I'm not imagining those, and a light beam stabs through the dark. A shadow by the window. I get up, my body fits perfectly behind the kayak and I stand at attention like a soldier, arms by my side to keep me from being discovered. My brain is straining for any sound of approaching feet.

"Security." I hear a man's voice outside, deep, dark, meant to intimidate. Not Edward, someone else. "Anyone there?"

"I looked there, I told you already." Edward's voice.

"Any broken doors?"

"No, no. Nothing like that. Why did you even come? No one called you."

Edward is upset, he wanted to deal with this alone, didn't want anyone to think there's a prowler on the loose. I'm catching on to him.

"I saw a flashlight. We're required to check when something suspicious—"

"That was me, we've been over this. Never mind. I'm fine. You can go."

"I'll have to write a report."

"Write your report. But go. Everything's all right."

"But you said—"

"I'm allowed to walk around my own property with a flashlight, right? I thought there was someone in the pool house. Obviously there's not. Thanks for checking but we're done here."

Say it, Edward. Say it. *My wife is here to hold me accountable.*

Without warning, I'm blinded by a beam. The sudden shift digs into my retina and I stand there, explosions of lights going off behind my lids. Everything goes dark. I'd give anything to step out into the light, to see Edward's face. Vera pops into my head, the thought of *when I tell Vera the story later,* I'll say *I came upon him in the most unlikely of circumstances.*

I wait for a long time. When I dare look out the pool house window, I see light in the upstairs bedroom. The security guard has left, down the road brake lights flicker, then disappear.

I have trouble focusing. Everything presents itself in shades of gray, like strokes from a charcoal stick. Except the pool, the pool is a shade of sapphire when I so clearly recall the tiles being sky blue. How long has it been since I lived here? Summer and fall went by at Shadow Garden but maybe it all blurred into one long stretch of time and there was another fall and another summer and somehow I have forgotten? Stung by a spindle, put to sleep. Was that a story I used to read to Pea or am I confused? How easily I assign Pea to the toddler, Penny to the child, and Penelope to the teenager, no longer sure if the names caused her to change or the change in her caused us to call her by different names. Everything is off—time, space, all of it.

I walk toward the house. Marleen pops into my head. What will she do once she finds my bed empty? It's still dark. I have plenty of time left. The house is a big rambling monstrosity and I will bunker down somewhere. Read the letters. Put it all together.

There are things Edward doesn't know. About Penelope. About this house. Like the fact that playrooms are perfect hiding places.

24

DONNA

The longer I've been in the house, the bolder I've become. The door to the playroom creaks open. The sound travels through corridors that snake in each direction. I enter. The shadows are long on the wainscoted walls, the light fixture sits flush against the ceiling, and the Victorian prints give the room a touch of whimsy: fairies and frogs and dragonflies. Dolls in strollers are tucked under blankets, an art easel sits in the corner with pastel chalks still resting on its ledge.

There's a rather peculiar story about this room and how it came into existence, given the fact Penelope was too old for a playroom by the time we moved here. It was designed with something in mind, but you have to know that to get the entire picture.

Hawthorne Court was on the Holiday Tour of Homes, an event created for charity with tickets and people being bussed from one architecturally significant home to another. It was Christmas and I had hired decorators who put up a tree in each room, and every fireplace was decked with fir garlands and red bows. I came up with the idea to spread out my pageant gown including the sash on the bed in the master bedroom as if I had just slipped off stage and out of the dress. The story of the house was as important as the people living in it, not just craftsmanship, landscaping, and design, but the essence of who we were.

But still I wanted more. I had put so much time into staging the house but I felt the need to stand out from the crowd. After all, there were so many beautiful homes on the list. I fabricated what I dubbed memory boxes and an entire playroom decorated like a childhood wonderland. The boxes were trunks with mementoes grouped by age: Penelope's first pair of shoes, her first dress, her footprint in clay, her first drawing, her first attempts at writing letters—all those things you hang on to and can't bring yourself to throw out. At the eleventh hour I concocted a teenage box, a spur-of-the-moment thing—the home tour was years after the house-warming party, Penelope was barely fifteen then—and I purchased a prom dress with a matching dried-flower bouquet, and a pair of shoes. I even scuffed the heels to make them appear as if a happy girl had danced through the night in them. I explained to Penelope that it was a make-believe space of childhood and adolescence.

Months of planning and preparation but Penelope found the idea disgusting. I included her journals of teenage angst poetry with bad spelling because I was committing to a theme, that's what I told her. I also wanted to display childlike drawings but Penelope's were disturbing to say the least. Back in Florida, I came across one of her doodles, a girl in black crayon strokes with disproportionate limbs and hair spreading around the head but it wasn't hair at all—so Penny told me when I asked—but waves, dark sketchy waves came out of the head of what looked like an alien. Not like ocean waves but more like a surge, twisted, gushing away from her brain. I threw it out, not because the waves unsettled me but because her answers later did.

How does the girl feel about what's coming out of her head?

Penny said in a childlike voice, *she's happy. She loves it.*

Perhaps that explains why I myself ended up drawing a generic house with a pitched roof and trees and a fence. But the stark reality consisted of childhood meltdowns so violent I had to physically restrain her. I'd strategically wrap my arms around her, holding her like a rag doll. Her rage caught me off guard and while I rocked her, smoothing her hair and kissing her forehead, I didn't trust her, never sure if her movements were attempts to get away or struggles to get closer.

"What's wrong?" Edward would ask whenever he caught the tail end of those moments and he'd throw me an icy look.

"She's upset. I don't know why," I'd say, one incident blending into another, not sure which one had reduced us to a teary heap on the floor.

Edward, the man who held the life of patients in his hands every day, the man whose noble intentions were to treat burn victims and put mangled limbs back together, was at a loss. In his eyes I was to blame.

There's another story that needs telling. In the aftermath of the housewarming party, Edward insisted Penelope get help. Not weekly therapist sessions but a place removed from her familiar environment. I don't recall the selection process, Edward handled all the details. It sounded like some sort of summer camp, with horses and goats and the kids having to clean stables and brush the horses and feed the farm animals, having responsibilities for meal planning and keeping rooms organized, basically an exercise in accountability.

I couldn't imagine Penelope being comfortable in such an environment, I frowned at the thought of horses, knew Penelope was deathly afraid of them. I questioned the strict policies in place—no visits, no packages, not even letters or phone calls—but Edward wasn't hearing any of my objections.

"How did you come up with sending her to a horse farm?" I asked him.

"It's not a horse farm."

"I don't know about this, Edward, I just don't know."

"Stop undermining everything, it will do her good. She will learn a lot there."

"Are we allowed to visit?"

"No visits. Leave it up to the professionals, Donna. Don't try to do this yourself. It's out of our hands."

"I don't see why a phone call or a Sunday afternoon visit would do any damage."

"Those are the rules, Donna."

"I can't imagine her having a good time. She's not very out-doorsy."

"It'll challenge her."

"Horses, Edward. What good will come of that?"

"Maybe that's the point. To teach her. To become better at things she's not good at," he said. He paused and for a second I waited for him to tell me something significant as if he knew facts I wasn't privy to.

"She doesn't like horses," I interjected, "and she'll fall behind on her schoolwork. Are they offering summer classes? You know how competitive her school is. She'll pay the price."

"Let's not talk about paying a price, Donna. We'll go down the wrong path quickly, trust me."

There were moments I was taken aback by Edward's comments. Why was it that all of a sudden Penelope deserved this kind of extreme attention? Did he know something I didn't, was he aware of things that remained hidden from me? I attempted to find out and called the therapist at the camp. During one conversation, I inquired about Penelope's progress. He told me she was making headway, writing letters to her victims.

"Victims?" I gasped. "What do you mean by victims?"

"Don't think of it as a crime, it's a breakthrough actually. It's her way of making amends, acknowledging people she's wronged. That's huge progress."

It took him all of two weeks to sing a different tune.

"Penelope isn't thriving in this environment as we thought she would. It would be best if she continued therapy while at home. On an outpatient basis."

"You think?" I replied.

"I will send a letter outlining her therapy and how she should continue on."

"A letter to who?"

"A therapist of your choosing," he added, his voice urgent as if he expected me to interject somehow.

"Do you keep files on her?" I asked, worried about someone finding out more than I knew about my own daughter. "What's in those letters?"

"I can't share that with you."

"She's a minor and I make decisions on her behalf every day. Where she goes to school, the friends she has, her diet, her entire life. If I feel, at any given point, she's putting herself in danger, I have to intervene. If there's anything I need to know, I think you are required to tell me."

"I can't tell you about our conversations in detail. Penelope requested that those remain private. If there was any concern, rest assured, you'd be included in the conversation. There's nothing really that I can share. We have clear guidelines as to the confidentiality between minors and—"

"I think we've said everything that needed to be said." I hung up the phone.

The insolence, the audacity of this therapist, I thought. And I'll never forgive Edward for having put her in such incompetent hands. *Horses*, of all things. What was Edward thinking?

Penelope returned home the following week. She had lost ten pounds and was pale but seemed upbeat and in good spirits.

It soon became apparent she had begun to retreat into herself even more than before, and the private child void of grand gestures or public displays of affection was now completely aloof. If you didn't demand to be let into her world, you'd remain an outsider. I felt grief for the girl she used to be, her—

I stop myself. Penelope was never easy and happy, never without trouble. I grieve the daughter I never had, I understand that now.

After she returned home from the clinic, I witnessed her hurriedly tucking something underneath a pillow or sliding a piece of paper inside a book when I entered the room. I felt compelled to act. One day, while she was in the shower, I checked every trite hiding place I could think of: beneath the mattress, between books on her shelf, in her nightstand, at the bottom of the clothes hamper, I even rifled through her underwear drawer. I found nothing.

What else was I supposed to do, how else was I going to find out—park at her school and keep an eye on her during recess as she stood huddled in a corner? Should I follow her to the mall and hide behind clothing racks, eavesdropping on her phone calls? What good would that do?

Pure luck intervened. Weeks after she returned from that dreaded horse farm, in the middle of the night, while I was in the kitchen getting a drink of water, Penelope made her way down the stairs in the dark, her feet in sandals, *flip* as her foot hit the bottom of her heel, *flop* as it hit the ground. I watched her slide open the glass doors leading onto the terrace. It was a chilly night, March, and unseasonably cold, and I instinctively wanted to call out to her, just a mother reminding her child to wear a coat in the cold. She marched across the lawn, her arms crossed in front of her body, clutching something to her chest. The cotton fabric hugging her body made it clear that she had lost even more weight than I had thought. She entered the pool house but reappeared within seconds. Less than a minute and she was back in her room and in her bed. Judging by the speed with which it all occurred, she couldn't have spent much time concealing anything.

What do you do when you imagine the worst, at the same time realizing that once you know you cannot unknow? And so I didn't go out to the pool house that night and not the following day. It took me three days of wringing my hands, but then I could no longer resist. I began to root through that old and grimy place, shabby floor of glossy terracotta tile that made it impossible to walk on with heels, pool supplies stacked in every corner and Adirondack chairs with peeled paint covered in spider webs.

I searched every corner, behind every piece of wood leaning against the wall, went through the dusty bin with deflated pool toys covered in dead bugs. Nothing. I bumped into a wooden structure hanging off the ceiling and it made a half turn just to pirouette back into its original position. It was that old wooden kayak. I had seen it before but never so much as wasted a thought on its peculiarity, no lakes were nearby and that was odd but maybe it was just decoration, a flea market find or a leftover from a previous owner. It had a Martha's Vineyard kind of feel in an authentic and vintage way and it dangled on a rope tied to a metal peg, swayed like a bicycle hanging off a heavy-duty steel hook. There was a compartment with a handle. I held the kayak in place with one hand and with the other I pulled the handle. It popped open. That's where I found a plastic bag folded over twice with papers inside.

I knew immediately those were the letters she'd written, her *victim* reparations, those declarations of guilt. Was I prepared to read something I would never be able to unread? I popped the compartment door back into place, knowing once I crossed that line, I had no way of remaining oblivious. The kayak swayed and the hook dislodged from the ceiling. I turned away and covered my eyes. When I opened them again, the kayak had come to rest against the wall, the bulkhead facing the corner. I took it as a sign and left it at that. I dusted myself off and left the kayak untouched in the corner, allowed it to lean in place as if it held up the entire structure and without it, my world would cave in.

25

DONNA

I listen to the house and there's not a sound to be heard. Edward must have returned to the bedroom but I'm no longer worried. I don't think he ever set foot in this room, given the disgust he had voiced when I staged it. Here I am in Penelope's playroom with the bag of letters I refused myself all those years ago.

I pull one of Penelope's childhood quilts from the top shelf of the closet, two chenille pillows and a blanket from the linen locker behind the door. Musty waves of mothball clouds come at me and a tinge of anger bobs up—the neglect Edward has allowed—but I spread them out on the floor though the blanket is dirty and unkempt. I need to rest. Following Edward around this house has taken a toll on my hip. Remembering the pain earlier from the pool house, I dip down with my pelvis in an anterior tilt and carefully lower myself so as to not aggravate my injury. I lie down and look up at the ceiling.

My final days here, before Edward took me to Shadow Garden, when tiredness came in both forms, physical and mental, are not days I care to revisit. All those weeks and months when I was up all night and felt like I was melting into the walls, every night a useless wrangle of conflicting thoughts, but that's not what this feeling is. Something else is happening.

As I'm about to discover my daughter in ways I might regret, finding things out about her that I didn't know, it finally comes to pass, stark and final: there will be no going back. But that's not all, is it? I will also find out things about myself, shortcomings I will have to face. Having gained distance from Shadow Garden, I see another *me*. A second identity, not apart from me but like a layer on top of the person I know myself to be. It's a double-edged sword in a way, finding out truths about yourself.

I brace myself and unfold the first letter.

The letter is about the day of the party. It's nothing like I remember it. The story was, *her* story was, that the boy left our property, and she didn't know what happened because she wasn't there. Heart in my mouth, I don't have to look hard for the next memory: We encountered the boy after that night, years later at a gas station, in the backseat of his mother's car. He stared at Penelope, a subtle tremor about him as if he was in a state of constant nodding. I mostly remember how untroubled Penelope's face was after she spotted him. Neither of us mentioned him.

I stop reading because I don't want to know more. No, I'm lying to myself. I don't want to read what I already know. If you hear hoofbeats, look for horses, not zebras, is what they say.

26

PENELOPE

All that rowdiness and how they'd been throwing toys and rocks into the pool and then there were the shards of glass. Leaving the property and going to the barn had happened quickly. Penelope was unable to hone in on what made her think of it at first, but after she had convinced Gabriel to go, had alluded to some sort of gratification—*you'll see*—there wasn't much more consideration or understanding of the reason. It was something to do, a spur of the moment.

It took Gabriel and Penelope a while to walk to the neighboring property. The road turned into a field. A farmhouse appeared, with a small barn to the left. Penelope imagined horses huddled together like penguins in the cold.

"Where are we going?" Gabriel asked and cut through the air with a stick like a sword chopping off the tops of the grass. He was sweaty from walking and his hair had parted, exposing a flat, pink area of skin on his temple.

"You'll see," Penelope said.

To the right, a few minutes' walk, was a pond on their property behind a line of trees and the field was rugged with solid pieces of dirt and she wore sandals and the grass was high and bugs would bite at her and make her itch for days, and so she took Gabriel to the barn instead.

"I want to know where you're taking me."

"First you say it's boring at my house and now you're being a baby about having some fun."

"I'm not a—"

Penelope began to regret having set the whole thing in motion. She prided herself on being convincing, had more often than not succeeded in making people do things they'd never consider doing, but here she was trying to talk some kid into getting into a little bit of trouble. And he was balking.

"Are you in or not?"

"How far is it?"

"It's not far."

"We can't be gone too long."

"Will you stop complaining?"

"I'm just saying."

"How old are you? Five?"

Boys didn't like to be called pussies, even in a roundabout way. That usually shut them up.

"Slide open the door," she said and pointed at the barn.

"What's in there?"

Penelope stepped past him and opened the barn door and everything came to life. Hooves pounded the ground, a dozen or so muscled creatures rocked back and forth in their stables, wondering what the late-night visit was all about. She had never imagined this place to be so dark, its corners so murky.

Penelope's imagination had already painted a somewhat threatening picture of horses but her mind hadn't accounted for the crosswind rattling the metal roof, the tree branches grating like giant nails against the corrugated building. Every gust of wind a cold hand reaching for her. It smelled like in a zoo but there was also a scent of leather and hay, and then another layer, buried much deeper in the wood and the floor and the barn itself. A damp aroma of ammonia. Feral.

The horses were huddled in the corner of their individual stalls. Penelope singled out the first one on the right and the hinges creaked as she pinned the lever to an iron hook on the wall. The horse, white with brown flecks, tossed back its head.

This is just a game, she told herself. *A game that doesn't have a name.*
Gabriel gasped behind her as the horse in the stall jerked.

"It's going to be all right," Penelope said more to herself than the horse or him. She unlatched the bottom part of the stable door.

Gabriel was easily fooled by her words, but the horse not so much. Animals have a smartness about them, a primal intelligence, but to Penelope she was powerful by showing the horse how unafraid she was, she displayed strength by overcoming her fear, by exposing herself. But that wasn't how things turned out.

The horse turned its head toward them, the eyes rolled backward. She moved closer and the horse blew air through its nostrils. What happened next wasn't planned or premeditated. She knew the meaning of that word: it meant specific intent to commit a crime for some period of time, however short, before the actual crime. It was more like getting to a fork in the road and turning the wrong way.

Gabriel stepped past her into the stall. He spoke gently to the horse, with innocence he extended his hand to the base of its neck, down where it turned into the withers. Penelope hated how fearless he was, how undaunted by the animal.

She stepped forward but the horse could tell she was terrified, regardless how confident she pretended to be. The horse knew that she was just an exposed quivering mass of nerves and twitching muscles.

It was like a movie: the rafters moaned, spiderwebs touched her arms, something stirred by her feet. Penelope exploded into motion and stumbled out of the stall and slammed both doors shut, but that made everything worse. So much noise, hooves, and dull thumps against the walls and then a crack. She imagined the horse kicking the stall door, splitting the wood, breaking it open and pushing its way out and coming at her. Gabriel was in there, that realization came to her after, that the stall was small, barely enough room for the horse to move or a boy to find a safe spot. She screamed, stretched out her arms to open both doors and let Gabriel out, but they were out of her reach. Not one more step could she take toward this feral animal and the only thing that remained was the sound of hooves. Too late to do or say anything.

Penelope ran home.

Later, in her room, she picked little flecks of sawdust and wood chips off her shoes, and held the curly bits in the palm of her hand. As her mother questioned her about Gabriel, Penelope stole glances at the dollhouse, the one with the miniature ash bucket the size of a raisin and andirons shaped like cats, the tiny blow poke, and the fireplace where she had placed the coiled pieces of wood from the barn. She wanted them out in the open for her to see but for no one else to know.

She didn't remember falling asleep in the closet but that's where she woke with a start when her mother called her name. Her sinuses were dry, it hurt to take a breath. An annoying pressure nagged on her bladder. Her heart raced.

How upset her mother was, how she felt the party had been ruined. Her father knew what she had done that night, she couldn't explain how she ended up with that conclusion, it was just a feeling.

First, it was the way he stared at her, then how he stopped making eye contact.

Her father sent her to a farm for therapy. There were horses. She didn't have to handle them until her third week. She couldn't even look at them. They had to take care of them, feed them, brush them, take them out to a pasture. Penelope learned that horses feel energy, though she knew that already. The horses bristled at her, didn't want to be brushed or petted. She refused and raged until the doctors agreed to send her home. Another disappointment. She tended to disappoint.

27

DONNA

Gabriel. I force myself to call him by his name. He had come up in conversations with Edward in the aftermath of the whole incident but the consensus had been that he wandered off to the neighboring property, entered the stables, was kicked by a horse, and broke three ribs. Suffered a blow to the head.

There was a newspaper article calling his injuries *horrific*. Edward told me the details: there was a forehead torn open. A crushed skull. Weeks in the hospital and major surgery—metal plates were inserted into his skull—what's the word, it won't come to me— they removed his scalp, a saw made an incision and the brain lay bare to allow it to swell without putting pressure on itself. *Craniotomy*. That's it. A craniotomy.

Even then, I felt as if Edward had mentioned the medical particulars to me as a means of punishment, as if I could have done anything to prevent this. Did he know Penelope had left Gabriel inside the stall with a thousand pounds of ill-behaved stallion? Because of Penelope, Gabriel ended up with a broken skull, a scar on his forehead, and weeks of his parents wondering if he would ever be the same. He wasn't the same. For one, he never told anyone about that night. Maybe he didn't remember. Maybe he was afraid of Penelope.

I place the pages on top of one another and fold them back together. Her confessions. What did she call it? I unfold them again: *The following are my recollections as to what happened on the night in question.* It's hard to gauge it but there are ten maybe fifteen more. More recollections. More confessions.

The next letter is different. For one, there are no complete sentences, it's not neatly written like the first one. It strikes me as a note one takes in the middle of the night, in the dark, as not to forget a dream. The handwriting is different, too. Shaky. I read the words but at first I don't comprehend them. They are disjointed and out of order but I catch on quickly, so quickly in fact that in hindsight I realize they've made sense all along.

Penelope, when she was younger, spoke in riddles. I call them riddles but they were the attempts of a toddler to communicate. A color wasn't a color but she assigned an object to it, *banana* meant *yellow*, like a placeholder, that sort of thing. I knew what the words meant. And I know what this next letter is. Not just part of a story, not something separate. It reveals her essence, how in her mind, wrong decisions demanded to be made. The letter is titled *The Night from Hell*.

I allow it to play out, to unfold, like scenes in a movie.

28

PENELOPE

In the cubicle next to Penelope, Jeanine Haney played jazz incessantly. Every time Penelope passed by the radio, that unsightly box of cheap chrome, she glared at Jeanine's back in that dreadful cardigan. The way she occasionally peeked around the corner of the partition, with her narrow gray eyes, that stubby nose that might look cute on a kid but hideous on a grown woman.

The jazz version of *Porgy and Bess*, over and over. Penelope didn't know much about music, but it was an observation on her part that jazz was rather random, the musicians just got caught up in an arbitrary scale that they, for some inexplicable reason, couldn't abandon. The notes gyrated in her brain, tore at her. *Summertime, and the living is easy.* The volume was low for the most part but she couldn't tune it out. Though tempted to tell Jeanine to turn the radio off, Penelope didn't dare because Jeanine was her sponsoring broker and Penelope couldn't risk coming across as rude.

The moment Jeanine was on the phone, Penelope shut down her computer, locked her desk, and left the building. It was Friday, the first of the month, and she realized the rent was due for the cubicle she had picked in the far corner of the first floor of the office building. She'd pay it online, later, but was worried she might forget. Maybe she should write it down, make a note of it.

She had a lot of time invested in this real estate thing and it had been fun for a while. Even her father thought it was a good idea but Penelope had been having doubts. She didn't mind floating from one career interest to another, was used to losing interest quickly, and had never seen it as failure on her part, but she couldn't fathom being locked into this job for the rest of her life. Her parents helped her financially every time she asked, had just bought her a Jeep Grand Cherokee a couple of months ago, a reward for *seeing something through,* those were her mother's words. "And you can't show houses pulling up in a car older than a couple of years. No one will take you seriously."

Penelope should've known there were strings attached. Right after her mother handed her the car keys, an ultimatum was given: one month to move out and . . . there was no further clarification as to the consequences.

She had been living with her parents, and their quarrels were tedious, draining, mostly unwarranted. Especially with her mother. That very morning they had gotten into an argument. As always, it started with something insignificant—burned toast or a careless dish left in the sink by Penelope—and every word Donna said was in turn a trigger to Penelope, that was a given, and before they knew it, it had gotten out of hand.

"Don't be such a bitch about everything," Penelope said, and that was the exact word that escalated every single argument, as if it signaled they weren't much better than some common women arguing in the streets. Penelope loved using words her mother considered crass.

"Don't take that tone with me. After everything I've done—"

"I never asked you do to anything for me."

"I'm so done with this. Why don't you just leave if I'm such a terrible mother?"

"I'm leaving, trust me, no one wants to hear this bitching every day."

"Then leave or I—"

"Or what?" Penelope had asked.

"Find an apartment. Move out. For good this time."

Penelope knew that they'd never kick her out on the streets but she couldn't be too sure now that she seemed stable, real estate license and all. She argued with her mother, *had she not finished all required classes, had she not passed the final exams, had she not taken the licensing examination, had she not submitted her fingerprints on time?* Penelope made it seem like she was juggling it all with newfound competence and a newly acquired sense of time management when in reality she had enrolled in an online course which was foolproof and even scheduled her tests and appointments for her. All she had to do was study and show up on time.

The month was up in a few days and her mother was going to bring it up. That thought, that loop of her mother questioning her the moment she walked through the door—*have you looked at apartments, have you sold a house yet, why is it only a cubicle and not an office?*—the anticipation of another quarrel had begun hours ago, out of nowhere, like a lightning strike. It was followed by a hop and a skip inside her chest, her heart pounding. Everything drilled at her, the idle chatter, the ringing phones. That damn jazz music. Sometimes she was convinced she was having a heart attack, could really get caught up in that thought, which made her chest tighten.

When Penelope was a child, her father had handed her his stethoscope and she had listened to her heart. It was the day she needed stitches in her hand from the broken window. The stethoscope was meant to be a distraction and so she listened to her heartbeat but it was frightening, how this thing—it's just a muscle, her dad had told her—inside her body flailed about. The cadence, the power of it all, something she had no control over, *thump ba-boom, ba-boom, thump ba-boom, ba-boom.* Every time she thought about that sound, she bristled.

In the wake of getting her real estate license, Penelope had experienced a surge of self-confidence and attempted to wean herself off her anxiety medication. Freeing herself had become more and more important lately, though she didn't quite understand what that was all about. She had quit cold turkey as if she had to prove something to herself. The results were heart palpitations so powerful they felt like drums inside her chest, long strides at a quick pace, and before she knew what was happening, she had a full-blown panic attack. She went online and read that she was supposed to wean herself off the medication slowly, over days or even weeks. She had three pills left. She'd half one, quarter the rest. Ten days from today she'd be good to go, that's what she told herself. This time it would work. She'd begun taking anxiety pills years ago, but she had promised herself she would see it through, she wouldn't waver, hell or high water. Start meditating, or yoga, or whatever it was they say helps with anxiety. Come tomorrow she'd be busy with appointments, open houses, and showings. Nothing to worry about.

The exit appeared and Penelope took it absentmindedly. She wanted to close the blinds and draw the curtains, prepare a bath with those expensive bath salts she had taken from her mother's bathroom, wanted to feel the suds, the warmth. Half a bottle of wine was the sweet spot, then a nap. The fantasy came to a grinding halt: she thought about her mother's meddling, though she had to admit that it might just be concern on her part, yet it felt like she couldn't even take a single breath on her own. One day at a time she could manage if she could avoid her mother. How she hated living at home, even for just a while now and then, but she couldn't argue

with the fact that nothing nagged at her, no bills, no rent, no responsibilities. Except the cubicle rent, something she kept repeating in her mind over and over, not wanting to forget.

Penelope parked her car in the lot of a grocery store. The green pills
rested in the palm of her hand, pale rectangles with grooves, easy
to break apart. The thumping inside her chest reminded her of the
hooves of a horse and that made her heart go even wilder. It was a
spur-of-the-moment thing, her brain wasn't involved, more a re-
flex, going out with a bang, one more drink for the road, one last
hurrah before a dry spell. She consoled herself; this was the last
time, *I will be free.*

She took all three. She chewed them, though the bitterness made
her gag but the tip of her tongue pushed the chalky substance
underneath that small membranous fold where it dissolved. Three
were a lot, even for her. Especially while driving. Better hurry and
get home. The car engine was still running, and putting the transmission in reverse and pulling out of the parking lot occurred simultaneously.

Penelope followed a white Honda into the street, honked at the
driver, who was too hesitant to weave into traffic. At a light, a police officer came to a stop beside her. She put her hands on the
wheel—ten and two—and looked straight ahead. Did he follow
her, had he seen her honk at that driver? There was a slight pull
behind her eyes, yet she was not afraid, she was young and good-
looking and the car was loaded to the gills, surely he could see that.
The officer stared at her but Penelope didn't care. Her heart couldn't
speed up if it tried, it was like she was floating in the clouds. No
sharp corners, no harsh edges, all fluffy all the time.

It began to sprinkle, barely a need for wipers, every other movement of the blade did nothing but lick a dry window, and then
the cubicle rent nagged at her again. She wanted Jeanine Haney to
know how responsible she was, wanted to transfer the money on-

line right then and there so she didn't have to think about anything for the rest of the day.

Her eyes got so heavy that Penelope got as far as White Rock Lake Park. She pulled into the parking lot. She'd been here before, on a weekend, last summer, when there were riders on road bikes in uniforms and helmets, joggers, dogs and kids, couples lying on the grass. She had sat on a bench and watched the dogs, had wanted a dog of her own but then she deserted the thought. She couldn't care for anything alive, she'd just mess it up. And her mother would never allow it, not at her house. "Take care of the cats out back if you want something to do," she'd say. To be honest, Penelope cringed at the thought of another responsibility. So much easier to just not bother with anything.

It was October, almost sunset but not quite, and White Rock Lake Park was all but deserted. She was glad there were no people around, the last thing she needed was someone to knock on the window asking if she was okay. One minute it was daylight, the next it'd be dark.

She pulled up her banking app and transferred the rent money, imagined a pop-up on Jeanine Haney's computer, *you received a payment from Penelope Pryor,* and then wooziness set in. Penelope let the car idle for a while but then she cut the engine and sat in the dark with her windows rolled down, hoping the fresh air would wake her up. Give her a jolt, a second wind.

Her eyes stared off into the distance. This place, it was beautiful. Peaceful. She had an epiphany right then and there—she hadn't thought it before but it had come to her sitting in this deserted park—there was nothing that suited her in this world, nothing. She was sure of it. Who was she kidding, this real estate thing wasn't for her, and she knew it. Too much talking to too many people, too much fakery. She just couldn't catch a break, couldn't find her *niche,* that's what her mother called it. It was so much harder since people expected so much of her, as if she wasn't allowed to fail, and she had given up on the interior design thing which took too much hustling. People didn't just show up at her doorstep, she had found that out quickly. She thought about buying houses and becoming a landlord and she'd run that by her parents, they'd have to put up the capital after all. She'd draw an income and hire a property manager—maybe that was her niche, having people do things for her—maybe that would work out. Do most people know what to do with their lives?

The rain picked up but came from the west so she left the window rolled down, the drops barely landed on the leather interior. The sound of a car door opening. And voices. Another car door. People talking over one another. High-pitched. Not in that order, but all at once.

To recall this all later meant to mix it up, forget the composition of the moment, like being asked how many gunshots you heard, you couldn't remember, it happened too quickly, jumbled, no one could recall how many or what came first.

On second thought, the voices hadn't been shrill at all, it was the fact that they'd jerked her out of her floating state that made them sound menacing. It wasn't even an argument, a slight raising of voices at best, nothing more.

The cold air had done her some good. Time to go home. It had been a long day, most of it she spent in the bathroom, in a stall, trying to get herself together. It was just the way it happened sometimes, months of relative peace and then something insignificant—was it the fact that she had approached the deadline for the move?—would throw her off and she was a ball of yarn, every single strand tight, unable to find the beginning or the end of anything. In those moments, she went overboard, alcohol, spending, men, forgot to pay bills, as a matter of fact she had been evicted for not paying rent at her last place, that's how she ended up living at home again. That posed a different kind of problem altogether. Her parents. She needed them but didn't want to need them and that's where she was stuck, between a rock and a hard place, or worse, going down a spiral. When she was like that, she didn't always catch herself in time, though her father did—she could tell by the way he looked at her, stern and concerned—and now she had just days left to get it together. She chuckled. One month to get out of her parents' house. As if she'd take that long if she knew how to get away from them.

Penelope started the car, followed the bike trail that ran along the lake, just to see if the car was where the people had shouted earlier. *It won't hurt to look, it won't hurt at all.*

There was a car with a driver's door ajar. She kept her eyes on it and stepped on the gas. Her movements were sluggish, as if packed in cotton balls, and her foot was heavy, she could tell by the way the car jerked forward. She wasn't buckled in yet, tried to untangle the twisted belt mess, free the buckle, and everything happened so fast that she didn't have time to think, to take it all in.

There was a thump. Not like something getting caught underneath the chassis of the car, some armadillo or animal low on the ground. It was more like a dull and faint bang. It wasn't a guardrail, it wasn't a bike left behind—there was no sound of screeching metal—but she hit the brakes and the car came to a halt, its front tires digging into the asphalt. She instinctively ripped the steering wheel to the left to keep from hitting it full force, whatever *it* was. (She remembered stories of deer flying through windshields, yes, it was a deer, it must be a deer.) She reached for the belt but couldn't find it, though she fumbled for it and what if a deer flew through the windshield? It would kill her for sure.

Her body propelled forward, and her chest made contact with the steering wheel. Penelope got out of the car and on a cloud she floated. She paused in the middle of the bike trail, the yellow line gray as if the world had lost all colors.

She saw something. On the ground. It looked mangled at first, some of it pointed up while other parts seemed to be stuck to the asphalt. It took her brain some time to catch up and she staggered toward it.

A woman.

She wanted to call out her name but she had no clue who she was. She wanted to tell her that she didn't mean to hit her but that it was dark and that she didn't see her, but the woman appeared fine. Dazed, yes, confused, yes, but moving, sitting up. A large purse, a tote, off to the side, items strewn everywhere.

Penelope bent down and she stuttered *are you okay are you okay oh my God what happened, where did you come from are you okay are you?* On and on she went, like a fountain, babbling along.

"Help me up," the woman said.

29

PENELOPE

There was a woman on the ground, but she talked, made sense—*help me up*, she said—and it wasn't bad if she could talk and wanted to get up, was it? She extended her arm, and Penelope put one hand in hers, the other underneath her elbow, and pulled her to her feet.

"What's your name?" Penelope asked, wondering if this wasn't a figment of her imagination, a name was going to make it real, and she wanted to commit it to memory.

"Rachel."

"I'm so sorry. I didn't see you. Are you okay?"

"I think so," Rachel said.

She seemed fine, her trench coat was belted, she hobbled, but only because she had lost one shoe, the other one was still on her foot.

In a fog, Penelope gathered that Rachel was beautiful. Her lips were painted red, and her hair was shiny, and she smelled of something clean, like soap or shampoo, maybe detergent.

Rachel stood and parted her trench coat, exposing a bloody knee for Penelope to see.

"What were you doing here?" popped out of Penelope's mouth before she could rein it in. She should offer to take her to a hospital, should do the right thing, make sure she got help and medical attention even though she looked just fine. "Can you walk?" she added quickly. "Should I call an ambulance?"

"No," she said, her voice fearful. "I think I'm fine," but she was breathing hard. Really hard.

Penelope didn't know if it was a *no* to the walking or a *no* to the ambulance, but the woman's breathing became more labored by the second, maybe that was what made her sound timid.

"I need to sit down," she said.

"My car's right there. Let me help you."

They walked together and Penelope held her up. Rachel staggered, still in that one shoe, but only two steps, then she kicked it off as if it just came to her that walking would be much easier without it.

Penelope opened the passenger door and the woman got in. Ladylike, she placed one foot just in front of the seat, lowered herself with her weight carried on her thigh, her head clearing the doorframe and she sat on the outer edge of the seat, then she bent her knees and brought her feet inside the car. She arranged her skirt to cover her bloody knee. Penelope couldn't help but think that her mother would like this woman, with her tasteful trench and her perfect hair, the way she slid into the seat of Penelope's car, so refined and elegant, even after what had just happened.

The woman's head fell back, hit the headrest.

"Let me get your stuff and I'll take you to a hospital. Just to be sure." Penelope shut the door, ran and grabbed the shoe, scooped the keys and other items—mints, a lipstick, a wallet—into the tote, then made one more effort to grab the other shoe, but the heel had come off. She stuffed the shoes into the tote and rushed back to the car.

Getting in and starting the engine happened simultaneously. Penelope made a U-turn, no reason going in the other direction, she didn't even know where it led and she must get the woman to a hospital. There was a medical center that Penelope remembered, on Highway 78, one of those urgent care centers. That was her best bet. It was urgent and the woman needed care, Penelope thought in a haze. She tried to be logical. No, that's no good. Come to think of it, they do stitches and strep throats, nothing major. But was it major?

Penelope was unfamiliar with her surroundings. She needed to get to 78, but her head hurt, her eyes burned in her head, she could no longer concentrate on directions. Will they take *her* blood? She hadn't been drinking but would they test for other substances? Her heart was calm, not a quiver there, but her mind did somersaults.

"I'm sorry, I have to pull over, I'm going to need a minute. I need to use the GPS," Penelope said and looked around for the nearest street address to input. She was in some sort of a residential neighborhood, small houses with siding and patchy lawns and no one was out, even though the lights were on behind just about every window. "Unless you know the way," Penelope added and turned to look at the woman. Her head was twisted in an unnatural way, like a baby in a carrier without a head support. Contorted.

"Are you okay?" Penelope touched the woman's hand. So pale and childlike, the hand of a twelve-year-old. "Hey," Penelope said and tugged on her arm. "Can you hear me?" Penelope wiggled her arm, trying to get her to stir. She wanted to call out the woman's name but she didn't. A red line emerged from the woman's left nostril.

A man approached, walking two large brown dogs. They stopped and sniffed the tree where Penelope was parked, their leashes stretched. The man was less than five feet away from her car and he looked at her, made momentary eye contact, but Penelope didn't say a word, didn't so much as reach for the button to lower her window, and he continued on down the sidewalk.

Penelope spotted a street sign. Bellfield, and she typed it in the phone but she couldn't comprehend the instructions. She switched to the map function and that she could understand, the highway around the next corner, down the access road and then take the next exit and one turn to the right. There was a red cross on the map, which meant hospital.

Penelope floored the gas and the tires squealed. She ran a stop sign, a car came straight at her, they both hit the brakes and came to a screeching halt inches from each other. The driver blew his horn, angrily, three or four times. Penelope raised her hand to apologize for her lack of attention.

She talked to Rachel without looking at her. *Everything will be okay don't do this to me the hospital is around the corner please please please.* Last time Penelope had looked, Rachel's chin had rested on her chest. People fall asleep in airplanes like that, in cars even, nothing to worry about. *She'll be okay, she's unconscious and everything will be fine. It will be all right.*

Penelope took the exit and then took a right, could see the lit-up red cross from far away, the illuminations, five or so stories, and she slowed down. There was a sign, outpatient, but she had to find the emergency room entrance. She turned right, then hit the brakes when the parking lot suddenly ended. There was a row of dumpsters, and she was behind a building with delivery ramps and this was all wrong.

She wanted to collect herself, for just a minute or so, wanted to come up with a story. No, *story* was not the right word, she didn't plan on lying about anything, she just wanted to arrive at some logical explanation so she wouldn't be rambling on and on, so she could tell them that the woman was fine, just fine, walking, talking, one minute she was grabbing her coat, pulling the lapel, the next her head was bent and there was blood coming from her nose.

Penelope got out of the car, hurried around and opened the passenger door. The moment the overhead light came on, when she saw the woman's face, she knew. The trickle of blood had turned into a tributary of red, leading from her nose across her cheek and down her neck. The woman wore a bright red silk scarf around her neck, tucked into the coat, now Penelope saw how bright the color was, poppy, almost candy-apple red.

Penelope's stomach dropped as if someone had dumped a bucket of ice water over her head. She wanted to shake the woman, get her to wake up. Wanted her to respond, in a coherent way. She wasn't sure what had happened—had the woman not gotten up off the ground earlier, had she not talked, had she not been responsive—and now she was contorted and lifeless? The word *dead* formed in her mind but before it manifested itself in all its consequences, Penelope somehow was back in the car, behind the wheel.

In the woman's lap, there was another scarf, red like a garnet. No, that's not a scarf, *no no no no no no no no no no*, that's not a scarf at all. Not around her neck, not in her lap. That's blood.

Penelope lifted the woman's head by her chin, but her head rolled to the side and her eyes stared straight at her, struck her with their broken beauty. And beautiful she was, even now, in a desperate and dramatic way, like a painting of a woman she had seen once, chained at the stakes and looking up toward heaven. Rachel looked like that, theatrical and exaggerated. Her eyes. Her eyes were so still.

Penelope sat in the darkness of her car feeling every beat of her heart. A narrow stream of light approached, painting the ghostly loading docks in lights and shadows. The silence was disturbed by an ambulance siren. Penelope held her breath. The ambulance passed. She remained perfectly still until the lights disappeared.

30

DONNA

Penelope sits in a parking lot of a hospital and does nothing. Nothing. A bleeding woman in the seat next to her doesn't rouse her conscience. Instead of rendering help she . . . waits? And just like that I'm caught up in a tangle of narratives. I've been without sleep for two days, I haven't eaten, my hands are shaking, that's how low my blood sugar is. I rummage through my purse for anything resembling a mint, gum, or granola bar. Nothing.

I flip to the next page. Speculations and opinions on my part are useless but before I read further, I should try to remember. Hear me out. I make no sense, even to myself.

First, I search my memory and vaguely discover a story resembling the one I just read. Doubt is my next instinct. None of it makes sense. None of it matches up with the narrative I've had in my head. And then it all turns peculiar because I know what Penelope did next—suddenly I know it and I can no longer deny it.

There's a conundrum I have inside. *Can I trust* this *Penelope?*

You'd think that's the most powerful thought in my mind but there's something else. I stuff the letters in my purse. A question demanding an answer: am I trying to recall something or shut something out?

A voice in my head answers. *Find proof.*

31

DONNA

I position myself by the stairs leading down into the garage with my hand resting on the banister. I step down—one, two, three, four—and reach into the darkness. The palm of my hands makes contact with the hood of a car. Running them down and back up, I feel a round emblem above the grill. Four rings. Edward's car. His Audi.

Five steps to the left and there's my Infinity. On the other side of the garage, the sprinkler display box illuminates the space enough to make out shadows. The third spot sits empty. It's where Penelope used to park. It feels wrong but I don't know what's wrong about it.

Four long steps to my left and I feel the partial wall of the storage cupboards. We used to keep bins full of Christmas decorations in those cabinets but they are gone now, the wall is boarded up. I take out my phone and turn on the flashlight option. The light centers on the wall. It has been fixed in a rudimentary way with a piece of plywood and nails, but there's no paint or stucco. A Band-Aid at best. My first instinct is I *know* if I take that plywood down, I'll find a large gaping hole behind it. I want to make this go away—all of it, the letters, the hunch I have—but I can't, it's too late, I knew that when I—

A door opens and light enters the garage. In my panic I can't find the button to turn off the flashlight. I press the phone against my chest to cover the light. I step behind the car and squat. My hip crunches. The pain is coming on searing hot, intense, like someone gored a hot poker into my groin all the way to the hip joint. I want to pinch my eyes shut in a childish notion, put my hand in front of my eyes, *if I can't see you, you can't see me.*

Something globular comes at me from another direction, hovering above like a full moon. I avert my eyes, cover them with my hands, but there's no escaping from the beam that burns into my retina, as bright as fresh snow accompanied by a momentary fear of going blind. I attempt to see what's in front of me but the world is a negative, light and shade reversed from the original, black is white and white is black.

My vision clears. Edward. Flashlight in hand.

"Donna?" Scowling, with a shaky voice. "I knew there was someone in the house."

I remain cowered. The beam lowers to the ground, illuminating Edward from below. He looks like a ghost.

Then, "You're here. You're really here."

It sounds more like a fact than a question, which takes me by surprise.

"What did you think was going to happen?" I ask. Edward doesn't respond. He's taken aback by me, I can tell, but I'm not particularly on solid ground myself. "Did you think I was just going to go away? Like that?" I snap my fingers.

Something odd is happening to me, something unexpected. The

fact-finding mission and the need for confrontation have turned into something else entirely. A doggedness. A realization. When I leave here, I'll know what needs knowing. Something I should have been after all along.

"I know things, Edward, I know things. And you do, too. We both know. And I've come . . ." I take in a sharp breath. "I've come here to find out what happened. To Penelope. To us."

"I'm worried about you, Donna. You don't look well," he says and cocks his head in a dismissive way.

"How does well look, Edward?"

"I mean, you look . . . Never mind. Do they know you're here?"

"They? Who are they?"

"I was told you couldn't walk. I was told you were recovering from your injury."

"I manage. I've been working hard on getting better. I'm much better now."

"I'm not your doctor. I wouldn't know."

"Are you afraid?" I ask.

"Afraid?" His brows furrow.

"Edward . . ."

I started out with so much confidence, but now I falter. All those weeks, months, all those questions and then not a word comes out of my mouth. All this buildup, all this preparation, all this pondering, this weighing every single argument. But perfect lives don't end this way so what did I miss? Once my mind forms this hypothesis, *what did I miss,* it's clear suddenly.

"I need to ask you something," I say. "I need to ask you something about Penelope."

32

DONNA

We end up in the kitchen, Edward leading the way. After I've been navigating through the house in the dark, everything is now bathed in lights. The kitchen counters expose fingerprints and flakes of food, stark and shameful. No one vigilant about wiping them down.

When I turn, Edward has taken a chair and placed it facing me. He has aged, his hair is grayer than it used to be, his eyes lie hollow within his head. I wonder if I look as old as he does. I hope not but I haven't really made an effort, not like I used to.

I tell him about the housewarming party. The horses. The boy, Gabriel. It all topples like Jenga blocks. I keep tugging but I'm determined to keep the tower steady, and before I know it I compromise the foundation and we both sit in front of a heap of wooden blocks.

"Stop," he says. Just like that. *Stop.* Edward stares at me. "Just—"

"I'm not sure you understand what's happening here," I interrupt with a tone I hope carries authority. "I'm telling you there's something wrong with Penelope. I need to understand what has happened to her. To us. I need you to fill in the blanks."

"Me? You need *me* to fill in the blanks?" His voice is measured and taut and looming. "I think you are the one who needs to fill in the blanks."

I shake my head. "Where's Penelope?"

There. Finally I said it though it doesn't carry as much weight as I thought it would.

"Donna—"

His eyes are blank.

"Don't Donna me. You've been ignoring my calls. You had me shipped off like I was no longer needed and you turned my daughter against me. She hasn't called or visited or made any kind of contact with me. I don't blame her for anything, I need her to know that I don't blame her for anything. And I'm so much better than I used to be. Believe it or not, even my hip is well. Here." I prance around. I take long strides, jump up and down, an almost-attempt at jumping jacks. Edward stares at me and I freeze. He's a doctor, he might call my bluff. Does he know that the problem with hips is range of motion and sudden movements, and jumping isn't all that difficult? Am I fooling him? I can't tell. "I'm well," I emphasize. "But I need to see Penelope. Edward, you don't . . ." How do I make him understand? How do I explain to him that . . . I don't even know what I'm trying to explain. "Every day, every single day I ask Marleen if Penelope has called and every single day the answer is no. I'm her mother, Edward. And you too, you can't even return a phone call? Where is she?"

"What does Marleen say when you ask her?"

What a cruel and menacing comment. *What does the housekeeper say when you ask for your daughter.*

"She says whatever you tell her to say, I assume?"

Edward swallows hard.

"Where's Penelope?" I insist.

I watch his Adam's apple, its up-and-down motion, and I know what's about to happen. He's about to choke on his own spit. A blockage of his airways keeps him from sucking in air and it sounds terrifying as he's forcing in a wet breath, saliva seeping down his trachea. Even he can't erase my decades of familiarity with his every move: he's about to lie to me. My heart might be racing and I have to wipe my sweaty palms on my thighs to keep them from leaving imprints on the black marble counters but Edward coughs and coughs until tears run down his face.

"What did you do, Edward? What did you do? To Penelope? To me? This house? Our life?" I want the evil part of him exposed, want him to bare his true self, the one who did our family in.

"I think I'm going to call—"

"The police?" I interrupt him. "Why?"

He pauses, recognizes the absurdity of it all.

"Why why why why why," I say as I slap the marble countertop with the palm of my hand. "No crime has been committed. I'm in my own house. An ambulance? No one is sick. No one is injured."

I need him to admit fault. Knowledge. Responsibility. But still, so much is missing, feels wrong. The oddity of it all. He doesn't act like a guilty man, he's more taken aback by me. I thrust those thoughts into the back of my mind to be dealt with later—but there's this rage, it prickles in my throat like acid. I want him to admit to *something* so I know I'm not the guilty one because only one person can be at fault. Right? And it has to be him.

"What the fuck's wrong with you?" Edward says.

Edward doesn't curse, not normally.

"Wrong with me?" I ask.

"Normal people don't forget what's happened to their child."

33

DONNA

The last solid memory I have of my daughter Penelope, solid as in if prompted I could give the date and time, was April first. I was reading one of those planted newspaper stories people take for face value until it dawns on them it's April Fool's Day.

Penelope came downstairs, looking disheveled. I remember thinking that a grown woman shouldn't be in public like that, stretched-out sweats, an oversized hoodie, hair matted, leftover mascara smeared. Her energy had been raw and frightening in the days prior and I insisted we go see somebody.

We drove to the hospital. Penelope turned on the AC and ran it on full blast. When I shut the vent—I knew better than to say anything—she rolled down the window. At the hospital, a resident, who didn't look a day over twenty, did an exam. I sat in a blue plastic chair while Penelope answered his questions.

He told Penelope she suffered from anxiety.

"She's on medication for that," I said.

"Her dose is pretty high," he said. "If she skipped one, it'll do a number on her. She needs to be seen by a therapist," he said.

He handed Penelope a prescription and sent us home with a list of counselors and doctors and urged us to follow up with her primary care provider.

See, I want to say, *I have not forgotten.* I took her to the hospital. She hadn't refilled her medication. There wasn't much more to it. I feel myself crumbling. Why is Edward acting as if there's something wrong with *me*? I don't have the energy to make a fuss, I came here for one thing but somehow now feel I lack the tools to finish this task. My resolve is gone, all that buildup, all that steadfastness I've had, just disappears. *Poof.* Gone.

How terrified I am of the thoughts in my mind. Not remembering everything I did or didn't do, and there are blank spots and being unable to fill them frightens me. I want to share all those questions that have been jammed like an old door but I don't dare.

Edward is watching me. He's so still, he doesn't even blink. I'm crumbling, and he can tell.

"Donna, you're a piece of work, you know that? I've about had it up to here." He waves his hand around eye level. "Come, come, come," he says and pulls me by my upper arm into the foyer. "How do you not remember?" He points down at the checkered floor then meets my eyes head-on. "Are you telling me you don't remember what you did?"

His eyebrows are raised. He doesn't know a thing. Thirty years of marriage, I'm no fool. I close my eyes. Images from that afternoon crowd my mind: Penelope's anger, her resolve, her bloodshot eyes. I can't bear another second of my heart beating like a runaway train.

"I want to know what *you* did," I say and poke a finger in his chest. "You go first."

34

EDWARD

Edward Pryor looked up from a book he was reading, a presidential biography Donna thought to be interesting. He'd never admit it but he'd been stuck on the first third of the book for days. He preferred crime fiction and an occasional Western—that, too, he would never admit—but everyone was going to talk about this book, according to Donna, so he thought he'd see it through.

It was eleven when he heard a noise, indistinct and faint. Edward exchanged a quick look with Donna, puzzled, as if to say *you heard that, too?*

Donna flipped through *Architectural Digest* and ignored him. She had called him earlier in the day just as he was going into surgery, and he had all but ignored her calls. She had had an argument with Penelope, she had alluded to as much, but when he had pressed her on the details earlier, she had clammed up. Little did she know that he had caught the very back end of the argument that morning, eavesdropped on his way out the door, and it wasn't so much the words they exchanged—those he could barely make out—but the tone of the conversation. Mother and daughter under one roof and all the arguments that came with that, but sometimes Donna cut Penelope to the bone. Donna knew better, it wasn't a note she wanted to hit but they pushed each other's buttons. A verbal rough-housing of sorts.

Donna and Penelope had been fighting since forever. For those two to get along was an abstract notion, an unimaginable thing. The older Penelope got, the worse the fights had become. It was like a boxing match, he was the referee, and he was tired of sending them to their corners between rounds. It was time to end this, time for them to be apart for good.

Edward listened for a follow-up noise. A knock, something falling down? A bump, boxes toppling in the garage, somewhere beneath them? Edward shut the book and stared at the TV. A rerun of *Law & Order*, the episode he had seen before—four high school girls make a pregnancy pact so they can raise their kids together—the occasional *chung-chung* indicating a progression in time, a fleeting bleat, unidentifiable, a sound that could be so many things.

There it was again, this time high-pitched, more of a shriek. His daughter, Penelope, coming home, maybe, but still, something about this was off. Edward stared off into the distance as if his hearing might improve if only he didn't focus on anything in particular. Maybe a deer had come through the clearing through the back of the property and got trapped underneath the awning with all the outdoor furniture. He imagined its slender legs and long neck trapped in a lawn chair, dragging it along the patio, bumping into things. Or those damn cats. He had told Donna so many times not to feed them, *dammit, dammit, dammit,* but did she ever listen to him? They had multiplied according to the amount of food she put out.

Edward muted the TV and chose his words carefully. "You just heard that, right? Those cats," he said to Donna. "We're going to have to do something about them."

He knew Donna had set out shelters, which were collectively frowned upon in Preston Hallow, and she had continued to do so even after she had been told multiple times not to. Someone had pulled some strings and the city had contacted her and told her not to interfere with the cat colony. Once he had come home late at night and as he turned on the high beams, dozens of eyes had reflected back at him. Someone claimed that entire hordes of cats, hundreds even, lived in the neighborhood. He thought that to be exaggerated but he couldn't be sure.

Donna continued to ignore him. It was mainly about him not taking her call this morning but she had been snubbing him for a while now, ever since she had booked a cruise to Italy for the summer without consulting him and he had told her to cancel.

"Just take three weeks off, there are other doctors at your practice. They all go on vacation. Don't be difficult about it."

Everything is so goddamn easy for her. Edward held those words back, didn't want to be rude, but Donna knew nothing about responsibilities. Taking weeks off would take just as long for him to prepare for and make the necessary adjustments to his schedule.

"You should have asked me before you booked," he'd said.

Before he could add anything else, she read from the brochure. "Charming villages, pristine beaches, and legendary cities, picturesque pastel towns from the Amalfi Coast to Sicily and Elba, and off to smaller ports and beautiful harbors, then off to Rome and Venice."

Truth be told, Edward didn't want to spend an entire month without his schedule of getting up at six, going to spin class, performing surgery in the morning, consulting in the afternoon, charting in the evenings. He took solace in the predictability of it all, needed to return every night to a pristine home where Donna handed him his favorite drink—two ounces of Old Tom gin, one ounce of dry vermouth, and a dash of Peychaud's Bitters—but Donna was relentless. She was working her way up to her final demand; soon there'd be talk of retirement and he imagined constant trips and charity functions and parties and he bristled at the thought of it all. He didn't even have time for the very thoughts he was having right then, it was eleven and his alarm was set for six. He had a full surgery schedule tomorrow. Eyes heavy, he shut off the TV and flipped over.

The pages of Donna's magazine rustled as he fell asleep.

Just on the border of sleep, he woke to a commotion. Disoriented, he reached for the lamp switch to check the time. A crash below— no more ifs and buts about it; a *crash*—made the walls shake. Not in a figurative sense, but the walls literally trembled as if the foundation of the house had been compromised. Those weren't cats or deer.

Edward Pryor reached for his phone, unable to decide what to do. Nine-one-one was a hassle, being put on hold and having to explain what was going on was nothing Edward cared for. After all he was on a first-name basis with the police chief, they played golf together—he hated golf but was fairly good at it—and they had an occasional cigar, and Edward could easily reach out to him. He decided to not do anything at all, someone would be here within minutes, he was sure. Their ADT account was up to date and the neighborhood was patrolled by a security guard.

Donna tossed the magazine to the side, put on her slippers, and threw on her robe, a silky silver thing that complemented her blond hair. Edward could sense her mind at work, the dominion of her logic which was off but predictably so: she didn't care to be robbed at gunpoint in her nightgown. She always thought of such things, even though it had dawned on him quite some time ago that her thoughts were the mental equivalent of a Tourette's outburst with flailing limbs and mental tics.

And so it began. Fracking was the first thing Donna went on about. She switched to the possibility of the hot water tank exploding— it had happened to a neighbor of theirs not too long ago—telling Edward to listen for water rushing through the pipes. Or maybe a small airplane from the nearby Skylark Field Airport had crashed into the side of the house? If he didn't know better, he'd wager that Donna was losing her mind, slowly but surely she was going off the deep end a bit more each and every day. None of this was normal. Her convictions manifested in random thoughts and she followed every rabbit hole offering itself, like the argument with Penelope that very morning. Donna was the adult, she ought to know better, and how often had he told her not to engage in those tiffs.

Come to think of it, it wasn't altogether impossible about that airport. He had to admit that even though Donna had a vivid imagination, there were sometimes small Cessna planes airborne overhead flying to a football game or a hunting trip, no more than six people. There wasn't a commercial flight route over his property but there was an airfield for small, private planes nearby.

Edward dressed in khakis and a shirt and slipped on his shoes.

"Maybe we're being robbed," he said but knew it was cruel to upset Donna even further.

"Shouldn't we stay here and wait for the police?" Donna called out and pulled the robe tighter around her shoulders.

Edward made his way out of the bedroom. "You stay, someone will be here any minute," he said in a hushed tone and closed the door with slow and focused movements to prevent it from slamming shut. He was pretty sure it had to do with that hobby airport, otherwise the alarm would have gone off. He realized he wasn't completely sure it would, ADT might just be one of those remote warning systems. He didn't know much about the system, Donna handled such things but she was worthless in her state. It was good to know this neighborhood was one of the safest in the area.

He looked down from the third-story landing into the foyer.

There was no light, no sounds, nothing but darkness and silence. Short and lean, he religiously went to his biweekly spinning classes, was fit by all accounts, in shape and limber for a man his age, but there was something he was not: a hero.

Edward paid people to do his gardening, the cleaning, and the cooking. He felt he had no choice but to investigate the noise, though he hoped the police would show up soon.

On the first floor he stood in the foyer and listened. In the kitchen the icemaker churned and the fridge motor kicked in. The moment his hand touched the front door handle, he heard a popping sound from the garage. It reminded him of a bicycle tire after you pull out a nail. He hadn't thought of that sound in decades, yet it returned to him as if to remind him of his childhood and happier times, or maybe, so he thought later, to brace him somehow as if fate whispered *there are good memories in life, still. Hold on to them.*

The motion sensor lights in the hallway lit up and he opened the door leading into the garage. He didn't move much farther into the space, stood on top of the stairs leading down into the three-bay garage, and his heart didn't have time to skip a beat, his intestines didn't have time to drop down.

Penelope had crashed her car into the back wall of the garage. The grill and part of the hood stuck in the wall. Edward peered through the driver's side window. Penelope looked disheveled. Her hair was unkempt, and she was staring straight ahead. Not so much as a scratch on her, as far as he could tell. He didn't have time to react because he heard the *woop woop* of the police car pulling up outside.

She must have been drinking, he thought. He pondered for a second if he should hit the garage door opener, to tell the police to take her away, to have her face the consequences. He wondered if neighbors stood by their windows gawking by now, not that they were bad people, but concerned about a prowler being on the loose after a police car appeared. Between the cats and a possible intruder they got worked up easily, they had talked about this at parties, their fear of burglars, the riffraff catching up with their way of life.

Woop woop.

He saw the blinking lights of the cruiser through a gap in the garage door.

Edward turned, walked up the stairs, out of the garage, and rushed out the front door.

It was all but dark outside but for the lights by the side of the driveway illuminating the landscaping. Making his way down the driveway, he waved at the officer in the cruiser. There was a brief conversation between them, a handshake, and the police car continued down the circle driveway and out into the road. He watched the brake lights come on, then it disappeared in the distance.

He knew without having to turn and look up that Donna was standing in the window, watching. By now she probably wondered if she ought to get her purse from downstairs but she'd be too confused to comprehend what was going on, given the fact the police had come and gone. Edward waited until the lights had completely disappeared and not until then did he turn and rush up to the bedroom, taking two stairs at a time and busting through the bedroom door.

"What's going on?" Donna asked. "Was there a robbery?"

Edward didn't answer.

"Why did the police leave? Did you send them away? Edward, what—"

Edward pushed past her, knocking into her shoulder, making her tumble backward.

Ever since they'd known each other, Donna had never heard a harsh word from him. Edward had never so much as raised his voice at her. His ways were the subtle digs and passive aggressive taunts, never anything physical.

"Edward, will you tell me—"

"Oh my God, oh my God." His words came out in short bursts, he was unable to catch his breath.

"What happened?" Donna shrieked as he darted past her and into the bathroom.

Edward bent over the toilet and vomited.

Donna followed him into the bathroom but didn't flick on the light, didn't dare expose him that way. Instead, she stood in the doorway, taken aback by Edward crouching in the darkness, heaving.

He rose and slammed the door shut in her face. He rinsed his mouth and flushed the toilet.

"I saw the police drive up. What was that noise and what's going on? I don't understand," Donna said, her voice hollow with her mouth so close to the door, her fists knocking and knocking, but she never entered.

"Get dressed," Edward said through the door. As if he knew she was still standing there doing nothing, he raised his voice. "Did you hear me? Get dressed."

Edward rushed past her and to the window and drew the curtains, didn't want neighbors to see them hastily rummage through the house, you never know who's about, even at that time of night, and he watched Donna as she gauged his outfit and slipped into a pair of jeans, a sweater, and a windbreaker. She put on a pair of boating shoes—she didn't own any boots—and flicked some cotton off her pants. She looked up and Edward stood a mere inch away from her.

"Why are we getting dressed?" How timid her voice was. He began to feel sorry for her.

"I need you to listen to me, Donna."

"I'm listening but I don't—"

"Now isn't the time to ask questions, okay?"

"You're scaring me. What is it? You're freaking me out. I don't understand? What's going on?"

His breath tasted sour and minty all at once. Edward was aware of the fact that in thirty years she had not seen him in this condition: unshaven, unkempt, boots haphazardly tied. He watched her put her cupped hands over her nose and mouth, partly because she was scared, partly because her throat closed up on her, the smell of vomit not something Donna was able to tolerate.

Edward took her hands and drew them off her face, squeezed them. He turned and pulled her with him, out of the bedroom, across the landing and down the double staircase, then along a hallway and into the garage, where Donna lost her footing on the steps leading down. Edward thought about this moment later and the best explanation he could come up with was that he wanted Donna to see what he had seen—he wanted her, in some small and petty and cruel way, to feel what he had felt.

The first thing Edward tuned in to was a hissing sound coming from the water heater. A stench of oil and gasoline, and everything was covered in a layer of *something* and he knew the water heater was spewing water. How funny, he thought, did Donna not just tell him to listen for water rushing through the pipes?

So much he hadn't seen earlier, hadn't paid attention to. Everything made perfect sense, but then it didn't: his daughter's car, the red Grand Cherokee, had hit the back of the garage, had crumbled the wall that separated the parking space from a storage area, and had hit the water tank.

"What's going on? Why is Penelope's car like this? She—"

"I need you to talk to her, Donna. I need you to talk some sense into her."

"Where is Penelope?"

"In the car. She's in the car."

Edward watched Donna step closer and wipe the condensation off the driver's side window with her right hand.

"Penny, baby, open up." There was no reaction. "Penny, unlock the door for me. It's okay. Just a little accident."

"Talk to her, talk some sense into her," Edward pleaded, knocking on the window.

He felt like that time at Whole Foods when a bagger had put the wrong bag in Donna's trunk and when they unpacked the groceries at home, they had stared at the items, knowing that they would never buy such things. That moment of not comprehending, the questioning of one's own faculties—this was such a moment.

Edward made his way around the car to the passenger side. The door was locked.

"Penny, open the door for me. It's okay. Everything is fine. Please open." With a wide swipe Edward cleared the passenger window from condensation and looked inside the car, cupping his hands against the glass. "Penny, please open up."

There was no reaction.

"Talk to her, Donna. She won't listen to me," Edward begged. "Penny, unlock the door for me. It's okay. Just a little accident." He found himself mimicking Donna's words.

On the other side of the car Donna kept pleading, "Penny, open the door. It's okay. Everything is fine. Please open."

Penelope's hand moved in slow motion, hovered over the door, and then lowered itself. A sound chirped twice. Edward ripped open the door and stared at the passenger seat. Penelope wasn't alone in the car. There was something next to her. Something scrunched together as if stuffed into the seat. A dummy? One of those mannequins in store windows? Edward stood and beheld what he knew deep down inside were not the distorted limbs of a plastic figure but a human. A woman.

And next to her sat Penelope. Crying. Crying so hard.

And there was blood.

So much blood.

35

EDWARD

Edward watches Donna like a hawk. As he relays the story to her, as she takes it all in, he fixates on her eyes, a series of saccades and intervening smooth anticipatory movements and then there are stationary periods. He wonders how well she is. He's no expert but he can't imagine, not for the life of him, that she can't remember. As a physician, he knows it's within the realm of possibility but he doesn't trust her.

He struggles to find the right words, doesn't know how to make Donna understand how terrible it was, even for him, a man trained to keep calm under the most difficult of circumstances, how he struggled to express the extent of the panic that had overtaken him that night, for that split second during which he believed that his only daughter had gone mad, had completely lost her faculties, had finally gone off that edge she's been teetering on for the longest time.

The stray cats, the ones Donna set shelters out for, they would sometimes bring a mouse as some sort of trophy. They'd fling the dead body around, catch it and paw at it, just to carry it off a few feet and watch it twitch. Edward couldn't help but think of the woman's body that way: an offering by his daughter. A reminder. *This is who I am.*

36

DONNA

I assemble the details of that day into bento boxes, neatly arranged and in perfect angles, separated and aesthetically pleasing. I can't commit myself to his madness quite yet. Another crack in the story I thought I knew? Now that it's told, it sounds plausible. But the question remains: is Edward a liar or is he telling the truth? I can't say he ever lied to me, not that I recall. At the most, he'd try to sway me in a direction. What do I know? Maybe *misleading* is a better word. He was good at that.

When Edward proposed to me, I had no idea what it meant to be the wife of a doctor nor did I spend any time thinking about it. It wasn't until he took me to his hometown that I caught on to his intentions. The town had a historic district and an art community selling landscapes to tourists, a picturesque civic square with a statue of a general on a horse, the kind of living that makes some sort of list for best places to retire.

He parked the car in front of an unassuming building and said, "I've got a surprise."

I hope he didn't buy this dump, was my first thought but my heart sank when we went inside. A practice with industrial linoleum and pencil drawings in crooked frames of a jolly man in a white coat with a head mirror illuminating a child's nasal passages. Stuffy noses and gout, I imagined, an occasional blood clot, and referrals handed out to specialists.

The waiting room was filled with elderly people, one person on crutches, a caretaker keeping an eye on a man barely in his sixties. A woman who was oddly dressed, her hair uncombed. People coughed and I turned my head. I saw myself having to pitch in, schedule appointments and keep files up to date and maybe Edward even expected me to learn how to draw blood? This was what I had spent all these years on, being frugal and living in mediocre apartments as he finished medical school? This was what was at the end of all the sacrifices I had made?

The months leading up to that, there was the pressure to have children. I was only in my late twenties but Edward had been pushing the issue. I wasn't opposed but wasn't focused on children quite yet, for a reason I couldn't put my finger on—there were no logical resentments there, it wasn't as if I had to raise siblings or anything like that, but it was just how I felt, or maybe I just hadn't given it any thought.

I was afraid of what we would become if this was our future. The waiting room made me nauseous, the queasiness from those smells. I had a hunch. I hadn't even seen a doctor yet, hadn't taken a test, but I knew, *I knew* though I didn't tell Edward. It only took me mere minutes and I considered the pregnancy a miracle, a sign. A microscopic cluster of cells, and I suddenly wanted more for this life inside of me. It was still an *it* then, too early to know, really, but this small-town-doctor's-wife thing, this I couldn't do. He couldn't possibly want this for me if he knew, could he?

Long story short, I talked Edward into plastic surgery by highlighting the advantages. "Think of all the people you can help," I said. "This is not about vanity. Mangled limbs need restoring, all those cleft palate babies. You'd do a lot of good." I laid it all out, how he was going to focus on his career and I was going to concentrate on the baby and that we could revisit the practice at a later point. "I won't say a word if you still want this ten or fifteen years from now, Edward," I said and meant it.

We moved to Boston and Edward started his residency at BMC. The move was easy enough, our belongings still fit in one moving truck then, we didn't own four sets of china but one which was still incomplete, there was no breakfast room or formal dining room furniture, and we hadn't filled two guest rooms to the brim yet.

I had never lived north of Oklahoma and the suburb we lived in was quaint, but the seasons felt different with winter showing up late and snow all through March and I was stuck in the house because I wasn't used to driving in snow, and the cold arrived in full force and winter never seemed to end.

Penelope was born and she was an easy baby, by all accounts, though I had nothing to compare her to. There wasn't a milestone she didn't hit or excel at, it wasn't a matter of her being slow or behind, nothing like that. She was different. And I had thoughts. I often wondered if I was explaining this well to Edward. I couldn't find the words to tell him that there was something off with her. If I told him that at birthday parties she was the one who wandered off and went from room to room while the other children played games and ate cake, that she had difficulty engaging with other children, that she pulled a girl's hair for no reason at all, and had a screaming fit after and snatched an entire table setting to the ground—would he have listened?

The years passed by quickly, *in the blink of an eye* sounds cliché, but there's much truth to long days and short years and before I knew it, we were in Florida and I enrolled Penelope in school. We lived in that shabby little house and it was then she stabbed that kid with a fork. Edward thought we should intervene, but I played it down like it was an isolated incident. I had this one job, raising this little human being, and I was clearly failing. Edward became more critical of me than he'd ever been. Everything was a point of contention: Penny's grades, how I didn't manage to stay on top of her schoolwork and if I just made her do things, everything would be so much easier. I spent those years doing what I was good at; I threw parties and organized charity functions, and along with that I reared the hope that Penelope would grow out of it, whatever *it* was. The less I told Edward about Penelope, the less critical he became. The house was a success, straight fringes on the rug, and I became relentless in my pursuit of the perfect family.

If Edward was the catalyst, if his name and his work was what had carried us to Hawthorne Court, it was my determination, my will to be extraordinary, that made us the envy of everyone. People were eager to attend our parties, to stand on the expansive lawn with the sun going down, pretending to be us. Colleagues, neighbors, friends, acquaintances—they eagerly ate off my china and wallowed in the luxury that I put forth before them. Edward knew nothing about the floor that needed replacing (*can we just patch it up?*), the money it took to keep up the landscaping, and I doubt he had ever heard of a retaining wall, and what kept the water from flooding the basement was nothing he concerned himself with. What he created, I sustained. And it wasn't an easy feat.

There was this silver maple at Hawthorne Court, must have been a hundred years old, according to the arborist. It had severe damage from a yellow-bellied sapsucker, which is like a woodpecker, only worse. The bird had pecked away at the trunk and left holes in horizontal lines with sap running down and bacteria entering, causing extensive damage. No one can fault the sapsuckers, all the bird is trying to do is to get at the sap, and it did what mothers do, it fed insects to its young, but the bird was about to kill the tree. The arborist said not to bother but against his advice I sprayed the damaged areas with hydrogen peroxide, filled in the holes with goop I purchased at a garden store, slathered the entire trunk in an attempt to save the tree. And I brought it back to life.

I can admit it now. I was embarrassed. Not for Penny but for myself. How did I manage to create this picture-perfect life while she ran through my fingers like sand? I had saved a tree from certain death, yet I couldn't help my daughter?

The reason I feel slighted when it comes to Hawthorne Court, the purpose of coming back was not to claim the house but to claim the truth, yes, the truth is what I'm after, I now know that all I ever wanted was a place for Penelope to be safe. But it didn't do any good. I want to spare myself the memories of what happened next but I've come this far, haven't I?

It goes against all reason that we should end up here, in this kitchen, in the middle of the night, the lights bouncing off the royal blue stove. Edward's words are like a beacon and once I catch a glimpse of something, though it doesn't come back all at once and it isn't there all the time, it bobs up just to withdraw as fast as it appeared.

How old and haggard Edward looks in this light. His left eyelid twitches. Is he still the man he used to be, still the surgeon people flock to? Can he still hold a scalpel steady, can he stay on his feet without tiring through eight-hour operations, and most of all, does he still have the power to make me believe I am the one to blame for everything?

PART III

HEAVEN

*Heaven wheels above you, displaying to you her
eternal glories, and still your eyes are on the ground.*

—Dante Alighieri

37

DONNA

The kitchen has a built-in desk where women used to sit and make grocery lists, a whimsical detail in an old-timey kind of way, but in reality it turned into a catchall spot for receipts and bills and newspapers. That's where Edward stands and stares at a framed photograph pushed into the corner of that desk; Edward and Penelope stand behind me as I sit on a chair. Penelope looks to be about twelve or so. I remember the day because we had an argument about her outfit. Looking back, it was unnecessary to quarrel about it but in the moment it seemed significant. Her eyes look empty, her smile forced. I shouldn't have been so hard on her, but that too is hindsight. I get lost in these moments, ponder every single action, every word I ever said to her. There's so much I'm not explaining right, so many things incongruent with what I remember and what I've forgotten. If I think about it hard enough, maybe I'll be able to pinpoint where I went wrong.

"What happened to Penelope's room?" I ask.

"That's what you want to know?"

"Yes, what's happened to it?" I insist. "There're holes in the wall."

"After all this time, you come here and ask me about holes in the wall?"

"Just one of the many things I don't understand." I panic for a second—the letters, where are the letters? Then I remember, I shoved them into my tote. "I want to know where my daughter is. I want to know what happened because nothing makes sense to me anymore. I fell and I hurt my hip and I was taken to the hospital. I recall nothing after that but not being able to get out of bed. And you deserted me because . . ." I can't finish the sentence. My voice sounds overly loud as I demand answers but this blame is a curious thing; Edward seems mad when prompted for details.

"How did you fall, Donna? How did you hurt your hip?"

"I don't remember. I had a car accident? A slip on the back porch maybe? I was out on a walk and a car hit me? It's all the same to me. I don't care, really. This isn't about me."

"Come with me," Edward says and marches me out of the kitchen and to the center of the foyer, his fingers digging into my arm.

"Here, right here," he says and points down to the black-and-white checkered tile. One has a crack. "Does that jog your memory?"

I pull away from him.

"Jog it for me, Edward, why don't you?"

38

EDWARD

If Edward were to get Penelope out of the car, it was going to be nothing short of a miracle. She clung to the steering wheel with such ferocity that he feared he might snap her joints out of place. Every time he loosened one finger, another one tensed its grip. As he managed to undo one hand, the other one clutched tighter. The steering wheel was sticky with blood and her face was smeared with what had by then turned into a brown mud-like layer, like sap from a tree. A trail of tears had made their way through the bloody landscape of her face and down her neck.

Trauma assessment. In sequence actions must be performed, preventing mortality. Not something he'd encountered in recent years, decades even. *Vital organs must be oxygenated, stop the bleeding if there's any.*

That's my child, my own flesh and blood—oh, the irony—my

daughter blabbering without rhyme or reason, shaking violently, her knees hitting the steering wheel, over and over.

He rattles the list off inside his brain. *Information gathering: time of injury, related events, patient history. Key elements of injury to alert the trauma team to the degree and type of injury.*

There were predictable patterns in which trauma mortality occurs and though he went through the motions, he wasn't equipped to do anything but an initial assessment.

Stabilize the patient.

He would suspect such blood loss from a gunshot wound but Penelope showed no signs of injury, her limbs were moving, her pupils—he shined a flashlight into them—reacted normally, constricted as they should. He couldn't think straight but he was aware that this was his child, half of his DNA in front of him, and everything he did to her he did to himself and never had he been so conscious of that fact and never had he felt so helpless and never ever had he been this aware of his failures as a father. He performed every motion like he did in the emergency room rotation so many years ago, did everything according to the book, had done it before but with his own daughter beneath his hands, it seemed crude. Edward patted his daughter's skull with his hands, moved on to her neck. Her pulse was racing but steady. Edward, by all accounts, couldn't find anything physically wrong with Penelope.

But there was a woman in the passenger seat. He couldn't help but be taken aback by the angle of the woman's head, the way it was touching her chest. He reached over and searched for the woman's carotid artery. Placing his index and middle fingers on her neck by the side of her windpipe, he felt for her pulse. Nothing. Not even a faint flutter.

Edward thinks drive-by. Penelope and the woman were driving and someone opened fire. Mistaken identity, maybe a stray bullet. So much blood, there must be a gunshot, if not on Penelope, then the woman had some sort of injury.

He should prepare the resuscitation area. Once the ambulance arrived, there needed to be airway equipment put in place, bag-mask ventilation, and endotracheal intubation. A line needed to be placed, IV fluids given, monitoring equipment hooked up. Guidelines on protection when dealing with body fluid should be followed throughout this and subsequent procedures. Did that even apply? How random his thoughts were, how he focused on insignificant details.

He asked himself *why don't you call 911?*

But he made no attempt. Neither did Donna.

Donna, in his peripheral vision, stood a few feet away and for once she didn't have an opinion to add. She didn't call 911 and it registered. After so many years they were in tune with each other, one look and they knew, understood the gist of it.

Edward's hands were sticky. Such an odd and peculiar feeling, he who had never touched blood without gloves, he who wasn't used to feeling the warmth and the stickiness, he who had always had a layer of protection between him and the blood of his patients.

There was so much of it. It had pooled on the mat by the woman's feet. On her lap, within a crease where the coat fabric had puckered, a crimson puddle where the plaid trench lining shimmered in the dome light of the car's interior. On the door, the handle, the window, even the glove compartment. So much blood. *Exsanguination* was the medical term.

Ex (*out of*) and sanguis (*blood*).

Meanwhile, within those spattered leather seats, his daughter was screaming without a sound. Her mouth, the gaping vastness of it, her wide eyes. And not a sound escaped. He'd never seen anything like it. He wanted, if he could have it his way, some sort of X-ray so he could understand her mind much more so than her body because there was not a mark on her, not so much as a scratch.

He was floating in a sea of adrenaline. As if an explosion had gone off and then died down, single auditory components of the world around him returned one by one. It struck him like a horror movie, everything over-the-top and too loud and too much, too much of everything, but this was real.

Penelope was in a state of madness. He needed momentum, needed to be quick about it. He wanted to lay her flat on the ground to do a proper assessment, maybe there was a break or a wound after all, but he couldn't get ahold of her.

Without warning Edward tipped his daughter's body to the left, put his arms underneath her from the back, locked his hands, and swiftly pulled her out of the car. Her hands let go of the steering wheel but she kept her fingers hooked like talons. She flapped her arms like a dervish, twisting her body as if she were prey and he was a raptor.

Penelope repeated words as if they were a recitation, as if in some sort of hypnotic state, then she broke free from him and whirled and hit his chest and then her body coiled—he couldn't think of any other word—and twirled as if she were dancing.

She said words he couldn't make out and all he wanted was for her to be quiet so he could think.

39

PENELOPE

Penelope didn't realize the extent of her actions until her mother had washed all the blood off her. She stood in the shower, hair shampooed, skin red from her mother's hands scrubbing every inch and fold of her body as if she were a child.

Penelope watched her mother as a film of sweat formed on her upper lip, as she struggled to get her daughter's arms into a shirt. When every last molecule of her recklessness had gone down the drain, as her mother awkwardly put a nightgown on her and her father turned to give them privacy, Penelope had a searing thought: Did Rachel have a child? Was she a mother? Did she have a husband and was he waiting for her, parting a curtain, expecting headlights to appear around the corner? If Rachel had children, who was dressing them? Who would care for them? That thought tumbled into another: Is this how Gabriel's mother slipped underwear on her son? Is this how she struggled to put pajama pants on him?

Penelope had been cleansed of all blood. Her sins were washed away but there was no righting this—that much she knew. Though her mother had washed the woman's blood off her, the guilt wasn't going anywhere. It was going to stick to her for all eternity. Her mind went on and on. This house. Those endless corridors that had frightened her as a child, the tedious staircases and infinite rooms were . . . *her*. She was a labyrinth with dark corners.

Her father had given her pills, had pushed a glass of water toward her. She chewed them like antacids. Penelope slid under the cover, her wet hair wrapped in a towel, but it leaned and dropped to the ground.

The way her hair stuck to her cheek reminded her of a summer, years ago. A memory she had been holding at bay. She was unable to diffuse it or make it go away:

How old was she then, sixteen, maybe seventeen? School was about to start back up, Penelope remembered being anxious, her mother had kept tabs on her all summer, involving her in errands and appointments and before Penelope blinked, summer was over and she was exhausted and just wanted to get away from the hovering. It was barely nine, the sun was about to go down, but the light had been draining away for a while. They pulled into a gas station. During shopping and running errands and dropping off dry-cleaning, it had begun to rain, a heavy downpour that had soaked the bottom of Penelope's jeans. Her feet were wet and then there was her mother's voice.

"Honey, fill up the car for me. My hair," she said and handed Penelope a credit card.

Penelope glared at her but rose from the seat, got out, and flipped the gas panel open like a little door. She unscrewed the fuel cap, swiped the card, inserted the nozzle into the hole, and squeezed the handle.

Ngggggggggggggggggggggg.

Penelope heard a noise but didn't know where it came from. She cocked her head but kept her eye on the pump screen. She turned when someone knocked on the back window of a car parked at the pump next to her. Was someone waving at her?

She walked closer to the car. The tinted window made her lean in but all she saw was her own contorted reflection. It was curiosity that made her cup her hands, shield her eyes, and stare into the interior.

Gabriel still bore some resemblance to the boy he had been years ago but if it wasn't for the birthmark on his left temple, Penelope wasn't sure she would have made the connection. His formerly poreless skin with a hint of conch pink was now dotted with cystic acne and his teeth had shifted into an odd assembly. His lips were moving as if he was speaking to her. His eyes weren't focused on her but drifted off somewhere upward and to the left just to sway to the right. Back and forth.

She had a sudden image in her mind of him with his mother, being fed, food dropping into his lap, his mother's eyes empty, a countertop crowded with medication bottles. How much reassurance that takes, Penelope thought, his mother telling herself that she can do this, can feed him for the rest of his life. Or her life.

Nggggggggggg.

There it was again. Shorter, cut off. A short but fierce thrust of air emerged from his mouth. No words formed, nothing she could decipher. He froze as if someone had hit the OFF button. Her mother had told her there were lasting injuries but Penelope had imagined a crooked bone or a scar on his temple. His head rolled back and forth. When the palm of his hand hit the windowpane, Penelope jerked backward.

Thunkkkkkk.

The tank was full. Penelope placed the nozzle back into its plastic sheath. She got in the car and her mother merged onto the highway and it was all behind her. She banished the moment, except the lolling of the boy's head. She couldn't get that out of her mind.

As her mother led her to her bed, Penelope saw her father's outline standing in the corner of the room. He was nothing but a distorted aura. When he stepped toward her, he seemed unreal, as if he were walking on air. She watched him, transfixed, waiting to see if he would speak to her.

So many conclusions rammed their way into her head, there was no more closing the gates to keep them at bay. All her life her father's approval had been important to her. His ability to make even the worst transgression seem like child's play would stop today. Even if she could suppress her guilt and everything that came with it, it would come to a full stop. That was what she was sensing, the end of it all. There was nowhere to go from here. This couldn't be swept under a rug or erased from memory. This would stick. Full circle.

At last her father opened his mouth. She couldn't hear the words, they seemed muffled. She realized he was whispering to her mother, who was sitting in a chair, *rocking, rocking, rocking.* Her mother spoke but the words made no sense, like she was answering someone Penelope couldn't see. Not one sentence was connected to the one that had come before.

She drifted in and out, from darkness to visions of guilt, and she did what she had always done when confronted with racing thoughts: she attempted to look as far back as possible into the Pandora's box which was her life. From the playhouse in the sparse backyard in Florida to the bluish light of the pool full of floating noodles.

Another memory lined up, one out of order, waiting to be acknowledged. Maybe it was her wet hair or maybe it was something else, but Penelope faced another memory then: one summer when her mother had cheered her on from the edge of the pool, the same pool she and Gabriel had thrown toys and rocks into. She had unsuccessfully attempted to do a perfect handstand in the shallow part.

You are almost there. Try again. Almost. One more time.

Finally Penelope managed to get her legs up in the air, the arches of her pruney feet stretched, her big toes touched. Her mother took a picture at this very moment and later, when Penelope came across the photo, she was surprised to discover how perfectly her hair rose around her head like a halo. She'd never realized that her mother, while relentless in pushing her, was her biggest cheerleader. It dawned on her that her mother had tried to be some sort of composed and solid presence in her life, a steady hand leading her along, and suddenly she saw her mother in a different light, saw her attempts to keep some sense of order, some perceived direction for her.

Penelope was joining her life midstream but something clicked in place. There was only so much the rooms of her mind could hold and she had reached the limit: stuff propped up to the ceilings, all those lies she had told, all those sins sat stacked, *tumbling, tumbling, tumbling,* had come to seek her out, had sat in waiting all those years, getting ready to strike.

When they moved into Hawthorne Court, after her father shook his head at the size of the house, her mother jokingly said *we have to live somewhere.*

Penelope couldn't live in her mind any longer.

"Hear me out," Penelope said to her mother then. "Hear me out."

40

DONNA

Like the corridors in this house winding endlessly around corners just to end up in front of a door, my mind has arrived at a haunting concept. Like a flower opening its petals in slow motion, one of those time-lapse videos, that's what it feels like. Here it goes: Something shocking happens; the mind shoves it into some remote corner of the unconscious but then it bobs up to the surface as if the anchor holding it in place has detached itself. It breaks through the surface and floats. Like a corpse. But how authentic is it?

More fragments have returned, and I want to believe I have a rich and detailed memory of that night. It's over the top, it has a tinge of Victorian asylum horror flick to it all, but it feels real enough.

It took us the better part of the night to get Penelope to talk. Not talk-talk, not a coherent stream of words, but a response. There wasn't much she said, and that was the challenging part, but we went at it for hours. We tried, over and over. We didn't know how to fix anything because we didn't know what was broken.

I felt like someone was pushing a pillow over my face.

"Is she all right, Edward?" I whispered. "Is she really all right? She has no injuries?"

Edward nodded. I was taken aback by his hands, the way they were clasped as if he'd been praying, fingers interlaced.

"Are you certain she doesn't have any injuries?"

"None."

"She'll be fine?"

"Yes."

"Are we going to ask her what happened?"

"If we do . . ." Edward said, letting his hands spring apart, but he never finished the sentence.

I turned to Penelope.

"It's okay, Penny. It's okay," I kept repeating. "Tell us what happened. Just tell us. Who is the woman and what happened? We can't make sense of it, you have to talk to us. Penny, please, talk to us."

Penelope stared off into the distance, her face cold and frozen. We tried for hours. In between she rested, closed her eyes and when her breath turned steady, Edward and I stepped outside the room. We stood in front of her door, where I cried, and Edward told me to pull it together. We whispered, hushed words of accidents and cars and police, and then we argued over what to do next and the conversation turned to lawyers.

"What do we do? Oh my God, what do we do now?" I said, words escaping with every breath in huffs of fear and panic.

"It was an accident. I don't know what happened but it was an accident. We need to find out where it happened, maybe we can do something," Edward said.

"Do something?"

"Yes, do something."

"What's there to be done?" I asked.

"Her phone," Edward said, and his eyes lit up.

"What?"

"Her phone. Where is it? Did you see it? There might be . . . I don't know . . . I'll have to check, did she use, you know, maybe she used her GPS. OnStar, does she use OnStar?" He sounded incoherent, so unlike him, a torrent of thoughts, so unfamiliar in his usually steady voice. The rock had turned into a quivering mess. "I think I can look it up, see where she's been. We have to find her phone. That's it. We need her phone."

We heard Penelope through the door moaning in her sleep.

"You go check. I don't know anything about that," I said. "Should I turn on the news?"

"It's the middle of the night. Nothing will be on the news."

"What if no one knows?"

We said nothing after that.

I had no recollection of falling asleep. I woke on the couch in the living room to a noise. A clatter of a chain, maybe the garage door? I couldn't be sure. I remembered Edward had given me pills to calm down. He was nowhere to be seen. I rushed to Penelope's room. She stirred. Helpless, like a child, her face so young and the shirt I put on her had sheep on it. *Sheep.* As I sat on the bed and swiped her still-wet hair off her forehead, I cried.

"Pea, we need to talk. Can you talk to me?"

The nickname from her childhood was supposed to soothe her. Never before had I attempted to con her into a false sense of safety, but there was a dead woman in my garage. She needed to understand what she had done. I can honestly say that there was no moral judgment, it was merely an assessment. *See what you've done.* Maybe that was what she needed to hear? Maybe she didn't understand the implications, the consequences of her actions.

"Pea, do you remember what happened? Tell me about the woman, tell me what happened?"

Her eyes were empty.

"That woman, the woman in the car, in the garage. Who is she?" No reaction.

"Pea, I need you to talk to me. We can't fix this if we don't know what happened. I need to know where you were. I'm trying to help you. So is Dad. Dad is here for you, Penny, we are here for you. Please talk to me, please."

Penelope's eyes opened. "Hear me out," she said. She attempted to sit up and I folded a pillow behind her back. There was this moment when she took in a deep breath and then held it as if she refused to take another. She stuttered at first but then she caught her stride, her voice low with a trace of rasp and much more determination than her frail body suggested. "I did a horrible thing," she said. Her eyes darted as if she saw this room for the first time. *How did I end up here,* her eyes seemed to say.

"Tell me what you did. Tell me what happened."

"I want to turn myself in. Take me to the police."

I knew Penelope. I knew my daughter. There was no convincing her otherwise once she was determined to go through with something.

"Tell me what happened, Pea," I said.

"I'm not telling anyone but the police."

"Tell me what happened," I insisted.

"You're just going to mess it all up. Call the police."

"You know what, I think I know what we're going to do. We'll get you some paper. You write it down, okay? Write it all down. Remember, the therapist told you, once you write it down, it'll be okay."

"That's not how it works."

"However it works, Penny," I said and watched her jerk as my voice went up an octave, "I don't care. Get it off your chest. If that's what you need, that's what we're going to do." I rummaged through her desk, ripped open drawers. A notebook, a pen. "Here," I said and pushed them hard against her chest. "Write it down. I'm begging you."

Penelope had closed her eyes as if she were resting before the inevitable downfall, preparing for a final blow.

"I'll get your father," I said and shut the door behind me.

In the hallway I stood and my heart was about to explode in my chest.

"I want to go to the police," Penelope screamed from her room.

The faint sound from before, this time I was sure. Chains pulling the garage door. I waited for a final rattle of the door coming to rest on the metal beams but there was none. I looked out the hallway window, down the driveway. Red lights turned into white and the jeep appeared and looped around the driveway, toward Preston Hallow Road.

I thought about opening the window. I wanted to open it, call out to Edward, *come back. We can't fix this but we can do the right thing.* In a vanishing second I reached for it, opened, then slammed it shut. *We are in too deep,* I thought. *So deep we'll never get out of it.*

In her room Penelope cried out with such force that I feared for her lucidity, no longer considered her sane, and I thought *she won't come back from this, this is the equivalent of the boy's crushed skull, a life of existing in some half world of derangement.*

I couldn't move, could only watch Edward drive off in Penelope's car. And next to him in the seat was the faint outline of a body.

I now know where I went wrong. The night I watched Penelope retrieve the key from the soil like a thief in the night. We found out later, she'd met up with friends on a hill a few miles down from our house. It was a cul-de-sac, undeveloped with half-paved roads and crooked streetlamps and large parcels of land with orange flags sticking out of the soil. Penelope and her friends broke into a house that was under construction. All the other teenagers with her were from other schools, we knew none of the parents.

I drove to the house after, in the morning before the sun came up. There were empty beer cans propped up and an old office chair sat in the dirt. Someone had dumped an old grill with missing wheels. There were condoms strewn about the area, flattened in the road. I couldn't enter the house because there was yellow tape tied to wooden poles sticking out of the ground, but there were shards of bottles with labels still intact—Captain Morgan with the picture of a pirate, KFC buckets, and cigarette butts—and the house was vandalized. I looked through a broken window; the damage they'd done boggled the mind.

"Penny, I saw what you did," I told her later. "What do you think is going to happen now?"

"It wasn't me, you know. I wasn't even doing anything."

"How do you not know that was wrong? Penelope, tell me you knew better."

"Well, you raised me."

It was this teenager logic, and what could I say? Yes, I had raised her. Edward called the chief of police to withhold Penelope's name but names weren't mentioned at all because they were minors. I asked Edward about the yellow tape—*Doesn't that mean it's a crime scene?*—and he said there was blood. "Was someone hurt?" I asked and held my breath.

"It wasn't human blood," Edward said, and I didn't ask any more questions after that.

Edward footed the entire bill to have the house fixed and he paid for paint and the labor to have the walls redone. He threw in free landscaping and the builder didn't press charges. Police were instructed to do frequent drive-bys and cameras were put up.

"She gets caught up in things, Donna," Edward said. "Those kids she was with don't exactly come from stellar homes. You just need to keep an eye on her, keep her busy."

I couldn't imagine Penelope partaking in vandalism when she had spent most of her life in a house like the one she had helped destroy. Had she not lived in luxury, in a home that a flier on the *Grand Tour of Homes* called *the elegance of past generations combined with modern updates*? Why destroy what sheltered you, why so much anger?

I found Penelope's clothes from that night stuffed behind the washing machine. There was blood on her jeans, as if someone had wiped hands in a sideways motion over the thighs. I disposed of them. It haunted me and I turned it over in my mind for days. In my panic I wondered—and I'm ashamed to say it—but I went out back and counted the cats but there was no way to keep track of them, anything could have happened to the ones that went missing and I didn't have an accurate count to begin with.

I allowed myself to go there and then I closed that door. That, out of all moments, that was when I should have done something.

Hear me out, Penelope said. *Let me confess*, she said. *Let's go to the police*, she said.

I knew what she was capable of. Birds of a feather, like calls to like. She'd done it this time. Though Edward had mentioned lawyers, we both knew no money in the world could fix this. It was beyond anything she had ever done.

Hear me out. I want to go to the police.

I needed a chair. A certain chair. If it was too short, it would just get pushed out of the way. In the library, below the window, sat a ladder-back chair, the thickness of the horizontal slats balancing out the height, one with its back higher than the doorknobs in the house. Carrying the chair upstairs, I hardly felt its weight.

Penelope's room was dark, her body a faint bundle underneath the covers. She must have calmed down, must have fallen asleep. Maybe that's what she needed, some rest, a reset of her mind so she could get back to her senses. I tilted the chair back on its legs and secured it in place. If Penelope pushed from the inside, the pressure of the door would wedge it even deeper, making it impossible to open the door. That was the plan.

I went downstairs and I waited.

My phone vibrated.

Wait for me it's going to be okay we are safe

What has become of us, I thought. We are not safe, we haven't been safe for a while. And we'll never be safe again. My life rushed before me, it felt like a dream in which Penelope was forever five years old as if that was the tipping point in this whole thing. *What if I talk to her, make her understand?* I imagined entering her room, draping a robe around her—*it's okay, Pea, everything will be okay, just listen to me, okay, just listen to me*—one more try, I said to myself, one more try. What was done was done, there was no going back. I will get her to realize this was much bigger than her, bigger than the dead woman.

I went back upstairs, forced the chair out from under the door-knob. Inside her room, I slid my hand upward over the duvet. "Penny, wake up," I said but the duvet was soft and pliable. There was no body underneath those sheets.

Penelope was gone.

I don't know this happened until I play it again in my mind. It's almost a parlor trick but that's exactly how it feels.

I ran through the house. Through every room, opened every closet door. From basement to attic, I searched. No one can imagine how long it takes to search a home that size. All those floors, all those rooms, those closets, under every bed.

The adrenaline that was going to make my heart explode. There was only one place left I hadn't searched: the pool house.

41

EDWARD

J ust a deer," Edward had told the officer. "It got trapped out
back, dragging furniture around. Sorry for bothering you." He
couldn't fathom how he had done it—the moment the police
showed up, before he knew the extent of it all, the way he had
played it off. That officer had been here, he had been close, and they
had been *so close* to being found out. Edward had played it off, had
done it so well, as if deceit was in his blood.

Edward heard the crying and pleading and carrying on through the
door. For hours Donna tried to talk sense into Penelope. He didn't
want to go in and add to it all, he was only going to make it worse.

Outside the room, Edward and Donna argued. It bordered on a
screaming match and he pulled her downstairs so Penelope wouldn't
hear them. He dissolved benzos in a cup of water and Donna gulped

it down and before long she was out, her upper body leaning against a pillow on the couch.

Somehow in that moment he gained courage. Resolve. That's when it all began, the collusion. That's when he made the decision to do what he did, for no other reason but to fix what had gone wrong and what was wrong was the dead body in their garage.

He came to the conclusion that there was no OnStar in Penelope's car but he found her phone. He dropped it twice as he skimmed over all those numbers and addresses and browser searches and it took him a while to figure out she was at White Rock Lake Park right before she attempted to locate the nearest emergency room. And he kept telling himself *you can still call the police.* Somewhere down the road, at some moment in the future, a lawyer might argue: *Did Mr. Pryor not call the police after he tended to his daughter? Did he not do the right thing? Imagine yourself in his shoes. He rendered aid and then he called the police.*

Stop it, he told himself. *That's a lie.* His hands held a phone, he was capable of dialing the number. He just didn't do it.

While Donna was passed out on the couch, Edward entered Penelope's room. The hardwood floor lay shiny and perfect in a herringbone pattern and he stared at that awful gaudy Victorian dollhouse she had loved more than the others, more than the garden cottage, more than the princess castle. The floor was sturdy and solid, yet Edward felt the ground underneath his feet give way.

That dollhouse. Inside was a small and tidy world where everything was in order, eagerly arranged and consciously moved about, organized to perfection. The only world Penelope ever had control over. Why didn't he catch on earlier? How everything had its rightful place in those houses, how she maintained order while her mind slipped. She was his. His DNA. Whatever happened to her happened to him, always had. As he raised his arms and folded his hands behind his neck, a small gasp left his lips. He began to cry. It felt good, like a release, like guilt was flowing out of him.

Penelope was asleep, her breathing deep and peaceful. He stared at her, thought of many things, in rapid succession, tidbits of images, never long-drawn-out scenes, then his mind switched to a faint childhood memory. Ashes deter snails and slugs in gardens—his mother was an avid gardener—and after sprinkling ashes on a compost heap, he watched worms slink along his palm and up his fingers. What had become of that part of his life? His family didn't see a need for three cars or ten bedrooms, they were pragmatic and salt-of-the-earth people who didn't understand the concept of housekeepers and staff and had declined everything he had ever offered them: cruises and houses and vacations. This was a gloomy memory altogether, and he tried to stay in the moment, think about his next move, but the corners of his mind were not nearly sharp enough.

Get on with it, a voice said in his head.

"Penny," he said and stroked her cheek until she opened her eyes. "Penny, I need you to listen to me."

"Don't yell at me." Her speech was slurred.

"I'm not, I won't."

"Mom doesn't understand."

"I know, Pea, I know."

"This will never go away."

"Everything goes away, Pea."

"I've been thinking about this. I just know it, it will never go away."

"You can't go to the police, you just can't."

"I have to, you don't under—"

"You can make amends, Pea. We'll figure it out. But you can't go to the police. You can't."

"We've been over this. Over and over—"

It went on for a while, neither one of them making any headway.

"This is madness," Edward said. *Madness. Madness. Madness.*

"I'm going to go to the police. With or without you," she said.

Penelope never wavered, and the amalgamation of things, her steadfastness and his fear combined, made him edgy, his heartbeat accelerated when she said *with or without you.*

"They'll crucify you," Edward said but what he meant was *us.* They are going to crucify *us.*

"Everyone is going to do what they're going to do," Penelope said, in a tone that was so matter-of-fact, so final.

"Go to sleep, Pea," he said. He stroked her cheek like he had so many times when she was a child as he watched her eyes close.

Her breathing slowed and everything shrunk into nothingness, his throat constricted, he began to choke. What else could he possibly do? Waiting this long to call the police had been a mistake but maybe, maybe he could still remedy it? He ought to try. That's all he could do. Try.

Edward hugged Penelope and told her he loved her. He tiptoed past Donna on the couch. He got into the jeep and drove off with the dead woman next to him.

He didn't so much as wipe away the blood. He draped a blanket over the body, tucked it underneath the woman's chin so she appeared as if she were sleeping. He didn't speed, he stopped at every stop sign.

His heart was beating out of his chest. He had been taught to react because seconds make a difference between life and death and he recalled once a healthy young body going into V-fib; recalled the hearts of vigorous men deciding to be temperamental on a moment's notice just when he performed the simplest of procedures; recalled a bleeder hidden so deep in the body that he had hoisted an entire colon out to find the source. He had kept composure all those times but this was different. The images played on repeat like a broken record but the blood was what got to him, his training in bodily fluids and the contamination, the impurity of it all.

Before he knew it, the park sign appeared. The parking lot was deserted but for a car abandoned with the front tires over the white line. A pack of gum in the street, a comb. A travel-size hairspray. An inhaler. A plastic casing that more than likely contained a mirror, more items women carry in their purses. To the careless eye it was just stuff but he knew better, he knew those were the woman's belongings. He looked around but there were no clues as to what had transpired here, what had happened. If he were forced to render a conclusion he couldn't come up with an explanation. While he tried to connect the dots, he imagined the headline.

Disturbed socialite . . . fails to render aid . . . stores body in wealthy parents' garage . . . parents cover up . . .

He looked down onto the asphalt. He hadn't brought a flashlight, hadn't thought that far, but had left the headlights on. There was no blood, not a single drop. Judging by the jeep's interior, the woman had entirely bled out in Penelope's car. The police would find a bloodless body and they'd scramble to explain that but that was none of his concern.

Edward moved quickly. He hoisted her body over his shoulder, didn't want to pull it along the asphalt, didn't want to leave drag marks on her. His spine curved under the weight of the body and he had to stop from time to time, gauging the distance to the spot where he wanted her to end up. He dropped her next to the package of gum, the compact, and the comb. He hadn't thought about anything beyond that. Not fingerprints. Not hair. Not fibers. There was blood all over his hands. What sprang to his mind were the dangers of infectious bacteria, like enterococci and vancomycin-resistant strains. He had watched all the TV shows, he was knowledgeable in DNA and the many ways this could go wrong, the evidence the smallest of pieces could render.

He stepped back to a vantage point where he could view the scene with ease. His eyes zoomed in on the lighter. A cheap and disposable lighter among the blades of grass by the curb. He stared at it. An accelerant. He needed an accelerant. The hairspray. Spray cans contain propellant chemicals, a liquid solution held under pressure within the can, butane and propane, two flammable chemicals. If it was still full, it might work.

He was cold, standing there. *Must be the sweat drying,* he thought, but then a flash ripped across the sky and Edward looked up. Rain. A fine mist like the faint spray of a sprinkler but judging by the sky it would come down hard any moment.

He saw it as a sign—not from God, he was a scientist and as a scientist he had no room for divine powers—and the fitting of shapes into place the way a silicone bag fit into a breast cavity. *Something* had pity on him, saw to it that the rain would wash away his daughter's sins and on and on he went in his head, justification after justification, and then the realization that he'd done something pretty awful when he had to argue so hard to justify it.

Starting the car and leaving the parking lot was one motion. He didn't need directions or instructions, as if the route was seared into his brain. Why his limbs worked, why his hands turned the steering wheel he couldn't comprehend. There was so much toppling over in his head—cameras, what if there were cameras, didn't parks have cameras?—and the phone, what if it was able to track the car, that was another risk he had to take. What if Penelope knew the woman, what if they had been seen prior to all this, what if—so many ifs and buts.

Everything was at stake. That's where they were at. There was a saying but he couldn't get it quite right, the wording escaped him. *We float, we don't sink,* was that it? Or was it *we float and then we sink?*

42

DONNA

Edward's made his case and he's laid it out logically and supported by evidence and therefore it appears to be true. The question is, can I trust him?

"She wrote letters, you know," I say and pull them out of my purse. I watch his face as if to catch him in a lie, a sudden blink or widening of the eyes, anything that might give him away.

"Where did you find those?" Edward asks as he stares at the letters.

I press them tight to my chest and when he reaches for them, I turn away like a child not wanting to share a toy.

"Penelope wrote them," I say. "The therapist told her to write down what she didn't want to talk about."

"I know what they are."

"You knew about the letters?"

"Look around, Donna. What do you think I've been doing here? Renovating?"

He wants the letters because he doesn't know. He has gaps. He too needs answers. Answers only I can give him.

"Let me see them," Edward says. His hands are shaking or am I mistaken?

"No. I want to keep them."

"You can keep them. I just want to look at them."

I relax my hands and allow the wads of paper to slip out of my grip. Edward lays them out on the foyer table, shuffles the pages around, rearranges them, puts some aside as if he can't tell where they fit in.

"Have you read them all?" Edward asks.

"Yes."

It's all wrong in my mind, like one of those three-cup magic shuffle tricks where the dealer puts a coin underneath one cup and starts shuffling them around all the while speaking frantically to disorient and confuse the onlookers. Does Edward take bets? If I guess correctly, I'll double the bet after that, if I don't, I lose it all? Remember, I tell myself, remember the game is a scam. *Never play against the house.*

"If you read them, you know what happened."

"What I know is that a woman died because of her, Edward."

"You think I don't know that?"

At the mention of the woman, his face turns ashen. I have never before looked at him in this light, I almost feel for him. My emotions are clouding my mind, I believe. That's what emotions do, don't they? They cloud everything and distort it and once you have time to give it a think-over, suddenly it all appears in a different light.

"What happened after?" I ask.

"After what?"

"After you came home. After you took the woman back to the park."

"Why don't you tell me what happened while I was gone?"

I take a moment to think. My mind can't do the heavy lifting quite yet.

"Tell me now," I insist.

"Would you believe me?"

I feel like I'm joining this conversation midstream. Edward is trying to confuse me with details, hoping I'll miss the big picture.

"You're trying to distract me and I don't trust you." I stand close in front of him, so close we are almost touching. "Where is Penelope?"

"I'm about to tell you."

Get on with it, I want to scream. *Just say it.*

43

EDWARD

Edward had given it his best shot. *Whatever will be, will be; what's coming will come and he'll meet it when it does.* He turned down the car display. He was unable to see the clock on the dash, didn't know what time it was but it didn't matter. Nothing mattered. That very moment he made a pact with himself: if he was able to get away with this, if nothing led back to Penelope and this accident, he'd make amends. Somehow he'd make amends. He wasn't sure what that entailed, but that's where his mind was.

He was spent. An eight-hour operation couldn't have drained him more. He had tried not to think about death, had pushed it out of his mind, had gone on autopilot like he did when in the operating room. He just wanted to wipe out the last twelve hours, remedy his mind, go back to some state of order.

The drum of rain on the window ceased suddenly as if he had driven into a tunnel. One minute the downpour was there, the next it was gone, and the street was dry. It wasn't really that strange, he thought, rain must begin and end somewhere. Everything begins and ends somewhere.

Edward parked Penelope's jeep in the garage. Horrified, he sat and stared at the blood. The pool on the doormat had begun to set, the outer edges were clotted. It was on his hands, the cuffs of his shirt, under his nails. It was everywhere. Did they own a steam cleaner, one of those small compact carpet and upholstery machines? Do they even still make those? He didn't know. He didn't know who cleaned his house, who detailed his car. He didn't know much, the genius he was in the OR, none of that mattered now.

He didn't know what to do about the car. He ran through the options, all of them came to him through movies he'd seen over the years: submerge in a lake, drive off a cliff, douse in accelerant and set on fire, and then . . . nothing. Those were his choices. Wherever he took the car, he'd need a ride home. There could be no trace of any taxi or even neighbors seeing him walk or drive by, he had to think ahead, not make any hasty decisions. Donna. Where was Donna? She would know what to do. She thought quickly on her feet, he had to give her that.

Edward dug his thumb into the red square to release the buckle and as the seat belt snapped upward, his hand made contact with something soft and giving. It was a leather bag stuck between the passenger seat and the center console. It was the woman's bag. Edward sat in the car, staring at it. With two bloody fingers he parted the opening and pulled out a black leather wallet. He unzipped it and looked at the driver's license behind a plastic shield. Should he rummage through it, take her wallet, dump the rest in the trash?

Here we go, he thought, the mistakes are already piling up. He had neither thought to look for it nor given it any deliberation, and come to think of it, what else had he forgotten to take into consideration? Should he drive back, back to the park, and dump the purse? It was too late now, daylight was looming. He assumed the heavy downpour that had fallen in chaotic waves with gusting wind had washed away all blood but to now drop a bloody purse there made no sense. *Think, think, think,* maybe, just maybe it was an advantage, some kind of confusion he could create once police began to investigate.

He tried to think clearly, patted his forehead with the palm of his hand as if to speed up his thoughts. Maybe that's why there was no perfect crime, *no one can think of all the possibilities, go down every rabbit hole, it's just impossible.*

All the wanting ceased and there was only room for one thought: to keep his family safe. He caught the peculiarity of the statement, the mockery not lost on him; they'd ever be safe again.

44

DONNA

The conclusion is that I have become my memory. How to explain, I don't know, but I'll try.

My memory is who I am. This isn't about pictures playing inside my head—it's a changing story, a story that conveniently fits into my narrative. What I've done is, I've picked and chosen memories. Like docking a boat and that's where the anchor went down so that's where I'm at. Am I explaining it right? I don't know.

First, a mediocre girl from an average town from a run-of-the-mill family, then Donna Pryor, wife of Dr. Edward Pryor. Then the part where Penelope crashed her car in the garage with a dead woman in the seat next to her. That's the part that didn't fit in the narrative. Depression didn't belong either, that too I pushed aside. Shadow Garden is a narrative I embraced—a rich divorcée living in luxury with a daughter who won't speak to her, that's what I've been living for the past year. Stories are believable if I give them my all—is that how it works? Some memories I kept, some I discarded? Some just didn't make the cut? Just like that? No wonder Edward is mad at me.

"What did you see, when you came home? After you took the woman back?" I ask Edward.

Those words hang between us.

What did you see when you came back from dumping the woman's body? That's the part I don't remember. I rest my hand against my hip. The accident. For so long I've been looking for answers and now he's about to offer me the truth.

"Tell me what you saw," I insist. His eyes are so cold.

I have to be careful. Memory is fickle. I've been saying it all along. But the truth is the truth. I think I've figured it out. There are Penelope's letters, and there's what I recall, and there's Edward's story. Once we put it all together, the puzzle will be complete.

45

DONNA

Should I tell Edward that Penelope disappeared while he was gone? That I found her bed empty and that I had visions of her shouting the truth into the night? Should I tell him what I did after I found her?

I have truths myself but I will not offer them to him. I will not tell him I found Penelope in the wet grass beside the pool house, the gentle raising and lowering of her chest the only assurance she was still alive. There was this sick feeling inside of me, a sickness that overpowered my thoughts, silencing my conscience, and a possibility opened up: we'd all live in a hole if anyone found out about what we'd done.

I don't know how I did it but I roused Penelope and dragged her back to the house. When she began to cry, I covered her mouth with my hands. *I covered the mouth of my daughter so the world wouldn't hear her scream.* Wasn't that what I'd done her entire life? I believe that's why it came so easy for me to do what I did next.

There was no reasoning with Penelope. I tried from every angle. From *you left the scene of a crime* to *I helped you clean up* to a stern *your father drove off with a dead woman in the car.*

"I've been thinking about this," she said, her eyes feverish. "I'm going to tell the police that you did this for me, that I lied to you, that you didn't know. I'll say whatever you want me to. We didn't do it on purpose, it wasn't planned. I'll explain it to them, it was all me, all you did was try to help. And I begged you to, but you told me to do the right thing."

"No, Penelope, listen to me. What's done is done. It doesn't matter if you did or didn't do this on purpose."

"I don't care what you tell me," she screamed. "I will turn myself in. I should have taken her to a hospital. I don't understand why you won't let me make this right."

"I understand how you feel but it's not something that can be undone now."

"Mom, listen." Her hands were shaking.

Nothing. Not a thing I could do about it. And worst of all, I knew she was right.

This was the gist of her every breakdown: *I messed up, help, sorry but not sorry.* Until that night. Suddenly she couldn't take another moment of her guilt. *I have to confess, I can't live this way, I can't do this. I. I. I.* Suddenly she had to make things right?

We were part of it. Though in my mind I had created this safety net: if all else fails, the lawyers will figure it out, that's what they're there for. They'll get paid a king's ransom and we won't ever have to speak to the police. We will insist on a period of time to get our minds straight, during which we will bicker back and forth about where to meet with the detectives. We will hire our own polygraph expert. We will employ lawyers for each one of us, more than one lawyer if need be. We will hire lawyers for the lawyers if we have to.

But something I couldn't argue with, one fear remained: there will be nothing left. Not our name, not our reputation, not Edward's practice. We will sign everything over to the lawyers and we will be penniless when this is all over. But above all, the fact that we'll end up in prison was likely, a possibility, no longer remote but conceivable.

And so it began.

I wanted to convince Penelope to let us make the decisions. She had never been equipped to see around corners, it was our job to do so. Isn't that what parents are for? My mind struggled for where to begin. That her father was the one used to pressure, that he was out disposing of the woman's body and that Penelope should trust him? If she didn't trust me, she could count on him to do the right thing? But Edward wasn't here. I was and I had to do what I had to do.

I'm not proud of what I did next.

I dissolved every last Xanax I found in water and made Penelope gulp it down. I held the bottom of the glass and when she lowered it, I raised it back up, watched the chalky residue slither past her lips.

And I tried to reason with her. I told her, *We will make this go away, take my word for it. No one knows. No one ever has to know.*

I *know*, Penelope cried. *I know what I've done. You can't make that go away.*

That's what I kept repeating over and over and over. *We can do this. This is not the end of it all. Trust me,* I said, *this is not the end. You don't understand what you are about to do, to yourself, to us.*

I jammed the chair under the doorknob from the inside to keep her from leaving.

I'm getting out. You can't keep me here.

A screaming match of filthy, hurtful words followed, words I don't want to remember. She flung her arms around, punching, scratching. I was in the crossfire. A punching bag. Holding her down like I used to when she was a child didn't work, she was like a wet bar of soap, slipping away from me. I took her blows, every single one of them.

Like an animal trying to escape a cage, she raged on and on. And so I let her have her wrath. I allowed her to destroy what needed destroying and I hoped she'd tucker out. Tucker out like she used to, collapse onto the bed, cry, sleep it off. Half of her childhood she'd spent tuckering out, *what was good enough then was good enough now,* I thought.

She stripped off the bedding, pulled the curtains from the walls. *None of this, I want none of this.*

There was nothing left whole in the room but the furniture. But as always, she took it one step further. She ripped open the closet doors and tossed everything out: floorboards and wooden slats and a toolbox with nails and drills and bits and tape measures and wood glue. When she spotted a hammer, she grabbed it and began to strike the walls. She banged and bashed until the room was speckled with marks of her frenzy.

We fought for the hammer. I won and she struck me with her fist. How she had the strength and faculties, I didn't understand, not after the amount of medication I had given her. I remember thinking, *all those meds and still she rages.*

By then her screams were so loud, I covered my ears. I closed my eyes for just one second. I should have known better than to drop my guard. She tore at the door and the chair screeched, dislodged from underneath the knob, and the door gave way and opened. I pulled her back into her room. *What a silly thing to do with a door that opens outward, to prop the chair from the inside,* I thought. *What was I thinking?*

She rammed against me, her body flew past me. Her screams

reverberated through the house and soon they'd echo through the neighborhood—a vision of her running across the front lawn in her nightgown screaming bloody murder, telling everyone what she'd done. That was what was going to happen next.

My hands clung to the doorframe, my body the only barrier between her and the door and the stairs and the outside. I gripped her upper arm but she pulled me onto the landing. There, we bumped against the banister. I stood my ground, railing against my back.

A push, a shove, a gasp, a scream. Who is to say who pushed and shoved and gasped and screamed? I don't even know who is to blame.

My heart was beating so fast, so *fast, fast, fast, fast. Ba-boom, ba-boom, ba-boom.*

In my story, in the story that is part of me, I held on to her to save her. I can honestly say that my only intention was to save her from herself.

We floated, but still I held on to her. I held on to her so she wouldn't get hurt. *Floating. Floating.* I braced myself. All those images, so quick, so sharp, *what have I done, what have I done.* Were those my thoughts, my words, Penelope's thoughts, her words, who is to say who spoke and thought? We were one.

It's done. This is it.

We hit the ground and it felt as if something was knocking the life out of me. Such pain. Searing. *That hip is ruined. I will never walk again.*

We lay scattered on the black-and-white checkerboard floor. I was still conscious then, must have been, because a thought bobbed up: look at this floor, a design from a fifteenth-century Roman painting, so geometrical, so perfect in its angles and contrast. It had cost a fortune. Imported. The floor was curved like in that movie . . . what's that movie . . . *Alice in Wonderland.* Distorted and twisted.

Not one sound but *humming humming humming* in my ears. Nausea. Head pounding. I opened my eyes and there was Penelope's body beneath me, as warped as the floor.

Penny. Penny. Penny.

"Why did no one tell me?" I ask Edward.

"Donna . . ."

"Donna what? What?" My voice is shrill, piercing. I don't mean to sound unhinged, yet here I am. *Hysteria.* Do people still say that? "No one told me about Penelope? No one?"

"I told you," Edward says, deflating somehow. "I told you many times."

"Tell me again," I say, my voice barely a whisper. "I need to hear you say it."

"Penelope is dead," he says.

46

DONNA

A sorrow so intense that for a moment I can't breathe. Penelope is dead. On the edges of my awareness I have *thought* it all along, but I didn't *know* it all along. I didn't know but now I do. That's the proper way of putting it.

What kind of platitude is this? *I've told you many times.*

Something flashes beneath the surface of my mind and I want to follow the flash, investigate it. It's too late, it has disappeared before I can identify it, like reaching desperately for a balloon that has long escaped, turning into a dot in the sky. The falling part, the one where Penelope fell to her death, makes me anxious. I can't elaborate on that quite yet, it's some sort of mental discord, but I'll get there eventually.

One step at a time.

I can't say I knew what happened, I can't say I was lying to myself either. I more or less kept the truth from emerging, if that makes any sense. The fact that my daughter took a life is hard to digest, a deed that seemed insurmountable at the time. I don't want to call the woman, Rachel, a deed, she was a human being, had a family, a life, and people who loved her, but in Penelope's mind her remorse must have been overwhelming. But why the guilt? All the things she'd done, if this was just an accident—though her actions after were negligent—it wasn't serious enough to take her own life. Was it?

I'm not sure if I should tell Edward the truth. The truth and nothing but the truth, so help me God. Poor Edward. I have always done my best, been the best mother I could be. I don't know if he can say that about himself as a father but I don't tell him that, it's not something I need to say out loud. He'll arrive at that conclusion in due time.

Penelope is dead. What am I supposed to do with that? It's like ending up in a story so much bigger than myself, a story that boggles the mind but Edward claiming he told me, *every single day* he said he told me, I wonder how often did my daughter die in my heart and in my mind?

"I need some time. Please give me a minute to take this all in," I say.

I step out on the back porch. Leaves and garbage have blown into the corners. Flattened paper cups and candy wrappers have accumulated, the outdoor furniture is covered in bird droppings and spiderwebs. Walking past the outdoor kitchen, past the bricked fireplace, past a dusty garden hose forgotten in a messy heap, I find a muddy bowl flipped upside down, unused for months. I step on something cushy and it squeaks, the sound digs into my brain as annoying as nails on a chalkboard. A torn piece of a Styrofoam box, a chest I used to set up for the stray cats as a shelter. Looking closer, I see what Edward has done, see the footprint from the rubber clogs he wears in the operating room. The wavy pattern so familiar.

He could've cared for the strays, could have had them trapped and picked up, but no, he abandoned them, left them to their own devices. I loved those cats, the softest pads you've ever felt, but still they were so scrappy, so feral, how they hissed and clawed at me, afraid for their lives all the while I was trying to save them. I imagine Edward stomping on the chest, ripping it apart. I look and look and look but there isn't a single cat out here. If I wait until morning, or maybe if I switch on a flashlight, will their eyes glow bright green in the dark? I feel rage bubble up as I imagine Edward dropping poison bait in the corners of the patio. Did he collect their stiff dead bodies, put them in a lawn bag and sit them out on the curb?

I jerk around when I feel his hand on my shoulder.

"The cats are all gone. I told you this was going to happen once you stop feeding them."

I search for words, any words, anything, but there's just an empty space in my head. My fickle mind refuses to participate. I turn and walk back in the house, away from him.

Inside, a sound in the distance makes us jerk. A clatter.

"What was that?" I ask.

Edward's eyes are focused. He stands still as if discomfort has frozen him into place. Another noise, above us, muffled in intensity. Barely a screech but it's *something*.

"Someone's up there," I say and make for the stairs allowing access to the second floor and the half floor above that.

I expect Edward to step in front of me but all he does is say, "Donna, don't—"

"You son of a bitch," I spit at him.

I've never cursed in Edward's presence, not even under my breath. I'm as surprised as he is about those words coming out of my mouth.

Be quick, *think think think*. What's above the kitchen? A room, a guest room.

Struggling to keep my balance, I reach for the black iron rail. I raise an unsteady foot onto the first step. My stiff hip keeps my legs from responding the way I want them to, but my brain keeps insisting *go go go,* and they move, do what I want them to do. I sway but catch myself, and I reach and clear the landing, rush down the hallway. The first room on the right. That must be the origin of the noise. I rip open the door and it slams into the wall.

Behind me Edward screams my name and other words I can't make out.

I rip open the door. The curtains are drawn. It's hard to see.

I've never seen a room with so much furniture cramped in every corner. Barely a path remains—chairs stacked, tables pushed to the perimeter of the room, a table propped sideways against a desk, a nightstand upside down on top of that. One wall is covered in framed photographs, not to display them but more for storage, haphazardly and crooked they hang next to one another. A baby in one photograph, a smiling child, a birthday cake, and balloons in another. Below them, countless frames lean up against the wall.

The chaos keeps me from taking a step without worrying about knocking over a chair, a painting, or a vase sitting dangerously close to the edge of a sideboard. Dressers and bedframes leaning randomly against one another. Is Penelope hiding from me underneath a table, behind one of the headboards, a dresser—some of the furniture is draped in sheets and I can't make out what they are—I'm reminded of the mirrors I shrouded at Shadow Garden.

I venture between a dresser and a chest to get to what looks like a person hiding underneath a bedsheet—a silly thought—but I pull at it. As it drops to the ground, dust swirls in a dance: a coatrack with an umbrella stand. The dust settles everywhere like winter's first snow. Another sheet, this one reaches all the way to the floor, the outline beneath an oval shape like a small bathtub. I rip at the sheet. It's stuck. I pull it, then yank at it, and the sheet lets go as if I have won the tug-of-war. A white rattan bassinet.

My body seems to extend either farther out or doesn't quite reach to where it should, my spatial awareness the equivalent of a clumsy child reaching to catch a ball. I attempt to step over a gaudy decorative flower planter. It has scratches, discolorations, and signs of repair along the bottom edge, it's dented—who would even keep this thing? My heel grazes against it. I keep my balance by holding on to a shelf. It's unsteady, slides and tumbles. A crash. I shield my eyes. It's not over yet. A crystal bowl falls and shatters. Then a glass lamp base—I see it slide off with my own eyes—and I want to scream. No one is here, this is nothing but untidily placed items toppling over in what looks like a cramped and overstocked consignment store.

"What's this? What's all this stuff? Why is it all in here?"

"Donna, don't—"

"Penelope's here, isn't she? She's hiding from me? Is she mad at me?"

"Donna, no, it's not—"

"Tell me where she is. Tell me what's happened. I don't understand what's going on. What's this room, what's all this?"

"You know, Donna. You know she's dead. You tell *me* what happened. You tell me *how* it happened."

"You lie," I scream. "All you do is lie."

47

EDWARD

Edward returned home after dumping the body. He entered the house and expected, like so many times before, to walk into the middle of a blowup between mother and daughter, blotchy faces and red-rimmed eyes. There was this hope they'd had, all those years, that those were just rebellious teenage years and that they'd pass. Yet here he was, the bloody purse in hand, and what he saw didn't compute.

There was no shouting. No slamming doors. Something eerie above him. A metallic sound, an unpleasant screech, high-pitched, followed by a squeal. Words failed to describe the sound but it reminded him of the *chung-chung* in the *Law & Order* episodes he watched every night before he went to sleep. Or was it *dun-dun*? What was that sound anyway? It occurred to him in that moment that it could be the sound of a jail cell locking.

Edward looked up and saw bulbs and fluted glass arms on a cable. He took a step and a crunching sound beneath his feet made him stop in his tracks.

It all happened at once. There wasn't one realization after the other, but an amalgamation, a fusion of images, his mind tumbling like collapsing blocks. On the ground in front of him, a jumble of limbs, of legs and arms, broken crystals, blood. More blood. How much more blood could he take?

The bodies seemed staged, Penelope perfectly underneath her mother, almost disappearing. He ran to Penelope. Her eyes were open and broken and he could tell, he could just tell. The fact that three times in one day, outside of an OR, he had frantically searched for a pulse, struck him as fated. Out of all the options he had weighed since he found Penelope in her car earlier, this hadn't been on his radar at all. The house might as well have been blown over by a storm while he was gone.

A voice in his head. *Detach*. His hands no longer shook. He placed his index and middle fingers on Donna's wrist. There was a heartbeat. A faint quiver, not a strong pressing outward. He wanted to snap, wanted to scream, wanted to perform CPR but he was afraid he'd just start pounding Donna's chest with a force that bordered on violence. And how was he going to explain that? He didn't render aid, he didn't check airways or wounds. He had the blood of three people on his hands not including his own. There'd be no sorting this one out. By then his hands were cut up by sharp pieces of glass and crystal, his blood and Penelope's blood and the woman's blood and Donna's blood all mingling into a concoction of guilt. What would they make of it: the police, the crime scene investigators, whoever else was going to be involved?

The chandelier chain above rocked back and forth, at least what was left of it.

It caught his attention, the way Donna was wrapped around Penelope, the way she was holding on to her. He wanted to think she had tried to keep her from jumping but his mind went to another place.

Detach. Death is the consequence of a disease, not your care.

He ran upstairs to Penelope's room. Holes in the walls gaped like wounds. The bed was stripped, the window nailed shut, covered with a board. Nails jutted, half in, half out, crooked, in a desperate attempt to shut out the world. It dawned on him, the strange scene he was looking at—something that hadn't occurred to him thus far—wasn't so strange at all. He had never understood his daughter, never understood the dynamic between her and her mother, but this room, this room in its chaotic state was the manifestation of their relationship: boarded-up windows and iron nails with pointed ends and crushed heads.

Edward rushed to the edge of the stairs and looked down. The railing was intact, the spindles were in place—and why wouldn't they be; this wasn't a dilapidated back porch where people tumble over and fall to their deaths, this was a solid staircase—and he didn't know what to make of that. Was there a logical explanation? There must be but he couldn't think of one, he couldn't explain it and he wasn't going to try. He shut the door to Penelope's room behind him.

He never even thought about covering this up, had been in over his head when he found Penelope in the garage. There was nothing he could do to remedy this.

He dialed 911.

Q: *911. What's your emergency?*
A: *Yes, yes.*

Q: *Sir, is this an emergency?*
A: *Yes.*

Q: *What's the address of the emergency?*
A: *The banister. They fell over the banister. Hurry up. 2011 Hawthorne Court.*

Q: What is your name? Explain to me what is going on. Who fell?
A: Edward Pryor. My wife and daughter. They fell over the banister.

Q: Are they breathing?
A: My wife is. She's breathing. I'm a doctor. Please hurry.

Q: What about your daughter?
A: She's not breathing.

Q: Can you perform CPR?
A: I'm a doctor. My wife needs an ambulance. My daughter . . .
there's no need for CPR.

Q: Sir? Please stay on the line. Are you there? Tell me what—
A: Hurry.

Q: Sir, please don't hang—

How was he going to explain this? And it dawned on him then that he didn't know what to say about his whereabouts, his alibi. Such an ugly word. What would he say to the police about where he was when this happened? Don't they play these recorded calls in court, ask the operator what they thought when they took the call, and if the person calling in the emergency sounded genuine? Normal on account of all the circumstances? Too calm? Too hysterical?

Edward didn't hear the ambulance coming. He didn't know why but there must have been sirens, there always are. The sun was up and, so he imagined, the neighborhood was rubbernecking. The phone in his pocket didn't vibrate. There were no calls, no voice mails, no texts. No one came over to check on them—they were friends but not that close.

He knew the paramedics needed free rein of the scene but his body wouldn't move. A pair of strong hands pulled Edward to the side. The medics wore black uniforms with neon stripes across their chests. They worked quickly, one pumped the manual ventilation bag and the other placed a central line in Donna's forearm. She looked pale and limp.

Three men in police uniforms. They didn't ask many questions but when they did, the words just bounced right off him. All he said, and kept repeating over and over, was *I don't know* and *I found them this way* and *how did this happen*.

He caught sight of Penelope. Gloved hands placed her on top of white plastic that reminded him of Donna's garment bags. She lay with arms stiff by her sides, head turned away from him. No one was rendering aid, no one was pumping her chest or administering fluids. White material bunched up by her sides. The blood drained from his face, and his forehead and cheeks and chin went slack as his pragmatic mind stumbled into reality; this was a body bag. One of the officers stepped in front of him and shielded his eyes from the unfolding scene but Edward knew that they were zipping up the plastic and placing his daughter's body on a stretcher. Outside, an ambulance took off, hurriedly with aggressive speed.

Edward stepped into an alcove and the foyer no longer was in his line of vision—*detach detach detach*—but something was knotted around his foot, attached to a bloody mess of leather. He yanked at it, flexed his calf muscle, but it didn't budge. It wasn't until he recognized the woman's bloody tote bag, which he had dropped in the foyer earlier among the shards and blood, that he began to panic. His heart clenched like a fist in his chest. He bent down and slipped the strap off his foot. When he tried to straighten his body, pain set in. Pain so searing he remained hunched over. A tightening had been building up for the past hour or so but he had dismissed it. *I'm having a panic attack,* he thought, *there's nothing wrong with my heart*.

Edward watched the dead woman's tote getting dragged across crystal shards and bloody beaded chains and shattered glass arms. The medics dragged their boots through it all, one tripped over a brass finial, then his foot got caught up in the tote but he kicked it loose.

His breathing was rapid and shallow. He felt clammy. He wasn't worried then, his lipid panels were perfect, he had just had a calcium scan. His lips must have turned blue or somehow he gave the medic reason to suspect a cardiac arrest because they put him onto a stretcher, moving slowly with all the blood and shards and glass on the floor.

He passed his daughter's body in the foyer. More pain in his chest. Ripping and searing, so strong he couldn't bring a single thought to completion. How could . . . ? Why did this . . . ? Into an ambulance where the odors of chemicals numbed his nose, speeding off as the drip and metal parts of the stretcher rattled.

Edward followed their commands. He opened his mouth when prompted and they sprayed nitroglycerine under his tongue. He took an aspirin, felt a prick in his forearm where the medic inserted a line. He wanted to cry, to lament what he had done, what they all had done, but all he could think of was how, if prompted, in answer to the question *where were you when your wife and daughter fell,* he'd say *I had a heart attack.*

Something tore at him. The image of a heart enclosed in a sack of tough tissue, the pericardium, attached to the breastbone and the diaphragm. Why did it feel like it was being ripped from his chest?

48

EDWARD

They stabilized Edward Pryor and the cardiologist confirmed his excellent health—any kind of cholesterol level or triglyceride value or any ratio thereof was in perfect range—and called it a stress heart attack.

"This was a lot to deal with, Dr. Pryor, you have our sincerest condolences. Your wife's recovering. You can see her as soon as she wakes up. Her hip was shattered but they were able to fix it. Brand-new part, top-of-the-line technology. It'll last forever. The orthopedic surgeon will brief you on that. It'll be a long recovery but she'll be fine."

The doctor didn't mention Penelope but for the condolence part. No one questioned him regarding that night. Not until the police showed up. A young man in a crisp suit appeared. A bulge on his right hip, under his jacket. A holstered weapon. Edward looked down at the detective's polished shoes and chose his words carefully; a troubled young daughter, the overwhelming grief, he used words like *gutted* and *beside ourselves*.

"Please don't talk to my wife just yet, she's in no condition," he added, well aware of how this could go wrong right then and there. What if there was an officer at Donna's bedside at this very moment questioning her?

But the detective didn't ask for details, *it's all just a formality, nothing criminal*, he assured him. They could talk *some other time, it was not necessary to get into it just now*. Edward thanked him. And just like that the encounter was over.

An hour later, they pushed his wheelchair into Donna's room. Her lower body lay elevated, her hips propped up. There were tiny cuts on her cheeks and the palms of her hands which would heal in no time. When the door closed behind the nurse, he leaned in.

"What happened while I was gone?" Edward asked quietly.

There was this implication, *while I was gone*, that unspoken part of that day, *while I drove the lifeless body of a woman away from our house. What did you do to Penelope?*

They looked at each other as long as either one of them could stand and then looked away.

49

DONNA

After I was discharged from the hospital, I returned to Hawthorne Court and a cloak hung over me. That's how I thought of it, a heavy cloak weighing me down, keeping me from moving. Aside from the hip injury, there was this fog. My mind was a black hole and it was difficult to make sense of anything. When I did get out of bed, those few steps from bed to bathroom and back, I'd pass by a mirror and wonder who that woman was.

Edward cared for me. Clumsily he brought me food I didn't eat, stacked books on the nightstand I wouldn't so much as touch, opened windows to air out the bedroom. His facial expression was dead, not like a poker face but lifeless, his eyelids drooping, his face beginning to melt like wax. Unshaven and slouching, drunk with fatigue night after night, caring for me.

My hip improved. I learned to sit up, then stand, then walk. Though the joint healed as expected, my limbs were no longer mine. They were too heavy for me, like I was straining against far more than gravity.

"Donna, talk to me," Edward said and held my hand, trying to pinpoint the cause for my behavior, trying to reason with it but always coming up short. His touch felt foreign to me. My mouth wouldn't move though my thoughts tumbled.

He went on and on.

Tell me what happened that night?

Try to remember, Donna.

Tell me, please.

I need to know what happened, please try to remember.

Donna. Donna. Donna.

It was like a game Edward played, all those demands, then he abandoned them just to repeat them the next day.

I had no words for him. My thoughts were foggy, his questions forceful and tedious. The answers in my head were unassailable. What was I to do? I lay there and rolled my tongue over my teeth, one at a time. I tasted the gold cap on the top left molar, metallic, like a piece of iron candy in my mouth.

As I learned to walk again, everything, including myself, was a puzzle I didn't know how to solve.

50

EDWARD

The longer Edward studied Donna, the more apparent it became that something wasn't right. Unlike the house, which had been restored to its former glory—minus Penelope's room, which remained unaltered behind the closed door—Donna's nicks, cuts, and bruises had faded, her hip had healed, but she refused to speak.

Donna ruminated in her room, only got up to go to the bathroom, and the woman who had always been so put together, who sat ramrod straight on the couch in heels to read a book, who never missed a nail appointment or skipped a root touch-up, lay in bed and couldn't be bothered to take a shower. There were moments it hit him that she was a mother who had lost a daughter, and he understood how she might be unable to shake that.

The doctors were as flabbergasted as he was; other than the hip, Donna was physically unharmed. It seemed as if the biohazard company had cleaned the house and scrubbed the floors and cracks in the marble tile, that floor the only witness of what had happened that night, had taken her tongue.

"Donna, tell me what happened while I was gone?" he'd ask her over and over. He couldn't bring himself to be more specific. What was he supposed to say . . . *while I was out disposing of a dead woman's body?*

He gave her an account of that day, blow by blow, as if he could lead her to the truth by concentrating on the facts. He told her the minute details of the day leading up to a certain point but what he wanted to do was ask the hard questions. *What happened in that room? Why were the windows nailed shut? Why were there holes in the walls? I was gone for two hours, what happened in those hours?*

And then he asked her, "Did you push Penelope?"

Donna stared straight ahead.

Edward did his best to convey to Donna the chaos in his mind. He didn't just want answers; he *needed* answers. Did she not see his desperation, did she not realize how haggard he was, how he struggled to understand? All those questions rattling around in his head—What happened? What did you do?—and he'd take her hand in his and hold it tight as if he could draw the words out of her that way, like some sort of parlor trick.

While Donna remained silent, trapped in her body, his days went on with full awareness of that night, and certain decisions he wasn't equipped to make, he had to handle, like arrangements for Penelope's body.

As Edward entered the funeral home, he was shaking as if he was hooked up to an epinephrine drip. The interior was somber, with lots of potted flowers and sconces, and heavy with the sorrows of people who had passed through. In the foyer, above a vase filled with flowers smelling sickly sweet, he caught a glimpse of himself in a mirror. His face appeared in his vision like a stranger's, mere skin stretched over a shaky jaw. The funeral director, a pudgy man in a brown suit, was too young for this business, in Edward's opinion. His handshake lasted too long, and the fact that he used the expression *she was called home* proved too much for him.

"What do I do now?" Edward asked, his voice quivering as he leaned against a wall.

"Have you decided on a burial or a cremation? Are you interested in a wake, a memorial service?"

They'd never so much as discussed a place where they'd be buried as a couple, they hadn't spoken about their mortality at all, never considered a family plot or a specific cemetery. The thought of a graveside disturbed him—wreaths and flowers and a funeral and people dressed in black, a headstone that said *Beloved Daughter*.

Edward pointed at the rows of urns on glass shelves at the back wall.

"Cremation," Edward said and stepped closer. All those urns, some metal, some ceramic, some so removed from their purpose, vaselike, nothing but the lid giving their purpose away. Picking an urn was not a choice he wanted to make himself, yet he stood in front of the display and his eyes wandered back and forth as if he was watching a tennis match.

"Take your time, Dr. Pryor."

"I am," Edward said and wondered if the man was naturally compassionate or if he had learned empathy the same way Edward had unlearned it.

"This is a very personal decision, Dr. Pryor. If it's too difficult at this point, we can always use a simple metal container and you can pick a final urn at a later date."

"I don't know much about these things. What happens with the urn after?"

"That's a personal decision also. You can have it deposited at a final resting place underground, you can arrange for a space at a columbarium, or you can scatter the ashes."

"What should I do?" Edward asked, more a question to himself than to the funeral director. "I don't know which one to pick."

"If you don't like any of the samples we have here, there's a catalog I can get for you?"

"That won't be necessary," Edward said and pointed at an urn. "This one will do."

He had Penelope cremated, without fanfare, but couldn't bring himself to pick up her ashes and so he had the urn delivered to the house by the crematorium staff. He thought about purchasing space at a columbarium big enough to hold three eight-by-eight-inch urns but didn't want to make that decision without Donna weighing in. He still had moments when he wanted her input, but then realized he had picked the urn Donna would have hated the most, a crackled container with gaudy leaves as handles.

51

EDWARD

Edward had picked out the urn and that very night he paced around the house, unable to come to terms with anything, unable to grieve. Something gnawed on him. He couldn't verbalize it, but it brewed in the back of his head. Donna's ability to shut it all out, to remain silent, to leave him in this misery. Donna faking some sort of condition was the only logical explanation. A more likely diagnosis he couldn't imagine and so he went with that and pretended he believed her. But what about him? Was he just another casualty? And if Donna wasn't talking, who could? And the cogs began to turn, the gears engaged, and an idea snapped into place. Rachel, the woman, though dead, had a lot to say.

What Edward did next was outrageous, he had to admit that, but desperation was known to push logic aside and so he did what he had to do.

It was a rookie move. He *had had had* to know how Penelope

ended up with the woman in her jeep. He *must must must* understand, had never wanted anything as bad, as if he was just going to
collapse to the ground if he didn't get his way. His need to know
was stronger than his need for self-preservation, he knew he was
teetering off the edge, the only part of his body clinging to the cliffs
were his fingertips, if that. This rookie move just added to his overall feeling of being found out sooner rather than later.

He called Dr. Price, a man he had met decades ago on one of his
rotations, and somehow they had ended up in the same city in the
same social circles down the road and attended many of the same
functions over the years.

Edward dialed his number and held his breath. When Price answered, after a minute of pleasantries, he forced himself to get right
to it.

"Edward, I've known you for many years. With all due respect,
may I ask why you are so interested in this case?" he had asked him
and rightfully so.

Edward had feared that question and hadn't come up with a believable reason. *A friend of my daughter's* might backfire, depending
on the course the case was going to take. That his office had performed surgery on her was far-fetched. He almost didn't care what
Dr. Price thought of his request and that was a dangerous state of
mind to be in.

"Professional curiosity. It's been a while since I attended one."
That wasn't a lie and it might get him in the room with white sub-
way tile and coolers for bodies like post office boxes.

"Okay?" Dr. Price sucked in air, then sighed. "That doesn't make
it any clearer but be my guest."

The next day, Edward watched Dr. Price's face hidden behind a
medical face mask and a plastic shield, positioning and then dragging the scalpel from shoulder to sternum, right shoulder first, then
left, and then down to the pubic bone, exposing her ribs and mus-

cles. He began to snip the ribs with rib cutters that reminded Edward of pruning shears.

Taking out the brain took the longest, a loud whirring saw cut off the top of the skull. There were hammers involved, then came the moment during the autopsy when his senses began to be assaulted: everything reeked. Gallbladder bile smelled sour and acidic, the bowels were earthy, almost muddy. He got light-headed but forced himself to watch one organ after another being removed. The medical examiner point at individual bruises on Rachel Dunlap's body.

"Cause of death?" Edward asked, attempting to speed it along.

"On appearance," Dr. Price told him, "a front bumper made contact with her hip and upper thigh region. An SUV probably, not a sedan. That impact caused the rotation of her upper body, the legs turned sideways before her right side made contact with the ground, her chest and shoulder region, to be exact. Resulting in multiple rib fractures."

Edward waited with anticipation. "I don't understand," he said and squinted, barely glancing at the body in front of him. This sounded as insignificant as a fall from a bike.

"She was struck by a vehicle traveling at an approximate speed of ten to fifteen miles an hour. She was not killed on impact. Internal bleeding did her in."

Edward blinked, trying to understand the implications.

"A perfect storm," Dr. Price continued. "There are not always outward symptoms to warn injured victims that they are in jeopardy. She probably felt fine for a while. A trip to an emergency room, a trauma center prepared for this type of injury would have saved her life. Once the lungs were perforated and her chest began to fill with blood, the injuries became life-threatening in a matter of—"

"What are the odds," Edward interrupted.

"Odds? Happens more often than you think."

"How long until it was too late? Until she bled out?"

"It started internally. See here." Dr. Price looked up at Edward and pointed at the vena cava. "There's the rupture. By the time she felt light-headed and had abdominal pain, it was too late. Twenty minutes from that point at the most. Give or take. She could have been saved but like I said, the perfect storm."

The perfect storm. So little time. How quickly Penelope would have had to act to save her. Calling an ambulance might not have been enough. She could have alerted someone, anyone who was better prepared to handle this situation, yet it seemed impossible to put all this decision-making on his daughter. It sounded so far out of her reach.

"You said an SUV?"

"You are looking for an SUV with very little damage," Dr. Price continued. "I found no glass on the body so the windshield didn't shatter." He had paused and taken in a deep breath. "You hit the right spot at the right angle and that's all it takes. Probably didn't know what hit her."

"What's the cause of death?"

"I'll classify COD as vehicular blunt force trauma. The crime scene was a riddle for me at first. Not a drop of blood anywhere and a body void of blood." He stretched his mouth into a grimace. "That's the stuff urban legends are made of." He cocked his head. "If it rained that night, that would explain it," he said and zipped up the body bag. "Depends on how heavy the rain was."

"Are there any leads?"

"I don't understand this, Edward. Is there anything you need to know specifically—"

"No, I just, I've taken an interest, ever since, you know . . . they died the same night and . . ." Edward didn't finish the sentence.

Dr. Price placed his right hand against his chest in what Edward took as an attempt to convey that he understood his pain. His desperation.

"Edward . . ."

"Yes?"

"I'm so sorry about your daughter, I know there are no words . . ." He paused as if he'd caught himself in a moment telling a grieving father how to mourn his child.

Edward left and when the door closed behind him, he was glad Price hadn't mentioned Donna at all. There was no telling what he might have confessed.

He sat in his car in the parking lot and it was then he remembered the tomatoes from his mother's garden, the way she lined them up in single-file rows with a walking path between each one and how puny they were and had to be left to ripen off the vine because there was never enough sun in Ohio. He attempted to escape from the present with those memories but even his mother's tomatoes reminded him of blood, and all he wanted to do was rest, pace his thoughts, and he'd be fine but at the same time he knew something was going to trip him up. He began to shake and he knew he'd go home and wash his hands over and over for the better part of an hour. Now that he'd seen Rachel again, he'd try to scrub away the blood he knew he still had on his hands after that night but they'd never feel clean. He was sure of that.

He still knew very little about that night, the state of the woman's body just a consequence of Penelope's action, yet what that action was motivated by, he still couldn't tell. Did Penelope know the woman? That had been tearing at him, the not knowing part a vampire feeding on him, sucking the life force out of him, as if knowing the why of the accident would extend to the why of his very own failings. In his mind he went over it but the gaps were going to claim his sanity, soon.

Though he felt as if he was searching for all those answers at once, he still had some fight in him. Some, not much. But some. Donna would come around so he could sort it all out. She had to.

52

EDWARD

Edward was unable to work. He spilled his coffee every morning. The tremor in his hands, which used to kick in while he was doing something, just to go away when he was not, had turned from intermittent into a steady rhythmic shaking. His fingers were slow, as if weighed down, and felt thick and clumsy.

What happened?
What happened?
What happened?
What happened?

How many more times could he ask Donna and not get an answer?

Weeks passed and Donna didn't so much as utter a word. Edward's life had become a never-ending circle of caretaking, of washing and dressing her, bringing her food.

There was a picture on the wall opposite from Donna's bed, and he saw her stare at it every day, some expressionist garden scene with women gathering around a table. In a spur of the moment, Edward tipped the painting slightly to the right.

The very next day Donna pointed at it. Two months into her silence, Donna had come back to life, gesturing and making demands to fix a lopsided picture on the wall. The day after, it was a chair turned on a wrong angle. The morning after that, Donna woke with a voice as raw as sandpaper.

"Where is Penelope?"

Edward was taken aback at first, thought her to be in a half-sleep state where reality hadn't quite set in yet. He caught something in her eyes that made him pause—there was no hint of knowing, just a mundane question to which she expected a mundane answer. *At work. In her room. Shopping. Out.*

Edward held her hand, stroked her cheek. He explained it to her. He told her about the cremation, about how he planned to buy a niche, a compartment within the columbarium at the cemetery, where Penelope's memorial would be maintained in perpetuity.

He cried. She cried. A burst of emotions, crying and carrying on. Then she descended back into silence.

The following morning she asked again. He stared at her but she wouldn't break his gaze and he realized she had completely exiled the truth of that night. He couldn't make sense of it. If she didn't recall that night, what was she mourning? If she didn't remember Penelope's death, who was she grieving?

There was only one logical explanation.

Edward drove Donna to the hospital, consulted a neurologist, the best money could buy. "She's faking it," he told the neurologist. "Nothing's medically wrong with her but she can't remember? Or won't? To be honest, she'd been making a lot of strange choices before this all happened." It was the only explanation he could think of, since any kind of brain injury had been ruled out. He insisted on it. "She's acting. What else could it be? We've exhausted every avenue there is."

"I have looked over your wife's file and the doctors have been thorough. I can't think of a single test I'd run. As far as pretending not to remember, that will prove difficult to diagnose, because it's not a diagnosis in itself. I want to caution you to not focus on that alone. It'll take time to figure this out. The decline more so than the state of a patient tells us the direction they're heading in and the subsequent diagnosis. We shouldn't jump the gun just yet. There's a number of things this could be. Or like you said, it's nothing at all."

"What else can I do?" Edward demanded. Certainly waiting for new symptoms to appear wasn't the answer here. He couldn't take this teetering back and forth between silence and absolute despair for much longer, every time she mentioned Penelope. "There must be something. Anything."

"Maybe you should take her to a psychiatrist. It might all be psychosomatic," the doctor said.

A week later they sat in the waiting room of a psychiatrist who specialized in emotional and behavioral disorders, as well as in neurology. Donna entered the office and emerged thirty minutes later.

"How did it go?" Edward asked as he helped her into the car.

She seemed slow to Edward, delayed in her responses, yet she was able to relay questions the psychiatrist had asked. Later, at lunch at a restaurant, their first real outing since Penelope's death, she complained about the apron color of the waiters and faint stains on the tablecloth. She was Donna, yet there was a sense about her that Edward, for lack of a better word, called *improvising*. Donna was improvising her life, if there was such a thing. And he waited for her to take a turn either way.

. . .

As much as Donna disregarded Edward's need to know, she was relentless in her very own pursuit of the truth. Every morning she posed the same question to him—"Where is Penelope?"—and every morning he relayed to her what had happened. The accident. The blood. His disposing of the body. His return to the house. Their bodies in the foyer. He whispered it to her at first, in an attempt to lessen the blow, but as days went by he changed from an elaborate account to a shortened version just to end up at a bare-bones description and a statement containing only three words: "Penelope is dead."

Every morning, he killed Penelope again with his words and every morning Donna relived the moment. Every morning she sat in shock, then cried and wailed and buried her face in her hands. Over and over and over. Every morning he showed her the urn on the mantel, and every morning she asked to touch it and she clenched it like little girls hold on to baby dolls.

Slowly but surely Donna came around, was quicker to respond, even began to brush her teeth and take showers on her own. One day, she demanded he dye her roots, and he applied the chemicals and then rinsed her hair while she sat in the tub. He stared at her neck, her vertebrae protruding, and he thought of his daughter and her broken C1, 2, and 3 vertebrae, and as the water ran down her neckline and the towel he had propped up caught the drops, they turned red and he pressed his eyes shut and when he opened them again, they were just water and Donna stared at him with a quizzical look on her face.

"Thank you, darling," she said and kissed the palm of his hand.

Then a phone call came from the police. A detective was coming by to ask Donna some questions.

53

EDWARD

Just finally paying you a visit," the detective said after the condolences, acting nonchalant as if he had decided to pop by while he was in the neighborhood. Edward had been declining the visit for weeks but there was only so long he could keep the police at bay.

Edward had made rules inside his head for the interview. He didn't want the detective in the bedroom upstairs, determined to keep him as far as possible from Penelope's room and the banister, the bare ceiling where the chandelier used to be. He led Donna to the top of the stairs and she held on to the railing with one hand and placed a crutch on the side of the injured hip. It took them forever to get to the bottom of the stairs and Edward had planned it that way. Who would interrogate a woman this fragile, this helpless, he wondered. From there, with the detective following them, he steered her into the living room and toward a chair, where he draped a blanket over Donna's thighs. She sat angelic and fragile in her blond and privileged beauty, her filled and peeled skin surprisingly holding up well, her perfectly capped teeth, her formerly Botoxed forehead, now frowning occasionally. But she was no longer passing for late thirties. And there were the bags under her eyes.

Detective Lee was in his fifties. Tall. Lean. Ill-fitting suit. Paying a visit. What a polite thing to do.

"Tell me what happened that night?" Detective Lee asked and leaned forward, his hands flat on his thighs.

Donna seemed hard of hearing and cocked her head as if she was listening to a voice coming from afar but didn't say a word.

"Can you tell me what happened?" The detective raised his voice, not by much, but it came across as strict.

Donna flinched. She wasn't used to being spoken to in a harsh tone.

"I need to know what happened so we can close the case. Like I said, a formality."

"Penelope, she, I just don't know, she . . ."

Edward watched his wife collect herself—the deep breath, the elongated spine, the lifted chin, yet her glossy eyes gave it away. She was approaching the edge of her calm state. Rub some dirt on it, he thought, but then regretted it. They were in this together, he reminded himself. What befalls her, befalls me.

Donna and Detective Lee were getting nowhere. She had paused to pour tea, and Edward wondered what was next. The more Donna got to talk, the more likely she'd slip up. Had he not told her to allude to an appointment or a migraine or something? He just wanted to get it over with, but at the same time he didn't want the detective to make the trip out again.

Edward watched the detective scan the rugs, the furniture, the paintings, down to the antique tea set with steaming earl or lord or whatever tea Donna had requested. She didn't brew it herself, he had made the tea and set it down on the coffee table and it was fragrant in a citrusy way, making him nauseous, and he wished she hadn't insisted on it.

The detective was drawing conclusions about his family, Edward could tell. The items in this room alone were worth more than a detective makes in a lifetime. It hardly qualified as a room, given the architecture, the size, and the ceiling height. The detective stared at the coffee table, at the framed family photograph at a cabin, a wooden sign on the door, *Carpe Diem. Seize the day.* The word *cabin* was misleading, the expansive porch with a lake behind them was somewhere between luxury and extravagance. Look at us, Edward thought, what an epitome of a successful family we are. Were, he corrected himself.

"Mrs. Pryor. I don't mean to rush you, but we are trying to close the file, figure out why your daughter did this. This is really just a formality."

Edward had to give it to the detective. He was diplomatic, sensitive, and appropriate. He was reminded of his very own bedside manner, something he was good at, there never had been one complaint in all those years. Not one.

It was then that Donna's composure took a turn. Something in her cracked.

"Wait, just wait," Donna pleaded, "just give me a minute. I have to think about this. I can't quite remember. Wait. Wait. Wait." She balled her hand into a fist, beating it rhythmically against her forehead. "I'm trying to . . . you know . . . I don't really . . ." Donna paused for a second. "All that blood, I had never seen so much blood. It was everywhere," she stammered, then collected herself. "We thought, you know, Penny sometimes took it too far, and when Edward told me—"

"Don't get upset. It's okay." Edward patted Donna's back, then squeezed her hand. "My wife is not well, as you can see. I don't think we should continue questioning today. I've tried. A psychia-

trist has tried. There's just no use, not at this point," Edward explained. "She's trying to come to terms with everything, I'm not
sure how much she remembers, if at all. I'm as confused as you are,
as she is. We are going to cut this short."

"I don't want to cause any—"

"Detective," Edward interrupted and paused as if he couldn't remember his name. It had been coming to this point for a long time
and it was only a matter of time until it all went down the drain, all
for naught. "Lee, was it? Detective Lee. My wife is hardly in the
condition to endure any more questions. She lost her daughter, Detective, her only daughter. Our only daughter. I doubt she'll be able
to tell you any more than she already has. We'll have our lawyer
draw up a statement and you can refer back to it. It will be as detailed as possible and if you have any questions, I'd appreciate it if
you contact our lawyer."

Detective Lee left and Edward sat in the spot where the detective had sat earlier. He looked around, wanting to see this room the
way the detective had, wanted to be able to judge what kind of man
he assumed him to be as if he was unclear about it himself. He
came up empty. Instead he wondered if the cleaning people came in
with ladders given the ceiling height of the rooms. A realization: he
had no clue. Where had he been all those years? Why did he not
know anything? Another one: from now on Edward had to be
afraid of someone insisting on speaking with Donna. He anticipated she would one day, out of the blue, tell a random person—a
doctor, a nurse, or a neighbor—what had happened that day.

*My daughter Penelope killed a woman and brought the body to our
house.*

The tower would crumble then.

54

EDWARD

Edward did his best but the care of Donna was overwhelming. He was ill equipped, he wasn't proud of that, but he wasn't cut from that kind of cloth. There was no end to her needs and at the forefront was always that one thought: he'd never be able to hire people to do the caring for him. He was afraid she'd let the truth slip. He didn't kid himself, there was still more rock to this rock bottom he was living in, they hadn't reached the lowermost rung of that ladder quite yet.

Donna went from silent to blabbering all day, a constant retelling of stories—the Tour of Homes with the Miss Texas gown and sash was one she kept going back to over and over. It left him wanting to rip her throat out. He had told her then how ridiculous it was but she was dead set on staging the house. She created an entire playroom, even. Who does that? No one in their right mind but she had committed herself to what she called *telling a story*.

But he was one to talk. Edward wasn't in his right mind either. The grief he felt for his daughter, this gasping for air at the most unexpected moments, as he awoke at night, every time the phone rang, that was something that would ease with time, but in the meantime he wasn't good for anything, hadn't been to work in weeks, had neglected all his obligations and was utterly useless in general.

Donna had half a million dollars' worth of X-rays and MRIs and ultrasounds, genetic analyses, and evaluations—insurance paid for everything but Edward had seen the paperwork, the outrageous dollar amounts spent to get to the bottom of it—and he even insisted on the most far-fetched hereditary genetic workups but not a single result presented a diagnosis. Money couldn't buy him clarity when it came to Donna.

There was but one consensus: there was no trauma, no injury, her daughter's body had all but broken her fall and if it wasn't for her shattered hip, Donna was unscathed.

The fall. Edward had suspicions. Not knowing what had transpired between mother and daughter tore at him. Had Donna caused the fall? Had she tried to keep Penelope from jumping? Why had it come to that? And the condition of the room, what was that all about? What had Donna done to his daughter? He was quick to assign fault, though he didn't like thinking of Donna that way, but he didn't trust her at all, hadn't trusted her in a while.

He'd get to the truth, if it was the last thing he'd do.

55

EDWARD

Sometimes, at night, he'd wake and feel someone touch his shoulder. He had no explanation for it, he didn't think it was Penelope from the afterlife, the dead capable of making contact was nothing he prescribed to, as a physician he believed in brain waves and loss of brain activity and therefore he categorically refused to believe in such silly notions. What he knew for sure was he'd be perpetually and constantly living with a sense of guilt and anxiety—did they find out, were they on to him?—and that insecurity, that painful anticipation he couldn't deal with. He'd never be safe and eventually the fear made way for some certainty, *it's a matter of time,* a nervous kind of energy that tingled through him like electrical sparks, gathering in his toes.

The day came when the urge to end this state seemed more pressing than ever before and he woke and no longer wondered where he'd find the strength to go on but with a sudden surge of momentum he opened the windows and let fresh air in the house. He went online and located an agency for domestic employees. When he spoke with a woman on the phone, her cheerful and bubbly voice reminded him of some sort of normalcy among the bleakness that were his days and he politely asked her if people still used the word *housekeeper* or if they had a new title, like *household employee* or *domestic worker*. He didn't wait for an answer and instead told her to send someone and if it worked out, that would be great; if not, she could just pick someone else for him.

"There's been a tragedy in the family. A death. I'm trying to cope," he said, aware that his voice was raw with emotion.

Marleen knocked on the door the very next day. She ordered groceries and called a cleaning service to give the house a good scrubbing, top to bottom. Edward told her to leave Penelope's room untouched as if at some later time, when he had gained enough distance and space, he'd be able to tackle that part of his life.

Marleen was understanding—or used to taking orders, he couldn't be sure—but she never so much as furrowed a brow.

There was something about Marleen that put Edward at ease. They'd sit and talk and Edward would find words that had been sitting on the tip of his tongue for months and she seemed to draw those out of him as if she recognized his suffering.

He did damage control the only way he knew how.

"Donna gets confused about things," he said. "About Penelope and what happened to her. Maybe it's, oh, I couldn't tell you, I don't want to guess, but she makes up things, like she can't help but fill in the blanks. And she has said horrible things. That Penelope killed someone and that, oh, I can't even talk about it," he added, covering his face with his hands.

Donna had almost let it slip before, the first time with Detective Lee, who had come to interview her, and if it wasn't for Edward cutting it short, she might have spilled it all. Then another time in front of a doctor, she had muttered something about *blood* and *car* and *death* and Edward had panicked, had ushered her out of the room. It wasn't until he met Marleen that he figured out what he should have done all along: tell people Donna was out of her mind. *Riddled with grief but unaware of what happened* were the words he used from then on.

Marleen assured him that she'd never tell anyone about Donna's *outbursts*—a word he'd also come to use—and she wouldn't tell a soul about anything regarding the death of Penelope.

"You know, maybe it's this house," Marleen added and rubbed her upper arms as if some chill had burst into the room. "Maybe she should recover in a different place. On neutral ground, so to speak. Where her mind can start fresh."

"You don't understand," Edward said. "Donna picked out every doorknob and every light fixture in this house. Every single piece of furniture. She wouldn't want to be away."

"There are places that can accommodate her," Marleen had said, and Edward leaned in closer.

As he listened to Marleen, for the first time in a long time he saw all that had been irking him, all that had ached inside of him, this jumble that had been his life lately, he saw it dissolve. Maybe he could solve the puzzle after all.

Two months later Edward looked into the place Marleen had mentioned to him. His initial hesitation turned into *that'll show her,* he thought. *If she can go on pretending, she might as well do it some place else.*

"Donna," he said in a stern voice, "we can't go on like this. I need you to get better. I found a place for you to recover and in the meantime just concentrate on that. And I'll do the same."

Where else was she going to go? She would be destitute if it wasn't for him. He'd watch the progression of it all but he had a feeling she'd play that blabbering idiot to perfection, that role she'd pull off like the flawless actress she was. Supporting her financially was a small price to pay as he considered the alternative: being trapped in this house with Donna until they both expired. If she was going to act like she was crazy he might as well lock her away and leave her to rot.

Marleen agreed to accompany Donna to oversee her convalescence at Shadow Garden. After Donna left, the house was empty, the scent of lemon cleaner hung in the air, the stuffiness that had seeped into the curtains had been washed away but he was alone and that was something he wasn't prepared for.

Edward stood by the back door, saw the woods in the distance, so menacing, as if they wanted to convey to him how utterly isolated he was. He stepped into the backyard for the first time in a long time. Not knowing what he would do in this big house all by himself—the outdoor kitchen neglected, the lawn chairs covered in the spatter of green and white droppings—all seventeen rooms and the expansive lawn, the pool, the pool house.

He could downsize. He could sell the practice, the patents were enough to guarantee him a pleasant life, maybe not one in Hawthorne Court with seventeen rooms, but something half the size. One third of this house would do, maybe a town house. Some distance and maybe he'd be up for performing surgeries again. He'd wait it out, see what was in store for him.

In the kitchen he found a ripped-open envelope and began making a list of what all had to be done to restore the house so he could sell it and move on.

He was hopeful. That day he was hopeful.

56

EDWARD

It started off inconspicuously, like the flu creeping up on him, with a general fatigue at first, followed by a headache and a sore throat, culminating into a full-blown fever. He smelled blood everywhere. He couldn't stand for doors to be closed, couldn't stand the scent of floor cleaner and silver polish, all those odors left behind by the people who cleaned his house because just below it, just beneath the pine scent, there was a stench of blood, a layer of stink he couldn't get rid of. The stench was everywhere, even in the basement. In the backyard. High and low, inside and out, near and far, here and there.

Blood. Iron atoms. Rusty. Iron cation (Fe2+).

He opened windows which in turn created a cross breeze that made the doors slam shut. Damned if he did, damned if he didn't. *Think about what you did,* the house seemed to say, mocking his every attempt to move on.

Months went by, he could tell by the changing of the seasons, but he didn't feel time pass at all. Often, he woke in the middle of the night and felt a pull toward his daughter's room, which had been sitting untouched since that night. Then one day it dawned on him that it was almost the day of Penelope's death and he could feel the looming anniversary creep into his bones. He was dreading it.

During those wakeful moments, his resentment for Donna grew. She lived carefree and without responsibilities, tucked away at Shadow Garden, and he wanted nothing more but to wash his hands of her but there was something reminiscent of a debt he owed her. He paid her extensive medical bills, she wanted for nothing and he felt he owed that to her. He paid Marleen to care for Donna at Shadow Garden and every so often he stressed the fact that Donna couldn't be trusted. He explained it just right so a possible confession would fall on deaf ears, about Donna's *situation*, and her *cognitive disabilities*, and he was proud of himself that he had managed to leave it basic and open for interpretation.

"She might get confused about what happened," he told Marleen. "She gets confused easily about Penelope and it would be best if you encourage her to stay busy and not ruminate too much. She makes up stories in her head. Wait until you hear the one about the Miss Texas pageant. She'll show you the dress. It's all made up, you can look it up. The sash. The dress, all of it. Just don't argue with her, just give her time to get better."

Not for one minute did he think about Donna returning to Hawthorne Court, for them to resume their marriage, their life together. But the cogs turned. In the back of his mind they turned and revolved around one thing: closure.

The grass had grown long, the seed stalks were higher than the turf by inches, and crabgrass had taken over. Mulch had been washed away by rain, the bushes impeded the view—not that Edward ever enjoyed the view anymore—the woodwork outside had begun to crack, needed a coat of shellac, but he couldn't be bothered. He was aware of the decline, the moribund state of it all.

The neighbors seemed to be waiting for Donna to return, and when she didn't, they began to talk. He noticed them disappearing into garages, stepping back into foyers, or hurriedly slamming car doors and spitting gravel as they sped away. When they saw him on the porch or on the lawn, they turned away without a nod or a greeting, unsure what to make of him, a man in faded pajama pants and a stained T-shirt, and a Scotch plaid flannel robe untied, two sizes too big for him.

Even the book club had moved on, no more selections appeared at the front door and two new houses had been built at the end of the cul-de-sac—New American style. Donna would have something to say about that. Builders had bought most of the parcels that were left and they had begun to divide the plats into smaller lots and cement trucks rolled in, and pneumatic staple guns echoed through Preston Hallow.

Once, at a gas station, he ran into a neighbor. He no longer recalled his name.

"How are things?" the neighbor asked, head cocked to the side, somber, empathetic.

"As expected," Edward replied and looked the man up and down, couldn't remember a single meaningful conversation they had had, though they had met frequently at parties and functions. The wives had their book clubs and lunches but what had the men really talked about? The brand of whiskey they were drinking? Sports wasn't something that was interesting to him, maybe investments, taxes, the best accountant in town?

"How's Donna?" the neighbor asked.

"As expected," Edward said again, as if he had no opinion about anything. It was what it was, and *as expected* wasn't far off.

Edward excused himself, cut the conversation short. "Run along now," he added, as if the man was a child, but he didn't care about him or the neighbors or the house or anything for that matter.

The weekly cleanings had ceased when Marleen left with Donna and though he meant to pick up the phone and hire someone else, he never did. Limbo was what he was in; he couldn't sell Hawthorne Court, had neglected it. No, he had done more than neglect it; he had all but abandoned it, and the list of improvements he had made lay hidden in some drawer. He contacted a real estate agency but avoided the well-known ones that handled luxury homes, didn't want word to get around, all he needed was to get a feel for what it would take to put the house on the market.

A real estate agent came by and as if fate wasn't done handing out suffering, the agent, a young woman in a designer dress, reminded him of Penelope with her flighty way of walking through the house and her attempt to grasp the property and numbers of rooms, randomly asking questions and not taking any notes. The woman was young and inexperienced and nervous and he bristled on the inside and thought of Penelope, who had probably been worse at this job than her.

Before he arranged for Donna to move to Shadow Garden with Marleen, he watched Donna like a hawk. Once, he had coaxed her out of bed, had taken her by the elbow and somehow they ended up talking about that ridiculous light fixture she had insisted on, a "piece of art" she said, a sunburst pendant he'd always despised and which seemed out of place in the otherwise classical style of the home. Donna told him a lengthy story about their trip to Italy, how she had seen a similar piece, and Edward knew this story to be true and so he continuously jogged her memory, and there were things she'd divulge if he jogged her memory just right. It was more Donna letting her guard down than him being sly, and a plan formed in his mind.

That scheme he'd come up with, foolproof one day only to be full of flaws the next, gave him a moment of pause. He ought to try.

57

EDWARD

The plan was as bold as it was far-fetched: he'd surround Donna with things that had some sort of emotional significance attached to them, and eventually, when it all came back to her and all the tiny puzzle pieces culminated into the larger picture—what happened the night Penelope fell to her death—he'd swoop in and she'd come clean.

Marleen had developed a fierce loyalty toward Donna and he had to choose his words carefully so she'd go along with his plan.

"You know about Donna's cognitive problems and the depression. Who could blame her, right, after all she's been through? If we just surround her with things from happier times, she'll perk up a bit. Make an effort to get better. Being here, where it all happened, it was just too much for her. You were right. But she'll come around. I know she will. Just imagine what she's been through. It's such a blessing for her to be able to recover and your help is instrumental, Marleen. I'm so glad I found you."

He began to pick furniture to send to Shadow Garden. Marleen planted items he gave her: a book, her vanity, silverware. A statue. He called them *little seeds of memory* and he hoped they would unsettle Donna enough to remember, and he thought of them like stoking a fire to get it to burst into flames. A slow but steady wearing her down, getting her to connect the dots, until the final breakdown when he'd finally know the truth.

Marleen was oblivious, thought his attempts to comfort Donna heartwarming. He'd let the phone ring twice then he'd hang up and later that night meet her by the door leading to the storage room, a room that she kept locked at all times. He showed up after Donna was asleep or had just taken her medication. He knew he had to be careful; if Donna ever saw him and Marleen together, she'd figure something was up. Donna was smart, she'd pick up on it, he knew that about her. She smelled rats everywhere.

Edward felt guilty in the beginning but eventually manipulating Marleen became easier and easier until it no longer concerned him. To her, the items he picked from Hawthorne Court—and he had an entire room dedicated to them—were meant to give Donna solace during her recovery: photo albums he had painstakingly put together with reminders of a trip to Italy, a picture of Penelope on the beach, a trip to a farm picking strawberries.

All he had to do was wait and Donna would come around. It sounded so logical, so easy, but nothing in his life had proven easy. And like everything else, it all turned sinister quickly.

In the beginning, Donna called him every day, sometimes more than once. He answered the phone for the first two weeks or so and then he let it go to voice mail. Those were just her ramblings, he could tell. *I was wondering* this, and *I don't know* that, on and on she went. Then she began to ask for Penelope, asking him to relay messages to remind her of things, and that's when he let the voice mailbox fill up and then changed his number. She'd get tired of this game soon enough, he thought.

Donna was in a state of flux, it seemed like, and soon she'd be ripe for the taking. That was the evil part of it, the way he caught himself using such phrases and he couldn't believe the person he had become. He had never treated a woman with disdain, had never so much as raised his voice at a nurse or at Penelope, had always been a gentleman and had been proud of it.

But there was more. During those nightly wanderings through the house—he had taken to storing all possible *seeds of memory* in an upstairs guest room—he did get carried away.

The door of a sideboard wouldn't open and instead of tugging at it and prying it open, in a surge of anger, he swiped vases and picture frames to the ground. He ripped the door off its hinges, pulled boxes of photographs out, took a nearby chair, and struck the sidebar once. There was this rush, this irresistible need to do damage and with the chairback—the legs had long come off and the seat lay on the ground—he beat away at the sidebar, at all those neatly organized things in Donna's proper home. He stomped on them, then stood, staring wonderingly at them.

The photographs wouldn't rip, which sent him into another kind of frenzy altogether. They slid out of his hands and he trampled on them but slipped as if on a patch of ice and he thought *accelerant accelerant accelerant* and *burn burn burn* this entire house down.

Pictures came to mind: his college days, the Greek mythology class he'd taken. After Troy was burned to the ground into nothing but blackened and partly melted buildings, the story was the gods were angry because the Greeks had shown such cruelty and therefore had to suffer great hardships before they reached home. The burning of Troy was mythology but nevertheless, Donna was his very own Troy, a city he longed to destroy, never to be rebuilt.

The Greeks couldn't take Troy but through trickery. Donna was Troy and the house was Troy and everything ought to *burn burn burn,* and he feverishly searched for matches but couldn't find any, no lighter either in any of the drawers he ripped *open open open,* sending corkscrews and ladles flying about, and then he found the fireplace lighter, the one with the long metal wand and he *clicked clicked clicked* it but it wouldn't spit out a flame because it had been months since it had been used. Troy was taken with a Trojan horse but he had been sending Trojan horses for months to no avail and he was *lost lost lost* without knowing.

Lighter in hand, he caught himself just in time, but those moments happened more often, he could never tell when he'd go from weepy emotions to anger, to an all-out rage.

Later, in the light of day, he'd see what he had done to his home and he wondered how long he'd go on this way and he knew he'd have to sell the house and start all over but those royalty checks, all that patent money, it kept pouring in and he saw himself spending the rest of his life knocking this house to the ground until it went up in an inferno.

His legacy, Donna had called it, as if bricks and wood and pipes and tile were anything, that was just his *doing,* but his *being* was the patients he had wanted to operate on, all those cleft palates and burn and acid victims, something he'd never got around to. All those years he'd put those causes on the back burner, and there was always something in the way—a house renovation, a vacation, a new plastic surgery suite, you name it—and most of all, Donna had made sure he was busy. But that was over with now, here he was, his hands shaking and trembling and God help him but he knew he'd never again be able to put a scalpel on a body without it slipping.

His *being* was also Penelope, his only child, who he had found in the center of this house, the foyer. Doomed they had been from the start, doomed, all of them.

58

EDWARD

E dward Pryor stopped his car and pulled into the gravel by the side of the road. It was a Friday, dusk was looming but still an hour or so away. He exited the car and stood there. The orange blinking four-way flashers dashed about in well-timed intervals. Through a grove of trees he saw ocher lamppost lights down the road.

This was where he had dumped the woman's body.

In the distance a heavy cloud rolled toward the area, wet and stormy. He shivered. A blue-black mass had been approaching southward, slowly but steadily. A cool, dry, high-pressure system shoved against the warm, moist air of the Gulf, and everyone had been talking about a Blue Norther fast approaching. It was announced on the radio, warning of temperatures about to drop thirty degrees within twenty minutes or less. No one knows the origin of the name, some say it's because of the blue-black sky, some say the sky goes from blue to black and back to blue after the cold front passes, others say one's skin turns blue from the cold.

Fuck if he knew.

He thought in curse words lately, as if some brute had slipped under his skin and taken over the entirety of his being. With his right hand he reached to check the half-Windsor knot but it was more a habit than anything else; there was no tie and he hadn't even bothered to button his shirt.

The wind picked up, swooshed at him. His pores contracted, jerking at the muscles at the roots of his hairs, turning his skin into a layer of miniature bumps. He rolled down the sleeves of his white shirt, buttoned the cuffs, and slid on his coat. His skin settled, the woolen coat keeping the wind at bay. His arms underneath the coat like the skin of a freshly plucked goose, a blend of fear and disbelief and also the drop in temperature, or maybe just another one of those useless feral reactions that served no purpose.

Edward approached the spot where he had dumped the woman. As he had watched Dr. Price perform the autopsy, he had listened to him describe the collision and the injuries, yet Penelope's involvement remained a puzzle.

And then there was information he had gathered from news reports: Rachel Dunlap, thirty-four, was a pharmaceutical sales rep, married, with two stepchildren. She suffered from asthma but had completed a half marathon just two months before she died. In the aftermath of her death, family and friends came together and talked about the best ways to honor her memory. They reflected on how Rachel was passionate about physical fitness and uplifted those new to long-distance running. A memorial fund was established in her honor.

Another report stated that the dispatcher received a call around 9:30 a.m. and that her body was found only a few yards in front of her vehicle, a Nissan, and the car itself was free of any damage yet void of her belongings, though some of them had been strewn about the accident scene. The car sat off by the side of the road on a bed of gravel, neatly parked and unlocked. It wasn't quite a robbery, but it wasn't just an accident either. It was up to the police to figure this out and so far they had been clueless. Not one news report mentioned the lack of blood, but there was always that one fact the police didn't release and it was an open investigation after all.

He had cut out a picture of her from the paper that he carried with him. Her face had become familiar by then, the gentle swoop of the bridge of the nose, the defined jaw, her teeth supporting the lips just right. That woman. It was still hard for him to call her by her name, preferred to refer to her as *that woman*. Crumpling the paper into a ball, stuffing it into the coat pocket, he knew he had to throw it away. Suddenly it felt unnerving to hold on to the picture. What if something happened to him and they found it, then what? Would someone put two and two together?

On foot he followed the road to the next bend. There was nothing but another bend around the corner, nothing to see there. He imagined how, in the dark, the woman might have parked and gotten out of her vehicle for one reason or another, Penelope had approached, unable to stop, unable to avoid her, the turn exposing her as an inattentive or inexperienced driver. Knowing Penelope, that was the likely conclusion to be drawn, but still, he was a scientist and not understanding the world wasn't an option for him, uncertainty equal to torture.

He thought he saw movement out of the corner of his eye but it was just a broken branch dangling off a tree. He took in the area. Another hour and the world would lose color and turn into shades of gray, but for now the orange flashes in the distance dashed about, dowsing the immediate perimeter in a tawny glow. Edward turned and walked in the other direction, past his car, past the park sign, and again there was a bend. He followed the curve, scanning the ground, though the road had been searched extensively, so he assumed, and Edward wasn't really looking for anything specific but it never hurt to keep his eyes open.

Headlights in the distance illuminating the bend in the road. It was an SUV—he couldn't make out the color, black or dark blue maybe—and it slowed down, then stopped. With a hum, the driver's window descended. A man in his fifties leaned out.

"You got car trouble?" he asked.

"What?" Edward stood still, slightly slumped over.

"Something wrong with your car? You need a hand? A ride?"

His mind tumbled. Was this a random person or a detective? Had he been lying in wait past the shoulder, in a gravel verge underneath a tree, invisible from the road? Was he here to catch the criminal returning to the scene of the crime? Edward didn't know if that was just a plot device on detective shows or if criminals really had an inclination to relive their handiwork.

"Your lights are flashing."

This place, this bend in the road. All those trees, the brush, even the painted line in the middle of the road and the cracks in the asphalt of the parking lot were silent witnesses. He wanted to spill it all, just get it over with, but not one word came out of his mouth. He was frozen.

"Are you all right?" A pause, then the man nodded. He pinched his lips. "Just thought I'd ask."

"Everything's fine. Nothing to worry about."

The window ascended and the car sped up and disappeared.

Edward buried his hands in his pockets, the crinkled sphere of paper unnerving as he enclosed it with his fist. He could've sworn he had just felt the temperature drop another ten degrees. Nothing was fine. *Not a goddamn thing.* The man probably was a detective— and what if he put two and two together? Penelope's death, the autopsy he had attended, maybe he got wind of that somehow, that would be the end of it all.

Edward got in his car and got back on the highway, where he

lowered the window just enough to fit the woman's crumpled picture through the gap. The wind grabbed it and in the rearview mirror he watched as it bounced a few times before he lost sight of it. Twenty minutes later he drove down a long winding road leading to Shadow Garden. The Monterrey oaks turned sparse and at the end of the road appeared a building within a circle of jade-colored grass, almost like a moat defending its tenants against some unknown enemy.

The deep-red terra-cotta brick building was the crowning center of the expansive lawn, surrounded by a cast-iron fence common around public parks, the building's border from the rest of the world was ten feet tall with intricate details of Victorian design. Even in the impending darkness he was aware of the comical appearance of it all as he considered the care it took to keep the place somewhere between formal English grounds and touches of whimsical cottage gardens. North Texas wasn't arid by a long shot, but it was far from conducive to elaborate and needy greenery. He imagined a crew of men in orange vests with mowers and hedgers and trimmers descending upon the place, sprinklers dispersing thousands of gallons of water within seconds, three times a day, which was proof that the illusion of Shadow Garden was about man's conquest over the elements, over nature.

Shadow Garden. *Fuck.* That's exactly where Donna belonged.

He slowed the car to a crawl as he approached the entrance, stopping in front of the cast-iron gate surrounded by crape myrtles. He loved crape myrtles because they'd been a favorite of his mother's, that's how he remembered her, on a bench, underneath sprawling domed canopies.

He thought about her as he spent the next ten minutes sitting in the car going back and forth with an invisible voice. The gate guard demanded his name, appointment time, and the name of the person he had an appointment with. He went along with it, didn't complain, and was mostly amused. During that time he called the number he had programmed into this phone, let it ring twice, and then hung up.

The guard's voice informed him through the speaker to proceed to the arched main entrance for car service drop-off and pickup. He parked next to a man in a chauffeur's uniform leaning against a black Buick, on his left a lime-green car with maid service decals.

From the central courtyard, a path led to the individual buildings and it was that walkway Edward took, past a fountain with a copper spigot. There was a certain stillness about the place, a memorial park for the rich where they hide from the rest of the world. He had an almost prophetic feeling then, saw the terra-cotta buildings not far removed from inevitable decay, withering blossoms drifting toward the dark earth, turning to sludge and slime.

Edward stood on the walkway and breathed in the dense air. It was like muddy water, thick and crisp at the same time. The lampposts gave off the faintest of lights, flickering about. They were so dim that they didn't produce any shadows but rather an overall layer of illumination, as if everything was important in this moment, everything deserved equal brilliance.

A hefty gust of wind impaled his pores. There'd been another drop in temperature between the time he had left the park and when he arrived at Shadow Garden and he buttoned his coat and made his way toward the center of the courtyard.

As he approached the building called the Ridge, he suddenly realized he hadn't seen a single soul about but the guards at the gate. Donna's apartment was the first one on the ground floor. He knocked and the door opened. Marleen stood, impeccably dressed, her eyes darting past him, not as if she expected someone else, but as if she was nervous being seen with him.

"Mr. Pryor, how are you?" Marleen asked.

"I'm well, thank you," he said but they both knew it was far from the truth.

"Mrs. Pryor is asleep."

"I figured," he said.

Edward handed Marleen a box. The flaps were open, within it a gaudy ceramic container. He held on to it because Marleen's grasp wasn't quite firm enough.

"Mr. Pryor, I don't—"

"Marleen, please. I would never do anything to cause Donna any kind of—"

"I have always supported your efforts but I'm conflicted about this."

"Please. We talked about this. I just need . . . I can't . . . please just put it on the mantel," he stuttered. "I have to go," he added. The moment Marleen shut the door, he turned and walked away.

Edward sat on a nearby bench with a view of the building. The unit next to the ground floor was clearly inhabited; an elderly woman stood on the balcony. He wasn't sure if he was watching her or she was watching him.

"Excuse me," he said and approached her.

"Yes?" She squinted but made no attempt to use the glasses that dangled on a chain around her neck.

"Do you know the woman on the first floor next to you?"

She eyed him suspiciously. "Who wants to know?" she asked and rolled up the top of a plastic bag she had rummaged through just then. Behind her, between an array of pots with plants and flowers of varying height, sat more plastic bags.

"Do you know her?" he repeated.

He observed her upper body slightly pulling back. She switched on the overhead light and he got a better look at her. The woman was sixty, maybe older. Her gray bob was immaculate, and she wore discreet makeup. She had been attractive once upon a time, and there was something to be said about the good old aging-with-grace thing. He couldn't imagine any scalpel making her more beautiful.

She looked him up and down, her eyes squinted, her lips pressed tight. "Am I required to give you an answer?" she said, then added, "I guess you can find out if you want to, right?"

"Do you know each other? Donna Pryor? Your neighbor?" He made his voice sound low and monotone, as if this was of no concern to him. "Do you ever talk to her?"

The woman pulled her shawl tighter.

"Did she tell you about her daughter?" he asked. "It's quite a tragedy. Does she ever, you know, mention her?"

The woman took a step toward the patio door. Edward didn't want her to just disappear into the building, and he scrambled for ways to prolong the conversation.

"I thought maybe you'd know something about her, being out here, with your flowers and everything."

"I'm not out a lot. I couldn't tell you anything."

"Those hydrangeas there, I didn't know they bloom this late in the year," Edward said and pointed at the bushy pink heads.

"Depends on the variety. Some do, some don't."

"Well, they seem to be doing well."

"A little care goes a long way," she said.

"I saw them from all the way over there. How do you get them to grow so large?"

"Just luck, I guess," she said and looked around as if to make sure no one was listening.

"I guess so," Edward said.

If she ever talks about Penelope, will you let me know? He wanted to say that but he didn't. He imagined a blank page with all his questions and below he'd scribble Penelope, Penny, and Pea, *if she ever mentions those names, call me, tell me what she said,* but that seemed counterproductive, it might only confuse her or make him appear unstable.

"Does she ever talk about her daughter?" he insisted, then caught himself. "Please don't think I'm a creep or anything like that, but she . . . she—"

"You act like one. Since you're wondering."

"Your name is?" Edward asked.

"Vera Olmsted," she said, with her voice so low he could hardly make it out. "And you are?"

"Edward Pryor."

"We value our privacy. I hope you understand." She nodded and turned, as if she realized she had said too much.

"Well, Ms. Olmsted, I appreciate your talking to me," he called after her.

Things were simple one moment, difficult the next. He stilled himself, like a bow in suspense. Above him the heavy clouds prepared to descend on the lush gardens, and cold air entered his nostrils. His body was overtaken by a scent, he couldn't tell if it was some sort of fertilizer the Olmsted woman used on her porch or if it was the gardens all around him, or maybe it was just his imagination, but he smelled—

It was just a moment in time, a fragment of a recollection he hadn't acknowledged in years. Yet here it was, alive. Urgent. The memory came hasty and unbidden in the form of a scent, dust and hay and ammonia. He had asked to see the barn and the residents didn't object, though he never told Donna—and he remembered a horse standing in a stall, so regal with the white coat and brown patches, skin pink around its nose. How its ears flicked back and forth, rapidly swiveling about.

That boy, Gabriel, he wasn't well. Would never be well again. A brain can only take so much impact, though there'd been hope with him being so young and one can never underestimate a body's capability to heal itself but his skull was no match for that horse. Edward had spoken to the boy's parents often over the years, told them he felt responsible somehow, their being at his party and all, but he never mentioned Penelope, never mentioned that he had put two and two together. He had seen tiny flecks of sawdust on the floor of Penelope's room the night the search for the boy was underway. At first he told himself those powdery particles could be anything but then he spotted larger curly wooden bits placed in the fireplace of the dollhouse and that's when he knew.

The wind picked up and Edward buttoned his coat. It was only going to get worse. That Blue Norther was coming, ready or not. It was coming.

It took Edward the better part of a year to achieve what he had set out to do: unsettle Donna.

All those carefully selected items, all those times he went to Shadow Garden, put up with security, dropped off a bronze statue, a photo album one week, one of her favorite dresses, the one with the animal print she used to love and wear often, a book the next, including a note he had found in Penelope's room, one she had written as a child, stuffed away in a box that contained everything from her first school year, an attempt at writing, first letters, then words, and finally sentences. He even found a children's book with a creepy dollhouse on the cover that had dropped behind a dresser drawer and had been stuck there for who knows how long. For months she didn't seem to react to any of it and he felt as if he was quibbling over scraps, wasting his time, but eventually, according to Marleen, Donna was beginning to become unglued. She had begun to ask questions, demanded to know where all those items came from, and Marleen remained steadfast. She believed in some sort of therapeutic component of it all until he dropped off the urn. He had felt her hesitation then and not only did he fear the end of the cooperation on her part, but he was also running out of things that seemed suitable. The room he had created for the collection of the items was filled with bulky furniture unfeasible for the task at hand.

When he called her to tell her he was dropping off the urn, Marleen was adamant that planting it might be a bad idea.

"How is her daughter's urn a positive memory? I think we might set her back months. When you approached me, you assured me you'd limit this, this . . . undertaking to pleasant memories. I don't think I'm prepared to go forward with this any longer. I think I told you once it doesn't feel right, I'll no longer be part of this."

No need to be surprised, Edward thought then, Donna had won over Marleen a long time ago. She's molded her to her advantage. Donna was like the mouth of a lion, swallowing everything and everyone.

"But Marleen," he said and clutched the phone in his hands, "the urn is all she has left of her daughter. She would want to be with her. Would want her near. Right?"

"I will remove anything that causes her any kind of stress, Dr. Pryor. Know that."

"I understand, Marleen. I understand."

Dropping off the urn was the last time he'd gone to Shadow Garden. He was done. No one could sustain this state of mind, this madness lingering in the bones, eventually it would reach to the edges of his body and do him in.

It no longer felt like he was coming out on top or getting closer to the truth—after all, he had arranged for Donna to be a recluse, with Marleen and the planted memories of her past being her only connection to the outside world—but she wasn't cracking the way he thought she should. His last trump, the ace in a hole, was all he had left and he had just handed it to Marleen.

. . .

One night he heard someone in the house, roaming around like a thief. He saw light in Penelope's room and for a second he believed in ghosts but then he knew it had all come to fruition.

Donna had arrived and Donna's memory was ready to let go, to expel the truth.

59

DONNA

I reach for the letters and Edward doesn't protest. I stuff them into my purse. I guess I've done what I came here to do. Edward on the other hand fell just short of getting the answers he was looking for. The letters are mine to keep, that's my punishment for him, I suppose.

"Just go, back where you came from," he says, slumped over, defeated.

He calls a taxi and gives the driver instructions to take me to Shadow Garden. I open the thumb turn bolt of the garage door leading to the front path and step outside. The taxi is parked down Preston Hallow Road, a short walk. It's barely daylight and I won't alert the neighbors. What would they say if they saw me, especially in this condition? I haven't looked in a mirror in days, it has seemed almost unnecessary to get a look at myself, it's always just a glimpse, never my true self. Was that the reason I shrouded them, because what's the point of looking at someone you don't recognize?

I get into the taxi and I realize how shaken up I am. My eyes are tired and I've seen too many things, heard too many explanations. I concentrate on the silver maples and the taxi takes a left. I turn and look back at the house. The entire upper floor is illuminated. There's a shadow but I could be mistaken—it could be the oaks and the branches swaying in the wind—and by all accounts Edward sat in the kitchen when I left.

I no longer understand what reality is, what it isn't, and what exactly is the opposite of it? Not a dream state, but an alternate reality that one lives in but never recognizes as such? Unreality?

I understand Edward. For the first time I comprehend his conundrum, his *need* to understand, this fervent obsession to assign everything a name, a reason, a cause, a motivation. Last night, he asked me over and over why Penelope would see a need to confess.

"After all she'd done," he said and wiped his forehead. "After everything, all the doctors and the therapy. That boy . . ." His eyes grew wide. "That boy, that poor boy. Why suddenly did she feel the need to confess when so much was at stake?"

Poor Edward. He will never know.

Say I know the answer. Say Penelope and I had a conversation about this while he was out dumping the body. Say Penelope told me, "No one can get away with this."

She saw the magnitude of it all and I understood. She couldn't hide in a closet, couldn't talk her way out of it, blame it on others. The dark. A horse. Pills. Doctors. She was to blame and there was going to be a consequence but this time *we* had risked it all. *We* had proven ourselves worthy, and maybe that was all she needed to know. In the end Penelope was a coward, and that too is not a judgment but merely an observation. Better to confess than to be found out. It was a new one but that was the world she lived in. Don't try to understand it.

I wonder, if people knew our story, would they question our love for our daughter? I imagine hearing a story like ours and I'd be the first one to question the parents' love for their child. I haven't spoken of my love for her yet. Though it's hard to imagine, considering her brazen ways, she was vulnerable. Know this, I want to tell them, know that she was all we had. We loved her the way you love the weakest, the most defenseless. We loved her the most. We defended her. We put it all on the line for her. We risked it all for her. What greater love is there?

I know this but I will never tell Edward. I won't give him the satisfaction.

The driver doesn't speak to me and I stare out the window, having nothing to say to him. Alone with my thoughts, I doze off. When the taxi turns onto Decatur Road, Shadow Garden lies in wait. The gate is closed, and I see Shadow Garden for what it is: a fortress. For the first time it dawns on me that getting in may be as difficult as leaving.

My mind is racing. I could go up to the gate and pretend I went for a walk and ended up on the wrong side of the fence, but this place is in the middle of nowhere and the walking trails are within the perimeters of the property. I look down at my scrubs. How do I explain those? And I'm not supposed to leave without a driver, not that that's a rule but an understanding we have. *Stay within the property for your safety.* I remember those words but not the circumstances of the conversation. Marleen will carry on about this for days on end and I think damage control, my first go-to response when something happens. Mitigate damages.

I walk up to the gate. Within the lush emerald landscaping there's the oval sign with gold letters on a black background set within a square of bricks. I stare at the keypad. Blank. My mind is blank. There's a number combination drivers use but I wouldn't know what it is. My fingertips make contact with the keypad but don't push any keys.

Above me, a camera hums, adjusting its angle to get a better look at me. I push the red HELP button. A crackling speaker announces the presence of the security gate attendant in the small square building.

"Welcome to Shadow Garden," the voice crackles.

Inside the fence, two elderly women with visors walk past, staring at me. "Can you open the gate?" I ask and lean closer to the speaker above the keypad.

After a short delay the voice asks for my name.

"Donna Pryor."

"Just a moment, please."

If he prompts me for anything else, I'll be reduced to tears. I can feel myself slipping.

"Can you hurry, please?" *Goddammitcutmesomelackmyhipispounding.* Two nights without sleep and I feel like something is amiss in my head. To ground myself, I picture my bedroom, lying in my bed with the ceiling overhead, the humming of the fridge from the kitchen, drifting off to sleep.

"Please look directly into the camera."

Another hum. I watch the shutters of the round black circle open then close, and open again.

"Welcome home, Mrs. Pryor. Please go straight to the office," the voice says and I breathe a sigh of relief.

The gate opens and allows a straight view of the leasing building. I walk past the front doors and though the guard told me to go to the office, I proceed toward my building. That's when I hear someone call my name. I can't be sure, maybe I'm imagining this. My gait is stiff and my legs are heavy. I'm dragging my foot, I can't even lift it off the ground. Footsteps sound behind me and when I turn, a woman working in the office extends a hand toward me. I'm not sure if she wants to shake mine, but she touches my shoulder. Virginia is her name, I think.

"Mrs. Pryor," she says, out of breath as if she's been running, "let me walk you home."

"I'm fine," I say and point in the direction of my front door. "It's right there around the corner, the first door on the right. I don't need any help."

Virginia lets go of my shoulder but stays put. Staring me up and down. She's confused by the scrubs I'm wearing, I can tell.

"Really, I'm fine," I insist. "I'm not a child. Please leave me alone."

She turns and walks away and I turn the corner and keep my eyes on my door and will my legs to move. There's a small concrete step in front of my door and as I fumble with the key, I turn around. Virginia stands by the corner of the leasing building but when I stare at her, she finally disappears.

Someone should have a look at that hip again, it's become progressively worse over the past few hours. I don't know if I don't lift my foot high enough or if the step is uneven, but with a thud I land on a bed of mulch. A sharp pain shoots through my right ankle. I end up on my left side and I manage to roll to avoid impact but still my head grazes the ground, just enough to send a sharp reminder that I have bumped my head. My brow, my cheek, they throb.

I rest for a second or two, then I straighten my back. Feeling exposed, I look around but there's no one there. I push myself up. My hip snaps and I can't straighten my leg. My left foot has to bear considerably more than its fair share required for walking and though I manage to take a couple of steps, I am hobbling now.

Inside, as I pass the mirror, right after I slip off one of my shoes, I want to get a good look at my cheek but the mirrors are still draped and I feel the blood more than I see it. I also taste it in my mouth.

I bend over to slip off the other shoe and that's when blood drips on the marble floor in tiny round splatters. Putting pressure on my brow with the back of my hand, I stumble past the kitchen and into my bedroom. I shuffle into the bathroom, peel off the scrubs, and stuff them in the bottom of the hamper. There'll be time to hide them later, laundry day isn't until Saturday. If Marleen finds them, she'll question me. If they were reported missing, there'll be an inquiry. An investigation. Theft is one of the worst things that can happen within the gates of Shadow Garden. Even small infractions related to missing items are frowned upon; even so much as a missing shoe from a front stoop, a potted plant by a door, or a misplaced purse triggers an inquiry as if Fort Knox's security protocol has been breached.

Pulling a small towel off the shelf among a dozen tightly wrapped into tubes, a good number of them topple to the floor. I wet the towel and head toward the foyer when I hear voices outside my door, cheerful, a casual greeting exchanged, then there's a key prying into the lock. It's too late and I have to just keep my fingers crossed that Marleen won't see the blood in the foyer. After all, it was just two drops, small at that. I use the wet towel to wipe my face. All I can do is take a guess where the blood is but now I can't recall if it was my left or right brow, so I just wipe the wet towel across both and around and around my face, the white fibers turning pink.

I climb under the covers, pull them up over my face. The towel, cold and sticky, I stuff under the pillow. I force my breathing to slow.

Usually, there's silence in the foyer, just the sound of the front door closing, a key pulling out of the lock, all those familiar sounds I have become accustomed to, Marleen's announcement, her proclamation of arrival—none of that is happening. Instead a shriek and the door slams shut.

Mrs. Pryor, Mrs. Pryor, are you all right, are you all right. Are you okay?

I continue to breathe, slow and deep. I exaggerate so Marleen doesn't think I'm dead but with all her carrying on and gasping, one would think she assumes I was. I give it a moment and then I stir.

"What is it?" I ask, my voice low.

Before I can protest, Marleen pulls the covers off me. She stares at me, a woman in her underwear with a swollen ankle. It's pounding and feels hot and I can imagine the look of it. I can feel her hand on my leg.

"Your ankle is swollen. What happened?"

"I twisted my leg, I guess," I say, hoping she'll just move on to breakfast. I'm famished. "I'm starving, Marleen, I'll have my breakfast in bed today."

"Why is your hair wet? Are you running a fever?"

It's an innocent question, really, but I hear a tinge of prying within the words. The wet towel, it must have been the wet towel. Marleen rests the back of her hand on my forehead.

"What's happened to your face? Are you bleeding?"

"A nosebleed. Please don't make such a spectacle of yourself."

I'm surprised that my voice is steady and scolding, that I'm pulling this off with so much confidence.

"There's blood in the foyer." Her eyes dart about the room as if to look for further evidence of what I have gotten myself into.

Marleen is frazzled and I feel sorry for her. Why can't I just tell her? Why can't she be my ally? Should I . . . No, I catch myself. I heard her talk to Edward. She locks doors and snoops, and kind she may be, but safe she's not. I can't tell her the truth. My very own despicable self is illuminated in the eyes of this very worried woman. Guilt? Just for a second, but the feeling passes. She's not friend but foe.

"Mrs. Pryor—"

"Breakfast," I insist. "Really, Marleen, I didn't fall, I'm fine, and it's just a swollen ankle. Bring me a bag of peas or whatever it is people put on such a thing."

"You need to have someone look at your ankle. It doesn't look good. Is it your hip? Is that why you fell?"

"Tea and toast would be great." I ignore her question and rip the duvet from her hand and cover myself.

"I'll make an appointment with the doctor right now. Have an X-ray, something might be broken."

"Okay, sure."

This entire exchange has me thinking about lies. And confessions. And that I must read Penelope's letters again. I'm already confusing facts in my mind. I panic. Where did I leave them? I turn and there they are, on the side table. Crinkled and wet, smeared with blood from my brow.

I get up and when I put weight on my ankle, I cringe. A sharp pain reminds me that I have done damage beyond just a sprain. I keep the foot suspended as I reach over to grab the letters. At first I don't know what to do with them, but the best place to keep them is the bathroom, the only place Marleen won't see me read them and question me. And I can keep an eye on them from my bed. It's a miracle she didn't see them just now.

Footsteps sound and I shove them under my pillow. Marleen packs my ankle in ice and when she tells me to sit up so she can fluff the pillows, I panic. The bloody towel—I have brushed my hair over my brow but it's only a matter of time until she notices the cut—is under my pillow. So are the letters.

"Not right now, Marleen. I need some rest."

I lower my head on the pillow. That's when she sees my brow. Of course she sees my brow.

"You fell, didn't you?"

"I would like to take a shower after I eat." I sit up and the ice pack tumbles to the ground. "And privacy. That's all I need."

"Mrs. Pryor, if you fell while you were alone—"

"Just for once in your life, live in the real world, Marleen. Do you think I'm blind? That I don't know what's going on? Who do you take me for?" My voice is sharp now, I'm done playing games. "I can walk. See." I get out of bed and suck it up. I take a couple of steps and manage to contain the pain. When I feel as if the ankle is giving out on me, I put all my weight on the other foot. "I want breakfast after my shower. Run along."

Marleen turns and leaves the room. I limp back to the bed and grab the letters and the bloody towel. I sift through the drawers in the bathroom and find a small white plastic bag. I put the letters and the bloody towel in the bag, fold it in half, and stuff it under the bin liner.

I step into the shower. I'm in shreds, body and mind. Unable to reach for the soap, I stand there, allowing the cold water to hit my face, washing the blood off my forehead. By the time the water turns warm, the day replays like a stack of photographs I'm flipping through.

I hobble back to the bedroom, where I find breakfast sitting on the side table. While I eat, I eavesdrop. Marleen attempts to schedule appointments with various doctors over the phone. They are booked for today and tomorrow, but the day after there's an opening with Dr. Jacobson.

Famished, I am famished. I want to ask for more food but Marleen is already suspicious. She tinkers around the house, cabinets open and close, the pipes hum and I doze off. I don't mean to, it just happens. When I open my eyes, Marleen is gone.

Alone with myself, I can't make head or tails of anything. I think about the therapist who told Penelope to write down what she couldn't say out loud. I had debated with the therapist over the phone but his argument was you can't go back on the written truth, it's a confession you can hold yourself to.

My very own motivations become less and less clear to me with every passing minute. Nothing short of a detailed account will do, something along the lines of *Before I leave, I want to tell you* . . . That day, I purge feverishly. I write it all down, everything. Page after page after page. I catch myself wanting to stop but I carry on. My hand shakes, but still I go on. *Before I leave I want to tell you about my daughter, Penelope. I want to tell you about a boy named Gabriel. A woman named Rachel. A little girl with fork marks in her arm.*

Between my account and Penelope's ramblings, I've come to a conclusion. I carry on through the next day and the next night. Once it's been written down, I can't revisit it, not because I don't want to but because I have decided to hold myself to a higher standard.

The second night, I add the pictures from the photo albums. They seem to paint a much clearer picture than words. It's more so for myself than for anyone else. At the end of the third day, I stop. But there's one more thing I need to write down.

I had felt myself slipping for a while. It began slowly, when I no longer knew how to drive. Does one unlearn how to drive a car? I don't know.

Yes, I do. I do know.

Like a flashcard, a memory pops up: I'm driving and the road is a tape measure about to snap back into its case. A moment of panic. Slowing to a crawl, cars honking and drivers gesturing, pulling over and gasping for air while the wipers went full speed and the lights flashed and the open door's *ding ding ding* left me breathless, the edges of my vision ruffled as a passing car blew gravel at me and the world around me had a reddish hue.

Forgetting to drive is not like forgetting to pleat a napkin into a rosebud fold. I felt a whir, I heard a roar, I didn't know what to do with my feet, what pedal was which, how to get the car to move. Traffic zoomed by me at high speed, my heart beating out of my chest. Driving was like a game and its rules eluded me and in that moment of panic I didn't recall what all the lights and buttons were for. How can that be? I asked myself. And what would come next? I fell apart and lashed out at the same time, said awful words to people who didn't deserve it. Half the time I couldn't follow a conversation but who would admit that? Those arguments with Penelope, I didn't know what they were about. I couldn't drive to a doctor if I had wanted to. Instead of an exit sign I saw a jumble of letters, my brain unable to make sense of the words. Then came the beginning of the end. That night in Penelope's room, I was *that* person. *That* incarnation of Donna Pryor stopped at nothing.

Before I leave I want to tell you . . .

The wainscoting boards stored in Penelope's closet. The hammer. The room.

It's confession time. These are my sins.

First I nailed the window shut.

"You'll go to prison, Penny," I screamed. "You know what that means, right?"

She just stared at me with big eyes.

Then I nailed the door shut. Two boards and it was done.

"This is how it'll be in prison," I yelled at her. "You'll have nowhere to go. Can't get out. It'll be all over then."

I looked like rage but I was all fear. I was afraid. So afraid. If she confessed, we'd have nothing. *Poof. All gone.* I wanted her to understand the implications of what we had done. It was no longer just her but all of us.

"Look around you. See what you are about to do! You will put us all in prison, not just yourself. All of us." I stripped her bed down to the mattress. "That's what you'll be sleeping on. A bare mattress." With one finger I toppled every single book. "There'll be none of this either. You'll just sit around thinking about what you did." I pointed at the dollhouse, the Victorian one. Her favorite. I flipped it over, the pieces came tumbling out.

That's when Penelope began to weep.

"That's all that'll be left of all of us. An empty house," I screamed, one word stumbling over the next, frantic, hysterical.

I got worse from there. She fought me and I fought her. She fought for her freedom, I fought for her imprisonment.

"You go to the police," I screamed. "You go and tell them what you've done. You might as well kill yourself. Why sit in a prison cell. Just end it now."

My rage came from a different place but I matched her just fine. I threw the planks I was unable to nail to the window at her feet, I drove the hammer so far into the walls that the room looked like a war zone speckled by shrapnel. The sharp and dangerous shards of my rage mottled the walls. I, a woman incapable of opening a jelly jar, had destroyed the entire room. That's how strong that Donna Pryor was.

I pushed open the door, and pointed toward the landing. "Why don't we all just end it here," I screamed and ran to the banister. My body didn't know where it began and where it ended. It was all or nothing.

Penelope reached for me, wrapped her arms around me. I clawed at her. I broke free—or so I thought—but my momentum had been too strong, too fierce, and as one we toppled over the banister. We were united for that moment in time, one body, hearts beating in our chests, and I have no way of knowing but I could swear that we both stopped breathing—*shit shit shit we are falling falling falling*— that's when we looked at each other, saw each other, maybe for the first time. For once she understood how far I'd go to save her, how far she'd go to save me. To the end of the world. I never knew how long a single second could be. Penelope was so close, in my arms. There was a pop, a screech, somewhere at the edge of our world but I knew what it was. The chandelier broke our fall and then we landed on the floor in the foyer.

I don't remember anything after that.

That's what happened and that's what I write down so I can't go back and change it. I wrote it down so I wouldn't falter. Knowing myself, I wouldn't want that stain on me. I can't ever take it back: I didn't push her, she didn't push me, it was just something that was inevitable. As if the universe had decided a long time ago that only in free fall we were able to cling to each other.

That's been kind of the whole story all along, hasn't it?

60

PENELOPE

Penelope had made her case in her mind. "Hear me out," she said to her mother but her mother wouldn't listen.

She wanted to tell her mother that while she sat in the parking lot with the woman in the passenger seat, while she allowed the ambulance to pass by without so much as rolling down the window or flashing her lights, the woman, Rachel, seemed fine. And then she wasn't. Penelope pulled on the lapel of the coat to shake the woman awake but she wouldn't budge. The lining of the coat was a synthetic fabric that repelled fluids and the blood just ran from her mouth into her lap and once her lap filled, the puddle ran down on the floor mat.

After she saw the magnitude of it all, Penelope tried to clean it up. She wanted her mother to know that she'd tried, that she took the woman's scarf and wiped her face but there was no use, blood smeared all over the woman's cheeks and neck. Even in that moment Penelope had trivial thoughts, how Rachel appeared ghastly as if she had applied a wrong shade of foundation or put on too much bronzer. And that synthetic fabric didn't absorb anything and that she had somehow come to the end of a line. And the end of the line was the case she had made in her mind. If only her mother would listen.

Later, in the shower, her mother scrubbed Penelope's skin in circular motions, rubbed so hard it burned. By the time she lathered up the pouf sponge with soap for the third time, Penelope winced as the suds stung.

Her mother scrubbed her so vigorously that her nightgown slipped off one of her shoulders and her bare breast was visible. Penelope stared at her mother's breast. How she scoured Penelope's skin as if there was a much deeper stain to be cleansed than the cherry-red rings under her nails. She made it her duty to return her to something sparkly and shiny.

Penelope tried to help, lifted an arm so her mother could wash it, but she just pushed it down and when Penelope tried to extend a leg for her mother to scrub her foot, her mother pushed her thigh out of the way and dug her nails into her already inflamed skin. Eventually she gave up, allowed her mother to twist and turn her to her liking until she shut the water off and ripped a towel off the bar on the wall and dried her body.

The entire time, her father stood turned at an angle from which he could supervise without staring. Penelope giggled. In her father's eyes she must have looked hideous and sickening. She didn't mean to, but this was a moment not unlike life itself: mother running the show, father standing by, idly wringing his hands. There was no eye contact between father and daughter. She thought she saw tears in his eyes but she couldn't be sure with all that water coming at her from the rainfall can above, the body jets from three sides and the hand shower her mother kept dropping, spraying beyond the walls of this Calacatta marble prison.

Penelope might have seemed like a rag doll without command of her limbs but her brain was working just fine. There were so many questions rattling around in her head. She wanted to ask her father *what could I have done differently?* But there was that look in his eyes. And she wanted to ask her mother *do you still love me, even now?* But none of that escaped her mouth, none of that her lips and tongue managed to verbalize.

Every time Penelope's thoughts raced, she told herself, slow down, and focus. She'd make her mother understand if she just listened.

In the end it took everything she had in her, and she managed to whisper in her mother's ear, "Do you think I'll get better one day?"

That chandelier. She could see if from her room, the very tip of it hanging from the ceiling. Those shiny crystals on the highest beam of the prettiest house on the most exclusive street, under a slate roof. Maybe that's what her mother had fought all along, the fact that nothing was special about any of them and so she had to wrap everything up just right to make it all beautiful, to make them somehow worthy to live in this house, on this street, in this abundance. Otherwise, what would be the point of it all?

Penelope allowed her parents to talk, and talk, and talk. Talk her out of turning herself in, talk her into going along with the cover-up, but then everything in her mind slowed. That's a thing backed by science, she thought, that slow-motion feeling when individual seconds expand and brief flashes turn into decades lived, a film reel of transgressions with all terrors reimagined. That's when Penelope got it.

Do you think I'll get better one day?

Penelope finally had an answer. Yes, yes, she would get better, and that dawned on her when her body hit the ground with such force it propelled the life out of her and saved her mother's in return.

And when Penelope asked herself the million-dollar question, as she held on to her mother—how far do you go to atone for your sins?—for the first time she had an answer: down, down, down, all the way down.

61

DONNA

I stuff my confession in with Penelope's letters inside the plastic bag and tuck it all in the bottom of the garbage bin, underneath the liner. For both our acknowledgments to be in such close proximity gives me peace.

I'm tired and I close my eyes. I don't know how much time passes but one day, I hear Marleen's square heels click on the marble floor, the front door closes, and I tell myself the ankle isn't as bad as it was before. I've been taking my medication, lulling in and out for what seemed days on end. The anti-inflammatory medication and ice packs hopefully have done wonders.

I get out of bed but I can hardly put any pressure on my ankle without gasping. In the bathroom I slip my hand underneath the liner. Nothing. Not the bloody towel, not the bag with the letters. I drop to my knees, rip out the liner, and turn the bin upside down. I shake it. I can hear my rapid breathing, the thumping of my heart.

I make an attempt to get up but I can't put any weight on my foot. I will need a cast and I won't be able to go anywhere or do anything, and I know what happens when I'm forced to lie in bed all day every day. I know what happened last time, when I hurt my hip. I lost it. I utterly and completely lost it. The memory of it knocks all other thoughts aside. Maybe I'm confused—it isn't Wednesday, today isn't garbage day at all—and maybe I put it under the liner in the kitchen? I've lost track of time. Maybe I'm mixing things up. I've been known to do that.

I hop on my left leg into the kitchen, I reach for the bin, about to dump the coffee filters and eggshells and tea bags on the kitchen floor when I look at the calendar on the wall. Sunday is crossed out. Monday is crossed out. Tuesday, too. It's Wednesday. I step on the pedal and the lid lifts up and it's empty. All I can think of is to go and run after the garbage truck and maybe it's not too late, it can't be too late, it just can't.

Outside, to the right, where the dumpsters sit behind a brick wall, that's where the letters are. Without them . . . I don't finish the thought, no, finish it: without the letters I'll make up another story and Penelope's death will be in vain.

I stagger toward the front door. I no longer feel my ankle, it seems fine, magically healed. I run toward the garbage truck, as much as you can call my staggering running. I fan my arms as if I'm attempting to paint a picture in the air. Swaying my arms like a dervish. I hear screams. They sound chilling.

Later, they tell me what I did. Like a drunk after a night of binging, in the morning people tell me I stood in front of the garbage truck. I wasn't moving, my hands were resting firmly on the truck's fork-lift. Screaming. No one could tell me what I was screaming and I don't know either since I don't remember. The packer packed and the tailgate rose and the dumpster flipped into the compress box.

I know none of those words but there is an official report of what

I did. Marleen read it to me. No one would know those words but the truck operator. *Lift bucket and blade slide and ejector push-out, inside and outside packer. Compressor box.*

The report said I mounted the truck and that I acted "desperate." The driver veered to the left when I stepped in front of him and the truck hit the brick wall constructed to keep the view of the dumpster hidden.

They tell me I hoisted myself into it. I doubt it, honestly. A woman my age? With that ankle? All I wanted was a small white plastic bag with papers smeared with my blood. My daughter's letters. My confession. If it wasn't for Edward and his weakness in carrying the burden, I might—

Wait.

The story of my family. The fall of my family. What will happen to it?

I can already feel myself slipping, committing to another narrative altogether. When I have to face that stain again, will I change my account, will I assign fault to someone else? I fear I will forget, I will forget all of it, I will tatter about this place twenty years from now, I will continue to ask for Penelope. That's what I can't take, the thought of every day before me being just like the days behind me.

My confession. The letters. What happens tomorrow, or the day after? When I don't recall how and why my daughter plunged to her death. Will I do this all over again? Look for the truth? Should I put a sticky note on a mirror?

But they are shrouded. I don't recall why.

I wake and for a second, I don't know where I am. The silence is peculiar. I'm alone in the apartment and the only sounds are the birds and their carefree song outside my window.

My mind wanders, trying to make sense of all the pieces that attempt to click into place. A pillow beneath my head, a duvet on top of me. Light seeps through the slits between the blinds, everything is defined and interpretable in the light of day. There are telltale signs that my brain is waking, it gains momentum like an engine that warms, springing to life. There are residues of moments grasping for significance above all others.

When I was a child, I had a rash. Obscure red blotches appeared on my cheeks and turned into fine pink sores that felt like sandpaper. Soon they spread to my ears, neck, chest, elbows, and thighs. Unassuming, taken for a sunburn at first, a diagnosis didn't come until a week later: scarlet fever. By then I had developed kidney inflammation. After a long recovery, one morning I awoke and the fever had broken and I was on the mend. I didn't know what it meant to be healthy or sick or getting over a sickness but I knew I was well. I feel like I have overcome a long illness. I wasn't well but now I am. The stitches have held and here I am, clear in body and mind. Everything makes sense. The mind settles.

The moment my bare feet touch the ground, I understand what has happened. It is irrevocably significant, I can't quite explain it and I talk to myself as if I'm talking to an audience. *I understand what has happened.*

A word pops into my head. Velvety, it slithers into my consciousness. I hadn't thought of it in years but here it is, sliding off the tip of my tongue. *Bobeche.*

In the big scheme of things the word is quite insignificant, referring to a chandelier part, a glass collar that catches candle drippings and holds suspended glass prisms.

I remember the chandelier at Hawthorne Court, three-tiered, with more crystals and drop pendeloques, baguettes, and fuchsia bells than anyone can count. The metal finish gleamed in silver leaf and was draped with beaded strands of jeweled chains. The bare bulbs were without shades. An Italian antique. Edward had argued with me over the price.

"It's too expensive," he had said.

"But it's imported from Italy," I had replied. "The glass is hand-blown and the metal is forged by hand. It's a marvel of artisan design," I insisted.

I get up. I don't remember when I went to bed, when I put these clothes on. What a hideous thing to wear, this smocked cotton nightgown. I would never wear such a thing.

I step outside. A blanket of fog hangs over the Shadow Garden grounds, lingering about, all but swallowing the world. A merry-go-round of random thoughts turn into some sort of order, they take shape like the word *bobeche* did, it forms in my mind and there it is.

A narrative emerges and if I just think hard and long enough, I'll make sense of it all.

I take stock of my life: hair and nails. Appointments. Chiropractor. My daily run, two if my hip allows. The constant glances at the clock, so pointless really, because no one is demanding of me.

I hear the door unlock, Marleen arrives. The keys jingle as she drops them in her purse. The purse slides across the accent table in the foyer. The gliding open of the kitchen doors. I get dressed. Casual attire, just an early morning walk, nothing more. Breakfast can wait. I pass the kitchen door and Marleen looks up, surprised.

"Everything okay, Mrs. Pryor? You look like you've seen a ghost."

"Going for a walk," I say, my voice lacking enthusiasm. Zipping up my coat, the scarf gets stuck in the zipper.

"But your breakfast?" Marleen's voice shakes. I'm not supposed to leave the house without breakfast. Blood sugar, I remember. I fainted once, on the back trails. I must have told her, she mentioned it to me the other day. Maybe someone saw me, I can't be sure.

"Okay," I say. "I'll eat something."

I want Marleen to fry an egg today. *Fry an egg.* I must have said it out loud because she stares at me. She knows I hate eggs. Hate the smell of them. She had fought me on that in the very beginning.

"Toast is not enough," she used to say. "Protein is what you need."
Eventually she gave up.

She fries not one egg but two. She never quits while she's ahead.

I sit at the table and watch her. Spatula. Butter. Salt. Pepper. It's all lined up and I know what does what, know it so well I could do it myself if I wanted to. Marleen heats up the butter in a skillet. She breaks two eggs and they slip into the pan. They sizzle as they make contact. The pan is too hot, the eggs will be tough, I know that not because I cook, but because I'm a picky eater. She reduces the heat to low, watches as the whites set. When the yolks begin to thicken, she slides a spatula under each egg and carefully flips it over. She looks at me with wide eyes, then sprinkles the eggs with salt and pepper.

Does she suspect anything? I don't know but I doubt it.

"Serve immediately," I say as if I'm reading instructions from a cookbook. What a pure soul she is, I see that now. But she is also a liar.

Marleen turns around. "Done," she says and unfolds my napkin.

The calendar on the wall with the closed-out dates tells me today is Saturday. Good. Saturday is perfect. I eat the eggs and the toast quickly, I more or less shove it all into my mouth.

"Going for a walk," I say and leave.

I hear Marleen call my name but I have long disappeared around the corner.

Outside, little wispy clouds move quickly. It's windy and cold and I'm glad I tied a scarf around my neck, otherwise the wind would leach underneath the woolen coat and chill me to the bone. Sometimes keeping an enemy from entering is half the battle. Down the breezeway, the rat poison is gone. I inspect the area closer and I find bait stations tucked away under the shrubs.

I look toward the buildings in the back of the estate. Straight across from my building, farther back, is the Oasis, and across from it the Gallery. There're four more, all facing each other like they are keepers of one another, enclosed by a steel fence. The path stops. I wait for signs of life, anyone walking about, but there's no one to be seen. The gate is latched but not locked and so I enter as if I'm supposed to be here, as if I belong.

Grackles. They are everywhere. They follow my every move with their yellow eyes, tracking me. My presence takes them by surprise, makes them scatter off into the nearby trees. The birds are only the beginning, the catalyst that gives my thoughts oxygen.

I think about my mother. She was diagnosed with liver cancer, and she refused treatment. I didn't blame her. Who in their right mind would want to go on, their last months putting their body through hell—what kind of life to be bedridden with strangers performing intimate tasks for you—and so I held her hand and told her about Penelope, how she'd be on her way to see her if it wasn't for finals at the university, and how perfect she was, how smart, how she was everything a mother could want in a daughter and all I wanted her to say was that she felt the same way about me. She held up her hand to stall the conversation, then looked away as if she knew—though she couldn't have—but I felt she knew me to be a liar.

"Give her my love," she said.

And I think about how, toward the end of our marriage, even before the depression, before we separated, that was when I began to slip. How my watch told me what time it was but I didn't trust it. I recognized that my perception of time was warped—I could clearly remember when a day began but not when it ended. What does one call that? A lapse? A failing? A breach? An oversight? A bungle? The words percolate and more bubble up to the top: a foible, a gaff, a fault, a blunder.

What I don't recall is the day I left Hawthorne Court. I don't understand how that can be. Did I leave in the dead of night, or did Edward make me? Maybe we shook hands—which sounds like something Edward would do, he is very clinical and tends to assume the role of a bystander, and there's a word for that I don't recall, oh, *detachment*, I think—and how good he was at that. He lacked something. Empathy. Understanding.

Edward assumed I refused to get well, I know that about him. Dr. Pryor—who could fix butchered patients, cleft palates, and infected saline inserts, a collapsing septum not remotely a challenge, a gangrene wound a mere obstacle to overcome—believed with all his might I refused to get well.

Saturdays are a late start for management. Skeleton crews they call it. There's a guard by the gate, a receptionist answers the phone. No nail appointments, no grocery delivery. A bursting pipe or a clogged toilet will summon someone in due time, yet there's no maintenance on the premises. Emergencies can be called in, but the offices are not staffed.

I enter the main building and walk down to the doctors' offices. Dome cameras watch me like bug eyes, in every hallway and at every corner. I wiggle the door to Dr. Jacobson's office and it is, as expected, locked. Through the glass door, the office suite sits empty, computer screens are abandoned, and printers are shut off. I leave the building and turn down a walkway leading to the Ridge. I pass through the breezeway and between the main building and the Ridge where the pathway comes to a stop, I cross the patch of grass and stay in the mulch beds where the ground covers sit slick with morning dew. No one but the grackles watches me, swooping in low arches, keeping their curious eyes on me. There's always one ugly side to buildings, the side they hope to keep invisible, where the utility boxes are, the AC units, where the power and gas lines disappear in between the grout of the red bricks.

Dr. Jacobson's office is the second to last window. I pick up a rock and gauge its weight in my hand. It'll do. I wrap my scarf around the rock and close my eyes as I swing it overhead against the glass. The impact barely creates a fissure, small, the length of a bobby pin, if that. I run my bare finger over the glass to see if the fracture runs all the way through but it's just a surface crack. I swing the rock again, this time as hard as I can. The crack widens, others emerge, ragged branches like a spiderweb. One more impact and fragments of glass rain down. My thick wool coat protects me from the tiny shards still stuck in the frame. I hurry and sit on the window frame and swing my legs across.

I expect to find my file by thumbing through the M through P section in Dr. Jacobson's office. I imagine the tops secured with prong fasteners allowing for two separate filing surfaces. Notes on the left side and labs on the right. I imagine flipping through the right, where my cholesterol and triglycerides are neatly highlighted, my blood sugar levels underlined. Lots of letters N, either *Normal* or *Negative*. I imagine finding the words, scribbled, lacking conviction, slanted. But this isn't the era of paper files, today's world is computers and passwords and medical information security. I slip into a nearby chair. I stare at the door to Dr. Jacobson's office. A conversation we once had comes back to me.

Do you know where you are? Dr. Jacobson asked.

I was taken aback by her friendly demeanor, her shallow way of pretense, the way she smiled at me.

Do I know where I am?

I know how this can feel, she said. *It can shake the very ground beneath your feet. The mind can grow a little muddled, familiar terrain can become foreign,* she said. *Everything's going to be all right.*

What a fool I am. I didn't understand a thing.

A light begins to flash red overhead. I should have known that the moment the rock hit the window somewhere an alarm went off, some blinking display indicating the exact spot of the break-in. A guard comes running, stops, and looks down the corridors.

When he sees me, he approaches me. Slowly, as not to frighten me. Because that's a rule at Shadow Garden; don't frighten the tenants.

I return and find Marleen is about the house. *Keeping house.* Something about her touches me deeply: her devotion, her resolve, I can't put my finger on it. I sit at my vanity. I open the folder, the one I've been hiding in my vanity drawer. The one I never bothered to read, just skimmed over the pages, admired the font and esthetic of it. The one about the butterflies roosting in the thick canopies of the Monterrey oaks, *the very generation that makes the journey south to Mexico isn't the same generation that went north the year prior, yet they always find their way back.* I assume it's some internal compass in their brain that allows them to end up at a specific location they have never been to.

I read on.

Once I finish, I throw the brochure in the bin underneath the vanity. I strip the mirrors of the sheets but I don't look. Not yet. What is the opposite of shrouding, I wonder, the antonym? *To lay bare.*

A moment comes to mind, the night at Hawthorne Court when I mistook a sliver of moonlight in my daughter's room for something it was not. My hands then seemed like something I had never seen before, old and gaunt. Bones protruded, veins bulged on the backs.

I look up into the mirror and stare at myself. I lean closer. I concentrate on my clavicle. My face. The skin is crepe-like, in stark contrast to my immaculate honey-colored hair and nude nails.

There's this man who sits outside by a table. I see him almost every day, pass by him as I go for my walks and runs, but I've never spoken to him. Vera and I refer to him as Watcher. Vera told me he lives alone but has kept all his late wife's belongings. I now understand him to be a man allowed to live in the past, surrounded by the fondest memories a man his age can have: his wife, her things, as if she still lived there, her underwear in the drawers, her bras lined up.

The framed dress above my bed, the Miss Texas gown, the sash. Nothing but lies. Made up. I'm not a former beauty queen. I staged the house with lies. I bought the dress and the sash, a facade to display in a mansion. Money buys you anything you want.

I have arrived at the truth: there are no smells of toilets, disinfectants, or overcooked foods. There's a private movie theater, a luxury spa, and a library stocked with books. This place is some warped Disney World where they immerse us in a world of normalcy, a theme park with everything we could possibly need, all we can possibly remember. The children and families in the park, the ones I see occasionally, are visitors. Employees are caretakers, not maids and chauffeurs. Vera Olmsted, not a friend but a fellow resident. My neighbors, eccentric at best and mainly obsessed with their privacy, are not tenants but patients tucked away where all seems well and no one is reminded that something is amiss.

The puzzle pieces fall and snap into place. The brochure states what not to do: never command, always ask. Don't argue, but agree. Never force, but reinforce. Surround them with things so that they recall their youth and happier times. Triggering positive memories helps calm anxiety, soothe aggressive behavior, prevent wandering, and improve quality of life. Never remind them their loved ones are dead.

Shadow Garden, as the brochure states, is a "living community" where we can spend the day exploring, safe and secure behind a fence. And if one dies, one does not speak of such things, as such talk unsettles us. Discover independently, the brochure says—nail salons and barbershops, literary readings, hikes, apartment spaces furnished with beloved furniture and mementos, familiar settings in a controlled space, safe confines, and expert supervisors. Reminiscence therapy makes those with dementia more content and happier because their minds return to a time in their lives when their memory was intact and they did not feel lost.

The day Edward dropped me off, I thought *all those years I've lived here but I never knew this place existed.*

That vase.

That ugly thing.

That's my daughter's urn.

What a shit show.

62

EDWARD

Donna's left Hawthorne Court but Edward isn't back to square one. He had his chance and he blew it but he's no longer concerned with the facts. Is Donna declining in a clinical sense or is she playing a cat-and-mouse game with him? She's ill. He can't know exactly what it is but she is ill. Donna isn't that good of an actress. He wishes he could tell her that and that it would register, one last ugly feeling for her to have.

Fuck if he cares. Whatever it is, it no longer matters. All those months, weeks, sleepless nights he's spent on cracking this puzzle have been in vain but the constant gush of emotions has stopped. He's almost at peace. Almost. And he'll get there, eventually he'll get there. There's no longer this space within him that needs filling with something, anything to help him see the bigger picture and move on, he no longer needs to approve of himself as the one who didn't fail his daughter. He had circled the wagons, what else could he have done?

There's a pep in his step as he makes his way into the kitchen and rummages through the drawers for matches. He's going to light a fire in the fireplace. *A hearth makes a home,* he can hear Donna's voice. He uses the pages of a book to kindle the wood. He pumps the bellows, which make the flames dash upward. It's not enough, he needs firewood. Somewhere in this monstrosity of a house there's firewood. The basement. That's where he'll look.

He chuckles. The kayak in the pool house, who would have thought? Leave it to Donna to just barge in here and know exactly where to look. Those ramblings of a disturbed teenager, whatever Donna read into them, the words she deciphered, he couldn't have done that, he didn't know Penelope well enough. All those months he had turned the place upside down and come up empty.

Hell, if there's no firewood in the basement, he'll burn that damn kayak instead.

On the basement stairs, he stands on the top step in utter darkness. A door slams, he doesn't know why, maybe the draft from the windows he keeps ajar, the doors he props open even when it's cold outside. There's a bare bulb hanging from the ceiling, he faintly recalls, and he reaches up and grasps for the string but can't get ahold of it.

This damn basement. It had cost a fortune. It smelled of damp and that stench. That foulness. What was that? He crinkled his nose. Sewer gas backing up into the house? He'd pour a few gallons of water down the drain and see if the odor is eradicated. If not he'd use bleach. That ought to do it.

His hand reaches and swipes through the air, catches hold of the string but only for a moment, then it escapes his grip. Grasping for it again and again, he absentmindedly takes another step. And another and another. His foot slips.

The step Donna told him needed repairing. The contractor

wanted to put in new steps altogether, he mentioned someone might have skimped on the basement. Edward can see the man as if he stood right in front of him, short, of average build with red skin, some sort of rosacea. "You have to do it right, you can't take shortcuts, the concrete down here stays forever wet, never cures." Donna had told him over the years to get that fixed. He was cheap about it.

Edward can't help but think of Penelope. How they'd done it all wrong from the beginning. *Head in the sand* is the phrase that comes to mind. Like an ostrich, burying its head in the ground when faced with attack by predators, stupidly believing that if it can't see its attacker then the attacker can't see it.

Edward holds his hands up in the air, thinking he must protect his fingers and his wrists above all else. He is a surgeon, he can't risk a broken finger, a shattered wrist—that would be the end of his career. He catches himself, holds on to the railing, comes to a stop but then his foot can't get a grip, his other hand reaches into nothingness—no banister, no railing, no nothing. He slips and there's an impact, elbow then wrist, then the head, but it happens so quickly, he can't quite wrap his mind around it but what he does notice is that the last step is his downfall. A tumble, a painful shock to his back like someone took a bat to it. His skull makes contact with the concrete floor.

The last image is that of a wine cellar with empty shelves. Edward, strewn across the cold concrete, bare bulb dangling overhead, feels the cold seep through his clothes. Soon he'll be shivering.

He thinks about the jeep suddenly, the blood-soiled seats, the clotted puddle of blood on the floor mat, and the night he drove the car to the stock pond at the very back of the property. He watched the jeep roll down the hill and submerge into the cold darkness. He had no clue if the pond was deep enough to hide the car and for a while it sat there, the bright-red roof like a beacon. He stood there, fingers laced above his head, *please, please, please,* he found himself begging some sort of power to have mercy on him, *please please please,* and then there were bubbles floating to the surface and the car sunk deeper as if there was a sudden drop-off and the roof was no longer visible.

As a physician, he has often imagined what death looks like, what people feel the moment they pass. He hadn't imagined it to be so insignificant.

Darkness comes with an almost anesthetic effect. There are hardly any thoughts left. Half a thought, barely: *the house has claimed me.*

63

DONNA

They told me Edward was dead. Fell on the basement steps. No one looked for him, no one caught on. They smelled him before they saw him. The mailman did and only because Edward had a habit of leaving doors unlocked.

Years ago, we talked about who of the two of us would go first. "I'll die first," Edward said and took my face in his hands. "Statistically that's a given. I'm older and men die younger. But I hope I won't because who will take care of you when I'm gone?"

I think of those moments often. The tender ones.

A black veil hides my eyes. I feel all alone in the world. First there's Vera. She's moved back to Sweden. She said she'd come visit but I didn't quite believe her. Yet I smiled. "You must. I can never replace you. Know that." Now Edward has passed. My eyes are red-rimmed from not sleeping but I have yet to shed a tear. I have complicated feelings for him.

Returning to Shadow Garden after Edward's funeral fills me with dread. If I can at all help it, my days here are numbered. I have plans but I haven't told anyone yet. I have to fight every single day to remain in good spirits and it's becoming increasingly difficult. I can go on all day but when daylight fades and time begins to slow, it all sloshes over me. I lose my rhythm and there is not enough oxygen in the room.

The car hits a pothole, raising my body temporarily off the seat. The driver lifts his hand to apologize. After a while, I nod off and when I open my eyes, my aspirations have returned. I wake with a vision: Shadow Garden behind me, the sun rising up ahead, beating down on my face. That vision tells me what I need to know—that I have to take control of my future.

A state of panic overcomes me. It begins unequivocally with a stumble of my heart, a gentle flutter. Then it throbs, speeds up, unwilling to surrender to its prior steady beat. I calm myself by imaging my new life.

I envision California. A thirties bungalow with a sloping roof and eaves with exposed rafters. A cozy atmosphere, nothing too formal, those days are over. A simple living room one enters directly from the front door—no parlor or sitting room—and a small kitchen. There'll be redwood beams and an attic under the sloping roof. I worry about the ceiling height. I get claustrophobic at times. From what I hear, bungalow ceilings are lower than Shadow Garden's Victorian architecture, still lower than Tudors, but I'll manage.

I imagine a lot of white. White walls. A white kitchen. White tiled floor. Old Hollywood style. I imagine a classic antique bar cart in brass finish and a gold jigger, a cocktail strainer, an ornate gold ice bucket, a corkscrew, and gold mixing spoons. I focus on this cart, I'm not sure why, but I imagine this polished vintage-style look on wheels, perfectly suited to tote around beverage necessities. Glasses for every occasion, I will even stoop to stemless wineglasses. They are a thing now.

California is expensive but I wouldn't mind listening to the waves all day. I'm thinking Berkeley maybe, or even close to the beach. They say the sound of water has a drowsing effect. From the pitterpatter of rain on shingles at Shadow Garden to the crash of ocean waves, that's a nice thought. *Imagine it and it will come true.* I'm so steeped in this moment, so deeply entrenched in the vision that I hear myself speak out loud. "Where is the sign? The Hollywood sign?"

My voice alerts the driver. There's a pause, a long look at me in the rearview mirror. He makes eye contact and then cracks a smile.

"This is not LA, Mrs. Pryor. We're not in California."

"Don't be silly," I say and keep my voice steady. "I knew that." A deep sigh, a smoothing of my black skirt. "I had a moment, is all."

He nods.

A cardboard box rests on the seat beside me. When I fastened my seat belt I almost reached around and buckled the box in, but then thought otherwise. That would have been silly.

Inside the box, underneath packing peanuts and balled-up brown paper, sits a handblown urn. I had it specially made for Edward, the glass shining in all colors of the rainbow. I spoke with the company over the phone and we deliberated colors.

"We roll raw molten glass in pigmented glass like you would roll an ice cream cone in sprinkles. Then the pigmented glass is heated on the ball of raw glass, merging them in a completely random pattern. We then blow and roll it into shape. It's not until then that the true color coverage will expose itself."

I was partial to purple at first, the color of blooming crape myrtles Edward loved so much, but then I thought otherwise. Rainbow colors will be more fitting on my California bungalow mantel. Edward's patent royalties and the sale of Hawthorne Court, even after all the damage he did, will support me for decades to come. Of course there will be an appropriate time of mourning and then I will have a talk with Marleen. I will offer her to accompany me to California. Her loyalty is second to none and maybe she'll take the leap with me.

I think about the letters often, by now discarded in a foul-smelling heap on the edge of the city. I want to think it was a sign, the fact Marleen threw them out, never to see the light of day. I am saddened by their loss, at the same time I have felt the pressure ease. No one needs to know what our family went through. Once you have been torn down and reinvented yourself, it's easier the next go-around. The beads are linked by the string, by time, but who am I to know what comes next?

64

The boxes had arrived the previous night and hours before opening, booksellers and store employees in every bookstore around the country displayed Vera Olmsted's book stacked up high on tables, and in special store presentations. Entire windows displayed the book, making for an eerie but beautiful picture. Published posthumously and to great fanfare, it was on every bestseller list even before publication, the preorder numbers so high it wasn't going to be outdone, not even by a presidential memoir.

Vera Olmsted's life had rendered more than anyone could imagine: a pragmatic childhood (the book *Maypole* told of the day she found her brother dangling off the rafters on her family's farm in Norrtälje) and the investigation which resulted in the conviction of their neighbor, a man she had called Uncle Ludvig all her life. Her decades-long friendship with an iconic fashion designer who rose to fame as they were rumored to be a couple. Her attendance at every

super-elite literary salon from Paris to New York since the late fifties, the first woman to be nominated and reject the position of
goodwill ambassador of the Council of Europe. Her affair with a
Canadian politician and the media frenzy that ensued; two failed
marriages, and her seclusion in an unknown location as she worked
on multiple short story collections, a book of essays, and a highly
anticipated novel. The last years of her life were shrouded in mystery.

Details were scarce and early critics were tight-lipped but what
booksellers unpacked on publication day was nothing short of a
surprise to the publishing world and the reading public: a novel
about an affluent couple and their daughter who plunged to her
death in the family's mansion. The novel drew significant parallels
between Donna Pryor and her daughter, Penelope, who fell to her
death in their home in an elite community. No one was prepared
for the frenzy that ensued on publication day, when Vera Olmsted
named Donna Pryor's late daughter, Penelope, as the hit-and-run
driver who was responsible for the death of a woman at White Rock
Lake Park, a case that had gone cold years ago and had prompted
documentaries, conspiracy theories, and YouTube videos.

Vera Olmsted and Donna Pryor spent a year living as neighbors
at Shadow Garden, a luxury estate that was home to over one hundred men and women living with dementia. Vera Olmsted blended
in so well because she played the part of a patient, even going through
the other tenants' trash occasionally. Depending on the severity of
the disease, residents enjoy almost completely independent lives or
assisted living with caretakers. The entire staff are trained geriatric
nurses who do everything from cooking meals to supervising ac-
tivities at the sprawling forty-acre estate.

The novel was titled *An American Tragedy*.

"This is, without any doubt, the next great American novel,"
said Peter Willoughby from FrontierBooks. "We are honored to
publish *An American Tragedy*. I speak for everyone at FrontierBooks
when I say we were blown away by it."

65

DONNA

The café is located between the market and the office buildings, the aroma of coffee enticing. Shadow Garden now has a bookstore and a farmer's market, and there's talk of building a spa including a pool and a state-of-the-art gym.

The barista has dark eyes, a narrow nose, and a softly shaped jaw. Her hair is pulled into a bun. She changes the coffee flavor daily and I never know what I'm going to get. I've learned to be less picky about things.

Today, there's a nutty scent in the air and it just might be a hazelnut day. I've read that there are over eight hundred known aromatics in coffee, but I could be mistaken. I come to the café daily but since Vera's move I have yet to make friends.

People rush by the window, some enter, and every time the door opens, I look up expecting her to walk in. The interior of the café is warm and cheery, with bright lights and colorful walls.

I ask the barista for a croissant. "Would you warm it up for me, please? Sorry for being so particular."

"That's all right, dear, I don't mind," she says and her eyes light up.

"Thanks."

"Have you found a place yet?" she asks and I must have a puzzled look on my face. "You were looking to move, remember? You were looking for a house?"

I laugh, though I don't remember having told her of my plan.

"I found a place. I think it's just perfect."

"I'm glad," she says and hands me a brown, warm paper bag. "Enjoy."

I have indeed found a house online. With Marleen's help and shortcuts that help me navigate, I have fallen in love with a house halfway between Santa Barbara and Ventura, in the small coastal town of Youngsport. The pictures of the moderately priced bungalow in short walking distance to upscale eateries and vintage stores looks like a dream to me. The bungalow sits on less than half an acre, a stark departure from Hawthorne Court and Shadow Garden, but it's all I'll need.

Youngsport is a picturesque Spanish-style town close to the beach and a cliff. I imagine standing on that cliff, listening to the layers of the sounds of the ocean; some waves come from afar, build up to a murmur, followed by a roaring surf when the waves crash against the cliffs, a sound I imagine to be closer, almost as if it took less time to reach the shore. Though Youngsport Beach has a moderate swell at best, it'll be perfect for swimming. I'll be able to watch sea lions flop around on the beach at the nearby sanctuary and I plan on making a sizeable donation to them. I imagine seagulls everywhere and their constant wailing and squawking, the chirping and the cawing in the distance nothing but white noise. It'll be a nice change from the grackles at Shadow Garden and there's a short uphill hike that culminates in some amazing ocean views.

With Marleen's help I'll make a life there. We'll go for daily walks in town and the historic buildings make Youngsport an attractive filming location with numerous movie productions underway. What a thrill. I'd never admit it but I wonder how it would feel to be a former actress who has retired after a long and prosperous career and maybe I'll pretend a camera is following me as I go about my daily life. But those are just games I play with myself.

I've got word Vera has passed. When the air gets thick, I tell myself she's somewhere scribbling away on those yellow notepads she loved so much. It's a lie I tell myself, but it makes mourning for her bearable. The bag on the chair next to me contains the book Vera published posthumously. I basically forced Marleen to buy a copy and eventually she gave in. I can be persuasive, I know that about myself. I'm proud of Vera and all she achieved, but mostly I'm proud of the friendship we had. Hearing her name makes me weepy and Marleen changes the subject.

I love the title. *An American Tragedy*. Marleen is critical of the book, maybe she's concerned about my obsession with it. There's an overall change going on with her. She, after the initial shock of Edward's death, has come into her own, she no longer wears black skirts and drab blouses but has taken my suggested casualness to heart. On one hand she seems to have adapted, in her wardrobe as much as in her behavior, though lately she's been up to her old tricks again. *Unrest* is the word that comes to mind, excessive attempts to keep me busy. I don't know what that's all about but I ignore it. The less said about that, the better.

I shut down the laptop and pull the book from my bag. It's a hardback with an embossed sleeve, glossy black letters on a white background. A chandelier shattered in pieces on a black-and-white checkerboard floor.

A simple dedication on the first page, all by itself. *For Donna*. And then Vera quotes Thornton Wilder, *we can only be said to be alive in those moments when our hearts are conscious of our treasures*. I ponder that one a lot.

The story is rather tragic. It's not the kind of book you consume in two sittings, it feels more like a true friend you return to at the end of each day. I form a quiet yet firm attachment to the characters and before I know it I've been sucked into the story. I finished the book quite a while ago but the moment I read the last sentence, I feel compelled to begin again. Some sort of loop I'm stuck in, as if I want to remind myself of something—I caught myself reading paragraphs over and over—and as the plot unfolds, it's like plucking petals, and I cry and cry.

I'm looking forward to a change of scenery and I imagine I'll be happier in California than I've been anywhere else. There is only one thing. Penelope. The images of her come and go as if I momentarily assume an alternate identity where I relive my memories of her. As they play out, there is always a sudden and unexpected fall from grace. The feeling reaches into my dreams, and my lungs fill with something crisp, cold, and sharp. Images are painted on my eyelids, images of falling, and a rush of fear shoots through my body, my lungs panic for air. My arms flail and desperately I'm reaching for something to hold on to, and then I feel Marleen touch my shoulder and I jerk awake.

I will forever remember Penelope with her hair blowing in the wind, a breeze catching her at a moment she wasn't prepared for. I get lost in thoughts of her, though *getting lost* isn't the right expression—it implies that one returns at some point to join the rest of the world—no, it's more a state of being.

We called Penelope "Pea" when she was little. She was a darling child, independent and strong of will, though brooding at times. As she grew older she insisted we call her Penny, but I remember her most fondly as Pea. Sweet peas come in pink, yellow, red, purple, and white, and Pea came with just as many personalities.

"Has Penelope called?" I ask Marleen every morning.

"No, she has not," Marleen says.

I worry about Penelope. She is grown, living her own life, but the mind is a fickle thing, there's only so much I'm able to process at one time, only so much weight a structure can hold before it collapses. I hope she is well.

The mind must take what it's given and make the best of it, never losing hope that more lies ahead.

Alexandra Burt

QUESTIONS FOR DISCUSSION

1. America is the proverbial land of opportunity, and Edward and Donna Pryor have achieved wealth and a high standing in their community. How do you think money played into the decisions they made on that fateful night? Do you see them making the same decision if they weren't affluent?

2. Was money a hindrance or an accelerator in the Pryors' downfall?

3. When you met Donna Pryor in the beginning of the story, did you feel empathy for her?

4. "If a child goes wrong, look at the family." Does that ring true to you?

5. We have all said "I'd do anything for my child." How would you have reacted coming upon the scene in the garage? Would

you protect your child from legal consequences? How far would you go to stretch the truth? Where would you draw the line?

6. Had Donna and Edward called the police that night, how might things have played out differently for the Pryor family? Would Penelope have changed how she lived her life if she had been exonerated? Would Donna and Edward still be together?

7. Think back to the initial quote in the book by William Butler Yeats. "Why, what could she have done, being what she is?" In what ways does that quote apply to both Donna and Penelope?

8. In your opinion, who is mostly to blame for the downfall of the Pryor family? Who can you forgive most easily?

9. Did the Pryors get what they deserved? Examine the consequences for each one of them. Does the punishment match the gravity of the crime for Edward, Donna, and Penelope?

10. "Dante's "The Divine Comedy" is a fourteenth-century poem telling of Dante's journey through hell. What do you make of the parallels of the three parts (hell, purgatory, and heaven) of the novel?

11. Shadow Garden is a character onto itself. What made the setting unique or important to the story? Did you know that places like Shadow Garden existed in reality?

Photo by the author

Alexandra Burt is a freelance translator and the international bestselling author of *Remember Mia* and *The Good Daughter*. Born in Europe, she moved to Texas more than twenty years ago. While pursuing literary translations, she decided to tell her own stories. After years of writing classes and gluttonous reading, her short fiction appeared in fiction journals and literary reviews. She lives in Texas with her husband.

CONNECT ONLINE

AlexandraBurt.com

Ready to find
your next great read?

Let us help.

Visit prh.com/nextread

Penguin
Random
House